EVIL TIME

Also by P. S. Donoghue

The Sankov Confession
The Dublin Affair

EVIL TIME

BY
P. S. DONOGHUE

DONALD I. FINE, INC.
New York

Copyright © 1992 by P. S. Donoghue

All rights reserved, including the right of reproduction in whole or in part in any form. Published in the United States of America by Donald I. Fine, Inc. and in Canada by General Publishing Company Limited.

Library of Congress Cataloging-in-Publication Data
Donoghue, P. S.
Evil time : a novel / by P.S. Donoghue.
   p. cm.
ISBN 1-55611-326-9
I. Title.
PS3554.O538E95 1992
813'.54—dc20   92-53071
CIP

Manufactured in the United States of America

10 9 8 7 6 5 4 3 2 1

Designed by Irving Perkins Associates

This novel is a work of fiction. Names, characters, places and incidents are either the product of the author's imagination or are used fictitiously. Any resemblance to actual events, locales, organizations or persons, living or dead, is entirely coincidental and beyond the intent of either the author or publisher.

ONE

Abarrotes Gomez was one of the last small mom 'n' pop stores still operating along the Franklin Park stretch of Hollywood Boulevard. Its bins offered reasonably fresh vegetables, shelves were stocked with canned goods predominately Mexican: chiles, enchiladas, refried beans, and plastic-wrapped tortillas. And a glass-faced cold cabinet displayed milk, yogurt, tamales, soft drinks, and beer. So far, my shopping basket held a head of romaine lettuce, half a gallon of skim milk, and a brown bottle of Lithuanian beer labeled Poummit's Brew.

I lingered at the frozen food bin long enough to compare prices and selected a turkey TV dinner. On my stringent budget it was all I could afford.

Mr. Gomez rang up each item, took my ten-dollar bill and handed me a jingle of change. As he fitted my purchases into a plastic sack he said, "You don't eat too good, Mr. Brent. Don't eat enough."

I shrugged, pocketing the change. "Losing weight. Doctor's orders," I lied, and patted my waistline. Gomez knew my name from a small check he'd cashed when we began doing business. And from the next-door stationer I knew that Abarrotes Gomez was no longer a mom 'n' pop enterprise, Mrs. Gomez having been knifed to death by two crack-crazed punks who collected eleven dollars and thirty-two cents from the old cash register. Mr. Gomez asked, "How long's the writers' strike gonna last?"

"Who knows? Started in March and here it's April—the cruelest month, Eliot said."

"Eliot?"

"Tom Eliot."

"Writer?"

"One of the best. Now occupying that big writers' annex in the sky." I hefted the plastic sack and started to leave. "Before then, he wrote *Cats*."

Mr. Gomez's nose wrinkled. "That play with all the crazy costumes?"

"That's the one."

"Made a lot of money, *si?*

"Mucho dinero," I agreed. "Shiploads. And the beat goes on."

"Well, good night, Mr. Brent. *Buenas noches."*

"Buenas noches." I stepped out of the store and heard the heavy iron grill swing shut behind me. It was dusk, purple and smoky, and Abarrotes Gomez no longer stayed open after dark.

As I turned west on the sidewalk I found myself hoping that April would indeed prove the cruelest month of the year, but I suspected that succeeding months could be even crueler. T. S. Eliot hadn't belonged to any Writers Guild, and in England, where he wrote and died, the ban on writing wouldn't have applied.

Six weeks since I'd collected a paycheck from Corinthian Productions via my agent, Morry Manville, and my legal spouse, Natalie, had cleaned out our joint checking the day after the strike began. She and her four-year-old son, Bryon—my legal but unadopted stepson—weren't going to suffer the vicissitudes of television unemployment—why should they? I should find scab work, she told me. I'd been a good provider when we married two years ago, I should scratch around and become a good provider again.

After hoisting it all in and deciding she was serious, I did an impulsive and impetuous thing: I packed a bag of clothes, grabbed my portable typewriter, snatched the Datsun keys from her grasp, and vanished into the night, leaving my dependents in our—now their—Burbank apartment to scratch for themselves. My present accommodations—toward which I was walking—were considerably less desirable: a second-floor studio furnished as scantily as possible while meeting the minimum lodging code. When I used the table for eating, the typewriter and a discouragingly small pile of typed pages had to be moved aside, then replaced when I resumed work on the novel: big money, sex, chicanery, and sex were the ingredients my agent recommended. Think big and I couldn't go wrong was Morry's philosophy.

So I'd decided on an action plot not unlike that of *Topkapi*, substituting St. Petersburg's Hermitage storehouse of art treasures for the Istanbul museum and the sultan's bejeweled dagger. That I'd never been in St. Petersburg wasn't an overwhelming obstacle. Edgar Rice Burroughs had never been to Mars, yet he'd written about it with credible familiarity and *his* books were still selling. Why couldn't Joe Brent do the same?

The L.A. City College library provided maps of St. Petersburg and color photos of the Hermitage collections, which I thought was enough research to start with. And I conjured up a gang of disaffected CIA operatives who spoke Russian and had larceny, if not burglary, in their hearts. Thin stuff, but I could always go back to the college libe. I still had a valid card issued the year I'd given night lectures on dramatic construction to would-be screenwriters, dramatists, and television scriveners.

That was how I'd met Natalie, I remembered unhappily. A night acting student, she'd had a part in the staged reading of one of my students' one-acters and had come on strong to me because I was the "professor," as she flatteringly titled me. But enough of that. Aside from unemployment, Natalie was my paramount problem, and they were interrelated. Why brood over what couldn't be helped? I had to hoard my thoughts and emotions for creative transfer to the typed page.

So thinking, I crossed Highland, carrying my bag from Gomez, and saw an extremely well-dressed young woman walking rapidly toward the intersection. She wore a beige dress, high heels, and what looked like a marten pelt across her shoulders. Overdressed for the neighborhood, I reflected, heard the squeal of tires, and saw a top-down purple heap nearly jump the curb before it slowed beside the young woman. The five youths in the heap looked like low-risers from East L.A.—ducktails, black jackets, and chromed chain necklaces. They began calling out indecent proposals to their quarry, offering to satisfy her—and their—sexual needs in a variety of bizarre ways. She ignored them and walked faster. The purple duster speeded up. The driver had a pimply face and a pink-dyed Mohawk ridge. His voice was the loudest and I felt a feral urge to shove his face against the cracked windshield.

Abruptly, the woman stopped, turned and caught sight of me. *"Darling!"* she cried, and hurried toward me. I walked to meet her, let her stand on tiptoe to buss the side of my face, and heard her whisper, "Please help me—you're my husband, right?"

"Right," I said, and gave her my free arm. The hoodlums stared at us in astonishment. Now I'm six-one, one eighty-seven, but no match, even when well-nourished, for five thugs wielding chains, which I wasn't at the time. So, holding her at my side, I turned to the hoodlums and bellowed, "Beat it, assholes, she's my wife!"

"Wife?" Pink-hair jeered. "She's a fuckin' hooker."

"Hooker?" I yelled, jerked the bottle of Poummit's Brew from my sack, gripped the neck and broke the bottle on the sidewalk. Jagged weapon in hand, I shouted, "Okay, *cabrones,* let's get it on," and started for the purple car. Pink-hair reacted, flooring the accelerator and screaming off, leaving exhaust smoke and burnt rubber in the air.

The young woman began to laugh—not merrily, but in a shaken, gasping way. Trembling, she clung tightly to my arm. I looked down at the dripping bottle in my hand and felt very, very foolish. Pulse pounding, I drew in a deep breath.

"Don't leave me," she implored, "they could come back and—"

"I'm only going as far as Cerrito—two blocks ahead."

"That's far enough—and thanks." We stood there for a few moments until her trembling eased, and resumed walking. Sure enough, before we reached the next corner, the purple heap tore around Highland and whipped past us, the riders gesturing and yelling, but their insults were lost in the roar of the decayed muffler.

We crossed Sycamore, arms linked, and at the first bush I discarded what was left of the one indulgence I'd allowed myself that day.

"Litterbug," she said, and when I looked at her face I saw a genuine smile. Her teeth were white and even, golden brown hair cut short and professionally done. She had high cheekbones, deep-set blue eyes, and a small turned-up nose. Considering the circumstances of our chance encounter, I found her extraordinarily good-looking, just a shade short of beautiful. Flash analysis made her a model, an actress, or a Junior Leaguer. The marten pelt and the over-the-shoulder kidskin bag murmured money. So I was surprised when she said, "Wanna fool around?"

"Well—"

"No French, no Greek."

"Ah—All-American girl?"

"Pretty much." Her eyes appraised me. "Vice?"

"Occasionally." Those punks were right, dammit!

"No—I meant the way you handled those hoods back there—scaring them off. You reacted like a cop."

"No way."

"So . . . ?"

"Lady," I said, "if I ever broke my oath and paid for it, I'd choose you—but I'm your day's worst prospect. If they were selling diamonds for five bucks a carat I couldn't buy one." I looked at her and sighed. "Sorry."

"Nothing to be sorry about. Ah—any reason you mentioned diamonds?"

"Unattainable," I said, "and I think you're out of danger now. Here's where I turn up." We'd reached Cerrito, and my place was halfway up the block. Gray stone façade and an *Apt. For Rent* sign beside the walk. Pointing at it, I said, "See what I mean?"

She nodded, and a worried look crossed her pretty face. "Would you mind looking around—see if we're followed?"

I turned slowly, saw nothing but sidewalk. "All clear," I said, "so I guess this is goodbye."

"Goodbye—and thanks. I was really scared back there."

"So was I."

"You're a real gentleman," she said softly, "and I haven't met one in a long time."

I patted her shoulder. "What I am is an unemployed TV writer, but I appreciate the compliment."

"Oh, you write for television? What show?"

"Nothing you'd remember," I told her, "if you have the kind of taste I think you have."

"That's a nice compliment, too. Shouldn't I know your name?"

"Joe," I said.

"Melissa."

"Really?"

"It'll do. Goodnight, Joe. Goodbye, really—I'll be in Vegas tomorrow."

"Lotsa luck," I said, and turned up the slanted walk toward my building. When I looked back she was gone.

I unlocked the first, second, and third security locks and walked up the dim flight of stairs to my door, where I used two more keys to get in. Once inside, I carefully locked the door and turned on the lights. Considering all the complications of access, the place didn't seem worth it.

I lighted the gas oven and slid the TV dinner inside, rinsed the romaine and got what was left of a bottle of russian dressing from the fridge. The Poummit's Brew would have been welcome about now but that had been sacrificed on behalf of a lady's honor. Or a hooker's honor. But whatever she was, I told myself, she didn't deserve the likes of the East L.A. delinquents—besides, she was damn lovely with her lean dancer's legs and slim, youthful figure. And there was no forgetting that appealingly innocent face. I'd remember it and her for a long time.

Melissa, she'd said. Good enough for short-term acquaintance; a trifle stagy, but with her looks it went well. And her voice suggested schooling and a degree of breeding. Well, there were hundreds like her around Hollywood—thousands, maybe.

And I'd settled for Natalie Faber. Good God, I must have been out of my mind.

Salad and turkey dinner disposed of, I cleaned up, drank a glass of skim milk, and brewed coffee on the range. While it was perking I reread the thirty-eight pages of my nascent novel, corrected a few typos, and began considering the next scene. When nothing came to mind I turned on my transistor radio to the Big Band station and listened to the Herman Herd do their thing. Bitter feelings toward the Guild flooded my mind. L.A. City College had offered me an extension instructorship at eighteen thou per annum, and for the first time since refusing it I began wishing I'd accepted. At the time I'd considered my low-paid lectures in the nature of *pro bono* work, because I was pulling down sixteen thousand every two months, less Manville's commission, and the Corinthian-produced series, *Frankie's Follies,* seemed destined to go on forever—or at least another two or three years. Eternity in TV land. Maybe it could recapture the audience share after the strike ended—whenever that was. Maybe.

As I thought about my thralldom I reflected that I was as much a prostitute as Melissa—she sold her body, I sold my mind. Both of us were trapped in uncertain professions.

I stared at the blank page in my typewriter. The novel was my way out—my lifeline, if I could manage it—but so far nothing I'd written suggested editors beating on my door for a first reading. Later. That would come later.

I poured coffee and sipped it black, hoping the caffeine would stimulate my thinking. From the scratchy transistor came the sounds of Artie Shaw's Gramercy Five. Ah, they didn't make music like that any more. Hell, most of the guitar groups rolling in gelt couldn't even read music.

How old was Melissa? I wondered. Twenty-three? Twenty-five? I had about a decade on her. Ten years in which I'd accumulated an indifferent wife with a bratty kid, and a heavily mortgaged twenty-six-foot Rollins-built sloop, whose dockage fee at Marina del Rey was a month in arrears. Pretty soon the dockmaster would slap a lien on my boat and then bank and marina could fight it out.

Damn the strike anyway! Source of all the evils that attended me.

No, not quite. Not honestly, because things in Burbank had been attenuating for a long, long time. The way molten glass spins out until its thread is nearly invisible—just before breaking.

And just before the strike Bryon had dumped a bowl of oatmeal in my Olympia electronic typewriter. The expense of repairs had been enormous, but why had I even bothered? I hadn't been able to write in the apartment for months. Between the brat and Natalie's calls to and from casting agents, the atmosphere had been far from conducive to creativity. So I worked in a cubby at Corinthian on Beverly Boulevard, my mind on auto-pilot as I spun out segment after segment of *Frankie's Follies*—a good-hearted chump saddled with a wise-ass family, a self-sacrificing idiot, like most husbands.

I could identify. Oh, could I identify with Frankie!

If Sol would go for it, I'd write in a retard nephew—Bryon—to give poor Frankie more trouble to contend with. *If* the sitcom outlasted the strike.

I was pouring another cup of coffee when I heard knocking on my door, then the buzzer. Doubtless Mrs. Haven, wanting another week's advance rent. Having come to that dispiriting conclusion, I set down my cup and listened.

"Joe! Let me in. *Please!*"

Not Mrs. Haven's high-pitched screech, but Melissa's voice, and she sounded pretty desperate.

I went to the door.

TWO

I slid both bolts, opened the door partway, looked at her and beyond her along the hallway. She was alone. Chest pumping, cheeks reddened, mascara dissolving, my lady of the evening stood shaking like a chilled waif until I said, "Come in."

Melissa slid past me, arms close to her body, as though for warmth. I locked the door and said, "How the hell did you get past the first-floor barrier?"

Her teeth were chattering. "I—I waited for someone to come in."

"Sit down. How'd you know this is my apartment?"

"J. Brent is on the hall list—you said your name is Joe."

"So far, so good. But this is like the opening scene of *The Purloined Woman*."

"*The Purloined Woman?* By who—whom?"

"Thackeray, of course. Those hoods keep following you?"

"No, I—" Her eyes narrowed. "Thackeray never wrote any such book. If you mean *The Purloined Letter*, that was Poe." She swallowed. "Edgar Allan."

"Just testing."

"Bastard! If that's coffee I'll have some—plus anything you can put in it."

"Well, there's a little cooking sherry I keep around for social occasions—don't let the Jim Beam label fool you." I poured coffee into the other cup that came with the place, and resurrected the Beam from its cache among cleaning rags and dishtowels.

She held the cup in both hands and drank gratefully. After a while she said, "More, please." I gave her what she wanted.

This time she drank more slowly, and when her shivering stopped, I said, "We could be sharing a bottle of Poummit's Lithuanian Brew, but you saw its fate."

She nodded. "Sorry about that, Joe. Can I pay you?"

"I'd rather drink coffee with you."

She put aside the now-empty cup and gazed at me thoughtfully. "How much was that beer?"

"Two eighty-nine plus tax—but I don't want the money."

"Want to take it out in trade, I suppose."

"Trade?" I stared at her, not quite getting it.

"You'd rather fuck me," she said matter-of-factly. "You do me a favor, I do one for you—isn't that how it goes?"

"Most places," I agreed, "but it's not as though I'd slipped you a ten-carat diamond. I may be broke but I like to think I can help a lady in distress without demanding reciprocity."

"My, my," she said loftily, "last of a vanishing breed. Can I have more coffee?"

"Till the can runs dry." While I was making another pot, she got up from the sag-bottom chair and strolled over to my work table. "So," she murmured, "you *are* a writer."

"Why doubt it? Nothing to brag about."

She shrugged. "In this town no one is ever what they seem—or pretend—to be. And, believe me, I've had experience."

"I can imagine."

"Not just with—johns. I mean upstanding, reputable figures. Men who are always promising a screen test or whatever, but it's always just a ruse, a come-on to fuck me."

"Now, listen," I said, "I'm a big boy, an ex-Marine, and I've kicked around places you couldn't imagine. But that word you keep using—to shock me, I guess—has no place in these surroundings. You came here for a reason, not just for laced coffee, and you're welcome to hang around a while—with the stipulation that you clean up your mouth. Okay?"

"Okay." She picked up the Beam bottle, tilted it and took a long draw. "Cheers," I said, and heard the coffee begin to perk. Melissa bent over and began reading the topmost page of my novel until I said, "Uh-uh, no one reads it until it's ready."

She looked at me. "When will that be?"

"God knows." I found a jelly glass and poured a shot of Beam for myself. While there was enough to pour.

"You mean it's not going well."

"It's my first try at sustained writing. Until recently I earned a pretty good living writing sitcoms but this is different." I sipped from the glass. "Much different."

"It's lonely, isn't it—I mean, cooped up here trying to force words onto a page?"

"Very lonely," I agreed. "Like being in an igloo without even Eskimos for company. Still—"

"—you wouldn't trade it for the world," she finished with a smile. "Or would you?"

"I'd trade it for almost anything where I could earn a few bucks. When the writers strike began, my wife took the cash and I got the typewriter—and my car."

"You could always sell your car."

"True—but it's a matter of pride. And I'm still eating."

She glanced around the room. "But not especially well."

"Also true. But if you're going to keep on sneering at my poverty then you can get the hell out."

She came over—glided, really—to me, and touched my arm. "Sorry," she said, "and I mean it. I've had a bad day—a bad week, and before that a bad several months."

"And you were all set to be in Vegas by sunrise. New setting, new leaf."

"And same old profession, right?"

"Pays better there, I hear. And Hollywood Boulevard isn't the safest place in California for an inviting stroll. Want my advice? Take Vegas."

"Would you go with me?"

I managed a short laugh. "Lady, I can't even play the dime slots. Forget it."

"I can pay you."

I turned off the gas ring and let the perking coffee simmer as I thought it over. "How much?"

"How much do you want?"

"I asked first."

Her lips pursed. "A hundred dollars, gas, and expenses?"

"You could fly there for less, Melissa. Besides, Vegas isn't my scene. You've got clothes, style, class—everything I lack." I poured coffee into our cups. "What are you running from? Or to?"

"That's my business, Joe—we'll keep it that way." She added Beam to our coffee. "Once a man offered me five thousand dollars to go to Las Vegas with him for a weekend."

"Don't tell me you refused."

"Not exactly. I married him."

"Well, that *is* different. Still married?"

"Legally, yes."

"But not working at it."

"You found me on the street, didn't you? Doesn't that answer the question?"

"It might—if all our cards were face-up, but they aren't." When she said nothing, I said, "You look hungry. I haven't much to offer but you're welcome to it: salad, bread, butter, milk, some apple jelly . . ."

"How about we send out for a big pizza—I'll pay."

"Or we could saunter down to Ruby Wing's Cantonese emporium around the corner—the sweet-and-sour is exceptional. You eat and I'll watch."

"Not even tea?"

"Tea," I agreed. "Let's go."

When she didn't move, I said, "Something wrong?"

"I don't want to be on the street tonight. Let's call for pizza, okay?"

"I can go down and bring it back—save time."

"I don't want to be alone." Stretching, she looked up at the ceiling. "Anchovies, pepperoni, extra cheese . . . the whole spread." As I walked toward the telephone, she said, "Yes, I can pay."

I called Vinnie's, placed the order and Vinnie said, "Half an hour, okay? Drinks?"

"Bottle of your rotgut Chianti and four bottles of iced Poummit's."

He whistled. "Big spender, Joe. Strike over?"

"Don't I wish." I replaced the receiver and turned back to my guest. "Good," she said. "Now, I have a proposition for you."

"Clean?"

"Absolutely. Rent me your bed tonight for a hundred dollars."

"Best offer this week. Burying my pride, the bed's yours."

"I'm hot, sticky, and smelly. Include a shower?"

I gestured at the bathroom door. "All yours."

First she took off the fur, then pulled the dress over her head. She dropped her slip and I saw a nylon money belt around her waist. She parted the Velcro fasteners and laid the belt across the chair. In beige panties and matching bra, she walked toward the bathroom. Semi-naked, her figure was even more spectacular than I'd suspected, and I suppressed a flash of desire.

Until the street doorbell rang, I drank coffee and wondered who she really was and why the hell she was with me. That she was afraid of something or someone was entirely apparent. The question was why, and she'd declined to answer, which was perfectly within her rights.

I opened a flap of the nylon money belt, took out greenbacks, and looked for a twenty—but there were only hundreds. Vinnie's delivery boy wouldn't like that, I told myself, and I was right. He told me he'd bring back change in an envelope and stick it in my mailbox. I said that was okay and keep five for himself. Then I carried the big box back upstairs with one hand, the sack of bottles in the other.

Wearing my old terrycloth robe, Melissa opened the door and I saw the same frightened expression cross her face. "Only Joe," I told her. "Relax. Chianti and my favorite, very expensive beer." I gestured at her money belt. "You can afford it."

"Let's dispense with small talk—I'm famished."

She ate ravenously. I helped myself to a slice to keep her company, filled and refilled her wine glass, and polished off two icy Poummits. When her intake slowed, I said, "This isn't a contest, Melissa—what you don't eat now will be fine for breakfast."

She delicately removed pizza crust from her lower lip with a little finger. "Don't know when I've enjoyed a meal so much."

"It's the superior company," I said, "plus the glitzy surroundings."

She sipped wine and smiled. "Is your wife crazy?"

"Moderately. Why?"

"Letting a good guy like you get away. She'd have to be bonkers all the way."

"Thank you, ma'am. Not every marriage works out—as you doubtless know."

"Just don't remind me—while I'm having fun."

Finally she pushed back her chair and said, "Enough already."

"There's change coming to you."

"Keep it."

"I'll subtract it from the night's lodging."

"Honest, too," she said in a tone bordering on disapproval. "Wish I'd met you, say, three years ago."

"Wish I'd met you, say, two years ago—before I married my present wife."

"First marriage?"

I nodded.

"Mine, too. But when I get to Vegas, that chapter ends." She added wine to her glass and I started my third Poummit's. An easy intimacy was developing between us, and I found myself liking this gorgeous streetwalker, not as a prospective lay but as a person of special and unusual qualities. "And after that?" I asked.

She shrugged. "Who knows?" She glanced at my typescript and said, "Your days and nights are planned, mine aren't—simple as that."

"Or as complicated."

She sat back and stretched. The robe neckline parted and revealed one small pink nipple. She noticed my glance and covered her breast. "I suppose you're going to ask me how a nice girl like me became a—whore."

"Not at all. I know most of the answers. Like you're from Kansas, won a beauty contest, and headed for Schwab's, planning to be noticed, only you ran out of money, worked at Burger King until you couldn't get the grease smell out of your hair, turned a few modest tricks, saved your money, bought good clothes, found a first-class beauty salon, and took to the better streets."

"My," she smiled, "you *are* imaginative. It sounds good—let's settle for your version. Now, how about you? Where are you from? Originally, I mean?"

"Small-town New York. High-school football and hockey. Four years as a fleet Marine, and two years community college. Wrote some short stories at sea and sent them off. Most came back, but two were bought—one by the L.A. *Times* Sunday Section. That gave me big ideas, so when I mustered out at Balboa, I came here and began making rounds of the studios. I got a lot of cheap talk from telephone-booth Indians until I decided to get smart."

"How?"

"What's left of the studio system wants presold properties, bestsellers that take multimillion budgets. They can't be bothered with original screenplays by unknown writers, but television—low-budget—can. At the City College library I read about thirty teleplays and absorbed the technique. Then I began turning out my own teleplays and taking them around to the Indies. Story editors are a funny breed—they resent anyone who can write, and see their job as keeping fresh material from the producer they work for. So the trick is to get your product read by a producer." Throat dry, I drank from the brown bottle. "It took a lot of trying but finally I got a producer to actually read one of my teleplays. He didn't buy it, but he had a proposition for me. He'd pay me scale to develop the pilot for a sitcom he'd been thinking about—the protagonist was a thinly disguised version of his own father." I shrugged. "Sol liked my work and I've been working for Corinthian ever since—until this damn strike put everyone on welfare."

"You're not on welfare," she objected.

"Well, it's called unemployment insurance—unknown in your trade—and I qualify in a couple more weeks. So—that's Joe Brent's story, unadorned, simplistic, and consonant with the American Dream."

She looked again at my thirty-eight typed pages. "I'd like to read your novel when it's published. Does it have a title?"

"Working title's *Hot Gems from a Cold Country.*"

"Too long."

"I have alternates." I set the uneaten pizza in the fridge along with the last Poummit's. Then I went back to my chair and studied my guest. Finally I said, "You're one of a very few women I've known who looks absolutely great without makeup. What do you do with your hair after a shower?"

"Shake it out doggy-style." She demonstrated, smiled, and said, "Sure you won't drive me to Vegas?"

"Only if you'll tell me why you're running."

"Sorry, Joe—can't do that. It would burden you with dangerous knowledge, a lousy way to return your kindness."

"Dangerous to me?"

"To both of us," she said and a slight shiver coursed through her body. "Have you got a gun?"

"Everyone does."

"Sell it to me."

I shook my head. "It's licensed and traceable. Anyway, even if you knew how to use it you're better off without. Long fingernails and a piercing scream are your best protection."

"For these?" She picked up her money belt, opened a flap, and removed an oblong chamois pouch. She separated the top and said, "Hold out your hands." I did, and about thirty shimmering stones spilled into my palms. The glitter was blinding. Most of the gems were five- to ten-carat-size and all were brilliant-cut—except one, the largest. It was heart-shaped, and as I stared at it, I seemed to see a soft lemon glow suffusing its center. Twenty, maybe thirty carats' worth—at least the value of a seagoing yacht. In a taut voice I said, "Diamonds?"

"Every one."

"You're crazy to go walking around with them." I swallowed. "Stolen?"

"Would I tell you if they were?"

"Probably not. Here, I get the shakes just holding them."

Casually, she returned the stones to the soft leather pouch. "Imagine," she said, "what these could buy in Vegas."

"Starting with a divorce."

She nodded. "That's number-one priority. After that—" She looked away. "Maybe I'll go back to the Kansas you described, find my high-school sweetheart and take him around the world."

"It's a good dream," I said. "Stay with it." My heart was still pounding from the sight of all that condensed wealth. I slaked my sudden thirst, emptied the bottle, and tossed it into the wastebasket.

She laid a hundred-dollar bill atop my typescript and said, "In case I leave before you get up."

"You don't need to, Melissa."

"A bargain's a bargain—and I can easily afford it. Now," she said, "I think I'll turn in. It's a double bed, and if you overcome your scruples during the night you'll be welcome to share it."

"Thanks," I said, and meant it, "but I'll try to write a while. Close the door and you won't hear the typewriter. Sweet dreams."

"I hope," she said, got up, bent over, and planted a goodnight kiss on my lips. Natalie had never kissed me like that—or if she had, it was so long ago as to be forgotten.

"You're a nice man, Joe Brent," she said as she walked toward the bedroom. "I haven't met anyone like you since I was sweet sixteen."

The door closed and I was alone with the debris of our dinner. I cleared off the table and pulled over the typewriter. Maybe it was the beer, the Chianti or just the unaccustomed warmth of human companionship, but ideas and words began to flow.

When my eyes got gravelly, I turned off the table lamp and lay down on the sofa fully dressed. As I stretched out I felt something under my back and pulled out Melissa's money belt. For a hooker she was a trusting soul, I mused, but it was her money, not mine. I draped the nylon over the sofa back, pulled a cushion under my head, and fell asleep.

I woke to sunlight piercing the blinds, sat up and looked around, gradually remembering the previous evening. The money belt was gone, but atop my typescript she had placed four more hundred-dollar bills. The bedroom door was open, the bed empty. My frightened hooker had gone.

But a note in stylish script said:

> *Joe, this is for you. Call it a down payment or retainer if I ever need your help again. I can't thank you enough for all you did for me. Please don't look for me or try to find out who I am. I said it would be dangerous for both of us and I wasn't lying. I trust you, and perhaps one day you'll hear from me again.*
>
> *Your friend,
Melissa*

I fingered the greenbacks and thought I'd rather have her than the money, but I hadn't encouraged her to stay and she'd made her own choice. I wanted to see her again but I was under obligation not to try. By now she was probably in Vegas doing her thing, but with all that money and those glittering gems, I knew she didn't need to.

Maybe it was just a game. Something she played for kicks.

After eye-opening coffee I dialed the LAPD Hollywood Division on Wilcox and found an old detective friend at his desk. I asked him if there had been a major jewel theft in the past few days. He checked around and said not to his knowledge.

So if the diamonds were hot, they hadn't been stolen in Los Angeles County. That made me feel better.

I shaved, got into clean clothing, filled the Datsun's tank, and drove down Highland to Santa Monica Boulevard, continued west to the San Diego Freeway, then south as far as Culver where I hooked over to Marina del Rey. The dockmaster's clerk nearly fainted when I handed over two bills on my account. I checked my boat, found it afloat and undisturbed, and drove to a nearby branch of the bank that held my marine mortgage. There I laid out another two hundred against arrears, leaving me with a single bill plus the seventy change Vinnie's boy had dropped off. It was more cash than I'd carried around in a month, and I felt flush.

At the Jamaica Bay Inn I took a poolside table and devoured an order of large Malaysian prawns, washing them down with two bottles of Poummit's Brew. On the way out I bought a paper and leafed through it as I walked to the lot where I'd parked my car.

In the second section, page nine, Personals, I saw a photograph that froze me in my tracks. Under the photo was a caption reading: *Reward offered for information concerning this woman's whereabouts. All information confidential.* A telephone number followed. The first three digits placed the number in Beverly Hills.

Even in black and white the photograph was easily recognizable. Same high cheekbones, upturned nose and full, smiling lips—not a posed photo but more like a party snapshot. Informal.

I hadn't looked for Melissa but I'd found her.

If only on the printed page.

At the exit booth I gave the attendant my franked parking ticket and noticed his plastic nameplate lettered *Chick*. Just beyond the booth there was a pay telephone stand. I left the Datsun, shoved a quarter into the slot, and began dialing the Beverly Hills number. *Wait a minute,* I rebuked myself, *is this the smart thing to do?* I broke the connection and heard the coin clatter free. As I reconsidered, I reflected that, welcome as a reward would be, I couldn't in good conscience endanger Melissa, not at any price. And I realized that I felt protective about her. Not just because she'd paid me a few hundred dollars nor because she was so damn beautiful. Rather, it was because she was a lady on the run to whom I'd given refuge. A lady whose complicated story was dismissable as fiction but for one undeniable fact: the pouch of glittering stones. Even if the diamonds were hers by right of possession, there were other claimants determined to regain them by all necessary means, including violence. Didn't matter, I thought, if she was pursued by pimp, husband, or strongarm thieves; in no way was I going to aid them. What I *could* do was call the number, ostensibly to find out about the reward, and try to learn who wanted Melissa.

So I deposited the quarter again, dialed the number, and waited tensely as the other phone began to ring.

THREE

After five rings a flat, computer-type voice cut in with recorded instructions to leave name and phone number at the sound of the tone. Happens I don't like answering machines of any description and the cyborg voice irritated me. So I growled, "I'm calling about your photo-ad. I have what you want and can verify—but not to any machine when I call five minutes from now." I looked at my wristwatch. "That'll be twenty-three minutes after the hour. Be ready to talk reward money. *Adios.*"

I hung up and walked back to the Datsun, sat in the shade, and decided I should have escorted Melissa wherever she wanted to go—Vegas, Seattle, Honolulu—armed with my .38 Cobra to protect her money and all those diamonds. If something evil happened to her, I'd blame myself. She'd asked me twice—no, three times—and I'd refused. Why? My only excuse, a weak one, was that traveling with her would take me from my typewriter and the novel I'd probably never finish. If the strike ended tomorrow I'd go back to Corinthian and the idiocies of *Frankie's Follies* and forget the fictional Hermitage heist. But I'd never forget the tainted damsel in distress; hooker or not, she'd cast a spell over me. I couldn't deny it. Melissa was beautiful, personable, intelligent, and running from danger. She trusted me, her note said, but I didn't at that moment feel particularly worthy of her trust. She'd asked for my protection and I hadn't responded. So I was angry with myself.

Something else bothered me: Melissa hadn't *acted* like any hooker I'd ever come across. In Beirut, Hong Kong, Bangkok, Nob Hill, or the lounge of any five-star hotel, a certain hardness emanated from pros looking for a trick. But not Melissa. Oh, she'd used some hooker language, but she could have picked that up from TV or a novel. I just wasn't convinced she was what she purported to be.

Or was that big-hearted humanist Joe Brent glossing over what he didn't want to believe?

What I had to believe was that the advertisement concerned the gemstones in her money belt.

Four minutes gone. I left my car and went back to the pay phone, quarter in hand.

After I dialed, the phone was answered at first ring.

A hoarse male voice grated, "You the wise guy who phoned?"

"It's alive," I said wonderingly. "Talks all by itself. Sure you're not a machine?"

"Cut the crap. Where is she?"

"Who'm I talking to?"

"Angelo. That's all you need to know."

"Well, Angelo, that's not quite all. What kind of money comes for the info?"

"A thousand—if it's the right lady."

"How could I forget her?" I said. "A beautiful blonde like her, dressed out of Rodeo Drive. But I couldn't finger her for less'n five."

"*Five?* You're crazy, man!"

"Forget it, then. But so you'll know she's the one, I'll mention this: five-seven, about one-twenty pounds, beige dress with matching shoes and bag, fur throw. A-cup bra, beige panties, mole under her left breast and a natural blonde . . ." I paused. "Worth five, Angelo?"

Moments passed while muffled sounds told me Angelo was conferring. Finally he came back on the line and said, "I'll bring the dough."

"Five large."

"Yeah—where you at?"

"Marina del Rey," I told him. "I work the parking lot by the Jamaica Bay Inn. Say when."

"Make it an hour. What's the name?"

"Chick," I told him. "Just Chick. Okay?"

"One more question, Chick. How'd you get that close to her?"

"That's for me to know and you to guess. Small bills, Angie, nothing over fifty."

I was about to hang up when a deep, coarse voice cut in. "She tell you her name?" The accent was Central Europe.

"We had a professional relationship," I said. "Short and pleasant. No names exchanged."

The same voice said, menacingly this time, "You screw her, Chick?"

"Bring the five," I said, "then ask her yourself."

"Listen, prick, don't jerk me around, or—"

"Threats? This is supposed to be a straight business deal, right? Threats make me nervous, so just one of you come. If I see more than the bagman, I'm gone—so's the lady." I slammed down the receiver, grinned at the telephone, and looked at my watch as I walked back to the Datsun. From Beverly Hills the drive should take no more than thirty-five minutes by the Freeway. Ten to fifteen minutes at a bank to collect five Gs, and Angelo—alone or in company—could be pulling in within the hour. Of course, if they weren't bringing money the bank delay wouldn't count.

I drove the short distance to Palawan Way and parked by the public beach. After locking the car I walked back to the Jamaica Bay Inn—the luncheon crowd was mostly gone—and chose an al fresco table from which I could observe the parking lot, in particular the ticket booth where Chick worked.

While ordering a frosted stein of Poummit's, I asked for a plug-in phone and the waiter brought both. I tested the phone, found it in working order, and eased back to enjoy the brew. And see who came looking for Melissa.

I was on my third stein when I saw a long black limousine pull up outside the parking lot and just beyond Chick's booth. Two men got out, the driver stayed behind the wheel. Light gray exhaust smoke showed the engine running. Neither man held a bag or a bundle as they walked toward the booth.

Lifting the phone receiver, I dialed 911, got an immediate answer, and said, "There's a robbery going on at the Jamaica Bay Inn—parking lot booth. Two guys and a getaway driver—black limo, plate" —I squinted to make it out—"California JA-797." I hung up and signaled the waiter for my check.

By then the two limousine passengers had Chick between them, marching him toward the car. Chick, a big guy, was white-faced and his lips were moving. The bald-headed one shoved him into the rear seat, got in beside him and slammed the door. His partner walked around the rear of the limo and was opening the door when two black-and-white prowl cars pulled up, one fore, one aft, blocking the limousine.

I paid the waiter and used the check stub to record the limo's license number. I left the restaurant and joined the crowd watching police in action. Four revolver-holding cops had Chick and the limousine trio spread-eagled against the limo. Beside me a bearded man in a yachting cap muttered, "This a movie?"

"Or something," I said, and moved closer to get a better look at the limo's personnel. The second strongarm wore a straw hat and a gaudily striped tie worth ninety-eight cents in any Woolworth's. The driver was the smallest of the three—short and bowlegged, spindly arms, and a face gray with worry.

Two cops began frisking all four men, producing revolvers from the two strongarms. Chick and the driver were clean.

Someone from the restaurant—day manager, probably—hurried out and began shouting. He pointed at Chick, and with obvious reluctance the cops let him stand away from the limousine. They preferred sorting sheep from goats at the station; for all they knew, Chick was the robbers' accomplice.

A third patrol car arrived, this one with a gold-braid lieutenant who got out with his walkie-talkie and began taking charge. After a while he pulled out the car's radio mike and started reporting to headquarters, staying outside the car in case any press photographers happened by. One did, along with a reporter, and the lieutenant began briefing them with a big, condescending smile.

I was fairly close to the scene, eyeing all participants and bonding the three heavies' faces in my memory. In the parking lot, horns were blowing, so Chick was allowed to return to his booth. Presently a waitress hurried out with a tall glass filled with dark liquid and chunks of fruit. She handed it to Chick, who downed the beverage in two long swallows and munched the fruit while taking tickets and making change.

Another five minutes, and the three handcuffed men were driven off in patrol cars, while one policeman followed in the black limousine. The crowd dispersed with disappointed mutterings—they'd hoped for a shootout and bloodbath.

Nothing there for me, so I strolled back to the beach parking section and unlocked my Datsun. I'd got everything I'd come for: confirmation that heavy people were looking for Melissa; the tag number of their limousine; and the satisfying knowledge that, even if I'd been willing to betray Melissa, the heavies wouldn't have paid me.

Cops in the wiretap business have reverse phone books, so if I'd had a cooperative police contact I could have called in the Beverly Hills number and gotten an address and a name. But there was another way of doing it, and when I got back to my studio-efficiency on Cerrito I phoned my car insurance agent, and, miraculously, found him in.

"Had a slight mishap," I said. "Some hit-and-run bastard scraped my elegant Datsun. What's my deductible, Art?"

"Le's see—here it is. Five hundred, Joe. Worth it?"

"Dunno. My car was parked down Highland so I didn't see the scrape. But a witness jotted down the plate number." I gave it to him. "If you can get the owner's name from the license bureau I'll give him a call, threaten him with something or other."

"Yeah, about all you can do." He repeated the tag number and said, "I'll call you, fifteen, twenty minutes."

"That's fine," I said. "I want to protect my claim record with your guys."

"Umm. Incidentally, the premium's due on your wife's car."

"She can pay it," I said. "I'm unemployed."

While waiting for Art's callback I changed bed linen and stuck damp bathtowels into a duffel bag, ready for the neighborhood laundromat, where they fluffed and dried for a slight extra charge.

There wasn't much in the refrigerator, but I used waiting time to clean out two limp carrots, some very brown lettuce leaves, and a nearly empty jar of apricot marmalade that had sprouted interesting growths in gray and green. I refilled the cube trays and was getting ready to scrub a few crusted dishes when the phone rang.

Art said jubilantly, "Man, you're in luck! That plate's registered to a real biggie. You were smacked by a Lincoln limo, Joe. Lotta parking violations, all fines promptly paid. Owner oughta make it right with you."

"So who's the biggie?"

"Ready for it? Well, none other than Borden Tarkos!"

"Tarkos? The guy who owns Falcon Productions?"

"Right, and a lot of diversification—theatres, talent agencies, a basketball team, a hotel-casino in Vegas. The Sagebrush. I got his phone number, too." He read it off, and I recognized it as the one in the photo-ad. "Where's he live?" I asked. "Beverly Hills?"

"Right again—Tahiti Way."

"Number?"

"Man, his mansion covers the whole street—but you'd never get past the guards. Better phone."

"I'll do that," I said, and, as an afterthought, asked if there was another car registered to Tarkos.

"Not him personally, but there's a Porsche in his wife's name—mucho speeding tickets, too."

"Hmm—a Porsche. What's his wife's name?"

"Melissa. Is it important?"

"Not particularly," I lied. "I used to date an actress who disappeared somewhere in Beverly Hills. Happen to have the lady's maiden name?"

"That I got. Here—it's Anders. Same broad?"

"Wish it were. The one I knew tapped two hundred from me three years ago; if I could find her, I'd like it back."

"Times are tough, eh?"

"You know it. But solidarity forever."

"You union guys," he said disdainfully, "never know when you got it good."

"Ain't it the truth. Thanks for the information, Artie. I'll let you know if Tarkos does the right thing."

"Yeah, I'd like to know. For the files."

I sat back and stared out of the grimy window at the wall of the next building. Borden Tarkos's wife had taken off with some of his gelt and he wanted her back—with greenbacks and glittering stones. The heart-shaped diamond, I imagined, was an engagement, wedding, or anniversary gift—assuming Melissa the streetwalker was Melissa Anders Tarkos, and it seemed very likely.

I'd never seen Tarkos but I'd watched two of his knee-breakers snatch Chick, and I could understand why Melissa was frightened.

If Tarkos had casino interests in Vegas, as Art indicated, then

Vegas was dangerous ground for the runaway wife. But had she gone there? And if not, where?

She needed help, more help than I could provide. She had money, but money didn't always buy loyalty—and Borden Tarkos had a great deal more than what I'd seen in her money belt.

I liked Melissa. I worried about her. I didn't know what I could do. Last night I'd had a chance to help her get far away but I'd passed.

Damn!

I went to the phone and dialed Tarkos's number. After the mechanical voice delivered its message and the taping tone sounded, I pinched my nostrils for nasal effect, and said, "Tarkos, you probably win most of them but you lost one today—at the parking lot in Marina del Rey. How do you like bailing out your strongarm guys and getting that big Lincoln out of the pound? The lesson is, deal honestly when buying favors. As for Melissa, she's doing just fine, and with some luck she'll never see your ugly face again.

"By now you're wondering if I'd have sold her out for five grand—well, the answer is no. I was curious how you'd respond and it went according to script—my script, not yours. And let me tell you, it was a boffo scene. Everyone enjoyed it except your three stars. They'll tell you about it, just don't let them minimize their astonishment. Oh, the way those cops cut your heavies down to size . . . gotta hang up so I can enjoy another good laugh." I replaced the receiver, waited a while, and redialed. After the tone sounded I said, "Me again, Tarkos. A couple of things to remember. You don't know who I am but I know who you are, where you work and live, and I can get to you whenever I want. That's in case there's any rough stuff with Melissa. Anyone lays a finger on her and I'll burn down your castle. Harm her and Falcon Productions disappears in a firestorm. In short, you have more than a wife to lose. So be a good citizen, you prick."

With all that off my mind, I walked down to Abarrotes Gomez and bought a supply of groceries. "Off my diet," I explained, paying with my last fifty, "so let's have a six-pack of Poummit's to wash down the calories."

Abarrotes Gomez beamed at me. "Strike over, Mr. Brent?"

"No—I decided to treat myself right for a change."

"Sure—why not? If you don't, who will?"

He was right there, I reflected as I left his store with two bulging sacks. And as I walked along, I remembered that it was just short of twenty-four hours ago that I'd seen Melissa striding down Highland.

Where was she? I thought of possibilities until I turned up Cerrito. Through my locked door I could hear the telephone ringing. I got keys out in a hurry, but by the time I was inside, the phone was silent. I took a deep breath and began putting away my groceries. That done, I uncapped a brew and sipped as I stared at what I'd typed late last night. Compared to what I *could* have been doing—sharing Melissa's bed—the pages were deeply unsatisfying. I tilted the bottle and was enjoying a long swallow when the phone began to ring.

FOUR

My subconscious thoughts—and subliminal hopes—were that my caller would be Morry, my agent; Sol, my producer; or, just possibly, Melissa—that is, Melissa Tarkos. Instead, the phone transmitted the voice of my wife.

"Joe? Natalie. How are you doing?"

"Why, splendidly here at the Hollywood Hilton. How else? Gourmet meals and a change of roaches daily. How's by you, Natty?" She hated the nickname, which was why I used it as often possible. Not having read James Fenimore Cooper's works, my wife wasn't familiar with Natty Bumppo. Anyway, she lacked the frontiersman's forthright wit and sinew. "Speak, Natty, what's on your labyrinthine mind?"

"Joe, would you like to keep Bryon for the weekend?"

Her question startled me. *"Here?"*

"Hardly. In my apartment, of course—I'll be rehearsing at the Long Beach Playhouse for—"

"—all night long?"

"I thought I'd stay over, save the long drive back."

"Mmmm. Prem Kushna directing the production?"

"As a matter of fact he is, but that doesn't mean there's anything between us—you have such a dirty mind."

"Not dirty, suspicious. So how *is* that sloe-eyed Bengali?"

"You know perfectly well Prem comes from Sri Lanka, and he's *extremely* talented. Now, will you look after Bryon? He *is* your stepson."

"Buy the cow, get the calf," I said unkindly, "but actually I have conflicting plans. Besides, you never let me lash the little predator when he deserved it so he's totally unmanageable where I'm concerned. I'm down to my last typewriter and have to preserve it from sabotage. So—tell you what: you and Prem work things out however you want, and when Bryon starts pulling your theater apart, dial 911."

"Oh, you *bastard!*"

"Better advice I cannot give."

"You'll hear from my lawyer," she said nastily.

"Why pay legal fees when I'll tell you for free how we'll divide our property. Let's see—you brought to the marriage two suitcases of used clothing, a box of cosmetics, one highchair, and a sheaf of dental bills. You get them all back—no contest. Including Bryon. So—"

The connection ended with Natty slamming down the phone.

I hadn't enjoyed the exchange but talking with my wife seemed a continuing obligation, even though I seldom initiated calls. If I'd really wanted to fight for Natalie I could have phoned INS and suggested they check Prem's green card. I didn't think he had one; Prem's eating-out story was that he'd journeyed from the East via Germany, Haiti and the Bahamas, stumbling ashore, dehydrated, in the Florida Keys. And there was a chance that, if the theater director stayed around, he would marry Natalie to legalize his stay in the hospitable USA. Much joy to them both. Not.

My wife's call left me in a dark mood and I told myself that if the Long Beach production was *Macbeth,* my wife could play all three witches. Simultaneously. Call her back and suggest it? No, that would be held against me, if not in heaven, then in judge's chambers. No way I could have fun and come out a winner.

Compensatorily, I opened a tin of smoked oysters and devoured them on English water crackers.

Poummit's Brew was just right for the snack, and soon my thoughts strayed far from Natty, Prem, and Bryon. I found myself wondering whether anything besides money had induced Melissa to marry the Tarkos creep. I realized she wasn't in or of the industry, because when I'd mentioned Schwab's famous pharmacy she hadn't known that filmland's legendary watering hole had closed down.

I analyzed Melissa as a spirited woman who wouldn't put up with house restraint or endless bullshit from her spouse. Maybe her acquisition of diamonds and money was an act of revenge for mistreatment. And being—or pretending to be—a hooker would be vengeance on a high, though self-destructive, scale. Assuming word got back to Tarkos.

After my snack I fingered the portable typewriter, felt no glimmerings of inspiration, and turned on the old black-and-white TV that came with the place. After considerable fine tuning I finally locked on the Lakers' game, and settled back in my chair to watch the fast-moving players. Up and down the court. Pass. *Bam!* Slam-dunk! The crowd went wild, and when the cheering subsided, I heard my doorbell ring.

My throat tightened. Melissa? Imprudently, I didn't ask who was there. I unlocked the door and opened it on two men standing in the hallway. My first impulse was to slam it in their faces, but the nearest man flashed a plastic-covered credential: LAPD. Swallowing, I said, "What have I done now?"

"Mr. Brent? Joseph Michael Brent?"

"Yeah."

"May we come in? Like to talk with you."

I shrugged, let them enter, and closed the door behind them. The first man said, "I'm Detective Sergeant Fallon. This is Special Investigator Ed Rinaldo."

I nodded at the shorter, olive-skinned man. "Also LAPD?"

Rinaldo shook his head. "Nevada Gaming Commission."

"I don't gamble," I said. "Can't afford to, and I'm unlucky. Sit down, and let's hear it." Reluctantly I blacked out the Lakers' game.

They sat side by side on the sofa, and Fallon got out a small spiral notebook. "When and where did you last see Mrs. Borden Tarkos?"

FIVE

I leaned back against my work table and stared at them. "I'm supposed to have seen the lady?"

Detective Sergeant Fallon sighed. "Let's have us asking the questions and you answering. It's more orderly that way, takes less of everyone's time."

My throat was dry but I managed to say, "Is this one of those official inquiries where I'd be well advised to have a lawyer present?"

"Suit yourself on that, Mr. Brent," Fallon said, "but I see this is as pretty informal—compared to what can happen at headquarters."

I took a deep breath, expelled it, and said, "Okay, guys, cooperation depends on the answer to two questions."

Rinaldo and Fallon exchanged glances. Rinaldo said, "Shoot."

"Is Mrs. Tarkos alive?"

Fallon said, "As far as anyone knows. Next question."

"Is she wanted for anything?"

Rinaldo stroked the side of his chin. "Mrs. Tarkos is not a fugitive from the law. What may develop, I can't predict."

"So you're doing her husband's dirty work?"

With a pained expression Fallon said, "The answer to that is also negative. It's your turn, Mr. Brent. Feel free to talk."

I sat down on my typing chair, unsure how much I'd tell them. "Last evening," I began, and described our sidewalk encounter, the low-riser delinquents who'd been bothering her, and said, "She told me her name was Melissa, no last name."

"But you found out she was—is—Tarkos's wife."

"I saw her picture in the paper. A reward was offered and I phoned the number given."

Fallon smiled. "You're too modest, Mr. Brent. You laid a rather clever trap to determine who placed the ad."

"I did?"

Rinaldo shook his head tiredly. "Yes, you did—at Marina del Rey and involving that poor clown, Chick. Then you phoned Tarkos and did some gloating, made some nasty threats."

The pit of my stomach was getting awfully cold. I considered the only possible source of his information, and said, "When you guys wiretap do you bother with a court order?"

"Definitely," said Fallon, "and you were overheard incidental to an interstate investigation. I used to think TV writers knew everything, but if you've missed this, there's a special electronic device that records the number from which an incoming call is made." He glanced over at my telephone. "From a number we get an address and a name. So we're interested in what you have to say."

"Since I'm not the target of your investigation, who is? Mrs. Tarkos—or her husband?"

Rinaldo said, "For the present, that's confidential, like grand jury presentments. We've traded what we can with you, and I encourage you to be completely frank with us. Cooperation is the theme, Mr. Brent. Cooperation. Because if you analyze your position, Mr. Brent, it could be termed delicate—extremely delicate. We have you issuing threats against a prominent citizen, and Sergeant Fallon's people could get pretty upset over someone making a false report to the police—a robbery that wasn't."

"If that's not enough to gain your full cooperation, Mr. Brent," Fallon said smoothly, "imagine what Mr. Tarkos might do if he were told—anonymously, of course—the name of the man who caused him so much distress and threatened to destroy his property."

"I'm imagining it," I said, "and it comes out a lot less pleasant than a weekend in Palm Springs. So, how can I assist your bi-state investigation?"

This was a scene I'd seen in scores of TV and feature movies: detectives move on a guy who has something to hide, threaten him, maybe beat him up, but the hero fends them off with shrewd, tension-breaking comebacks, manages to maintain the integrity of his secret, and the frustrated detectives finally give up and go away.

That was the cliché but the present scene wasn't going to play that way, not entirely. I readied myself for the first question, which came with Rinaldo saying, "How long was Mrs. Tarkos with you?"

"Seven, eight hours. She slept in the bedroom, I slept where you're sitting. This morning she was gone."

"Just like that?" Fallon asked. "Didn't leave a phone number or an address for contact purposes?"

"Why should she? She was broke, frightened, I gave her shelter—a simple human transaction."

"Very compassionate," Fallon said dryly. "You pick up a hooker—or a broad *pretending* to be a hooker—let her sleep here, and—"

"There was a meal involved," I told them. "She was hungry."

Rinaldo shook his head incredulously. "A dame with all that money—*hungry?*"

I said, "Whatever money Tarkos has he must be pretty close with it. She said she wanted to go to San Francisco but didn't have the fare by train, bus, or plane." I cleared my throat. "She asked if I'd drive her there, but I told her I didn't have gas money myself."

"Was that a true statement?" Fallon asked.

"It was."

Rinaldo said, "So she wanted to get to 'Frisco, did she? Nothing about Las Vegas?"

"The words never left her lips."

"And she didn't talk money with you—big money?"

"Not other than I've described."

Fallon eased forward. "Did you search her purse?"

"No, I didn't. Why should I? I wasn't checking I.D. and I was convinced she had no money—even if I'd been inclined to take it."

"Which you weren't," Rinaldo said suggestively. "I got to say you're coming off cleaner than a Supreme Court candidate. For a man in depressed economic circumstances, you express an amazing indifference to money."

"It's the way I was brought up. Like the TV ad said, I get money the old-fashioned way—I earn it. Of course, with the writers' strike in full swing, I haven't seen a paycheck in quite a while."

Rinaldo came back at me: "Did Mrs. Tarkos mention gems of any kind? Jewels?"

I shook my head. "She didn't even have a ring on her finger. The only thing of value I noticed was an animal skin around her shoulders. One pelt, probably stone marten."

Fallon muttered, "That checks—and her Porsche is still in the garage." He looked at me. "I don't like asking this, Mr. Brent, and I don't do so from prurient interest, but did you lay the lady?"

"If I had, I might lie about it—as one gentleman to another—but the fact is, we had no physical contact."

"Any particular deterrent?"

"She didn't suggest it, I'm married, and there's an epidemic of that lethal something called AIDS."

Rinaldo said, "Did she know you're married?"

I thought about that one. "I can't recall it coming into the conversation, sir. However, *I* knew I was married—"

"—though separated," Fallon interjected.

I shrugged.

Fallon put away his notebook. "Too bad you didn't take that five grand you asked for, Mr. Brent. Then we could put you away for extortion and taking money under false pretenses."

"I never intended to take reward money," I said angrily. "The tape tells you that."

"Still," Rinaldo said, "I have a little way-back feeling you haven't been totally forthcoming with us."

"Like hell I haven't."

"You're a writer, you have a creative mind. If I can ever prove that any of what you've told us was invented to cover for her, yourself, or anyone else, you'll do hard time, Mr. Brent. Very hard. No country-club prison for you."

"That all, gentlemen?"

"One final thing," Fallon said as he rose. "In the event Mrs. Tarkos crossed your path again, you'd let me know, wouldn't you?"

"Why, of course, Sergeant," I said as insincerely as possible. "Absolutely. And, in return, you or Special Investigator Rinaldo will tell me all about the casino skim investigation you're running against Borden Tarkos. That's really FBI and Treasury business, of course, but you've dealt yourselves in and you'll want to follow through. Unless, of course, Treasury and the FBI should hear of turf violation —anonymously, of course—and take it away from you." I smiled. "None of us would want that to happen, would we? No commendations for you guys, and I'd have lost a couple of pals who tried to keep a secret investigation secret. I think you're scared to go after Tarkos—too much power, money, and influence for a pair of sneaky Petes like you. So you're after the runaway wife as a purported accomplice, regardless of whether she may have had personal reasons for getting out. Her you can bulldoze and intimidate without reprisal. Real gutsy—which one of you thought it up?"

Fallon's face reddened as I talked. He held back until I finished and then he exploded. "Don't tempt me, wiseass! A lot of bad things can happen to you."

"That's the chance we take living in this crime-ridden town," I said, and gestured at my typewriter. "The night's young. I'll put in time composing a memo of everything we've discussed. Let's see, the Nevada Special Investigator is Rinaldo—would that be Edward or Eduardo? And your Christian names, Detective Sergeant Fallon?"

"Fuck you," he said, and gestured at his partner. "Let's get out of here before I throw up."

While they opened the door, I called, "I'll think up some better exit lines. Call me next week. No charge."

Rinaldo turned, glared at me, and they were gone, door slamming behind them. I went to the cupboard and pulled down what was left of the Jim Beam and swallowed most of it. The warmth defrosted my stomach and presently I felt better. A lot better.

One problem with law enforcement, I reflected, was that right and left hands seldom knew what each other was doing. I could visualize the Nevada Gaming Commission getting a tip on Tarkos's Sagebrush casino operation, and assigning Rinaldo to it. He would have had to contact someone at LAPD who could lay on a wiretap, and together they'd conduct a covert and very private operation. Maybe they were going to collect evidence and turn it over to constituted authorities. Or, I mused, maybe they planned to use that evidence to shake down Tarkos and set themselves up for life—with points in the Sagebrush operation or shares in Falcon Productions.

I had no reason to doubt that Sagebrush profits were being skimmed; it happened at a lot of Nevada's gambling casinos, and many quasi-respectable people got rich on the undeclared skim. They got it out of the country one way or another to Nassau, the Caymans, Liechtenstein, and, less frequently these days, Bern and Zürich.

For such clandestine transfers, though, a courier was needed. Someone above suspicion.

My thoughts turned to Melissa Tarkos.

Focused on her custom-made money belt and all it contained. Say, ten thousand in cash—travel money—and millions in concentrated form—diamonds. I began to think of them as skim destined for some offshore bank account. Skim that hadn't reached destination because Melissa had decided not to make delivery.

Conjecture, sure, but interesting, nevertheless. And possible.

Reasonable, too, when you considered why a man involved in illegal monetary transactions would use his wife as a courier: he could keep her nearby and watch her; but most significantly, however much she knew of his illicit dealings, the law protected a husband from his wife's testimony.

That immunity was not necessarily complete. A vengeful wife could still tell investigators where bodies or valuables were hidden, and her leads could be used to build a case against the husband. She would never have to appear in court and testify.

Tarkos's lawyers were certainly aware of his vulnerability and it seemed ample motive for Tarkos attempting to get his hands on his missing wife. Free of his control, Melissa could be anywhere, telling what she knew of Borden's hidey-holes. Her freedom endangered his.

Pieces of the puzzle were coming together, the focus sharpening on domestic estrangement with criminal coloration.

Tarkos didn't want Melissa merely confined in his Tahiti Way chateau; he wanted her deep underground, forever silent.

I drained the last drops from the Beam bottle and put it in the already-full trash basket.

The phone rang. I answered mechanically, heard Morry Manville's voice, and suddenly felt optimistic. "Joe? Read the *Reporter* today?" he asked.

"Can't afford it."

"Then I've got bad news and good," my agent said. "The bad is that Sol and Corinthian filed for bankruptcy."

"Oh, God!" I swallowed hard. "After that, what news could be good?"

"The remaining assets are in escrow. Your holdback two weeks' pay is safe."

"Morry, I really need it. When can I collect?"

"Ah, well, that's more bad news—a year or so before the bankruptcy referee releases it. With nothing coming in, Sol couldn't keep paying production staff and other creditors. He had no option but to file. Sorry, Joe—I'm in a bad way, too. Until the strike's settled, everyone stays broke."

"Aaagh! I need a respirator."

"The Guild office is making small loans while the strike fund lasts. And you can start collecting unemployment." He paused. "You could sell your boat."

"Or torch it for insurance." I said miserably. "Goodnight, Morry."

"Take care."

I stared at the phone as though it were a cobra that had fanged me deeply. Bad enough to have been laid off because of the strike, but to have no workplace to return to . . . that was really heaping disaster atop misfortune.

Was there no solace? Ah, there was: I wasn't the only one affected. There were others similarly hit; plenty of misery to share out there in Tinseltown, and lots left over.

Because a strike's effects weren't limited to the strikers. Cameramen, sound and light technicians, video editors, grips and electricians, costumers and makeup artists, script and continuity people, front office personnel were all suddenly unemployed. They skimped on groceries and gasoline, postponed rent and mortgage payments just to get by; for every writer like myself, I figured a dozen others were hit equally hard. Like all disasters, this one had a ripple effect extending far beyond the causative core.

What to do?

There was a time, I'd been told, when writers seeking inspiration could stroll the streets of L.A. for night air and a change of scene. Now the air was poisonous, and dark streets were controlled by gangs, dopers, assault artists, pimps, and hookers. It was their turf and I had no inclination to invade it.

So I went to bed, tossed and slept restlessly, and in the morning drove down to Marina del Rey.

SIX

Semmes & Co. were the yacht brokers who had sold me my modest boat. Madeleine Gossons was the broker who handled the transaction, and it was at her desk that I pulled up a chair.

She wore frizzed hair and very thick glasses, through which she appraised me. "You look familiar," she said by way of greeting.

"Joe Brent," I said, "and nineteen months ago you sold me a fiberglass contraption with frayed sails that I optimistically named *El Dorado*."

"Brent," she murmured, went to a file cabinet and brought back a thin manila folder with my name on it. "Let's see," she said, opening the folder. "Ay, yes, Rollins-built twenty-six-footer. Price thirty-two eight." She peered at me. "Trading up?"

"Selling out." I passed the papers to her. "Bank mortgage is about eleven thousand. What can you do for me?"

"Bad market," she sighed. "Has your boat been recently surveyed?"

I shook my head.

She sat back and gazed at the low ceiling. "I remember you, TV writer. Well, in the past few days four screenwriters have come in to unload their boats, and only one could pay for a marine surveyor."

"I'm benched with the other three," I admitted. "Can't come up with four hundred for a survey."

"What's your bottom price?"

"How about thirty?"

She shook her head and the Medusa curls rolled back and forth. "I could try at twenty-five, but the market's so depressed I think you'd be lucky to realize twenty. Deduct the mortgage and you'd come out with nine. Is that okay?"

"Have to be."

She handed me a sales authorization form and I signed at the bottom. "Can't promise a quick sale," she said in tones that suggested she enjoyed my fall from affluence, "but we'll do all we can."

"Sooner the better," I said, walked outside with her and pointed out the buoy where *El Dorado* was tugging at the tide.

"Keys," she said, and I turned them over to her, blowing a parting kiss at the boat that had given me so much weekend pleasure cruising to Catalina and San Clemente, wind and spray in my face, sun silvering the crested combers. "I'll clean out my gear when you have a live prospect."

"That may be a while," she warned, "but who knows? Miracles happen."

"Plenty of storage space," I said. "Could bring up quite a load of grass from Ensenada."

"I'll remember that," she said, "if I spot a buyer who might be interested in a quick run. Boat's never been impounded?"

"No."

"Good selling point." She gave me a firm, muscular handshake. "I'll go over your boat today and order a survey, deduct the fee along with our commission, if that's satisfactory."

"Has to be," I said glumly, and left the brokerage office.

As I walked to my car I glanced over at the Jamaica Bay Inn, where I had devoured those delicious Malaysian prawns and watched the police action I'd provoked. I was in high spirits then, I recalled, no thought of Corinthian's bankruptcy and the end of *Frankie's Follies*. Ah, but how quickly one's fortunes fade, and now I was at the mercy of a yacht broker who had given me scant hope of a timely sale. For a while, at least, I would have to survive on beans and day-old bread, travel on the fumes in my Datsun's tank.

Nevertheless, I drove north into Beverly Hills and found Tahiti Way. As Art had said, the Tarkos estate was huge and walled, with a guardhouse inside the heavy iron-grill gate. I drove around the perimeter, noting closed circuit TV scanners, and reflected that life within could have been hard on its chatelaine, Melissa.

Driving away, I rebuked myself again for failing to provide the escape route she so desperately wanted. I hoped she would be able to remain free of her husband's pursuit and out of Fallon's and Rinaldo's hands.

Now, totally and completely unemployed, I had time and motive to help her, but opportunity had come and gone. I drove back to Cerrito, left my car, and checked my mailbox for whatever bad news it might contain.

All the box held was a folded piece of paper that bore the following message:

Mr. Brent—Please come see me rite away. R. Gomez.

Why would Ruben Gomez want to see me? Had a check of mine been returned? I didn't want to see Gomez, but neither did I want him out of pocket. So I walked down to Highland, turned east, and entered the store.

He was ringing up a customer and motioned me to wait. When the customer left, Gomez came around the counter, wearing a large, white-toothed smile. We shook hands and he said, "I have a message for you. Wait." He went back behind the counter, rang No Sale on the register, and extracted a small envelope. The sealed envelope bore the engraved name and address of the Roosevelt Hotel, a few blocks away, and was addressed to Mr. Joseph Brent.

"Who gave you this?" I asked.

"A man."

"Good, that establishes gender. Did he have a name? What did he look like?"

"No name. He was shorter than you, and older. Maybe fifty. Gray hair, beard not so gray. He paid me to get this to you."

"Which you've done. Thanks, Ruben." I pocketed the envelope and went back to my room. Before opening the envelope, I held it to the light, saw nothing resembling a letter bomb, and opened it carefully.

There was a folded sheet of notepaper with writing on it, and a hundred-dollar bill. I fondled the bill voluptuously and read the handwritten message:

> *Because we share concern for the welfare of a certain young woman whom you succored, it will be to your advantage and hers if you will come circuitously to my room—407—where*

we can converse in private. The enclosed money is a good-faith token.

George D. Anders

Well, well, I thought, a relative of Melissa's, or someone pretending to be. The message wasn't particularly informative, but the green enclosure had bought my time, and the Roosevelt was nearby.

I took my suitcase from the storage closet, opened it, and got out my .38 Cobra, leaving the shoulder holster in the bag. I opened the cylinder and found the expected six soft-nosed cartridges in place, snapped the cylinder into position, and fitted the .38 between my belt and spine. Anyone could sign himself George Anders, I thought, and the man who wanted to converse in private had better be legit.

The hundred-dollar bill went into my nearly empty wallet; providentially, it had arrived at a time of great need, and I was prepared to listen to what Mr. Anders had to say.

At the Roosevelt I climbed the wide marble staircase to the lobby and looked around. No suspicious types in view, and I had decided not to announce my arrival on the house phone.

Fourth floor. Room 407. Chicana maids were cleaning rooms and dusting the hallway. I rapped on the door, rapped harder over the noise of a hall vacuum cleaner, and heard a voice call, "Who's there?"

"Fellow you sent a note to."

"Be with you."

Presently the door opened and I saw a man fitting Ruben's description. He was wearing an open-collar shirt, worn corduroy slacks, and a luxuriant beard, beginning to gray. "Come in," he said. "I'm glad you came so promptly."

I closed the door behind me. "So you're George Anders?" I said. "Mind if I see some I.D.?"

"Of course." He moved toward the coffee-table sofa and I watched his hands. One went into his hip pocket and produced a billfold. Handing it to me, he said, "I'm Lissa's father, Mr. Brent."

I looked at the plastic insert in his billfold: the credential card showed his photo and gave his name as George D. Anders, Professor, School of Communications, San Diego City College. "I'm satisfied," I said, returning his billfold, "now, what about your daughter?"

"Coffee? Or would you prefer a drink?"

"Coffee's fine." I sat down while he poured two cups from a thermal carafe.

"As you know," George Anders began, "my daughter is on the run, attempting to evade her husband."

"Borden Tarkos." I reached for the cup and sipped.

"Oh, you know his name? I didn't think she'd told you."

"I found out."

"Through his newspaper ad?"

"Plus a little initiative of my own."

"Interesting," he said musingly, "very interesting. So you know that her husband is a very wealthy man who is able to spend a great deal of money to regain possession of my daughter."

"And the trinkets in her money belt."

Anders nodded. "The product of illegal gains, the proceeds of money diverted from the State of Nevada and the IRS."

"So a Nevada investigator informed me. Casino skim, specifically Tarkos's Sagebrush operation. The LAPD is involved, too, in what appears to be an unofficial way."

"Unofficial?"

"Could be private initiative," I said, "looking to a large payoff from Tarkos."

"I—I don't understand."

"There's a tap on Tarkos's phone," I told him, and sipped more room-service coffee. It wasn't bad, but what my percolator turned out was a lot better.

"I see," he said finally. "You've certainly become well informed in a very short space of time."

"Your daughter impressed me," I said, "and I don't like people like Tarkos."

"Well, you impressed Lissa, Mr. Brent, and she doesn't like Tarkos either—I guess that's been obvious all along."

"She must have liked him once, enough to marry him. Or was it gold and glitter that attracted her?"

He grimaced. "She was young, vulnerable, and very human. Tarkos gave her a life of luxury with strings attached."

"Working as his foreign courier."

Anders's eyes widened. "The police know that?"

"I surmised it; they can, too. The problem, Mr. Anders, is that Melissa is criminally culpable for having taken illegally large sums out of the U.S. and deposited them abroad for Tarkos's benefit. The authorities would like details from her, while her husband seems determined to keep her from talking."

He nodded. "That is it—in a nutshell. The question is, what can we do?"

"I've wondered about that myself," I said, "and I think the best all-around solution is hiring Melissa a good lawyer, who then makes a deal with the feds in return for the diamonds and her cooperation. She avoids prosecution, divorces Tarkos, and gets half of whatever Tarkos property isn't confiscated. But as long as she has the stones she's in double jeopardy."

Anders stroked his beard thoughtfully. "How right you are. Borden Tarkos is a ruthless, unscrupulous, amoral man. My daughter fears him more than the federal authorities, unfortunately. What she did was impulsive, hence the present appalling situation." He sat forward. "I love my daughter, Mr. Brent; she's my only child. I raised Lissa from age twelve when her mother died. We've always been close—until she was drawn into Tarkos's magnetic field. After that, for the past three years, we lost contact. I assume she didn't want to tell me the role her husband had cast her in. I wouldn't have liked it but my lips would have been sealed. She should have understood that."

"Give her credit for keeping you uninvolved," I said. "Already too many people are in the know." A thought occurred to me. "Tarkos doesn't own Sagebrush outright, does he?"

"Something under fifty percent."

"And the majority owners?"

He looked away. "From Lissa I've inferred that certain organized crime figures are the actual owners."

"That's not surprising," I said. "Which makes me wonder if Tarkos was skimming from them. That's not an easily forgiveable offense. In fact, wiseguys have been disappeared just for trying."

He shrugged. "If you say so—it's not a world I'm familiar with."

"But what I can't understand is why Tarkos should set up a skim operation. He's supposed to be fabulously wealthy, got a movie studio, a basketball team, and—"

"His last three or four films have been box-office disasters, and his Rebels are at the bottom of the league."

"So he's been covering those deficits with money skimmed, not only from the feds and the Nevada authorities, but from his partners in the Sagebrush." I shook my head. "Then his wife runs off with two or three million dollars he shouldn't have and can't admit losing."

"Quite a predicament," Anders observed with that stodgy earnestness typical of professors.

"At least," I agreed, "but you didn't ask me here to evaluate Tarkos's problems. Melissa has plenty of her own."

"Yet they're interconnected."

"Absolutely. If a time machine could take her back to that moment when she decided to run with her husband's loot, this time around she wouldn't. She'd take the stones to their intended destination and no one would be looking for her, threatening her life. Tarkos would be able to replace the skim if his partners came looking, and the two of them, man and wife, would be as safe and snug as two borers in an ear of corn." I finished the rest of my coffee, saw Anders was getting ready to say something, and held up my hand.

"But we ain't got no time machine, Professor, and Melissa has to play out the scenario that's writ—that, in fact, *she* wrote. Why did she skip, Professor? Infected with her husband's greed? Or revenge for having been slapped around, beaten up and abused by her husband?"

Rather stiffly he said, "Lissa didn't confide in me—you'll have to ask her."

"Well, motive isn't all that important right now. What's important is extricating her from a dangerous situation, preferably through a very sharp attorney and protection from the feds."

He thought it over as he refilled our cups. After a while he said, "Suppose she didn't elect to take that course—what alternatives are there?"

"Neutralizing Borden Tarkos—if you know an assault team for hire."

"I could never recommend that, Mr. Brent. I'm not at all a violent man." His gaze was penetrating. "Are you?"

"Not for a lot of years. But you set me a hypothetical situation, I gave a hypothetical reply." I added sugar to my cup and stirred. "What's your impression of what your daughter really wants to do?"

He sighed. "She's numb with fear, incapable of framing logical thought."

"Well, that's not the quick-thinking Melissa who braced me on the Boulevard—of course, she could have been on a high."

"I don't believe my daughter takes drugs."

"Oh, c'mon," I scoffed, "you teach kids her age, you know the milieu. A joint's a joint, a pop's a pop, and if you haven't seen glazed eyes in your classroom, I'll jump out that window."

"No need to," he said apologetically, "it's just that I don't think my daughter uses drugs as a matter of course."

"Well, being around Tarkos, and in the Beverly Hills-Las Vegas settings, she probably knows how to snort a line or two, wouldn't you say? Incredible as it may sound, even in the rarefied atmosphere of TV studios it's been known to happen. There's shit all over the place; no one has to ask for it. Open your beak like a baby robin and the stuff is there. Handy as vitamin C and Alka-Seltzer. It's hardly a subject of discussion. But, okay, let's say Melissa is a lady usually in control of herself. Now, she's scared to death, frightened by the consequences of what seemed a compelling move at the time. Does she still have the stones with her?"

"She didn't say and I didn't ask. I'm here because she asked me to contact you surreptitiously; she wants your advice."

I half-grunted, half-laughed. "Let's be frank, Professor—what I write is dream stuff, no relation to reality. I have no credentials at all as an adviser. And who came up with the idea of using Gomez—surreptitious, sure, but why him?"

"She said you bought groceries there. She didn't think you'd deal with someone who wasn't okay."

"That's a far stretch," I remarked, "even though it connected."

"She said not to telephone you or go to your apartment, in case I was followed."

"That was good advice," I acknowledged, "and what I wonder is whether you were followed *here.*"

"I don't think I was, but I'm no expert in such things."

"The initial premise was sensible. Tarkos knows about you—he'd think it logical for Melissa to take refuge with you at some point." I stared at his deep, cloudy eyes. "She's not at your place, I hope."

He shook his head. "We both decided that was a poor idea. No—she's stashed herself away in what we think is a safe place and wants you to come to her."

"You can pass along the advice I've given."

"Of course, I can parrot it, Mr. Brent, but Lissa wants more than advice. She wants—needs—protection until the situation is somehow resolved."

"Why me? Why not a licensed security service?"

"Knowing her husband, she doesn't think she could trust them not to sell her out. Whatever passed between you in those hours, she was your guest, Mr. Brent, a bond of confidence formed. Lissa trusts you, and she's more than willing to pay for your time."

I grunted. "My time comes pretty cheap these days, Professor, but I'll talk things over with her. The hundred bucks buys that."

He nodded, relieved. "It's for expenses to San Diego. Is it enough?"

"Easily," I said, "and I'll need an address."

From his shirt pocket he took a slip of paper and gave it to me. Maude Arkwright had room 201 at the Beach View Motel on Harbor Island. Like most runaways, she'd kept her own initials. I used a hotel match and ashtray to burn the address, finished my coffee, and stood up. "I don't know where all this is leading," I said, "but I'll try to guide her to an attorney's office. I was a Marine but I'm not a gunslinger. Both of you should understand that. And I certainly don't kill for hire."

"There was never any suggestion of that," he said somewhat primly, "and had there been, I wouldn't be talking to you."

"Fair enough. Call Maude from a pay phone and let her know I'm on my way—no names. Discreetly."

"Discreet is the word," he smiled, then his face went taut with worry. We shook hands and I left his room and the hotel.

I took I–5 south through Santa Ana and along the coast, past La Jolla and Mission Bay, then over the airport cutoff and west on Harbor Drive to the Harbor Island access road.

I was familiar with San Diego, beginning with the Marine Corps Recruit Depot and the North Island Naval Air Station just across

San Diego Bay. And I knew the bars and strip joints around Camp Nimitz and Point Loma. I knew the Naval Hospital, too.

The Beach View Motel was easy to find. A two-story unit of about fifty rooms, iron-grill walkway facing the Bay, curtained glass doors and a scattering of Mexican maids making up vacated rooms. As I climbed the outside staircase, a V-formation of navy fighters soared up like silver arrowheads and thundered over the motel.

The door to Room 201 was like all the others. I pressed the button and waited. Pressed again, and saw the curtain part an inch while I was inspected. The door opened, snub chain rattled free, and I stepped inside.

Facing me was a woman with shoulder-length black hair and thick black eyebrows. For a moment I was baffled, then I realized it was Melissa gone into disguise. "Joe!" she said breathily, and hugged me. "I'm so glad you've come. Thank you, oh, *thank* you!"

She stepped back, pulled off her wig, and smiled weakly. "I was so afraid you wouldn't come."

"Your dad made a convincing case," I replied, "and so I'm here." I looked around the room, saw a small kitchenette, table and chairs, and an unmade bed. Touching the side of my face, she said, "I'm making sure it's really you."

The sight of this woman who had come to occupy my thoughts almost totally, the sound of her voice, the soft touch of her fingers thrilled me in a way I couldn't remember having been thrilled before. My heart was beating faster and my lips were dry. I licked them and asked, "How did you get here?"

"Daddy met me and brought me here." She looked at me searchingly. "Do you think I was followed?"

"You haven't been snatched yet, so the answer is no. However, we're getting out of here."

"Why?"

"Because word will be out for a single woman. If we're together you're less noticeable, and safer."

"Of course—you're absolutely right." She glanced around. "I haven't anything to offer you—not coffee or even a drink. I've sent out for meals."

"Hungry?"

She nodded, and began folding things into a nylon shoulder bag, including the beige dress and marten stole she had been wearing at our first encounter. Now she had on a cheap white blouse, a black drawstring skirt, and woven leather sandals. Wearing the black wig, and with eyebrows darkened as they were, Melissa couldn't readily have been recognized. In a few moments she said, "I'm ready."

"Bill paid?"

"As soon as Daddy called."

"Leave the key in the door, let's go."

Once in my car I said, "I assume your valuables are in the usual place of concealment."

She nodded. "Where are we going?"

"El Cajon. About twenty miles northeast."

"Why there?"

"Because I just thought of it. Meaning no one else will think of it. I know—La Jolla is more your style, but it would be a likely place to scout for you. Besides, there's an airfield near El Cajon—in case a fast getaway is in order."

I turned back along Harbor Drive, picked up the freeway heading north, then hooked into I-8 through Mission Valley and La Mesa. Nearing El Cajon, I slowed to begin looking for out-of-the-way lodging and found a walled bungalow-type spread that offered RV facilities and a small convenience store. Pulling up in front of the registration office, I said, "We can't use credit cards, so everything has to be cash."

"How much do you need?"

"Give me a couple hundred."

She took bills from her clutch purse. "I haven't had a chance to talk about paying you. How—?"

"We'll have time together," I said. "After all, we're a runaway couple who want privacy. The owners will understand."

A gray-haired woman in curlers and a calico duster showed me a fair-sized double with twin beds, card table, gas stove and a working refrigerator. "Fresh towels and bedding every day," she announced. "How long you plannin' to stay?"

"Several days, but it could stretch to a week. I'll pay the weekly rate."

"That'll be one-sixty including tax."

I shoved two bills across the counter. She eyed them and said, "No major credit card?"

"Cash illegal?"

"I'd like to see your driver's license, please."

"Revoked," I said. "My wife does the driving. But I've got my Coast Guard service record in the car if that'll help."

She shrugged. "Got to be careful these days," she muttered, and gave me a registration card, which I filled out: *M/M Michael Phillips, Spokane, Washington.*

She gave me back forty dollars change and studied the card. "You got California plates."

"You get them when you buy a California car," I told her, and decided the lady was a bit too nosy for my taste.

I drove around to the bungalow and nosed the Datsun into the porte-cochere. Fifty yards away some oldsters were clustered around the shuffleboard, and a spirited game was underway.

I opened the door, beckoned Melissa inside, drew a glass of water from the tap, and went out to the car again. With driveway dust I made a handful of mud and plastered the visible plate with enough of it to make two numbers illegible. Then I washed my hands at the sink, and while Melissa was taking a shower I walked over to the store and bought beer and soft drinks, bread, mayonnaise, lettuce, cold cuts, pickles, milk, instant coffee, sugar, napkins, paper plates, four TV dinners, and a nosegay of violets. After paying, I asked the elderly cashier where hard liquor could be purchased.

"Over on Magnolia," he said, gesturing, shoved up his spectacles, and stared at me.

"How far?"

"Mebbe half mile. Now if you was suffering from scorpion sting I could help out—emergency."

"That's a blessing," I said. "My wife's got a swollen toe from one of those desert devils and I was planning to apply a poultice of Jim Beam."

"Beam?" He fumbled under the counter. "Fresh out of Beam, partner, but Wild Turkey does as good—they say." He tucked a bagged pint into my grocery sack. "Ten dollars an' mum's the word."

I paid him and hoisted the bag. "Pleasure doing business with you."

"Wouldn't accommodate you, but you're from out of state an' all."

"Courtesy of the road, and I appreciate it." Lugging the bag, I went back to the bungalow and let myself in.

While I was distributing the groceries Melissa emerged from the shower, towel wrapped around her body. I knocked ice cubes into two glasses and added enough bourbon for an authoritative slug. We drank, and she said, "I needed that almost as much as my shower."

"I needed it, period," I told her and drank again. Eyeing her, I said, "You'll need clothes, shoes, and eyebrow dye that doesn't rinse off in the shower. We can shop tonight or tomorrow. Right now—ah, would you mind getting into a skirt or something? You're distracting me."

"Oh? I thought you were invulnerable to my charms," she murmured and gave me a naughty smile, "but if you insist . . ."

The teasing, provocative tone, her lack of clothing, made me want to crush her in my arms and kiss her deep and long. I managed to swallow and said, "Right now—as I was saying—it's time for realistic talk."

"About money?"

"About you—the danger you're in."

She nodded. "For your time, advice and protection how much do you think would be fair?"

"You left five hundred at my apartment, and that's plenty for now. Let's keep it to expenses."

She shrugged. "If you prefer." She ran one hand through damp hair and said, "I'll be right back."

While Melissa dressed I built myself another drink and boiled water for instant coffee. Then I made sandwiches and had two plates ready when she reappeared in skirt and blouse, looking fresh, clean, and luscious.

After biting into a sandwich she said, "You do everything, don't you, Joe? It's as though you'd taken care of lots of strays."

"I was a Marine and a bachelor, and after I married I found my wife wasn't much on kitchen arts."

"You said you were separated. Does that mean divorce?"

"In our case, yes." I started on my sandwich and realized I was a lot hungrier than I'd thought. I finished my Wild Turkey and opened a Coors. Melissa added Coke to her bourbon and we sipped silently. After a while I said, "Some ground rules, Melissa. You don't phone from here or anywhere, not even to the professor."

"Agreed."

"When you go out, you go with me, wearing wig and such."

"You have a plan?"

"I discussed one with your father and he agrees on its general wisdom. Do you know a good lawyer who's not connected to your husband?"

"I'll have to think about that."

"A criminal lawyer, not a real estate or probate type."

She swallowed and sipped from her glass. "I'm afraid I don't. Do you?"

I shook my head. "What I can do is call the Bar Association for names."

"So what will this lawyer do for me?"

I put down my glass and told her. As I spoke her face tightened and she looked away. When I finished she said, "I don't think I like your plan."

"Give me an alternate."

"Go to Europe, sell the diamonds, and enjoy life."

"A short life," I said. "You don't seem to understand that people like your husband and his Sagebrush partners have connections all over the world. You might last a week in Paris, Rome, or Monaco, then lights out. You'd be tortured for the money and killed. I don't know what possessed you to take off with all that loot, but you didn't think things through. Otherwise, you wouldn't have been playing hooker and pleading protection from a stranger—me." A thought occurred. "Do you have a boyfriend? I mean, someone you're seriously involved with, someone you can trust?"

Her mouth tightened. "Last year—God, it seems so much longer ago—I was seeing the beach club tennis pro—after hours. Borden found out, bought him off, and relocated him in Vegas."

"Which is where you told me you were going."

"Well, I decided against it. If Rene was that mercenary once, all he'd do is call Borden and I'd be back in my special prison. Worse off than before."

"That was good thinking," I said. "Now, how much do you know about your husband's business affairs? I don't mean Falcon Productions, real estate, or the ball club—I mean the covert side, where you were operating."

"You mean how much money he skimmed and where I took it?"

I nodded. "Like that."

"Just about everything. Shall I tell you?"

"Save it for the lawyer and the feds."

She thought it over. "You're not giving me any choice, are you?"

"Melissa, you sought my advice, paid for it, and I've given it to you. I can't force you to accept it, but I have your interests at heart—only yours." I sipped more Coors. "Does your husband love you?"

"I thought he did—when I married him."

"Do you love your husband?"

Her face became an ugly mask. "He's a horrible man. I loathe him."

"Enough to put him behind bars?"

"Enough to kill him."

SEVEN

With all that on the table, I decided the time had come for action. From a pay phone outside the store I phoned the San Diego Bar Association, described the kind of attorney I was looking for, and received three names.

The first lawyer, Severino Sanchez, couldn't give me an appointment for five days—busy at trial. The second, Mark Levin, was attending a bar meeting in Acapulco. The third, Joel Hatfield, had his secretary put me down for an appointment at five. Initial consultation: one hundred dollars. I gave her my motel alias, Michael Phillips, and said I'd be there. His office was on Union Street, near the courthouse and the Performing Arts Center.

Melissa was cleaning up after our meal and looked at me expectantly. "We'll leave now," I told her, "and while I sound out the attorney you can do some shopping around the Gaslamp Quarter—suitcase, spare clothing, nothing too fashionable, don't want you attracting attention."

"I understand. Other than the attorney's name, what do you know about him?"

"The Bar Association said he's from Santa Clara Law, four years Assistant U.S. Attorney, and a substantial practice in the federal courts. That means he'll have contacts and know where to deal."

She closed her eyes briefly. "You'll be with me?"

"Part of the way. Once there's a lawyer-client relationship, Hatfield won't want me around. And," I continued, "I won't want to be privy to all those secrets. Tarkos may go down the tube but the Mafia remains—and I don't need their kind of trouble."

She gazed at me then, eyes smoky, face remorseful. "I've brought you nothing but trouble, Joe—I'm sorry."

"Forget it. I didn't have to follow through—my choice."

She began putting on her black wig, adjusted it in the bathroom mirror, and blackened her eyebrows again. When she turned to me she said, "How do I look?"

"Like what you were pretending to be when we met."

She sighed. "That bad? Well, I'm ready as I'll ever be."

During the drive to San Diego she told me that her mother's death from cancer had devastated her, that her father had done all he could to be a good parent while teaching and studying for his doctorate. "But I was alone a good part of the time, got involved with the wrong high school crowd and barely graduated. Daddy had friends at Mills, so I was admitted. Stayed two years and dropped out to study acting at Pasadena. Borden saw me in *Lady Windermere's Fan* and invited me to test for Falcon. He gave me the usual one-year option contract and we began going out together. Instead of a film part I got a marriage proposal." She looked away. "I told myself it would work out, even though I was pretty sure it wouldn't. But I wasn't much of an actress, I guess, and I was overwhelmed by Borden's presence, his wealth, the respect he commanded wherever he went. I mean, you get accustomed to the best tables in the best restaurants, waiters bowing and scraping, limousines, weekends in Vegas and Palm Springs and Acapulco. I didn't want to give it up, so I married him."

"Any marriage is a gamble."

"I suppose. But I soon realized I was bought merchandise, the way Borden buys everything. And he began insisting I do things that revolted me—"

"Taking his money abroad."

"That was the least of it." I sensed her shiver.

"So you rebelled."

"I wanted to get back at Borden the only way that would hurt him—taking his money."

"Well," I said, "money is something he understands and desires."

"Do you think of me as a criminal—a thief?"

"No," I told her, "because I'm not sure it's a crime to take stolen money. Even if it is, there are mitigating circumstances." I patted her hand. "The lawyer will sort it out, get things squared away."

"I hope you're right, Joe. I'm tired of running, tired of being afraid."

At the entrance to Hatfield's building, we parted. Melissa was to shop, then come to his office on the seventh floor of the new highrise. I took the elevator and walked down the corridor to a stained oak door that bore the gilt legend: Law Offices of Joel R. Hatfield.

The receptionist had me wait on a comfortable leather sofa in a room carpeted in thick pile. There were current magazines on a Chinese rosewood table, and a number of framed Oriental scrolls hung on the walls. When she said Mr. Hatfield would see me, I went into a handsomely decorated office and shook hands with a short, smooth-faced man of about forty, who was beginning to bald. He wore a three-piece suit, white shirt, regimental tie, and a Phi Beta Kappa key on the watch chain that hugged a developing paunch.

"Joel Hatfield," he said. "What can I do for you, Mr. Phillips?"

We sat across a low coffee table on which I placed one of Melissa's hundred-dollar bills. "Before I go into anything," I told him, "I want lawyer-client confidentiality established."

Nodding towards the greenback, he said, "It is."

"I'll begin with two things. First, I'm using the name Phillips because I don't figure in what I'm about to tell you. Second, I'm acting as an intermediary on behalf of a potential client who feels herself in jeopardy."

"Is she a fugitive?"

"Not to my knowledge—or hers." I leaned back against the soft cushion, studied his face, and saw no reaction whatever. All he said was, "Coffee? Or something stronger?"

"A little Beam, if you've got it."

"Good idea—it's that time of day." He pressed a button, the receptionist came in, and he ordered two Beam highballs. Before she left he handed her my hundred dollars and told her to make out a receipt.

When the door closed I said, "The potential client is a young woman who married an older, very wealthy man with widespread financial interests, including participation in a Vegas casino. I've inferred that the majority shareholders are O.C. figures shielded by front men. A time came when this lady's husband began skimming from the casino—large amounts that he forced his wife to take abroad from time to time. These illegal runs were distasteful to her, and for reasons I'm not familiar with, the marriage deteriorated."

Hatfield said, "I don't do divorce work, Mr. Phillips."

"Not asking you to."

The door opened and the receptionist entered with two icy highballs on a silver tray. She set one before me, the other in front of Hatfield. He lifted his glass and said, "Good health."

"*Salud.*" I sipped and picked up where I'd left off. "Some days ago the lady was given a quantity of diamonds to take abroad for conversion and deposit in a clandestine account."

"How much money are we talking about?"

"I'd say two to three million."

He whistled, sipped again, and said, "Go on."

"Instead of following instructions, the lady took off with the diamonds, not wanting to commit further illegal acts, but wanting to take revenge on her husband for what I assume were abuses inflicted on her."

"And she has possession of these diamonds?"

I nodded and sipped more of my drink. "Earlier her husband became suspect by the Nevada Gaming Commission, who assigned an investigator to come up with the facts. The investigator—a man named Rinaldo—and a Los Angeles police sergeant named Fallon have been tapping the suspect's phone—probably illegally."

"Illegally? Why would they do that and ruin a case?"

"I think they want to shake down the suspect—it's happened, you know."

"I know very well. So the runaway wife has the diamonds and her husband wants them back. Her, too, I imagine."

"And you can imagine what her fate will be if he finds her."

"Bones in the desert," Hatfield said soberly. "Yes, she's got a problem. What does she want to do?"

"She's disposed to turn the diamonds over to federal authorities—if that's your advice—and cooperate in any prosecution of her husband in return for immunity and protection."

Picking up his glass, Hatfield sipped slowly and thoughtfully. "Protection from what?"

"From her husband, his associates, his O.C. partners. Are you interested in the case?"

He nodded. "To avoid possible conflict of interest, I need a name."

"Have you the guts to go up against Borden Tarkos?"

The name had impact. "Tarkos," he muttered. "I'd enjoy taking him on again. Last year I represented an actor who had a contract dispute with Falcon Productions. Tarkos tried to screw him out of a picture percentage, spent a lot of money in the effort but finally settled out of court. So I know a little about Borden Tarkos, and he's a real bastard. Can't say I'm surprised by what you've told me."

"As I see it," I said, "your job will be negotiating with the feds on behalf of Mrs. Tarkos."

"And the Nevada authorities," he added, then smiled. "I may need some protection myself. Tarkos is pretty ruthless, not to mention his associates. That would be the Ambrosino family—old Raf and young Dino." His eyes narrowed. "I had a case once—but that's history. When do I see my client?"

I looked at my watch. "She'll be here in a little while."

"Until I can make appropriate arrangements with the U.S. Attorney's office, what protection does she have?"

"Me," I said, "so I hope you won't delay making the necessary contacts."

"Assuming I have a satisfactory interview with Mrs. Tarkos, I'll start in the morning. Can she be specific about diverted sums and depositories?"

"She says so, but that's for you to determine."

He nodded. "And your role in all this, Mr. Phillips?"

I laughed shortly. "I find it hard to define. I befriended the lady through sheer chance, and she's come to trust me. I must have an honest face."

"Then there's no—how shall I put it?—romantic involvement?"

"I'm married but separated, with divorce on the horizon. I work in television, currently unemployed, and with no prospects."

"I see. Will Mrs. Tarkos be able to pay me?"

"If you'll take a diamond or two."

"My wife is very fond of jewels."

"As I recall it," I remarked, "an informant supplying fraud information to Treasury is entitled to a percentage of what's recovered."

"That's so," he agreed, "and I'll see that her interest is protected.

Of course, the jewels have to be appraised before a determination is made."

The door opened and the receptionist said, "There's a lady to see Mr. Phillips."

"Have her come in." I got up when Melissa entered. Joel Hatfield rose and said, "I've agreed to represent you, Mrs. Tarkos, and now we need to talk."

She looked at me uncertainly until I said, "I've told Mr. Hatfield as much as I know. It's up to you to tell him the full story, no holding back. Okay? I'll wait outside." I picked up my glass and went out, closing the door behind me.

The reception area held a new fabric suitcase and a nicely wrapped package, representing Melissa's purchases. I made myself comfortable on the sofa, accepted a refill from the receptionist, and leafed through *Time* without reading. I felt relieved that Melissa was finally in professional hands, but I couldn't ignore my sense of regret that our relationship—whatever it was—was coming to a close. In a day or so she'd have no further need of me and I'd be back with my unwritten novel, wondering what in hell I could do for a living.

Ms. Gossons might sell *El Dorado* tomorrow; then again, a sale could be a couple of months away. I was in a hell of a bind, and I loathed the idea of crawling back to Natty for food and a place to sleep.

Christ!

The receptionist was long gone when Hatfield's door opened and Melissa and her new lawyer came out. To me he said, "How can I best contact Mrs. Tarkos?"

"We'll call you."

"Around three o'clock tomorrow," Hatfield said. "By then I should know pretty well where we stand."

"Then what?"

"Assuming I get the agreement we want, I'll surrender Mrs. Tarkos to the U.S. Attorney's office." He glanced at her. "That could be as soon as tomorrow afternoon."

Her face was taut. Thinly she said, "Then I disappear into the federal underground."

"For a time," Hatfield said soothingly, "and for your personal security. Take my word, nothing disagreeable will happen."

She was silent in the elevator, and when we emerged on Union Street I said, "I think we owe ourselves a good dinner."

"Yes, that was pretty stressful—answering all those questions of his."

I carried her suitcase to a nearby restaurant, checked it and her package, and we were shown to a cushioned booth. The place was nicely decorated, with plenty of Tiffany-style glass, aproned, mustachioed waiters, and a softly functioning player piano at the far end.

We ordered whiskey sours and the steak-and-lobster dinner, and after the waiter left Melissa said, "I've never really dealt with a lawyer before, Joe. Do you have a good feeling about Hatfield?"

"He asked the right questions, said he wasn't afraid to move against your husband, and is ready to act. Given his background, Hatfield has to know the right people. I don't know what more we could want."

"Suppose Borden tries to buy him off?"

"There won't be an opportunity. Besides, you're not going to be surfaced for a long time. They'll want to keep your husband guessing."

We had a second round of whiskey sours, enjoyed a leisurely meal, and then we went to the parking garage, put her things in my Datsun, and drove back to El Cajon.

Melissa unpacked in the bungalow, took out a pair of pajamas, and disappeared into the bathroom. I turned on the television set—a Lakers-Utah Jazz game was scheduled—and caught the tail end of a news program. From Los Angeles a reporter announced that the bodies of two men had been found in a car abandoned at the Long Beach airport. Both men had been shot to death. One of the victims was identified as Los Angeles Police Sergeant Rodney Fallon. The other, a Nevada State investigator named Eduardo Rinaldo. No motive for the double killings could be immediately ascertained, and police were investigating.

I stared at the screen as a commercial came on. My mouth went dry and my hand trembled as I reached for my drink. Two down.

Whatever their game, it had ended in death. Had they talked? Did Tarkos have their tapes? Did he know about *me?*

I drank deeply, feeling cold and clammy all over.

Without willing it, I began to hypothesize the chain of circumstances that had brought about their murder. Then the bathroom door opened, and Melissa appeared.

The wig was gone, her light brown hair was freshly washed and fluffed, her eyebrows were her own again, and in translucent pajamas she looked absolutely ravishing. Coming toward me, she flicked off the TV, sat in my lap and encircled my neck with her arms. Her lips found mine and they were soft and inviting. Her tongue caressed, and she murmured, "We have two beds, you noticed?"

"So?"

"Your bed or mine?"

"Lady's choice."

"Joe, even if we're never together again, let's make this a night to remember."

Our lovemaking was more than memorable—for me it was magical. The silken touch of her skin, the sweet resilience of her youthful body, the soft, seductive murmurings transported me to a realm of enchantment I'd never known before. Long abstinence enhanced desire and made me voracious to possess this female until I lay utterly spent beside her.

Hands clasped, bodies gently touching, we lay together in darkness while our breathing—so recently urgent—decelerated and left us relaxed together. After a while she said softly, "It's never been like this for me before."

"Nor for me. It's unbelievable."

"I felt as though I'd become part of you and you part of me. Is that what love is like?"

"I want to think so. And I don't want to lose you."

"I'll be here for you whenever you want me, Joe." She kissed my cheek, then my lips. "I won't ever want to be with anyone else. Just you. For the rest of my life."

"I feel the same way," I confessed, "and it's going to be hell without you."

"For a while—only for a while." We kissed languorously, and she said, "You're so different from Borden. You're tough and brave and intelligent—a man in every way. I never knew anyone like you before."

"I like your saying that, because I've always thought of myself as pretty average—a guy with a knack for writing comedy, nothing of lasting value. And I don't even have the silly series to go back to."

"But you're so good, and other jobs will open up—they'll have to."

"After the strike," I said unhappily, "and competition will be savage."

"But you won't surrender—you were a Marine."

"I was a Marine," I said slowly, "but I try not to remember too much of that."

"Why?"

"Guilt for having survived."

"I—I don't understand."

"Beirut," I told her. "I was in a jeep scouting the coastal road for infiltrators when that bomb-car blew up our barracks. From a mile away I heard the explosion, sensed something terrible had happened, drove back like a maniac, and for the next four days pulled bodies and wounded buddies from the rubble."

"Oh, God."

"It was fiendish how they destroyed us, then boasted and bragged about it in their papers and radio. If I'd had ammo for my weapons I'd have killed every Arab in sight—but we were a peace-keeping force," I said bitterly. "Unloaded weapons only. Nearly two hundred and fifty of my comrades murdered—and there was never any retaliation. Never."

"So you left the Corps."

"My time was nearly up—and I didn't want to serve a country that had become so passive. I came back, had therapy at Balboa until I could pull myself together, and then I went to college. So I'm not as brave and courageous as you think."

"You're human and compassionate, and that doesn't detract from courage." She lifted my hand and kissed it. "I saw you react to protect me—smashing that bottle and going after those car punks. I'll never forget it, Joe."

I kissed her forehead. "I'll never forget the beautiful hooker I declined. Why did you pose as a whore?"

"Useful camouflage—and if Borden found me, I wanted to be in a degrading situation, to degrade him as he degraded me." She rose on one elbow and her breast brushed my cheek. "Drink?"

"Please."

She brought back Wild Turkey on the rocks, and our glasses touched. For a while she sat silently, then said, "I want you to know about Borden and me so you'll understand why I left him."

"You don't need to tell me anything."

"But I want to, it's necessary—and I told Joel Hatfield, so it's only right that you know."

"I don't want anything to hurt you, not even memories."

"I know, I know," she said gently, and looked away. Light from the shuffleboard made the curtained window barely visible. I waited while she sipped her drink, and then she said, "When Borden and I were going out together—before we married—he never touched me, didn't try, just a gentlemanly kiss at parting. I thought well of him for that, believed he was showing me respect and I appreciated it. But when we married it turned out that he was impotent or nearly so. He said his sexual energy was absorbed by business, that it took special situations to arouse him. I was his wife, he kept saying, and I should accommodate his desires.

"I thought he meant whipping and leather, but it wasn't that. It was worse. He wanted to watch me with another man—or woman."

"A voyeur." My stomach tightened.

"Before we'd been married a month he took me to Vegas—the Sagebrush—and got me drunk. When I came to, a man was in bed with me—screwing me. My husband was nearby, doing things to himself and loving it. I screamed and tried to fight off the man but he choked me unconscious.

"In the morning I started to leave, but Borden showed me a photo —the man on top of me—and said if I ever left him, he had proof of adultery, so I wouldn't be able to collect anything. Then he became very kind, very solicitous, and thanked me for the pleasure he'd enjoyed. He gave me an emerald necklace to make it up to me, and for a little while I thought that was the end of his obsession. But later he said since I'd fucked one stranger, fucking another made no difference, and he brought a man to our bed." She looked down at me. "Understand why I posed as a whore? I felt like one. It isn't something you can wash off like dirt from your skin. The feeling's deep inside."

"But you were a victim, not an aggressor."

She sighed. "I felt hopeless, defeated, became submissive, almost an accomplice. Borden had a former girlfriend—Sondra—under contract to Falcon Productions. He brought her home, we smoked some grass, got high, and at Borden's urging I let her make love to me—if you can call it love. So that became a pattern, and when he started having me take money abroad, I welcomed the trips because they kept me away from him and his kinkiness. True, he gave me every luxury a woman could want, except one thing—love. And I didn't want it from him. So when I took the diamonds I was supposed to deliver in Vaduz I told myself it was what I'd earned through degradation."

"So when you said you hated him enough to kill him, you meant it."

"I still do." She bent low and her bangs brushed my forehead. "Blame me?"

"I can't," I said, "but let the law take care of him. Don't think of anything else."

"Despite his voyeurism, Borden's possessive of me, crazily jealous. If he knew about you he'd try to have you killed. You should know that."

"He didn't have your tennis pro killed."

"Rene was soft, easier to buy off than murder." She paused. "Though I suppose it could come to that if Borden went into one of his rages. So as long as Borden is free, anyone I'm with is in danger."

"I'm not worried about myself, I'm worried about you."

"I'll be protected—Hatfield said so. And no one will be looking out for you."

For a very brief moment I thought of telling her about the two murders—Fallon and Rinaldo—and just as quickly decided against it. The knowledge would only upset her. Besides, I didn't think Tarkos's strongarm boys had done the deed; more likely his Mafia partners, the Ambrosinos, had ordered it to protect themselves from extortion and at the same time shield Tarkos.

I put my arms around Melissa and held her very close. Her warmth flowed into me, the vital warmth of life, in such contrast to the chill corpses in the abandoned car. I had to stop thinking about them. "I treasure you," I told her quietly, "and everything you told me we'll now forget. It happened to someone else, a story you once heard. It's not important. It doesn't affect you or me. We go on from here."

She kissed me deeply. "I wanted you to say that, hoped you would. I want my future with you—only you."

"We'll get there," I promised. "Loving and trusting each other."

Her mouth opened on mine, her body moved sinuously against me, and very soon we re-created the indescribable miracle of love.

In the morning I got eggs and bacon from the little store, we made breakfast, and stayed in the bungalow for most of the day. Then at three o'clock I went out to the pay phone and placed a call to lawyer Hatfield.

EIGHT

When Joel Hatfield came on the line I said, "How's the situation developing?"

"Quite well. My friends are impressed. But before signing a commitment they want to talk with your friend."

"You can do better than that," I told him. "Tell them no free lunch, and that's what I'll advise my friend."

"Well, I've said as much."

"Then say it again emphatically. Mutual confidence begins when the document is signed, not before. Now think back to what I told you last evening about two wiretap men. According to a late news report, they were found at the Long Beach airport—executed. Tie that to my friend's situation, and if your friends have any sense of reality they'll understand the meaning of urgency." I looked at my watch. "I'll call you back in half an hour."

"Do that. Your information is going to be very useful."

In the bungalow Melissa said, "Do I start packing?"

"Might as well. I have a follow-up call to make to verify all paperwork's completed."

"Joe, I don't know what I'd do without you. God knows where I'd be—dead, maybe."

"Don't think about that," I said. "Think about this—advice your lawyer won't give you."

"I'm listening."

"Only Tarkos and you know how many jewels you took. Before the feds inventory and appraise them, I'm going to suggest you set aside a reserve for yourself—to cover legal expenses and comfortable living for, say, the next year."

She smiled puckishly. "Would that be honest?"

"Listen to the lady thief. Don't worry about morality, just do it."

"Yes, of course. But where would I hide them?"

"With your father—I'll take them to him after you're in safe hands."

She undid her drawstring and the black skirt pooled on the floor. Taking off the nylon money belt, she opened the gemstone pouch, dipped into it with her fingers. I gave her an envelope of motel stationery and said, 'I don't want to know how many you keep, but don't skimp on yourself. Just seal the envelope and give it to me. Your father needn't know the contents."

While she was doing that I poured Wild Turkey into a glass and drank it straight. When I turned back she handed me the envelope with one hand, and in my other she laid a two- to three-carat sparkler. "You have expenses, too."

Holding the diamond between thumb and forefinger I said, "I wouldn't know how to sell this for anything like its value, so I'll hold it in trust. And if I hit rock-bottom, I'll pledge it with Uncle Nathan, okay?"

"You mean, pawn it?"

"Put bluntly." I thumbed the stone into my trouser pocket. "Thanks, darling."

"Meanwhile," she said, "you'll need cash," and opened the banknote section of her money belt. "I have, oh, about thirteen thousand and I want you to take all or any part of it."

A lump rose in my throat and I swallowed hard. "You'll need money yourself—for send-out pizza and Cokes. But pride flees before poverty. I'll take a thousand and make it last."

"Two," she insisted, and gave me twenty one-hundred-dollar bills. I kissed her and put the bills in my pocket with her diamond. "You're a lifesaver."

"You saved mine."

She positioned the money belt around her waist and drew the skirt up over her hips and blouse. "Now, do you have any idea what my protectors will do with me?"

"Probably settle you in a comfortable safehouse where you can be guarded while interrogation goes on."

"How long will that take?"

"Couple of weeks. They'll want to check the offshore bank accounts you'll tell them about, and the Swiss in particular work at a leisurely pace."

"There's the Caymans, too, and Panama."

"So it will take a while. Then, once they have everything down pat, you'll be given a statement to sign. Make sure your lawyer goes over it, and follow his advice. I'll call Hatfield from time to time to check on you."

"When will I be able to see you?"

"Probably not until after the interrogation. Then a conjugal visit will be in order."

"I'll be eager, believe me. And, Joe, I want to start divorce proceedings right away."

"The feds should cooperate in that—the U.S. Attorney can't take you before a grand jury to testify until you're free of your husband."

"But I thought I wouldn't have to testify."

"Not in open court, but grand jury proceedings are secret. Before that happens the Feds will be building their case against the alleged suspect." I smiled. "If they handle the investigation right they can probably go for an indictment even without your grand jury appearance."

"I hope so. I just don't want to tell everything to a lot of people I don't know."

"Who does?" I put my arms around her and held her very tightly. When I released Melissa she looked slowly around the room. "I'll miss this place, darling; I'll think of it every night we're apart."

"I'll think of it, too," I admitted. "Warmly and reverently. Now, I'll make that follow-up call while you finish packing."

This time Hatfield sounded self-assured and confident. "All signed and sealed," he told me. "The double murder was unanswerable. When can I see my client?"

"In about an hour, but not at your office. Let's agree on a locale where you can surrender her to your friends in a tranquil way."

"I'm agreeable to that. Let's see, you know Balboa Park?"

"I was in the Naval Hospital there."

"Then you know the Casa del Prado."

"I know it."

"Let's say the main entrance, just inside the archway."

"If you can get your team together we'll meet in an hour."

"I don't see a problem. Well, let's hope everything goes smoothly."

"It had better," I told him, and hung up.

"All arranged," I told Melissa, and described the rendezvous while she snapped her suitcase shut. We had a final embrace in the room and then I carried her suitcase to my car.

The old woman stepped out of the office and yelled, "Checkin' out?"

"No," I called back. "Paid for a week, right? We're taking a side trip. See you later."

As I drove away from the bungalow Melissa said, "Why the secret meeting place—Balboa Park?"

"Neutral ground. Like in spy stories when an exchange is made."

"I'm an exchange item?"

"Sure—the Bartered Bride. Say, you have a dimple I hadn't noticed."

"It only shows when I smile, and I haven't smiled much lately. Until I met you, that is."

I drew her head over so I could kiss her cheek. "You can do better than that," she reproved.

"Well, I'm in a learning mode—teach."

She kissed me sweetly, and when I took the ramp onto Interstate 8 she said, "What if I don't like my new protectors?"

"Frankly, I don't expect you will. If you're under the U.S. Marshals Witness Protection Program you'll see a lot of guys who wear shiny polyester and couldn't make it into the FBI, CIA, or the Secret Service. Not a high intellectual level, but they're supposed to be good gunslingers."

"Better than you?" Her hand crept behind my back and touched the .38 Cobra. "Much better," I said, "I haven't been on a firing range in years."

"But you can teach me—you will, won't you?"

"Honey, on our Caribbean island the only danger will be from falling coconuts and sunburn."

"So we're going to the Caribbean, are we?"

"For the first year or so—long enough to work all the foolishness out of our system."

"Take longer than that, dear, much longer. You stirred new lusts in me. I could become a nympho very easily."

"I think I'd like not having to whine and beg for sex."

"Never—that's a lifetime promise."

So with more banter like that—to keep our thoughts from parting—I drove through Mission Valley and turned south on the freeway along Cabrillo. By then we were in Balboa Park and I cut over to Park Boulevard and entered the big public parking area. I steered to the south end, braked, and turned off the ignition. "I'll go first," I said, "check with Hatfield, and if everything's okay I'll come back for you."

"Why shouldn't everything be okay?"

"I don't know, but I keep remembering that your husband has a very long reach." I was thinking of Fallon and Rinaldo and wondering how they'd been trapped. I kissed her lips and walked down past the carousel and the Photo Arts Building, then took the path around the formal gardens. My timing was good; it was just under an hour since we'd left the bungalow I was beginning to think of as Honeymoon Hotel.

I kept to the side of the path in pace with other visitors until I could make out the façade of the Casa del Prado. I'd always thought of it as an architectural horror, a baroque version of the Alamo, with spiral-garlanded columns and lots of swoopy, deep-sculpted ornamentation. A frontage of skinny desert palms shaded the stone walkway, and as I came closer I saw five men approaching from the left. The shortest was Joel Hatfield. Two large, polyester-suited men had to be deputy marshals, and I hoped the other two were highly placed Assistant U.S. Attorneys. The party turned into the main archway, stopped, and stood looking around. I came up on their blind side, put my hand on Hatfield's arm, and said, "Hi." He jumped, then smiled sheepishly. "Where's my client?"

"In a secure place, waiting for my okay. Got the agreement?"

He tapped his breast pocket.

"Well, let's see it."

One of the deputies said, "Who'n hell's *this* character?"

To Hatfield, I said, "Don't bother with introductions, Joel. Dirty fingernails tell me they're deputy marshals."

Hatfield swallowed. "And Messrs. Frick and Golden from the U.S. Attorney's office." He glanced at them. "Mr. Phillips."

I moved into better lighting and began reading the three-page, single-spaced agreement. No prosecution of Jane Doe in return for full cooperation; physical protection as long as deemed necessary; and a third of any fraudulently diverted monies recovered.

The agreement was signed by Archibald F. Ballantine, U.S. Attorney for the Southern District of California, and by Roger E. Blistein, Chief of Enforcement, Department of the Treasury. I folded the document and returned it to Hatfield, who said, "Well?"

"Lacks waivers from California and Nevada."

Hatfield said, "I secured verbal agreement. I'll have the papers in a day or so."

"Other than that I'm satisfied."

"Yeah," the belligerent deputy said, "let's get this show on the road."

His partner weighed in with, "Mebbe we'll take this character along, cool him off for a while." He snickered and blew his nose using thumb and forefinger.

To Frick and Golden I said, "And these apes are the ones you're entrusting the lady to? They'd better clean up their act or you'll have an uncooperative witness."

Nervously Hatfield said, "I'm sure my client will be treated with the greatest courtesy and consideration."

"I have your word on that." I looked at Frick and Golden. "Care to reassure me?"

Frick said, "What Mr. Hatfield said goes for us too. Now, if you're agreeable we'd like to assume custody."

"Wait here. Joel, come with me."

He detached himself from the deputies and walked with me back to the parking lot. Before reaching my car I said, "From time to time I'll be calling you—to check on Mrs. Tarkos's well-being."

"Of course."

"I've told her to sign nothing without your concurrence."

"I'll restate that to Frick and Golden. Anyway, this thing is too big to take chances; no one's in a mood to play games."

"Fallon did," I said, "and Rinaldo. Remember that."

We were at the car. Melissa lowered the window and looked out. Hatfield leaned over and said, "Everything is going to be just fine, Mrs. Tarkos, just as you and Mr. Phillips wanted."

She opened the door and I took her hand. To Hatfield I said, "She has a suitcase and a package in the trunk." I handed him keys and took Melissa in my arms. We kissed lingeringly, and Melissa murmured, "So this is goodbye."

"For a while."

"I love you."

"I love you," I said, and heard the trunk lid shut. Hatfield came around and returned my keys.

There was nothing else to say. She smiled wistfully, turned, and began walking off with Hatfield. I watched them a few moments, choked down the lump in my throat, and got behind the wheel.

For a while, as I'd said, it was over; just memories to comfort me. Well, there was a diamond and two thousand dollars that I'd have to spend carefully. With luck and her money I could last out the damn strike.

After starting the engine I felt in my pocket for the envelope that contained her reserve. Professor George D. Anders lived on Russ, near Balboa Stadium and the college where he taught.

I drove out of the parking lot and turned down Park Boulevard, past the huge Naval Hospital where I had spent unpleasant weeks. Where Russ intersected I turned east until I found the number I was looking for, parked my car, and entered the old apartment building.

A small, creaky elevator took me to the fifth floor. I left it and walked down the hall to Anders's door. I pressed the call button, heard it ring emptily. Pressed it again, repeated.

Finally a weak voice called, "Who is it?"

"Joe Brent."

Presently a key turned, the snub chain dropped, and I saw a man with bandaged face and forehead, one arm in a sling. Skin around the visible eye was purplish-black. Through puffed, swollen lips he croaked, "Is Lissa safe? Did they get her?"

"No," I said, "but apparently they got you."

He toed the door open, and I went in.

NINE

Anders limped toward a coffee table set between two sofas. There was a bottle on the table and glasses. He poured three fingers in one glass and looked at me. I said, "I'll take about half."

"Painkiller," he said hoarsely, gulping from his glass and pouring my drink. I sat across the table from him and listened to what he had to say.

Yesterday afternoon, as he was nearing his apartment on foot, two men forced him into a car at gunpoint. They drove around behind Balboa Stadium and asked him where his daughter was.

"What did they look like?"

"One was short, heavy-set, and balding. The other was taller and had a black mustache. He called the short fellow Angie."

Tarkos's men. "Go on."

"When I said I didn't know Lissa's whereabouts they began beating me up, knocked me down, kicked me." He drank from his glass. "Threatened my life."

"But you held out."

"I was terrified—you have to understand—and in great pain. One said he'd blind me if I didn't tell. So—" he looked away—"I betrayed my daughter."

"Told them about the Beach View Motel."

"I was cowardly." A tear streamed down his discolored cheek, vanished in heavy beard. "But you say she's safe."

"We moved out before the strongarms got there."

"Thank God! Where is she?"

I eyed him over the rim of my glass. "Under the circumstances, you'll agree it's better you not know."

His head lowered and he stared at what remained in his glass. "You despise me, don't you? Because I couldn't hold out."

"Pain is subjective," I said, "and everyone has his own threshold. They passed yours and you talked. So it's enough that you know your daughter is safe. And you can thank your son-in-law for those contusions."

"Tarkos? I—I wasn't sure. But you're certain?"

"Those men are his retainers, bodyguards, gofers—I've had dealings with Angelo."

"They left me lying in the dirt, drove away. I managed to hobble to the college clinic, where they fixed me up." He looked at the sling suspending his left arm. "I've been in a lot of pain." Lifting his glass, he swallowed the final ounce.

"Did they ask about me?"

He started to shake his head, winced, and said, "They were interested only in Lissa." He wet his lips. "They'll come back, won't they?"

"It's possible. So I suggest you get out of here, take a couple of weeks' sick leave and disappear." I sipped my liquor and judged it reasonably good bourbon but not Beam quality. "Make sure you're not followed, take a bus to anywhere."

He managed a brief smile. *Erehwon.* Nowhere."

I watched him refill his glass. After swallowing a jolt, he said, "I'll do as you say, thankful you saved my daughter." Another tear appeared. "Makes my betrayal not so bad."

"She's safe, no one can get to her, so the prime thing is to take care of yourself."

"Can you talk to her?"

"I can get a message to her."

"Please don't tell her about me—this thing's on my conscience."

"No need for her to know." I stood up, Melissa's envelope still in my pocket, undelivered. Entrusting it to Anders would be the same as yielding it to her pursuers. "For a few weeks," I told him, "we'll stay out of contact with each other. When the time is right, I'll get in touch." I started to move away but noticed a framed photo on the bookshelf. The subject was a teenage girl in black cap and gown, graduation scroll in hand.

"Lissa," her father said. "She never made it through college."

I went closer to the photo. Face calm and innocent but showing the considerable beauty that would come. Seventeen, eighteen? Her poise was unusual for one so young. " 'When woman is beautiful'," I quoted—probably imperfectly—" 'what more can be asked of her?' "

Her father said, "They sense that intuitively and seldom try to make anything of themselves." He sighed. "You'll still help Lissa, won't you? Protect her?"

I turned to Anders. "I love your daughter," I told him. "Anything happens to her will be over my dead body."

He sighed. "Then I hope everything works out—for both of you."

I left him standing there and walked back along the hall to the elevator, and heard the cage rising. It stopped, the doors opened, and two men stepped out. One was Angelo. His partner glanced briefly at me, then they walked together toward Anders's door.

I followed them, and when they stopped, I got out my Cobra and stuck it in Angelo's spine. "Hands on the wall," I snapped, "feet back and spread, you know the drill." I stepped back and the mustached partner said, "Hey, fella, what's this, a heist?"

"You should be so lucky. Police. Now, move."

Slowly they got into position and I patted them down, took a .45 pistol from Angelo's shoulder holster, a .38 Special from the other man's belt clip. No ankle guns. I toed their pieces along the hall runner, and said, "Drop your wallets, slowly."

A billfold and a wallet hit the floor. Angelo said, "Let's work it out, man, I don't need this kind of shit."

"Professor Anders didn't need that beating. He lodged a complaint and I came 'round to write it up. Fastest collar I ever made. Now ring that bell."

With one hand Angelo pushed the button, and when Anders asked who it was I said, "Me again."

The door opened, and Anders stared at my captives in horror. "Back up," I told him, "and we'll all come in."

When we were all inside I shifted grip on my Cobra and slammed the butt against Angelo's bald skull. Before he hit the floor I dropped his partner. Anders stared at them with an agonized expression. "Get rope or twine," I said, "we'll truss up a couple of turkeys."

From the hall I recovered their guns and wallets. Moving dazedly, Anders brought me a ball of parcel twine, and I began tying their wrists behind them. Angelo groaned and moved, and I slammed his skull again, close to the first purple butt-mark. He stopped moving.

In a thready voice Anders said, "Isn't this going to cause me more trouble?"

"Think of the trouble you'd be in if I hadn't spotted them."

I tied their ankles together while Anders got himself a drink. Finished, I got up and poured one for myself. Then I emptied their wallets and learned from driving licenses that one of the strongarms was Angelo DiLirio, the other, Harold Tisch.

I dumped their money on the table. Angelo's wallet yielded eighty-seven dollars, Tisch's fifty-three. I replaced seven dollars in Angelo's wallet, and three in Tisch's. "The rest is yours," I told Anders. "For pain, suffering, and clinic repairs. Now you're going to call the police and say you've got a couple of intruders. When the cops come, tell them about yesterday's beating and say the hoods appeared here with drawn guns. They forced their way in when, fortunately, a man appeared and made a citizen's arrest, saving you from another beating. You don't know who the man was but think he was a Crime Watch type." I paused. "Got that?"

"Yes, I'm pretty sure I have."

"Now, this is important. Swear out a complaint for assault, battery, and forced entry, and anything else the cops suggest. Don't be intimidated by these two pricks. Give the cops their guns and wallets. The guns aren't licensed, so that's plenty to hold them for a while."

"But they'll get out of jail and come after me again," he said tremulously. "Kill or blind me."

"Not this pair," I said, "though Tarkos may send backups. So do as I said, and when you're finished at the station take that vacation. The further away the better." I tilted my glass and swallowed the rest of the liquor. "Use your phone."

I stayed beside him while he made the call because I could see he was reluctant to get more involved. After he hung up I said, "Follow the script from now on and you'll be reasonably safe."

"This is all terrible, just terrible. I could never imagine something like this happening to me."

"It happened," I said, "so take it in stride and put these guys away."

I was starting to leave when Tisch's eyes opened and he looked at me. "I'll get you, motherfucker," he grated. "You don't know who's behind us."

"But you'll tell," I said, knelt and shoved the Cobra barrel into his mouth. Tisch gagged. "Talk, baby."

"Fuck you!"

I thumbed back the hammer and the cylinder clicked as it turned. "A name."

Eyes wide, face white, he blurted, "Borden Tarkos."

I rose, put away the Cobra, and spoke to Anders. "Remember that," I said. "Harold Tisch freely confessed."

I left the room and closed the door behind me. The elevator cage was still at the floor so I rode it down to street level and got into my car. I drove half a block away, parked again, and waited. In about five minutes a prowl car screamed up, light bar blazing, and two uniformed cops piled out. They hustled into the apartment entrance, leaving the car in a No Parking zone.

Dusk had settled over the street. San Diego was a nice, very livable community with lots of public pride and spirit. If that pride was reflected in the police force, Angie and Harry were in for considerable trouble. I liked it that they were being arrested here rather than in L.A., where a sort of revolving-door policy was in effect. Well, nothing else I could do to help Anders or his daughter. I still had her reserve diamonds and I'd have to get them to a safe place. Hatfield's office was the best I could think of, so I drove to a pay phone, called his office, and found him there. "I just got back," he told me. "Anything wrong?"

"Not really, but I want you to stay until I can get there, say, half an hour."

Hatfield agreed to wait, so I went into a drug store and bought a padded mailer envelope. I slid Melissa's diamond envelope inside and sealed the mailer. Across it I wrote: *Property of Melissa A. Tarkos. To be opened only by Melissa A. Tarkos.* Then I drove down to Union Street and went up to Hatfield's office.

He said, "The lady is comfortably settled and in good spirits."

"Good to know." I handed him the mailer. "Keep it in your vault," I told him. "I don't know its contents and neither do you."

"I understand."

"There's been a development you should know about, but it's not for Melissa's ears." I told him about Anders's beating, and the episode just concluded at his apartment.

Hatfield nodded thoughtfully. "Do you think they killed those two men at the airport?"

"Fallon and Rinaldo? More likely the Ambrosinos, but their guns should be tested for bullet comparison. Maybe you could suggest it—in a discreet way."

"I can manage that. Anything else, Mr.—Phillips?"

"I'm worn out, too tired to think. It's been a long day."

"For both of us," he said, opened his combination safe, and laid the mailer envelope inside. We shook hands and I left him and went back to my car.

I was too tired to drive to Los Angeles, so I went back to the El Cajon bungalow, poured some Wild Turkey, and made dinner for myself.

Without Melissa it was a lonely place, even though it was crammed with memories. I missed her and wondered what she was doing, if she was thinking of me.

On TV the L.A. Clippers were playing and beating Tarkos's Rebels. It was a one-sided game, and as I drowsed in my chair I reflected that Tarkos would soon have more to worry about than a losing basketball team. Two of his gofers were in the slammer and a secret, high-powered federal investigation was about to begin.

Borden Tarkos was its the target.

What, I wondered, was Tarkos going to do about me?

TEN

Next day I relinquished the bungalow and drove back to Los Angeles at a leisurely pace. No reason to hurry, I told myself, the only work in sight was my Hermitage heist novel, and I didn't expect to see Melissa for at least two weeks. Her absence depressed me even more than my unemployment, but there was nothing I could do about either.

Before reaching my apartment I stopped at a newsstand for a copy of the *Reporter* and grew even more depressed by a story that said negotiations to end the writers' strike had broken off with no indication of when they might resume. My mailbox held a couple of bills—forwarded by my wife—and a card printed with the name of Detective Lieutenant Jaime Nero, LAPD. On the back was a handwritten request that I contact him as soon as possible.

Standing there in the small lobby, I considered the detective's request until Mrs. Haven opened her door and barked, "Your phone's been ringin' an awful lot, Mr. Brent—you been away?"

"Yes," I said, "I've been away," and, carrying bills and Nero's card, mounted the staircase to my apartment.

The air was stale, the apartment stuffy. I opened a window and let the smog drift in.

On the table I laid out and counted my assets, the diamond among them, all from Melissa. For a while I pondered a secure cache for the diamond, then went to the freezer compartment and emptied an ice-cube tray. I dropped the diamond into one of the cavities, filled the tray with water, and replaced it on the freezer shelf. In a couple of hours my "ice" would be indistinguishable from the real thing.

I hid ten hundred-dollar bills in the bottom cover of my portable typewriter and returned the other ten to my wallet. Naturally, I intended to report my cash income to IRS. Naturally.

Just as Borden Tarkos reported income from his skim . . .

I didn't need to visit Abarrotes Gomez for supplies. I had enough for a couple of days, including the leftover pizza I'd shared with Melissa that first night. It was looking a little dry and the crust was curling, but twenty minutes in a medium oven would restore edibility.

I took a shower, shaved, put on clean clothing, and decided I was ready to respond to Lieutenant Nero's request.

He wasn't at the given number, so I left my name and invited him to phone me when he could. Then I picked up the typed pages of my novel and reread them to get back into the story line.

The phone rang, and a voice identifying the caller as Lieutenant Jaime Nero said, "You're a hard man to reach, Mr. Brent. Been away for a while?"

"Obviously," I said, "or I'd have been here when you called."

"Hmmm. So, now you're back, how about coming down to Wilcox for a chat?"

"Why would I want to do that, Lieutenant? I've got a lot of catch-up here. A writer's life is not a happy one."

"It could be even less happy if you fail to cooperate, Mr. Brent."

"What's on your mind, Lieutenant—Nero, is it? Possibly we can handle the matter by phone."

"I think a face-to-face would be a lot more satisfying. So if you'll be there a while, I'll drive up, we'll talk, and hopefully put the questions to rest."

"Questions about what?"

"The murder of a colleague and his associate—Sergeant Fallon and his Nevada pal, to be specific."

"You haven't collared the killers?"

"Not yet, but it's early in the game, and I have the feeling your input could be useful."

"Unlikely," I told him, "but I'm always prepared to cooperate with the authorities in the unending fight against crime. You'll be here when?"

"Oh, half an hour, fifty minutes. I'll get a chili dog on the way."

"Unmarked car, I hope. Prowlies give the neighborhood a bad name."

"Where *you* live? The neighbors should be grateful."

"I'll make that point at the next Crime Watch meeting."

Nero took his time arriving. I spent mine thinking about Melissa and wondering how things were going for her. Tomorrow or next day I'd phone Joel Hatfield and find out.

Detective Lieutenant Nero was a tall, spare man with long fingers, who looked as though he might have played basketball on a community college team. Before coiling himself into a chair, he glanced around my quarters. "What I'm interested in, Mr. Brent, is learning why your name got into Sergeant Fallon's notebook. But before that I'll ask the inevitable question: Did you kill them?"

"No."

"Got an alibi?"

"Probably—if I knew when they were killed."

"We'll let that rest for the time being, since we don't know the time of death. Both bodies were stuffed in the trunk of Rinaldo's car, and the heat that builds up retards rigor mortis and makes time of death only an estimate."

"The M.E. could try carbon-dating."

He looked at me sourly. "Very funny. Now, why did that pair call on you?"

"Very simple. They were tapping a number I happened to call."

"A Beverly Hills number."

"So it turned out."

"And why were you calling that number?"

I explained about seeing the photo-ad and said, "The sought lady had spent the night here. I'm unemployed and thought the reward would come in handy."

"Unemployed from what?"

I told him about *Frankie's Follies* and the writers' strike, and he nodded understandingly. "One day beluga, next day nacho chips."

"How true."

"And you never saw them again."

"No. However, it was apparent they wanted to track down the lady —the wife of Borden Tarkos, they told me."

"So they told you that. Did they tell you why they were tapping Tarkos's phone?"

"They gave me a story about casino skim in Nevada and how Rinaldo had enlisted LAPD help in laying on the tap. Ah, Lieutenant, I'm thirsty—shall we dip our beaks?"

There was enough Wild Turkey left for two highballs, so I made one for Nero. He sipped thoughtfully, said, "Thanks," and showed no disposition to leave. Stretching out long legs, he said, "And what did you think of their story?"

"I thought it contained elements of truth."

"But you didn't buy the whole thing?"

"I felt that if they had the resources of the LAPD behind them they wouldn't have come to me—wouldn't have needed to."

"And you couldn't really help them."

"I didn't tell them where Mrs. Tarkos had gone from here because I didn't know."

"You hear from her later?"

"I did."

"In what context?"

"She phoned to ask if I could recommend an attorney."

"Did you?"

"Eventually."

"A Los Angeles attorney?"

"No," I said, "and if you want more on that you'll have to get in touch with the U.S. Attorney for the Southern District. Name's Archibald Ballantine. But that has nothing to do with your investigation. Nor, in fact, does she."

"What makes you think that?"

"Because she didn't kill Fallon and Rinaldo, and has no reason to know who did."

"How about you?"

"What about me?"

"You're licensed to carry a handgun, .38 Cobra, I believe. Have it handy?"

I went to the closet, opened my suitcase, and brought back the Cobra. Nero took it by the butt, swung out the cylinder, and sniffed the muzzle. Then he peered through the barrel and said, "Dusty, with a buildup of lint."

"Could have dandruff for all I know. I haven't fired the piece in two years. Now, for the record, Lieutenant, you're in charge of the murder investigation?"

He nodded. "And when a cop's killed—"

"—you gotta produce," I finished.

He shrugged. "Tradition. And, of course, the media expect a full court press, so we explore every nook and cranny."

"But as of now you have no suspects."

"Why assume that?"

"If you had, you wouldn't be wasting time on me."

"Oh, I'm not wasting time. Just following up a lead. Your name was the last one in Fallon's notebook."

"And the others?"

"Police information." Lacing his fingers, he cracked his knuckles loudly. "I'd sure like to interview Mrs. Tarkos. Wouldn't care to facilitate that, tell me where she is?"

"I don't know where she is—Ballantine's your contact point, and I told you that."

"Getting through to a U.S. Attorney means a lot of paperwork and more time than I've got." His eyes narrowed as he gazed at me. "If you knew her location, would you tell me?"

"In answer to a hypothetical question, a hypothetical reply: No."

"Why not?"

"Privileged information, and the lady knows nothing of those two murders."

"How can you be sure of that?"

"We never discussed it."

"And her husband, Borden Tarkos?"

"Never met the man."

"Maybe not—but you're involved in this somehow. Could be a material witness."

"On that basis, anyone could be. But to get things in focus, Lieutenant, forget about citing me as a material witness. More profitably, you could look into that wiretap the dead men were operating. I got the feeling it was a venture of their own, lacking legal authorization."

"They said that?"

I shook my head. "Fallon *said* it was legal. Check with the judge who issued the order."

"In due course. Meanwhile, why would Fallon and Rinaldo be tapping Tarkos without a court order?"

"Do I need to be specific? Tarkos is a wealthy man, perhaps involved in something illegal. The boys may have figured he'd finance early retirement."

His cheeks reddened. "Nasty accusation."

"Speculative," I said. "Of course, if there *is* a court order, then everything was done by the book." I paused. "So there'll be tapes and logs and transcripts of conversations intercepted during the wiretap." I cleared my throat. "The *legal* wiretap."

When Nero said nothing, I said, "You have access to all that stuff, of course."

He looked away. "So far they haven't turned up."

"Then you have to consider who benefits by the tapes' disappearance and the deaths of the tappers."

"Obviously—if we can't locate tap product." He stood up. "But that's down the road. I'm confident the product will show up during the investigation."

"I hope so," I said, "and thus ending speculation I had anything to do with knocking off those two exemplary investigators."

Finishing his drink, Lieutenant Nero set down the empty glass. "But you don't think the tapes will be found."

"I think the men were killed for the tapes and the knowledge they gained from eavesdropping on Tarkos and people who phoned him. If I'm correct, the tapes have probably been destroyed."

"Not an encouraging thought. It's all very baffling, isn't it?"

"If you say so, Lieutenant."

He gave me a sharp glance. "I'll probably want to talk with you again, Mr. Brent."

"If you come to that decision, give me a little notice, will you? I'll want my attorney present."

"Like that, is it?"

"It's like that." I unlocked the door for him and he went out. I lighted the gas oven, and while it was heating for the leftover pizza, I reviewed the interview and felt my story had held up. I hadn't lied to the lieutenant but I'd rocked him with the suggestion that Fallon and Rinaldo were working Tarkos for felonious reasons. If Nero could prove otherwise, so much the better—but this was L.A., where not every cop was a model of rectitude.

Anyway, if Nero's investigation began edging toward Bordon Tarkos, he'd soon find that the feds had more at stake than solving the murders of two possibly rogue cops, and the killer(s) might never be brought publicly to justice. Nero wouldn't like that; I didn't care.

The telephone rang. I slid the pizza into the oven before answering, and heard my wife's voice. "Joe? Where in hell have you been?"

"What's it matter?"

"It matters to me because men have been here looking for you and I've been scared to death."

"Well, climb down from your tree and relax, because I've seen the man—Detective Lieutenant Nero."

"Joe—" her voice quavered "—it *wasn't* the police."

My spine began to prickle. "Who, then?"

"I don't know, but they were ugly-looking types."

"What did you tell them?"

"I said you were on a business trip—didn't know where."

"Natty, I owe you one," I said fervently. "They come back?"

"No, but I've seen them watching the building." She was silent for a while. "One said he hoped you'd get back soon—wasn't safe for Bryon and me without a man in the house. So—oh, Joe, what have you got yourself into?" she bleated.

I tried to keep my voice even. "Bill collectors try all sorts of stratagems."

"Joe, they *weren't* bill collectors, they made threats very coldly. So who could they be?"

I had a pretty good idea what they represented, but if I shared it with Natty she'd collapse. "Did you see their car? What did it look like?" I asked.

"Well—" Natty's memory was an unreliable thing "—it was brown. Dark brown or maroon."

"Big? Small? How many doors?"

"Two doors, Joe."

Easier to keep victims from jumping out, I reflected. "Any idea of the make?"

"You know I'm no good at that sort of thing."

"All right, if they come back tell them we've separated and I don't report in. That ought to discourage them."

"Oh, I hope so. It was very frightening."

"Then do as I say—but for God's sake don't tell anyone where I am —not even my phone number."

"What are you going to do?"

"If they approach me I'll call in the police."

That made her feel better—I could tell from the tone of her voice as she said, "Promise you will."

"Have I ever lied to you?"

She thought it over, sighed, "Not on important things."

"There you are. And you do the same."

"All right," she said doubtfully. "So what have you been doing? Where are you?"

"Looking for work."

"And . . . ?"

"No luck," I said mournfully, "but I have to keep trying. Sol's bankrupt, Corinthian's gone, the series is dead, and I'm the one to tell the tale."

"Oh, Joe, I'm so sorry."

"Happening all over town," I told her, "so you better find steady work for yourself—and I don't mean the Long Beach Playhouse."

"That wasn't necessary," she said resentfully.

"You know what I mean. Whoever wants to eat has to work. Natty, I appreciate your call and warning. I'll take it from here. Otherwise, you and Bryon okay?"

"We're doing all right—for now."

"'Bye." I hung up.

Curls of smoke issued from the oven. I pulled out the pizza and found the underside scorched. When it cooled down I scraped off the charred portions and ate the remains with a bottle of Poummit's Brew.

While eating, I reflected that Natty's visitors hadn't come from Borden Tarkos but from his associates, the Ambrosinos. They had the wiretap tapes, and the tapes had provided them with my name.

To get the tapes, I realized with a sick feeling, they had killed Fallon and Rinaldo.

Now they were coming after me.

ELEVEN

In an effort to reroute my mind from mounting problems, I worked on the novel for a while, realized I was getting unsatisfactory results, and telephoned Professor George Anders. His phone rang a dozen times before I hung up, reasonably satisfied he'd followed my advice and taken to the hills.

Next, I phoned Joel Hatfield and asked about Melissa. Things were moving along on schedule, he told me, though she was incommunicado as far as the outside world was concerned. One hopeful note: he thought I might be able to spend an evening with her next week.

I then told him about Lieutenant Nero's visit and the uglies who'd intimidated my wife. "No way they could have gotten my name other than through the Fallon-Rinaldo tapes. And to get the tapes they had to liquidate the tappers."

"Logical," he said, "so I advise you to be careful where you go and what you do. Can I help?"

"All I can think of is getting the feds to put the Ambrosinos under surveillance—and letting them know about it."

"I'd have to have a reason—murder isn't a federal crime."

"Obstruction of justice is. Fallon and Rinaldo were potential federal witnesses against Tarkos; eliminating their testimony adds up to obstruction. Right?"

"Good point. But I'm pretty sure the Ambrosinos have been under technical surveillance for years now. They make their contacts out in the desert."

"Where they can be tailed. I want them harassed, Joel. Maybe they'll think twice about taking my life."

"I understand your concern and I'll see what I can do. There's a jurisdictional barrier, but I know some Nevada Strike Force people, and a phone call might be enough to lay something on."

"Any help will be appreciated." I gave him my true name, address, and phone number, saying, "Since the other side has I.D.'d me, you might as well know."

"I appreciate it, and I'll use the information with circumspection."

"One last thing: did Tisch and DiLirio bond out, or are they still in the slammer?"

"They were denied bail because they'd bailed out on a previous L.A. charge—attempted robbery—and were set for a hearing on that. Plus carrying unlicensed handguns in San Diego—that's a no-no for convicted felons. So as far as I know, they'll be getting free meals for quite a while."

"Best news today." I hung up, relieved that those two scumbags wouldn't be paying Melissa's father a third visit.

I had my own concerns, of course, but they came more from the direction of the Ambrosinos than from Borden Tarkos. Natty had been menaced because of me, and although our love had died or worn away, she was still my wife and I felt responsible for her welfare—and Bryon's, much as I disliked the little monster. He and his mother would be better off in Prem Kushna's ashram, but I didn't know how to bring that about. Perhaps time and propinquity would work a miracle advantageous to us all.

The typewriter sat there, inanimate yet reproving. I pulled over my chair, reread the five last pages, and forced myself to start typing.

For whatever reason, the flow of words improved, became fluid, and I worked through the afternoon until dusk.

By then my neck and back were stiff from hunching over the machine and I got up to stretch, telling myself I'd put in enough effort for one day. I decided on a stroll. And with money in my wallet I'd examine Abarrotes Gomez's inventory of delicacies, get some fresh milk, a few bottles of Poummit's Brew, then settle down to watch whatever NBA game was being televised. Of late, I hadn't had much time to myself, and the prospect of doing what *I* wanted to do pleased me.

I left my apartment and walked to the end of the hall, where an unwashed window overlooked the street. I looked down toward Franklin, then up Cerrito in the direction of the big Yamashiro shrine that dominated the hill.

There, on the far side of the street, fifty yards away, a two-door car was parked. Fading light made its color ambiguous—dark brown or maroon, as Natty said—and I felt a chill of recognition. Squinting, I tried to see if the car was occupied, but distance and shadows foiled me. So I walked back to my apartment, unlocked the door, and dialed 911.

When a female voice answered I said, "Franklin Park Crime Watch. There's a suspicious car parked on the east side of Cerrito, north of Franklin. Dark color. It's been there a while with two men in it. Could be casing for a burglary after dark."

"Thank you, we'll respond. Your name—?" But I'd hung up.

After looking at the time I uncapped my last bottle of Poummit's and carried it to the front window. From there I watched the two-door, and after a while two men got out and began walking down the incline in my direction. They came diagonally toward my building, so they were on the street when a prowl car, light bar flashing, turned down Cerrito and caught them in its headlights.

The men stopped, looked back, then faced each other, deciding whether or not to run. I heard the police loudspeaker order them back as the cop car stopped behind theirs. A patrolman got out and stood, hands on hips, as the pair slowly trudged back to their car. I couldn't hear what else the police had to say, but the two men were positioned hands against their car, feet back, while the patrolman patted them down, and found two handguns that glinted in the headlights.

Handcuffs also glinted as they secured two pairs of wrists behind the men's backs, and I took a long pull from my bottle.

At gunpoint the anonymous visitors were seated in the back of the patrol car. The light bar went dark, the prowl car backed up, then headed down Cerrito past my building, leaving the two-door parked where it was.

Darkness had fallen, streetlights went on. I returned to my apartment and shoulder-holstered my .38 Cobra, left the building, and walked down to Hollywood Boulevard. Two blocks west, I came across four hangouts on two motorcycles who seemed to be looking for action. One wore a dented Wehrmacht helmet with a black-and-silver swastika. All had black jackets, jeans, and heavy gauntlets. To the helmeted youth I said, "Not far away there's some prime transportation."

"Yeah? Why tell me, man?"

"It's my neighbor's car. He's given me a lot of aggravation, and he's out of town for a few days. East side of Cerrito, up the hill from Franklin. Dark two-door. New."

Helmet turned to his companions. "Hear that? What're we waiting for?"

Both bikes kicked off in unison. They roared off into the night.

I took their direction and walked up to Abarrotes Gomez where Ruben was setting his night-grill in place. Peering out, he saw me, unlocked the door, and let me in. I made my selection promptly and paid for my purchases. As Mr. Gomez was bagging them he said, "Ever see that fellow who left that message?"

"I saw him. *Gracias.*"

He locked the door after me, and I walked back to Cerrito. The street was quiet and uninhabited. Either the two-door's occupants had left keys in the ignition or the four bikers had done a fast hot-wire job, because the car was no longer there.

They'd take it to a chop shop, I reflected as I unlocked the entrance door, and within hours what had been a car would be a collection of spare parts ready for resale.

In my apartment I put things in the refrigerator and the freezer compartment, which also held Melissa's ice-camouflaged sparkler. I drank a glass of skim milk and settled down, with a considerable sense of accomplishment, to watch Seattle wallop Phoenix in a bruising Pacific League game.

Unlike most recent nights, I enjoyed a long and restful sleep. Toward ten o'clock next morning, while I was preparing breakfast for myself, the phone rang and I heard the voice of my agent, Morry Manville.

Before he could speak I said, "Strike over?"

"No—but I got something for you, kid. Assuming you're available for assignment."

"I'm Mr. Available, but I don't want to buck the Guild."

"No problem, this is Mexico."

"Mexico? Whereabouts?"

"Down the tip of Baja California—Cabo San Lucas."

"Never heard of it."

"It's location work, Joe. Mexican production being shot in two languages—English for export. Seems the English-language writer took sick and they can't continue shooting until they get a replacement. Two weeks' work guaranteed, thousand a week, plus transportation."

I thought it over. "My Spanish isn't anywhere good enough to translate a script into English."

"They've got a translator, so that's no worry. You have to put dialogue in English for lip sync. You can do that."

"I guess so. What do you know about the producers?"

"Producciones Zaragoza"—he stumbled over the pronunciation—"listed in the register. No black marks against them. And Señor Evaristo asked for you by name. You'll take it?"

"Why not?"

"They'll Telex tickets to the Mexicana counter at L.A. airport. Three o'clock flight today."

"I'll be on it," I told him. "Thanks, Morry," and hung up.

No sooner had I replaced the receiver than I had second thoughts about the deal. I didn't know whether the production was comedy or drama, even the name of the film. And why Señor Evaristo wanted to hire an obscure writer of TV sitcoms was a question that bothered me. But I told myself if Morry was satisfied with the deal, I should be too.

Besides, I'd been living so long on Melissa's bounty that I was eager for honest work. So I finished breakfast, washed what needed washing, and packed some warm-weather clothing in my suitcase.

Reluctantly I put my revolver in the closet, deciding I couldn't chance wearing it through security checkpoints. Not for two thousand gross, which was under Guild scale. Anyway, if I didn't like what I found at Cabo San Lucas I could board a return flight tomorrow, having lost nothing but time.

I phoned Joel Hatfield's office but the secretary said he wasn't in. Using the Phillips alias I told her I'd taken a writing assignment for Producciones Zaragoza at Cabo San Lucas, and asked Hatfield to make my apologies to Jane Doe and assure her I'd be back in two weeks. She said he would and wished me a pleasant stay in Mexico.

Morry rang back to say I'd be met at Los Cabos airport by Evaristo or one of his assistants. I'd be staying at the Hotel Vista del Mar with the cast and production crew. "Look on it as a paid vacation," he advised, "a change of scene from Hollywood's grime and intrigue."

"You said crime?"

"That too. When you get back we'll have lunch and you can tell me about the bilingual experience."

"Chasen's," I said, "on you."

I looked around the apartment, glad to be away from it for a while, and thinking it was just as well I didn't have a pet to board at a vet's. I'd wanted a cat or dog at my Burbank apartment, but after appraising the latent cruelty in Bryon's pale eyes I decided not to risk it. Anyway, Natty informed me, her son didn't like animals: a puppy had nipped him, a kitten had clawed his delicate hand, and a budgie had pecked his skinny nose. I could imagine why. So no pet. My portable typewriter substituted.

Before leaving I again considered the desirability of bringing along my .38 Cobra. I could wrap it in a towel, conceal it in my suitcase, and check the suitcase through without examination. Then I'd have it on location.

Only, why was I thinking of taking a piece? Mexico was fairly civilized, and if drug-runners decided to shoot up the location, they'd have automatic weapons—MAC–10s, Ingrams, Uzis, or AR–15s— against whose firepower my .38 would be useless. So reasoning, I discarded the thought and stopped at Mrs. Haven's door on the ground floor.

Telling her I'd be away for a couple of weeks, I paid in advance and asked that she give no information to any callers who asked for me. Then, to satisfy her curiosity, I said, "I'll be in Schenectady doing a training film for GE."

She found the news exciting. "You'll be sure to tell me when it's showing?"

"Absolutely. But because of the strike, I don't want it known I'm scabbing—or where."

"I understand, Mr. Brent. Have a good trip. I'll hold any mail."

"Appreciate it." I went down to my Datsun and, with my suitcase riding beside me, drove along Hollywood Boulevard to Santa Monica, cut south on the San Diego Freeway, and found the long-term parking lot at LAX.

The Mexicana counter produced computerized R/T tickets in my name and gave me a tourist form to fill out. When I'd done that and checked my suitcase I strolled over to the duty-free shop and bought two bottles of Jim Beam for delivery aboard the aircraft. On my way to the boarding gate I glanced at the Mexicana check-in counter and saw a long line of grizzled field hands in blue jeans and straw sombreros. They were dragging and shoving along large suitcases and rope-wrapped cartons labeled Sony, Amana, GE, and Hitachi—name-brand merchandise representing weeks of sweaty stoop labor in the fields, orchards, and vineyards of Southern California. I hoped the folks back home in their adobe huts would appreciate what their men had gone through to buy the gifts.

My window seat was toward the rear of the stretch 727, and after we were airborne a steward who looked like Raul Julia announced that complimentary beverages would be served: Mexican beer and wine.

The field hands helped themselves so liberally that by the time the beverage cart reached me it held only a few cans of cabin-temperature Coke and Sprite. The stewardess smiled wanly, said "Sorry, sir," and shoved the cart back to the galley.

Hell, I thought, the *campesinos* needed the stuff more than I did, and it was only a two-hour flight. But I uncapped a Beam and sneaked a long pull while the plane cleared U.S. airspace and flew south over the tranquil Sea of Cortes, where the gray whales sing, frolic, and mate on holiday from the Bering Sea.

The snack, served an hour later, turned out to be a styrofoam tray bearing rice, guacamole, and a tepid tamale. The *campesinos* wolfed down their rations and clamored for more. I swallowed a little rice and washed it down with straight Jim Beam while my fellow-travelers got beerily noisy and unruly. The three flight attendants lounged around the galley, oblivious of the general high spirits; they were accustomed to the homeward run and never let passengers interfere with their own gossip and conviviality.

I turned my attention to the long land finger below that was Baja California. Against the western side the Pacific rolled whitely. The Gulf shore was a thin silver beading far, far below. The land between was a barren moonscape, sculpted, ridged, and fractured by volcanic action and eons of hostile elements. No wonder the few widely spaced settlements I could see were on the shoreline; nothing to venture inland for. You lived by the sea and the sea sustained you.

The plane swung south of the Baja tip, lost altitude, and came back and down onto a landing strip set back from the sheltered harbor with its shrimp trawlers, sport-fishing fleet, and low-lying hotels. A palm fringe broke the view and there was only the airport building, a scattering of tied-down private planes, and a Pemex oil tanker.

The *campesinos* helped their buddies stumble off the plane and we walked in a long file toward Immigration and Customs. My tourist form was stamped and returned to me, and I went to the baggage carousel to claim my bag. First on, last off, and for a while I was lost among the jumbled mountain of consumer goods. Finally I lifted my suitcase to the inspection counter and was about to open it when a man appeared at my side. "Brent?"

"Right."

He gestured at a female Customs inspector who nodded back, came over, and made a chalk mark on my suitcase. "Let's go," he said.

"You Evaristo?" I asked as I regained my suitcase.

"Call me Diego," he said, and led the way out of the building. A tall, well-built, rather handsome man, Diego was wearing a white embroidered guayabera shirt, loose cotton trousers, and reptile skin boots. A breeze lifted the fringe of his guayabera and I saw a holstered .45 on his cartridge belt. Nickel-plated, with mother-of-pearl handle, it was the kind of showpiece worn by affluent traffic cops in Mexico City. A jeep pulled up and Diego got on the back seat with my suitcase. I sat next to the driver, a short, squat Indian with the stolid long-nosed profile you see on Aztec bas-relief.

I'd expected to check in at the Vista del Mar Hotel but the driver took a road leading away from town. "How far off is the location?" I asked Diego.

"A few kilometers—miles. Evaristo needs you now so he can start shooting."

"It's nice to be needed," I remarked. "What's the name of the picture?"

"*Lágrimas y Sonrisas*," he told me. "*Tears and Smiles* in English."

Gilligan's Island came to mind but I erased the thought as Diego said, "The film industry here is government-subsidized and controlled. Sixty percent of all films exhibited have to be Mexican-made, but the export market is limited to Spanish-speaking communities in the American southwest. Which is why this is being shot in English, too. Better chance at U.S. distribution."

The one-lane road entered a zone of coconut palms that thickened the farther we went. The dirt surface was potholed and dusty, and I wondered how heavy production trailers managed to make it. But in Mexico maybe they used smaller trucks to haul lighting, film, and sound equipment. RVs for actors and crew. I had to grip the seat's iron frame to keep from being bounced off the jeep, and when I looked at the driver for relief I saw him staring fixedly at the road ahead. "Hey, Pepe," I said loudly, "how's to slow down before I cough up my pancreas?"

From behind, Diego said, "Pancho doesn't speak English. Anyway, we haven't far to go."

So I clung to my seat for another half mile of jungle road that gave out into a clearing. Coconut palms had been felled and their trunks used to make a fair-sized cabin in the center of the clearing. The jeep engine died and I heard a new sound—an electric generator engine chuffing away behind the cabin.

From the palm-thatch roof, a radio aerial led off beyond the edge of the clearing, and I wondered if the cabin had been erected for the picture. I climbed down from the jeep, glad to be stable again, and from behind, Diego said, "He's inside—go on in."

So I followed a narrow trail among palm stumps, razor-grass, and cactus, and opened the wooden door.

A low-wattage bulb hung from roof timber above a rough table and a couple of chairs. Behind the table sat a man in a blue guayabera who said, "Take a chair. Glad you got here."

"Evaristo?" I asked, sitting down.

"Evaristo's on location," he said indifferently, "and you and me got some talking to do." His olive skin was close-shaven and slick with perspiration, but his eyes were cold as an undertaker's. I heard the door close, looked around, and Diego was standing before it with folded arms.

"Yes," the man said, "you're a valuable, property—how valuable, you have no idea."

My neck hairs began prickling but I said, "My agent indicated you were in a bind."

"Sure—that's what he was told and that's why you're here." He eyed me for a few moments before saying, "Ever see me before?"

"No."

"Any idea who I am?"

"Not without a name."

He looked beyond me at invisible Diego and shrugged. "Why not?" Then his gaze returned to me. "I'm Dino Ambrosino. I've gone to some trouble to arrange this meeting away from eavesdroppers and wiretappers, so you could tell me what happened to Mrs. Tarkos and the money she stole from me."

TWELVE

I looked around, but by then, of course, Diego had his nickel-plated pistol in hand, so I looked back at Dino Ambrosino while fear chilled my blood.

"This isn't the script I expected," I told him. "No translation required."

"It's a shooting script," he snickered. "You get shot unless you play the part right."

"I was never much of an actor."

He leaned back again. "Oh, I don't know I'd say that. Different voices, different names. You put on a pretty good show . . . while it lasted."

"Amateur night," I said, "but you're the pro—even to the picture's name. *Lágrimas y Sonrisas.*"

"Diego thought it up. *Tears and Smiles.* Not bad. The grins are mine, Brent, you get the tears."

"I'm not crazy about the split but it's your scenario all the way."

"Has to be. Glad you understand that."

"Just to clear up any lingering confusion—I suppose there's no picture in production."

"Not around here. Happens my family and some Mexican associates own Zaragoza Productions as a convenience. It transfers funds, gives some of us reason to travel to Mexico, and is an occasional source of really good-looking young *chiquitas.* Just like Hollywood, the chicks here go limp at the idea of appearing in front of a camera. Of course, not all the roles are Shakespeare quality and I won't pretend the pix qualify for *Good Housekeeping* approval . . ." He laughed lewdly and Diego echoed him. "But now and then Zaragoza turns out something good enough for export and the firm shows a profit." He paused to light a cigarette. "We're businessmen, Brent. Profit is the motive, and loss is unpardonable—a heavy loss like the one Melissa Tarkos is responsible for. Where is she?"

"If I told you I don't know, would you believe me?"

"Probably not."

"I don't know where she is."

He nodded at Diego, who slammed his pistol on the back of my head. As I pitched forward I felt intense pain, saw blinding lights, then darkness. When I came to I was lying on the dirt floor, flashes of pain shooting through my skull. My brain felt squeezed in a vise. "I don't know," I managed to gasp, "but before you hit me again, hear me out, okay?"

"Okay," Ambrosino's voice. "Tell me why I should believe you."

"Look at it through my eyes. The woman came into my life by chance, I didn't even know who she was until after she left and I saw that photo ad in the paper. I was broke, saw a chance to get the reward money, but set up a test for Tarkos. He didn't send money, he sent two knee-busters. That made me mad, so I made a couple of phone calls to upset him. End of story."

"You got a thing for her, right?"

"Like I'm crazy about the Spiderwoman. Listen, she's been nothing but aggravation from the time she braced me on the street. And now this." I ended with a quaver in my voice that wasn't just pretend.

"But she talked, told you things. How much did she tell you?"

I wet dry lips, squinted against pain and pushed myself upright. Now I could see young Ambrosino across the table top, his smooth, wet face. I was trying to calculate how much he knew but my brain wasn't cooperating. "She gave me a sob story about bad treatment from her husband, said she'd taken money from him. Later she said it wasn't really her husband's money—he'd juggled casino books, cheated on his partners—"

"She name them? Me? My family?"

"No. Treated the whole thing like a prank. Said she wasn't worried about her husband coming after her because his partners would find out what he'd been doing, and he'd suffer. I figured she was trying to convince herself she wasn't in danger, because she was uptight about being followed." I licked my lips again. "She left my place before I woke up."

Ambrosino thought it over. "When did you see her again?"

I tried to think fast but my brain was in low gear. "I didn't—wait, she phoned a couple of days later."

"Why?"

"A confused dame. Thanked me for the overnight and said she was considering giving her husband back his money. She didn't like her husband but she didn't want him killed by his partners."

"What did you say?"

"As little as possible. I had my own problems—still do—and wanted no part of hers. I wished her well and that was that."

"She say where she was going?"

"No—and I don't think she knew herself. Hell, she's probably back with her husband. Ask him."

"He claims he hasn't seen her since she took off."

"Look," I said, "this is a goofy dame, right? To do what she did and think she could get away with it. She gets a dose of reality and runs for the best cover she can think of—home and husband. I don't know where Mrs. Tarkos is. I don't have her and God knows I wish we'd never met."

In a thick voice Ambrosino said, "I don't like what I'm hearing, not any of it." He nodded at Diego and the toe of his pointed boot kicked the base of my spine. Pain shot up to my skull, ricocheted around like a speeding bullet, and my legs went numb. I groaned and retched. Bile filled my throat and mouth.

Through the pounding in my ears I heard Ambrosino say, "The diamonds, what'd she do with the diamonds?"

"I never saw them," I groaned. "She just talked about them. Far as I know they're imaginary."

A grunt was his only comment. Feeling slowly returned to my legs. I retched again, spewed out Mexicana's rice ration. Ambrosino growled, "You got to be crazy to try protecting her, man. Or you're in love with the bitch."

"*Love?*" I spat threads of bile from my mouth. "If I loved her, knew where she was with her goddamn mythical jewels, would I come down here for a two-week job at less than scale? Be logical. I'd be living it up with her in the Caribbean—Jamaica, Barbados—bouncing her every hour. I'm not her accomplice, for God's sake. I gave the woman a night's lodging and she paid me."

"Paid you? How much?"

"Seventy bucks." The amount Vinnie had returned.

"Seventy lousy bucks," Ambrosino giggled. "And for that you buy into this kind of trouble? Chumps like you don't come around every day." Behind me, Diego snorted contemptuous agreement.

I thought of trying to grab his pistol, but I wasn't confident I could get up, that my prickling legs would support me. All I could do was keep spinning out the tale, make it convincing.

I felt like Scheherezade: as soon as the tales stopped I was finished. I knew it but I wasn't sure they knew I knew it. So I said, "Okay, I was suckered, I see that. She had a pretty face, a good figure. She came on to me as a hooker—I thought her pimp was after her—"

"A *hooker?*" Ambrosino rasped.

"She spoke the lines, asked if I was a vice cop. When I told her I was broke, couldn't afford her, she said she'd pay me to put her up overnight. Until I saw her photo and the Beverly Hills number I thought she *was* a hooker."

"A true fool," Ambrosino said pityingly.

"And the last thing she said that night before she turned in was not to try finding out who she was."

"What did you think of that?"

"I thought she was some housewife turning tricks for Christmas money. She didn't tell me her husband's name or how much money he had."

"Well, he's got less now," Ambrosino said in a hard voice. "A lot less, thanks to that sly cunt of his."

Unseen, Diego said, "Dino, maybe you oughta check out Tarkos— this clown makes a certain amount of sense."

"You're not paid to think," Dino snapped. "When I want advice I'll ask for it."

I'd planted a seed of distrust. I wanted it to bloom into a poisonous flower.

Fast.

Dejectedly, my head hung down, chin on chest. I didn't have to pretend dejection, fear, and despair because I felt those emotions.

But they were submerged in a flood of cold hate, resolve to get even. Revenge.

"What else should I know?" Ambrosino asked in a flat, deadly voice.

Without looking up I mumbled, "I don't know anything else. You can pull me apart and you won't get more because I don't know more about Mrs. Tarkos, her loot, or her husband. You gotta believe me."

"Maybe I do," Ambrosino muttered, "but where does that leave you and me? I brought you down here, gave you some pain. Suppose I put you on a flight back to L.A., pay your agent—can you keep your mouth shut?"

"Oh, God, yes," I bleated. "If I don't—and I swear I will—you could always have me hit."

"Got a point," Diego said, unasked. Ambrosino glared at him. "Will you for Christ's sake shut up? If we're gonna talk it'll be away from this clown, *capisce?*"

"*Entiendo,*" he said obediently, and I knew he'd just as soon blow my head off as squash a roach under his fancy boot. When Ambrosino told him to. At least Dino was *talking* about an arrangement. That he even bothered gave me a small crumb of hope, too small to feed on. *Prepare for the worst,* my D.I. had snarled at Pendleton and I'd taken it as gospel. Too bad our colonel hadn't sensed how vulnerable our Beirut barracks was and—

"So," said Dino Ambrosino, "I'll think it over—what you said, how it fits in."

"I'll certainly be grateful," I said humbly, and heard Dino tell his gofer to tie me up.

Diego did it with nylon cord around my wrists and ankles, not quite tight enough to cut off circulation, then knotted a length to my ankles and looped the other end around a table leg, using a rusty machete to part it from the nylon coil. I knew the kind of line it was, having used it aboard my boat. Four-hundred-pound test, the line didn't stretch, freeze or rot. It was tough to cut through, but flame melted it like wax.

I lay on my right side and looked up at Ambrosino, who was looking down at me, amusement on his soft, slick face.

"Cocktail hour," he said, "so we'll hit town, have a few margaritas, check the local action."

"Love to go with you," I said. "Maybe next time."

"After I make a phone call or two. We'll see."

"Could I trouble you to bring back a little food for me? Some water?"

"I'll consider it. Meantime, search your memory for anything you forgot to tell."

"How long have I got?"

"You'll see me later. That's a promise."

"*Adios,* chump," Diego said, and they left the cabin together. At least the single bulb was still lit, the generator plugging away outside. I turned over on my back to ease head and spinal pain, and after a while I reflected that the way the situation had developed I was lucky to be drawing breath. Dino had given me what I was to interpret as hope of survival, but I wasn't convinced I had the slightest chance. Once he'd squeezed all he could from me, Dino would make sure I'd never see Los Angeles again. Shoot me or chop off my head with the machete was the plan, drag my remains into the jungle for the fauna to feast on. Hatfield and Morry knew where I was—roughly speaking—but neither had any idea I'd been lured away and captured. When I didn't return from two weeks' employment, they might ask questions of Evaristo, who could deny anything and everything. Scores of *gringos* never made it back from rural Mexico; I'd be just another disappeared gringo, name added to the depressing total. Unfortunate.

The jeep engine started, and I heard its wheels bump over the road, the sound of its engine fade through the jungle trees. Was Pancho driving, or was he lurking outside, an unseen guard?

As they left I'd glimpsed the outside world and seen that darkness had fallen. I couldn't see my wristwatch but I judged the time to be around seven o'clock. At least the cabin door was shut against predators; no worry there. But the human predators would return. Before that, if I wanted to live, I had to escape.

How?

The old machete was in the cabin, wherever Diego had tossed it. Could I somehow find it, manage to use its blade on my wrist bonds? With that in mind I lay silent, listening for Pancho's footsteps, the jeep's raucous engine, anything that signaled danger.

For a long time I listened, my hearing eventually filtering out the generator engine's throbbing hum. But I couldn't hear soft sounds because of the closed door.

When I told myself an hour had passed and Pancho hadn't looked in nor the jeep returned, I sat up, almost fainting from pain in my skull. Gravity surged blood through my arms and legs until I judged them usable. I looked around, but my view was blocked by Ambrosino's table. My ankle tether was fixed to one of its legs, and as I reached a decision I was also listening very carefully for hostile sounds.

Hearing none, I scrunched forward on my buttocks, ignoring an explosion of pain where Diego had kicked my spine. I lay back and planted my shoes against the heavy table, took a deep breath, and shoved with all my strength. The table toppled back on one side, and my ankle tether slipped free. Now I could stand.

But I didn't get up. I rested, fought pain, and listened, afraid the sound of the falling table might bring Pancho. When he didn't appear I breathed more easily, squatted yoga-style, and forced my legs to lever my body erect.

The motion made me giddy, so for a few moments I leaned against the table, looking around the cabin's interior. The first thing I saw was a radio set in corner shadows. It looked like a ham outfit, earphones and hand mike lying atop it, mated to the aerial I'd noticed earlier. It didn't look powerful enough to reach Las Vegas or Los Angeles, but what did I know about radio transmitters?

My gaze left the radio and traversed the uneven earth floor until I saw Diego's machete. It lay about ten feet away, and as I hopped toward it like a kid in a sack race, the jarring unleashed new bolts of pain that seemed to penetrate every portion of my body. But finally I reached the old machete, knelt and studied how best to reach, hold, and use it. I decided to sit down, clawed behind me until my fingers touched the cold steel. Slowly, I pried the machete off the floor so that its edge was upward. I tried to saw my nylon wrist bonds against the edge, but the blade wobbled and flattened on the dirt. Tried again, same result. Almost sobbing with frustration, I positioned the machete a third time and managed to cut one wrist.

Forget the damn machete.

From the floor I looked around for anything else that might sever my bonds and saw nothing. The generator's humming invaded my mind, bringing with it an idea. So I forced myself upright and hopped painfully to the door. No lock, it was simply shut. I leaned against it, the door swung outward, and I toppled into the night.

Lest the interior light bring Pancho, I shouldered the door shut, and began hopping around the cabin toward the sound of the generator's engine. Presently my eyes adjusted to darkness, and I was able to see, as well as hear, the generator.

From a yard away I studied it, smelled the smoke of its exhaust, and located the exhaust pipe running atop the two-cylinder gasoline engine. I turned around slowly and backed against it until I could lower my wrists toward the exhaust pipe. Miscalculating, I scorched my left palm, readjusted quickly, and centered my nylon bonds on the hot metal pipe. I pressed downward.

At first nothing happened. Then I smelled burning nylon and exerted sideways pressure to spring my wrists apart. Slowly the melting nylon gave, and when the cords parted, my right hand snapped against the pipe, burning the palm. I sucked and licked my burns, sat down and untied my ankles. Now I could move, pain permitting.

I massaged my ankles, then my wrists, as I made out a stack of gasoline cans, five gallons each. My impulse was to drench the cabin and burn it, but reason took over and I realized destruction was a flourish that could wait.

I needed transportation, meaning the jeep, and to get the jeep I needed a weapon. Walking was a novelty and much easier on my concussed skull. I entered the cabin and quickly shut the door, picked up the machete, and sat in Ambrosino's chair to rest and gather strength.

My thumb tested the machete's dull blade and I began looking around for a sharpener. Toward the rear of the cabin I saw a stone embedded in the dirt. After prying it out with the machete point I honed the blade with it until the edge was sharp enough for my purposes. Then I righted the fallen table, got on it and unscrewed the light bulb.

The cabin was now darker than the night outside.

Carrying the machete, I left the cabin, closed the door, and went around to the generator. When my eyes gained night vision, I bent over the engine and looked for the fuel cutoff valve. When I found it I turned it off. The engine stuttered, coughed and died.

Let them think the cabin was dark because the engine ran out of fuel.

My next problem was tactical: ambushing three armed men with nothing but a machete. I retraced my steps and sat down beside the cabin door to think the problem through. I'd hear the jeep coming from far away, giving me time to get back inside the dark cabin—if that was what I wanted to do.

As my mind searched for solutions, the thought occurred to me that they'd have flashlights. Good for them, bad for me. One more handicap, I mused, as if I didn't have far more than I needed.

After a while the moon came up—a spindly, silvery new moon that shone with the special clarity of the tropics, away from factory-polluted air. Its light showed palm stumps in the clearing, the road that led out of it, and when I looked up I noticed the radio aerial suspended there like a delicate silver strand.

The radio. Ambrosino wouldn't have installed it unless it was of some use to him. For me it was useless, so I went in and hacked at the wiring, smashed the microphone, and pulled the headset apart. Whatever Ambrosino had used his radio for, he couldn't use it now.

And while I was doing physical things, my mind had sorted out one part of my problem and was now telling me my sole asset would be surprise.

I returned to the generator engine and opened the cutoff valve—in case they checked. I didn't want them to suspect I was free and moving about.

I sat with my back against the log frame, knees up, machete cradled in my lap. It was a warm night, still but for the occasional high-frequency squeals of bats swooping on nocturnal prey. My eyelids were heavy, eyeballs gritty with fatigue. I found my head drooping, chin almost touching my knees, started, and sat erect, rubbing my eyes.

Time passed, the moon rose, crickets chirped in the razor-grass, lizards croaked in the trees. Dino and Diego would be in good spirits when they came back, assuming they returned tonight. In town they'd be celebrating the success of their ruse, congratulating each other, maybe taking a whore or two to bed. Acting like the scumbags they were.

I remembered Dino's mentioning phone calls he'd make from town. If he was serious, one would be to Tarkos, the other to old Raf, his dad, who headed the rotten clan. Raf would say if I lived or died, although I was sure Dino had made his own lethal decision. Dad was in Vegas, Sonny was on the spot, free to do as he chose. Remembering the pain he'd caused me—pain barely tolerable—and the death he planned for me, I felt my hands draw into tight fists. My body was tense, my stomach taut and filled with nothing but hatred for him and his sidekick.

I had no trouble deciding what to do with them—if I could manage it—but Pancho had never done me harm. Still, he had a mouth, he could talk, tell a tale, and I didn't want that, couldn't have it and live long if I somehow got back to L.A.

For a time my mind dulled, went vacant, and still I hadn't formulated an ambush plan because my mind had taken me into a future beyond the cabin, with the jeep mine . . .

Easy, I told myself, slow down and concentrate on what happens when the jeep returns with three armed men.

If I was lucky, the two prime targets would be drunk—but not the Indian. They wouldn't let Pancho take strong waters because he was their designated driver. But for height he was built like a Raiders nose tackle and I was in no shape to take him on hand-to-hand. In my best day I never was. And even drunk, Dino and Diego could still pull triggers.

During its down cycle my mind had produced two ideas for survival; both could work in the dark, one might even work in daylight if my captors didn't turn up until morning.

Carrying my machete, I walked around to the silent generator engine and sawed a small opening in the underside of the copper feed line. Drop by drop, gasoline began to drip onto the engine block. I opened one of the gasoline jerricans and filled the engine's tank to make sure there'd be plenty of fuel in it when they started the engine again. Then I carried the open jerrican into the cabin and stowed it under the radio equipment.

For a while I sat beside the cabin door, looking up and trying to identify constellations I'd learned as a Boy Scout, but I was so far south the stars weren't located where I used to find them.

I saw the blinking lights of an aircraft and heard its breathy jet as it slanted down toward Los Cabos airport. I was wondering where it came from and where it might go on the return flight when I heard the faint oncoming sound of Ambrosino's jeep.

Involuntarily my muscles tightened. I stood up and prepared to fight for my life.

THIRTEEN

Entering the cabin, I closed the door and stood near its opening side. Whoever came in would be silhouetted against the starlit background and maybe the jeep headlights too.

As adrenalin charged my veins it amplified the jeep's noisy progress so that it seemed much nearer than it was. Gripping the machete like a baseball bat, I heard blood pounding in my skull. The back of my head throbbed brutally but that was unimportant. This was my one chance to live and get back to civilization. Rage at what had been done to me filled my mind.

The jeep came closer, its engine noise reverberating through the palms. Poised, ready, I glimpsed its lights through the door crack. The beams bounced up and down, finally lighting the clearing stumps, turning them into grave markers.

The jeep rolled to a stop, its engine died, but the headlights stayed on. I heard Dino Ambrosino say, "The damn generator's off, go fill it while I check on Brent."

Footsteps on gravel coming nearer. They parted as Diego went around the side of the cabin and Dino continued on toward my door.

He paused outside to listen, then kicked the door open and burst in, pistol in hand. Profiled by the jeep headlights, he made a target no one could miss. With two hands and all my strength, I slashed the machete at his middle, felt it bite into soft flesh, jerked the blade free, and slashed again, nearly severing his gun hand. He screamed, the pistol dropped, and Dino Ambrosino went down on his knees, clutching his open belly. Blood spouted between his fingers, and silver-blue intestines writhed like fighting snakes.

From the generator Diego yelled, "Dino—you okay?"

"Okay," I called back and scooped up Dino's pistol.

Machete in one hand, pistol in the other, I waited and heard Diego pulling the starter lanyard. The mechanism whirred and died. Diego cursed and jerked the lanyard again.

This time the engine sparked and exploded with a concussion that shook the cabin. Diego screeched in pain, and as Ambrosino toppled forward, dying, I shaded my eyes and looked toward the jeep for Pancho. If he was there I couldn't see him. I looked down at Ambrosino. One eye glinted at me and his lips moved, *"Bastard,"* he mouthed.

"Addio, amico," I said, crouched, and left the cabin in a weaving run that took me around the side.

Flames were climbing the cabin wall, streaking high, firing the dry roof thatch. A few yards from the exploded engine Diego was rolling on the ground, trying to smother his burning clothes. His face and arms were seared and blackened by the explosion. Pancho, the Indian, was tossing handfuls of dirt over Diego. I walked toward them and pointed the pistol at Pancho. "Get away from him," I said. *"Fuera. Rápido."*

The Indian looked at me, shook his head, and in perfect English said, "I need him alive."

"I need him dead. Move away and lie face down."

"I'm Treasury, man, don't interfere."

"I don't care if you're President," I said harshly. "Move." I fired at his feet and earth spurted over his shoes.

While this was going on, Diego was screaming horribly as he rolled frantically, trying to smother flames consuming his clothes. The stench of burned flesh was nauseating. Pancho got down on his knees and I saw one arm reach toward his ankle. My next bullet hit three inches from his leg and I spat, "Don't try it."

"I'm a U.S. government officer," he called as he lay face down. "Treasury."

I went to him, toed up his pantleg, and saw an ankle holster with a gunmetal derringer. I jerked it out and stood back. "Treasury? Prove it."

"Undercover—no I.D."

"Tough shit. This is Mexico, you have no authority here."

"Let me try saving Diego—he could be a witness."

"Forget it," I said, "he's gone. And you, you cocksucker, to protect your cover you'd let them kill me." I knelt and shoved the pistol muzzle into thick black hair that covered the back of his head. Pancho squirmed. I said, "Your life's on a thin edge, T-Man. I don't owe you a fucking thing and I don't like loose ends. You're a loose end."

"If you let Diego die I'll have you charged with obstruction."

"Fuck you," I rasped. "You tell that story, I'll say you were found out and killed them both."

Diego's screams were lower and less frequent. His body jerked spasmodically. Charred hands clawed at his eyes. Probably the blast had blinded him. From where I knelt I sighted the derringer and blew off the top of Diego's head. His body arched, writhed, and lay still. Fire crept across it, consuming the last of his clothing, licking at his cartridge belt. Pancho yelled, "Damn you, Brent! You won't get away with this!"

"Hell I won't," I said, and tossed his derringer as far away as I could. "Now get up and drag that body over by the gas cans."

He got up slowly and said sullenly, "Man, you fucked up an entire long-term operation."

"What I did was save my life—something that didn't matter to you. Grab his shoes, get moving."

I covered the self-styled government officer while he dragged the smoking body close to the stack of fuel cans. Dropping Diego's feet, he turned and stared at me. I said, "You've got a choice: either you stop giving me trouble and help me get away from here or you'll be the third body. What'll it be?"

He licked his lips, glanced down at the corpse, and said, "I'll do it your way."

"And no bullshit about obstruction?"

He shook his head. "You've got the aces."

"Damn right," I said, "and no thanks to you. Now move away but stay where I can see you." As he started moving off I fired a round into the topmost jerrican. Gas spurted from it, trickled downward, drenching the other cans.

By now the entire cabin wall was aflame and burning noisily. Sparks from the roof whirled upward. Flaming thatch would crash down in another minute or so, igniting the gas stowed under the radio.

"Time to go," I said. "You'll drive, I'll sit behind you, covering you all the way."

Walking ahead of me he said, "Where to?"

"Well, if you were in my circumstances, where would you want to go, dummy?"

"Airport."

"Good thinking." We got into the jeep. Miraculously, my suitcase was there, down in the rear footwell. One Beam bottle was gone, the other half-emptied. Uncapping it, I swallowed a long sweet slug, capped it again and kept it upright between my thighs. Dino's pistol—a 9–mm Browning—pointed at Pancho's back. He saw it when he turned around, and said, "I could use a drink too."

"Buy your own whiskey," I told him. He started the engine, backed around, and was just straightening the front wheels when the cabin exploded with the force of an ammunition dump.

I ducked as pieces of burning logs rained around the jeep, stamped on sparks atop my suitcase. Pancho gunned the engine and the jeep bucked and bounced as he steered back along the way he'd brought me.

When we pulled into the parking area by the airport building, I opened my suitcase, stowed the Beam inside, and took out the lightweight coat I'd intended wearing on cool evenings in town. I shoved the Browning 9–mm in my right hand pocket, closed the suitcase, and told Pancho to give me whatever he carried by way of a wallet. "You rob as well as kill?" he sneered, but surrendered a worn, alligator-hide billfold. It contained about eight dollars in pesos, and the mandatory Mexican voting credential in the name of Francisco Gonzalez V. Nothing else.

"What's the V for?" I asked.

"Ventura—supposed to be my mother's name."

"I'll keep this for now."

"Why?"

"Puddinhead Jones," I said pityingly.

"Puddinhead—? Don't get it."

"Puddinhead Jones—dumber'n sticks'n stones," I supplied. "I'm holding the I.D., see, because if you make a ruckus before I board the plane you have nothing to identify you, give you standing with the authorities. See, Puddinhead? *Comprendes?*"

He seemed not to have understood. Stubbornly he said, "I need I.D."

"And you shall have it. Now, back to your Pancho role, T-Man. Grab my gear and take it inside."

"You're a real sonofabitch," he muttered, picking up my suitcase.

"Maybe, but not the kind who'd stand by while a fellow citizen was tortured and killed." I leaned close to him. "That's *your* kind of sonofabitch."

He went ahead of me to the Mexicana counter. Hardly anyone was in the building. A sleepy girl behind the counter roused herself while I scanned the departure board. Local time was 11:19 PM. The next flight left at midnight—destination San Diego, California.

Pancho stood beside me while she fixed my return ticket so I could take an onward Mexicana from San Diego to L.A. She took my suitcase, gave me claim check and boarding pass, and wished me a pleasant flight.

Near the departure gate was a small bar. I motioned Pancho toward it, ordered a Tequila Sunrise for myself, a bottle of Tecate for him. After a long pull on the bottle he said dispiritedly, "This is gonna wash me up at my field office."

"Not if you use the sense God gave you. Is it your fault your targets fooled around with a gas engine and got blown up? They're hoods, not mechanics—or were."

He drank moodily, glanced around at arriving passengers. Several were sport fishermen, expensive rods enclosed in fiberglass tubes. They wore long-bill marlin caps and flowered shirts. Two dreamy couples were obvious honeymooners, and the rest were Mexican laborers headed back for another dreary stretch in the broccoli and asparagus fields of Southern California. They wore stained straw sombreros, blue work shirts and pants, and carried small cloth bags or cardboard boxes. No TVs or stereos headed north; that traffic was all one-way.

Pancho was looking at me uneasily. "Speak up," I said, "what's on the peanut mind?"

"Ambrosino," he said, "in the cabin—how'd you kill him?"

I sipped my Sunrise and stared at Pancho over the rim. "Well," I said, "and we wouldn't want this to get back to ol' Raf—Dino experienced one of those lightning conversions. Filled with remorse, he came in, handed me his piece, and begged for the machete. I figured it was an advantageous trade, so he got the machete."

Pancho's eyes were as black and shiny as wet flint. "Then what?"

"Well, the hump squatted down Jap-style, said he couldn't stand thinking of his evil ways, and dug that big ol' machete right into his middle, twisted it around, *seppuku*-style, and never said another word."

"I heard him yell."

"Didn't say he didn't *whimper* some. What'd you expect from him, a lifetime confession?"

He looked away but not before muttering, "Bullshit."

"You weren't there, T-Man, what do you know? You were out back helping your *compadre*, Diego, and don't forget it." I eyed him steadily. "*I* won't."

The flight was called, I finished my Sunrise, and told Pancho to wait while I visited the *Caballeros*. "If you want that I.D. card."

I left him there and entered the men's room. There I dropped the Browning in a trash receptacle, rinsed dirt and dust from my face, and got in line for the security check. Beside me Pancho said, "When do I get it?"

"Stay alert," I said. "Keep your eyes on me." I moved forward and showed my boarding pass. The last thing Pancho said to me was, "When I get back to the States I'll be looking for you."

"Sure," I said. "Bearing in mind you're easy to spot and could be drilled as a drug-crazed wetback. *Adios.*" I passed through the electronic screener and walked out to the waiting plane, last in line.

As I neared the top of the mobile stairway leading into the cabin I held up his wallet, waved, and dropped it to the tarmac.

Inside I said to the steward, "Save me a couple of drinks, will you? On the way down I was shorted."

"Glad to," he said and gave me a white-toothed smile.

The cabin door closed, I found a seat, strapped in, and heard the engines start.

Not until the plane began its takeoff run did I relax. True to his word, the steward brought me two frosty cans of Modelo. I opened one, drank gratefully, and presently the cabin lights went out. I finished the first can and stuck its twin in the magazine holder for later referral. I yawned, my body went limp with fatigue, and before long I was asleep.

A bumpy landing woke me. I filled out the blue-print Customs declaration before the plane came to a stop, stood up with the other passengers, feeling worn and old and full of pain.

There was a flight in two hours for LAX but I was too tired to take it. Besides, what was waiting for me but the same small room and a hostile typewriter?

So I checked into the airport hotel that had a courtesy van standing by, pulled off my clothing, flopped on the bed, and slept nine hours without moving.

I woke to sunlight flooding the room—I'd neglected to draw the curtains—and ordered room service breakfast while I enjoyed a long soak in a hot tub. There was even time to shave before the breakfast cart arrived, room service being what it is most places.

After orange juice I ate Belgian waffles, scrambled eggs, sausage, and downed two cups of yesterday's room service coffee. I scanned the morning paper, saw nothing of interest, and put on fresh clothing.

I was in San Diego, I told myself, why not contact Hatfield? Since leaving Mexico I hadn't had much time to think about Melissa but I was thinking of her now. Besides, having left Hatfield a message yesterday I wanted to let him know what had happened down in Baja California.

His secretary put me through, and the first thing Hatfield said was, "Where are you?"

"In town. Is that important?"

"Damn right it is. She with you?"

"She who?"

"My client, of course."

"I'm confused," I said. "If anyone, you ought to know where she is." I gripped the receiver. "What's happening?"

"All I know," he said, "is the marshal's office phoned me about an hour ago. They're looking for her."

"Looking for her?" I repeated idiotically, still not getting it. "You mean—?"

"Hear me," the lawyer said angrily. "She sneaked out last night. She's gone, vanished, and I need to see you."

"Why?"

"Tell you when you get here." He stopped talking but the connection stayed alive. "Oh, I almost forgot to mention it—the U.S. Marshals are drooling to talk to you."

FOURTEEN

"So," said Joel Hatfield, gazing with satisfaction at his well-buffed nails, "I learn Melissa Tarkos has run, and naturally I put it together with that message you're in some cockamamie Mexican village. To me, that added to a joint maneuver: my client's taken off with you." He looked at me across his desk. "You not only say it didn't happen but you spin me a bizarre tale of capture and killing that your own producer wouldn't buy—and he deals in fiction."

"Comedy," I said, "only comedy." I leaned forward. "Feel the back of my head—gently." He stretched out one arm and did so. "What do you feel?" I asked.

"An egg and a scab. Proves nothing."

"Well," I remarked, "I've heard lawyers don't like lying clients, so I told the truth to *my* lawyer and he doesn't believe me."

"Neither will the marshals when you tell them."

"Hadn't planned to. They don't fit into my program."

"Arch Ballantine is madder'n hell, mad enough to subpoena you before a grand jury."

"Before which—on your advice, of course—I'll take the Fifth. Look, Joel, you'd hardly expect me to incriminate myself confessing to two killings, even though I regard one as an act of mercy, *coup de grace*."

He sighed heavily. "Guess not. Besides, it was south of the border, where anything can happen and frequently does." He gave a final glance at his nails and put away his hands. "What about the Treasury agent—Pancho?"

"*Alleged* Treasury agent. What about him?"

"Any trouble expected?"

"I left him depressed, concerned about his future, but the guy's built like a tree. If he ever grabbed me he could snap my back like a twig. Anyway, I contrived a tale for him to tell his supervisor—*if* he's really Treasury." I sat forward and braced my elbows on the desk. "The feds—of which you were once a part—have been trying to bury the Ambrosinos since time began. When word gets around Dino didn't make it back from Mexico the Nevada strike force should throw a celebration banquet."

A shrug was his only response.

"Anyway," I continued, "there's still old Raf soaking up Vegas sunshine. They can keep working on him—and Tarkos."

He looked over at a large, professionally maintained aquarium on the window ledge. Gaudily colored fish darted to and fro among strands of swaying kelp. The five-inch diver replica belched streams of bubbles. Hatfield seemed to be counting his rented fish.

"They'll multiply," I offered.

"What? What's that?"

"Your fish—nature's way. Also the way trouble multiplies. My recent life is a textbook example."

He exhaled a long-drawn sigh. "So Melissa's disappearance surprised you."

"Shocked me. Still does."

"She wasn't under guard, actually, I mean not like prison. She was the one who sought protection—you know that better than anyone."

I grunted. "At this point I don't know what I know. When did you last talk to her?"

"Yesterday afternoon."

"And—no problems?"

He thought for a moment. "Problems—no. However, Tarkos's lawyers got a *habeas* writ and served it on Ballantine. He allowed a lawyer to visit my client and check into her welfare—that was the writ's stated purpose."

I felt myself getting tense. "Did you fight the writ?"

He looked at me condescendingly. "You don't fight a writ—that's between the petitioner and the U.S. Attorney. The judge granted the writ and Ballantine had to obey."

"You weren't present at the interview?"

"My client didn't ask me to be. Anyway, I was in court most of yesterday."

I sat back and stared at the muted ceiling. "Who's the lawyer who saw her?"

He shuffled through desk papers, produced a folded legal document, opened it and said, "Stanley Parsons, Esquire. Williams, Ermentrude, Byerly and Parsons, P.A., Century City, Los Angeles." He refolded the writ and eased back in his swivel chair. "So?"

"I think you should have been present when Parsons came calling."

"Telling me how to practice law?"

"I'm suggesting that, had you been there, Parsons wouldn't have been able to accomplish the purpose of his visit—intimidating your client."

His eyes narrowed. "A lawyer is an officer of the court."

"Lawyers have been known to do reprehensible things—even go to prison." I shook my head. "Melissa disappears and you jump to the conclusion *I* lured her away from her safehouse, maybe even to Mexico. If Ballantine wants to go after anyone over her disappearance tell him to grab Parsons's balls. He's responsible for making her take off."

"How? Why?"

"Ask Parsons. The whole purpose of protective custody was to safeguard Melissa from Tarkos—yet a Tarkos man gets to her and a few hours later she's gone. Jesus, Joel, put it together!"

A flush spread across his face. "I don't like your tone or the implication of negligence."

"Don't like it? Well, I don't like what happened—and I'm a fellow who killed two men less than twenty-four hours ago, so go gentle with me, lawyer-man."

"Am I to interpret that as a threat?"

"Interpret it as you prefer. My intention was to respond to your expressed resentment."

He held up both hands, palms outward. "Okay, okay, we're both upset, let's cool down. She's still my client and I stand ready to respond to any communication from her."

"I'm also a client of yours," I reminded him. "I have a receipt that says so."

He nodded. "So you are, no argument. Of course, she's free to go wherever she chooses."

"I was assuming flight nullified the no-prosecution agreement."

"It may—technical thing. Depends on her degree of cooperation. I don't think Ballantine will try to indict her—he's got mud all over his face. Too embarrassing for him."

"Any idea how Tarkos-Parsons learned where Melissa was?"

"Court papers, I guess. They're supposed to be confidential, but any number of clerks have access to them."

"And any number of U.S. Marshals." I stood up. "So much for secrecy. I'll go home and soak my bruises. If Melissa contacts you and wants anything, I'll be available."

"Think she will?"

I glanced at his vault, the one holding Melissa's diamond reserve. "Probably," I said, waved goodbye, and left him behind his desk.

On Union Street I hailed a taxi and went to the airport hotel, packed my suitcase, and paid the overnight bill. The courtesy van deposited me at the terminal, and I used the rest of my ticket to ride the shuttle to LAX.

Before picking up my car I phoned Morry Manville, who said, "Where are you? Mexico?"

"That was a wrong deal, Morry. Evaristo makes porno films, both sexes. I was supposed to manufacture lewd giggles and declined. Just got back."

"Jesus, Joe, I'm sorry!"

"Not your fault," I said, "but you might footnote Producciones Zaragoza in the register. Also, the outfit is owned by a well-known O.C. family. So I had a trip to Baja, a few tequilas, and now I'm home and ready for work."

"I'll call."

"Sure," I said, and hung up.

The skin of my Datsun showed a layer of oily grime from jet exhausts and the inside was broiling hot. I opened windows to air it out before driving back to Cerrito Street.

I unlocked my apartment door, opened it, and dropped my suitcase. The rear window was open, curtains waving in the draft, and from the slashed furniture and overturned drawers I saw that the whole place had been savagely searched.

My head began throbbing. Fear chilled my flesh until it was cold as the belly of a snake.

FIFTEEN

When I brought up Mrs. Haven, my landlady took one look at the damage, shrieked, and began to sway. I helped her to a chair and brought her a glass of water. After gulping some, she wiped her forehead and moaned, "This is terrible. What am I going to do?"

"Notify the police and your insurance agent."

"Insurance?" She snorted bitterly. "Who can afford it?" Her gaze traveled over the destruction. "What were they looking for?"

"Money, I guess, and stereos. The TV's too big to get out the window."

"Your typewriter's still there. Why didn't they take it?"

"Too old to sell, not worth the trouble." Before bringing up Mrs. Haven I'd checked the portable's lid and found my thousand dollars undisturbed. I knew what the burglars had come for, but I wasn't confiding in my landlady.

The bedroom was a mess, too, mattress overturned and slashed, pillows slit open, bureau drawers dumped; bathroom cabinet emptied, toilet lid removed. . . . Closet clothing had been stripped from hangers, pockets turned inside out, my .38 Cobra lay exposed on the floor—it hadn't been taken because the number was traceable through my license.

Also before informing my landlady, I'd taken out the ice-cube tray and found Melissa's diamond still encased in ice. So my belongings hadn't really suffered, just her furnishings.

I said, "You heard nothing up here? They must have made some noise."

"Well, *I* didn't hear anything." Her eyes narrowed. "You were supposed to be gone two weeks—how come you're back the day after you left?"

"Bureaucratic foul-up," I said. "The guy in charge of production wasn't ready for me to start."

She sighed and heaved herself out of the damaged chair. "If only you'd been here . . ."

"Yeah, but I wasn't."

"Well, I'll phone the police, but I don't expect they'll ever catch the robbers—do you?"

"Probably not."

"I'll get Pedro to help you straighten up—I haven't the strength."

"Thanks," I said, and steadied her toward the doorway.

"So what are you going to do, Mr. Brent?"

"Tape the slashes, make my bed—life goes on."

"Well, I'm glad you don't expect me to replace everything—some roomers would."

"I try to be realistic," I told her. "Not your fault, not mine. After the cops leave I'll be ready for Pedro's help."

She went away and I heard her footsteps descending the stairs.

I tucked my thousand out of sight, and sipped a Poummit's while waiting for the cops. One was a short, pear-shaped female, the other a skinny rookie of twenty-two or so. They poked around, made notes, took my name and expressed sympathy. The lady cop said, "But nothing was actually stolen, Mr. Brent?"

"Nothing—there wasn't much to steal."

"Winos'll take anything they can get a dime for," she informed me, "and druggies."

The rookie came back from the window, saying, "You need a new latch but the wood's pretty dry and old—near rotten. Screws pulled out clean when they pried it up."

"So I noticed," I said. "Hardly worth the effort, eh?"

He shrugged. "Window bars would help."

"Hard to withstand a determined assault," I remarked, "Not to mention the expense of protective devices."

"That's the God's truth," the lady cop said, and tucked her notebook in a taut hip pocket. "What we got looks like vandalism pure and simple. Lucky you didn't get hurt, Mr.—"

"—Brent," I supplied. "You're so right. Well, thanks for your time. The owner will sign the complaint."

They went away, and after a while old Pedro came up and together we righted furniture, got the mattress back on the bed, and generally restored a semblance of order. I gave him five for his help, he thanked me in broken English, and left, closing the door behind him. Pedro was humble and grateful for any kindness, as illegals usually are. I wondered if Mrs. Haven ever paid him anything beyond his garret room and meals. Being Mexican—even in Los Angeles—wasn't easy.

I rehung jumbled clothing, unpacked my suitcase, and separated the items that needed washing and dry-cleaning. Too late in the day to visit the laundromat, so I sat in my typing chair and considered phoning Lieutenant Nero. There was a chance he'd see my name on the burglary-victim list, an equal chance he might not. Informing him would imply a connection between the search of my apartment and the murders of Fallon and Rinaldo. Also, I'd have to explain where I'd been while the vandalism was taking place.

So, I vetoed the idea, checked my Cobra to make sure it hadn't been sabotaged, then realized the searchers wouldn't have bothered. They knew I was away and didn't expect me to return.

Ever.

I'd kept Melissa in the back of my mind, but now that the cops and Mrs. Haven had gone I had to think about her disappearance. But what more was there to think about? I'd expressed my thoughts to Hatfield and I still felt he'd been damn remiss in not being there when Tarkos's lawyer spoke to Melissa.

She'd then left protective custody of her own volition, and was either on the run again, or home with her hated husband.

The latter—as I'd told Hatfield—seemed more likely, because she hadn't tried to contact me, directly or through her lawyer. And if the emotions we'd shared meant anything at all, she would have.

I assumd the feds had relieved her of Tarkos's diamonds, so if she had gone back home it was with empty hands.

How would Borden Tarkos feel about that? And of equal importance was the question of what kind of pressure he'd applied to make her leave the safehouse. What threats? Against whom?

In the jungle cabin I'd aired the proposition that Tarkos had been cheating on the Ambrosinos, and my hope remained that Dino had conveyed the thought to his father when he phoned.

If Melissa surfaced with her husband, old Raf might well feel he'd been defrauded by conspiracy, especially if Tarkos couldn't make restitution. *My money,* Dino had said. *Heavy loss . . . unpardonable.* I couldn't have said it better myself.

I wondered if Tarkos was under active investigation, or whether the heavy machinery of government hadn't yet started to roll. Before Melissa disappeared she must have given the feds enough for probable cause and that was more than they'd had before. Her testimony wasn't essential, in fact it could never be used; just the leads she was to supply during interrogation could tear Tarkos down forever.

My lower back and skull still pained me plenty. I swallowed four aspirin with water and looked around for a liquor chaser. But Nero and I had finished off the pint of Wild Turkey, and I hadn't gotten around to laying in more Jim Beam.

Before leaving the apartment I closed the window through which the burglars had entered, strapped on my shoulder holster, and then I walked down to the Boulevard pharmacy. There I bought two fifths of Beam and a large roll of silver-colored duct tape. Walking back, I realized that the aspirin was dulling pain, so for a while it would be part of my daily diet.

Back home, I iced a glass and partly filled it with Beam, drinking as I applied duct tape to the slashed furniture. That done, I taped mattress and pillows and remade the bed.

While I was doing this my mind churned with memories of Melissa. I felt abandoned, and the apartment seemed dismally empty.

Still, I told myself, last night she might have tried to reach me—while I was in Baja. Or this morning. I looked at the silent telephone. Perhaps she'd call tonight.

Of one thing I was confident—she hadn't returned to Tarkos because she wanted to, but because she was forced to in some way. But then I wasn't sure she'd gone back to her husband—not if all she'd told me was true—and I didn't want to believe she had. So she was somewhere out there, on the run again, hiding. Full circle, back to the time we'd met.

Whom would she encounter this time, beseech to take her in? No, she wouldn't do that; she trusted me, would come back to me if she were able.

Unless . . . and the thought expanded like a poisonous cloud . . . she believed me away from Los Angeles.

Or dead.

Parsons, Tarkos's lawyer, could have told her that, persuaded her she had no one to turn to but Tarkos.

If he'd done that, then Tarkos knew I'd been lured to Mexico, and he was part of the deadly trap.

Tilting my glass, I drank deeply, emptying it.

When Dino didn't call in and couldn't be raised by radio, people would visit the cabin site and find the remains of two bodies. Were there three, the supposition would be that I'd died, too. So if I'd shot Pancho and left his body to be destroyed with the others, I'd be safe for a while.

But that was an evil thought and I suppressed it. I wasn't so far gone that I was down to killing the innocent.

How did I feel about killing the two villains? Justified. And I felt no guilt, no remorse. After what I'd seen in the bloody shambles of the Beirut barracks, I'd become inured to horror. Navy shrinks had accomplished that and I had more than a little reason to be grateful.

I looked at the telephone again, and thought of changing my number, making it unlisted. Then Tarkos/Ambrosino could tell with a single call that I was alive. Or I could move out and find a remote place to wait out the strike. But if I did either, Melissa could never find me, and I wanted her to. Badly.

Besides, I couldn't hide forever. A time could come when they'd find me, so I might as well stay where I was, remain alert to the first small sign of danger, and live my life as best I could.

The telephone rang. I let it ring four times before deciding to answer. When I did, I heard a female voice saying, "Mr. Brent? Maddy Gossons here, Semmes and Company."

"Oh, yes," I replied. "Got good news?"

"Maybe—depends. I tried to reach you this morning. A customer's interested in your boat."

"How interested?"

"Firm offer of eighteen thousand."

"Not enough," I replied. "I'll hold out a while."

"Up to you," she said somewhat huffily, "but an offer's an offer and you can't expect a lot of them. The marine surveyor's report isn't all that good."

"Oh? What's the problem?"

"Deck and woodwork's weatherbeaten, two sails ragged and black mold. Engine needs work. Auxiliary prop nicked and slightly bent. Estimate four thousand to make everything shipshape."

"I see," I said, as a thought flashed through my mind. "Any objection to my living aboard while I do some of the work?"

"Not at all—in fact, it's a good idea. Then the next customer who sees *El Dorado* will feel you're keeping it up."

"That's what I'll do," I told her. "Would it be asking too much to arrange dock space for me? I'll need utility hookup."

"No problem. When'll you be down?"

"Maybe tonight."

"Fine—you'll save a lot of labor cost, you know."

"I know. Boatyard gets about forty an hour for simple manual labor."

"At least," she said, and hung up.

Well, I'd made a decision. Tarkos/Ambrosino couldn't trace me as a boat owner, and I'd give the dockmaster's phone number only to Morry and Joel Hatfield. Then if Melissa called her lawyer he'd know how she could reach me.

Assuming she wanted to.

But I still had faith in her, still believed she shared our fantasy of an island where coconuts and sunburn would be our only dangers.

So I'd stay put a few more hours in case she phoned, then head for the marina.

After putting the thousand dollars in my wallet I closed up my portable and slipped my novel's draft pages into an envelope. I bagged my dirty clothing—there was a laundromat and dry cleaner near the dockmaster's office—and folded clean clothing in my suitcase.

I mixed another drink for myself and turned on the television set to kill time. No NBA game, but a hockey game was beginning—Islanders and Hawks. I enjoyed hockey while the puck was moving, but not when a game deteriorated into pitched brawls on the ice, organ thundering in the background. I liked contact sports but not when opponents started maiming each other.

I sat through one brawl in the first period, and when the second began, I switched channels and, lo and behold, found a rerun of *Frankie's Follies* in prime time. That meant residuals for me—eventually—and as I watched the segment I'd written last year and barely remembered, I was painfully distressed by its inanities. Canned laughter bridged the shots when Frankie turned to the camera and mugged helplessly, mouth agape. That was Frankie's shtick, a prime ingredient of every segment I'd ever written.

The humor, I had to admit, was slapstick and juvenile, and I felt a flush of embarrassment as one contrived situation after another played across the screen. The network had to be hard up, I told myself, to rerun *Frankie's Follies,* but then there was a saying in the industry that there was an audience for anything. That explained why the formula Sol and I had developed kept the show running so long and made me reasonably affluent.

Unable to watch longer, I turned to the Fox channel and found a watchable chase story in progress. Hoods were hunting down the female lead, who reminded me of Melissa, as did her plight.

When the inevitable auto chase began I darkened the set and sat finishing my drink and speculating on Melissa's future.

Suppose she *had* gone back to Tarkos—would he trust her enough to let her live? After what happened to me in Baja, I doubted it. And there was the problem of the diamonds. She couldn't regain them from the feds, I was sure of that, and as I saw it, Tarkos needed the diamonds far more than he needed his wife.

Possibly lawyer Parsons would have Melissa recant her story, swear the diamonds were hers alone, and demand them back. If the feds refused, Parsons could sue in her name . . . a smart lawyer could do a lot of things, and Tarkos hadn't hired Parsons because he was dumb.

But the diamonds weren't my problem. I had one of them, and it was going to remain in the ice tray for the present. Searchers had raked the apartment without finding it; they wouldn't look again.

By eleven o'clock Melissa hadn't phoned, nobody had, so I gathered food from the refrigerator and, in two trips to the Datsun, carried down my typewriter and draft pages, laundry, food, and Beam.

Before turning out lights I lingered a few more minutes, hoping Melissa would call, then gave up and locked the apartment.

At the front door I scanned the lighted street for surveillors, saw none, and went down to my car.

Southbound traffic was light and I reached Marina del Rey in forty-odd minutes, found a parking place, and checked in at the dockmaster's office.

"Your boat was moved to Pier Three," the lady in charge told me, "with utility hookup. Want a phone aboard?"

"No, but I'd be grateful if you'd take messages for me."

"That's what we're here for." She passed me a form to sign, I paid an advance and we said goodnight.

After stowing my gear aboard I rinsed out the small refrigerator and turned it on. The galley range and oven operated on butane and there was plenty left in the tank.

Bunk bedding smelled damp and moldy, so I changed sheets, mixed a drink, and set up my typewriter on the table. But I wasn't up to writing, I felt bone-tired. Just twenty-four hours ago I was at the Cabos airport, having avoided almost certain death, the Indian watching me with surly mien.

Well, he'd been lucky, too. I hadn't shot him, and I'd given him back his false I.D. He ought to be grateful, I reflected, but I didn't expect gratitude from Pancho. And I didn't want to see him again.

It was one o'clock when I stretched out on the bunk. The boat moved gently, soothingly, and when I fell asleep I dreamed I was tied in a burning house and a girl I didn't know came in and tried to drag me out. I could feel the flames' heat, her arms under my shoulders . . . then the roof crashed down and I saw her vanish in a sheet of fire.

I woke, drenched in perspiration, stared around until I could orient myself. Gradually the trembling stopped. I swallowed four aspirin with a long shot of Beam and got back on the bunk.

It had all been so real, so terrifyingly authentic, that I half-thought Melissa had been there at the cabin. Then the nightmare faded, the boat's gentle motion lulled me, and in a little while I was asleep.

SIXTEEN

I felt better in the morning, made breakfast in the galley, cleaned up, and went over to the boatyard where I rented a disc sander, bought sanding pads, brushes, a gallon can of polyurethane varnish, and a pint of thinner.

The morning was bright, water calm, boats came and went, gulls cawed and skirmished, and I got into dungarees and skivvy shirt to begin work. Railing and deck first, then the cabin. Brightwork could wait, and I'd check the engine last. I didn't know much about marine engines but I could replace plugs, distributor, and condenser. With scuba mask and snorkel I could check bottom and keel, even remove the damaged propeller.

Assuming the weather held, I estimated four to five days' work ahead of me. If rain interrupted sanding and varnishing, the work would take that much longer.

I hung the holstered .38 just inside the cabin doorway for easy reach, put on old work gloves, and connected the sander to a dock extension cord. For half an hour I sanded blisters and worn spots on the port rail, then the breeze shifted and dust began blowing against my face and mouth. I stopped to wipe my face, glanced over, and saw a man standing on the pier staring at me. When he saw I was looking at him, he shuffled his feet and said, "How's it going?"

"So-so," I said. "Time for goggles and dust mask."

"Don't bother. You done all you're gonna do."

"That so? Who says so?"

"The union. We got a contract here, see? You wanna work on your boat, tie up at a buoy."

I smiled at him. "Doesn't apply to me."

"Yeah? Why not?"

"'Cause I'm a union man myself."

His feet moved nervously and his mouth sagged. "Whyn't you say so?"

"You didn't ask."

"Okay then, sorry, brother."

"No problem." I watched him walk down the pier and was glad he hadn't asked which union I belonged to. The Writers Guild didn't carry much clout along the waterfront.

I went back to the boatyard for yellow safety goggles and a dust filter to cover mouth and nose, banged a can of Sprite from the vending machine, and got back to work.

Now that I was into it I took satisfaction from what I was doing. I used diminishing grades of sandpaper, coarse to very fine, to achieve the smooth finish I wanted, and by noon I'd completed the port railing. I knew it was noon because the boatyard whistle blew, and I could see riggers and carpenters digging into lunch pails, eating in the shade of boat hulls.

In my galley I washed up and heated a can of vegetable soup while I made a liverwurst sandwich. The under-the-counter fridge worked marvelously well and provided me with a chilled bottle of Poummit's Brew.

Eating at the table I listened to midday radio news and heard nothing of interest other than a Mideast report saying Syrian President Hafez Assad hadn't been seen in several days, and there was speculation that he had stomach cancer.

I hoped it was cancer because I wanted him to die as horribly as had my barracks buddies in Beirut. But the old man was so permeated with evil, I doubted cancer bugs would dare attack him.

After lunch I cleaned up, stretched out on the bunk for a brief nap, and remembered I hadn't called Hatfield or my agent. The dockmaster's number was on last night's receipt, so I went to a pay phone and relayed it to Morry Manville. "Just in case you need me."

"Let's hope I do, Joe."

I used a handful of quarters to phone Hatfield, who said, without being asked, "She's still missing."

"I figured that. Anyway, I'm staying on my boat for a while, but the dock office will give me messages." After I repeated the number to him Hatfield said, "It's a big mess, isn't it?"

"Hardly be worse," I agreed. "Let's hope she's still alive."

"I'm with you there."

Using damp cloths I wiped dust from the railing, decided to let it sun-dry, then laid on a coat of primer to seal the open grain. The finish would be smoother and last longer and I was willing to do the extra work because there was always a possibility I wouldn't have to sell my boat. There'd be less upkeep later, whether for the buyer or me.

While I was waiting for the rail to dry I checked the deck mahogany and decided to sand from bow to stern, half one day, half the next. I saw a shadow on the cabin, glanced around, and saw a scantily dressed female looking down at me.

She was wearing a tie-dyed bandeau around medium-size breasts, and white shorts so tight I could see the roll of her panties. Black hair rolled back with a gauzy kerchief, and drops of perspiration rolled down her middle. "Hi, neighbor," she said cheerfully.

I shaded my eyes and saw a tan, sun-lined face, with a skinny-bridged nose (nose job?), full lips, capped teeth, and a weak chin. I said, "You from the union?"

"What union?" She giggled and swayed coltishly. "Why'd you say that?"

"My last visitor was a union checker."

"Oh. You're working, aren't you? How long you gonna work?"

"Till sundown." I wiped water from my forehead.

"Well, I'm Glenda Gray, who're you?"

"Joe. Joe Phillips," I decided to say.

"We saw your boat being docked last evening, so, being neighbors, I thought I'd say hello. After work how about coming up to the *Carefree?* That's three boats ahead. We could have a few cool ones and talk."

"The wife'll like that," I said. "What time?"

"Wife?" Her eyes narrowed and her mouth drew into a pout. "Maybe it's not such a good idea."

"Maybe not," I agreed, "but thanks for the thought."

She walked away on cork wedgies, rolling her hips to show me what I was missing. Ah, well, I thought, it's nice they still try. I tested the railing for dryness and began laying on the primer coat.

I worked until the breeze shifted, became cooler, and I realized it was time to close down for the day.

As I stepped down the companionway I admired the smoothly varnished rail, thought of all the effort I'd put into it, and decided union sanders and painters were probably worth their twenty or thirty bucks an hour. I'd want that for working on someone else's boat.

In the cramped head I took a cool shower, got into shorts, and heated a TV dinner for myself. I ate at the forward end of the table so I could see stars through the cabin's open doorway. Only last night, I recalled, I'd looked for constellations in the sky while waiting for the killers' return. Now they were history but the stars still hung there, and I was alive to watch them.

After dinner I went into the dockmaster's office and checked my box for messages: nothing. The lady in charge invited me to watch the basketball game, so I brought a couple of bottles from the boat, and sat behind the counter with her while we made small talk between baskets, and watched the Lakers destroy the Celtics in an interleague game.

After the game I went back to *El Dorado*, tired from work and sun, drank Beam from the bottle and lay down on my bunk. Melissa came into my mind but I tried blotting her out with memories of my childhood in Cobleskill, and my mother and father. Good memories, for the most part. But my most vivid and painful memory was of my little brother, Billy, who'd been playing in the street and was killed by a hit-and-run driver. Something went out of my parents then, and I understood now they'd lost the desire to live. The house was gloomy, never any laughter, so I felt isolated by their grief, and angry because they didn't understand I'd lost Billy too.

His killer was never found, and for years I prayed I'd meet him face to face one day, then kill him as callously as he'd destroyed little Billy's life.

I still hoped that day would come.

Gradually body and mind relaxed, I pulled up the sheet, turned over, and slept.

My life followed that first day's pattern until an afternoon rain squall on the third day ended topside work. So I sat in the cabin, listened to a call-in radio talk show, and drank myself senseless. Next day, fighting a major hangover, I resumed topside work, and

Glenda Gray, whom I hadn't seen lately, stopped by long enough to say she hadn't noticed my wife around.

"She's sort of a recluse," I said. "Sleeps daytimes and gets up at night for the meeting."

Her plucked eyebrows lifted. "AA?"

I nodded.

"Sorry," she said, "didn't mean to pry. But my first husband was a bottle fighter so, believe me, I know what you're going through."

"It's tough all around," I said wistfully. "So you're on your second husband now."

She giggled nervously. "I wouldn't exactly call him my *husband*—if you know what I mean."

"Gotcha."

"But he's an okay guy, doesn't booze more'n I do, and he's got this nice boat where me an' Twinkie live."

"Twinkie?"

"My girlfriend. We do cabaret together. Right now we're laying off, enjoying the good life. Only trouble is, lacka men."

"Your, ah, husband is a man," I observed.

"Sure is, but he's got a family, y'know. Wife and kids in Downey. Hard for him to get away." She smiled roguishly. "That's what I mean."

The conversation was going nowhere and I was tired of her confidences. So I gave her a vague smile, said, "See ya," and ducked below.

I made sure she was gone before I surfaced again, and didn't see her for several days, and then only in the office, getting mail.

Over the weekend I put on scuba mask and snorkel and went down to take a look at the fiberglass bottom. There was marine growth, of course—there's always marine growth on your keel and bottom—but aside from that the hull looked sound. The auxiliary engine's propeller, though, was another matter. As stated, it was nicked and slightly bent, and I had to wrestle out the cotter pin that retained the lock-nut before I could bring it up.

On Monday the boatyard charged me forty for straightening and welding the prop, the mechanic telling me they'd have charged ninety if they'd had to take it off and bring it in. So as I lugged the heavy prop back to my boat, I told myself I was fifty ahead of the game. Not fifty to spend on a fab dinner at Stone's, just fifty unspent; it gave me a feeling of thrift and accomplishment.

Ms. Gossons was standing on the pier, viewing *El Dorado* with a pleased expression. When I arrived beside her she said, "Looks great."

"Less filling."

She gave me a baffled look, then her expression changed. "I get it, those jocks in the TV ad for some kind of beer."

"Right."

"For a moment I forgot you're a TV writer."

"It's forgettable." I stepped aboard and carried the prop to the stern where I laid it gently down. Turning to the broker I said, "So what's new?"

"We advertised your boat over the weekend; two people are coming separately to look it over."

"When?"

"Mid-to-late afternoon. Can do?"

"No problem. I'll have the prop on in an hour. After that I check the engine."

She frowned slightly. "I thought you'd have checked it by now."

"And have an unbalanced prop ruin the innards? Uh-uh. First things first."

"Of course—should have thought of that. Well, ta-ta, see you later."

I bowed deeply and she went away. Must be an old-fashioned girl, I told myself; they stopped saying ta-ta around the time I was born. I couldn't remember hearing it on TV except for late-night reruns of the old *Maisie* series. Maisie, the flirtatious, imperfect secretary whose style had vanished by the time the Libbers came in. Well, some of my Frankie dialogue would sound pretty antique ten years from now.

I got into the water and, by holding on to the diving platform with my left hand, managed to center the heavy prop on its driveshaft. The lock-nut came next, then the fail-safe cotter pin that was supposed to sheer on impact. After doing all that I was winded and my head and spine ached in memory of blows taken from now-dead Diego.

In the head shower I soaped off oily water and shampooed it from my hair, washing the face mask while I was at it.

After dressing, I activated the bilge exhaust, sniffed for gas fumes, and turned on the engine. It caught with a powerful burble, and I let it run a while to pick up any roughness. Satisfied no prospective buyer could complain about it, I cut the engine and pocketed the ignition key.

I was curious about the advertisement for my boat, so I went to the newspaper vending boxes outside the office and found a few copies of Sunday's *Times* remaining. Two quarters opened the lid, and I carried the bulky paper back to my cabin, where I turned to Classifieds. If I had to talk with the buyer I wanted to make sure La Gossons hadn't exaggerated my boat's merits, as salespeople tend to do when they want to unload merchandise.

Under the Marine heading I found it listed: 26′ Rollins-built . . . good condition . . . CG certified, blah, blah, blah, asking $25K.

To me, "asking" meant the owner was willing to go down plenty, and since Maddy had employed that ambiguous word she should have set the asking price at thirty. *Then* I could come down to twenty-five and the buyer would feel he'd gotten a bargain.

As it was, he'd get a newly refurbished boat, everything prime condition but the sails. I could drag them out of their bags, unroll them on the pier, and scrub them down, but what the hell, let the next owner have the pleasure, I told myself. If he was a novice sailor/yachtsman he'd soon learn what it takes to keep your boat trim and in the water: thick billfold and a sturdy spine.

Mine ached from underwater effort. I popped two aspirin and swallowed them with Beam. Very little left in that second duty-free bottle, I noticed, for I'd been guzzling fairly steadily. Galley supplies were also low; I'd pick up milk, bread, cereal, and meat when I walked to Washington Boulevard for liquor.

But I didn't want to walk those few blocks until my pain diminished. Meanwhile, I read the first and second sections. Normally I had no interest in what passed for the Society section, but a six-by-eight photo on the first page caught my eye.

It showed two people leaving a launch to climb a yacht's slanting ladder. The man wore yachting cap, blazer, and white trousers. The woman ahead of him had on striped shorts and a loose-knit short-sleeve top. The photographer had caught her unsmiling profile, and my heart pounded as I recognized Melissa.

> TAORMINA, Sicily. Back together after a rumored separation, financier Borden Tarkos and his wife, Melissa, are enjoying an extended Mediterranean cruise aboard the Tarkos yacht, *Flaminia*. Owner of Hollywood's Falcon Productions studios, a Las Vegas hotel, and a professional basketball team, Mr. Tarkos is scouting Mediterranean locations for his studio's next production, whose title will be announced at a later date.

I stared at the photograph as my stomach contracted. Tarkos looked much as I'd imagined him: stocky, swarthy, a scowl on his face.

Melissa was as I remembered her: long-limbed, poised, and breathtakingly beautiful.

And Tarkos's possession again.

The fantasy world we'd created shattered, fell apart in worthless shards. She'd abandoned me to resume a life she abhorred. Or did she? For a moment I felt like killing her, killing them both. When sanity returned I was laughing at myself with pent-up bitterness. Before the seizure ended I heard her voice whispering, *I love you . . . I want my future with you, only you.*

Lies, or she wouldn't have done it.

The words were wrenched out of me as I spoke to the empty cabin: *Why did she do it? Why?*

SEVENTEEN

Joel Hatfield asked the same question when I was steady enough to phone him.

"Isn't it obvious? Tarkos made her an offer she couldn't refuse."

He was silent for a while, and when he spoke again he said, "Through his lawyer—Parsons."

"Exactly."

"And you blame me."

"You should have been there shielding her."

"In retrospect I should have, but she didn't notify me."

"Did she try calling you any time before she fled?"

"There were no messages, and I checked the machine particularly, in case she'd phoned after office hours."

"What are you going to do?"

"What's to do? Everyone interested in my client has seen the photo—she's out of reach, even if there were legal cause to bring her back. I explained to you she was free to leave. That she went abroad with her husband was an option she exercised. It's not up to me to question her motives. Nor—if I may say so—is it your problem any longer."

"Just the residue."

"Eh?"

"Raf Ambrosino, Joel. He knows damn well I was down there with his son. When he realizes I'm alive he'll want questions answered."

"I'm afraid you're right." A long sigh. "Ah—what's to be done with that envelope you left for my client?"

"Keep it in the vault pending further instructions."
"So what are you going to do?"
"Join the unemployment line."
"Really?"
"Really." I had nothing to add and neither did Joel Hatfield, so I hung up and walked to my car.

At the Unemployment Office near City Hall, there must have been five hundred people ahead of me. Most were seated at school-type desks filling out forms, and I was reminded of my second day in the Corps, when recruits took I.Q. and placement tests.

Following instructions lettered on a large sign, I took a number and waited on a wall bench until my number was called.

I stepped up to the glass-faced counter, behind which a patient but tired-looking black man said, "You keep the same number. When you filled out these forms, take them over there"—he pointed at a desk—"an' you'll be called."

When a desk was vacant, I sat down and read over the application questions; they wanted a lot more information than name, rank, and serial number.

I wrote in the answers: date and place of birth; SS number; married/single/divorced (and oh, how I wanted the last category); last place of employment; salary; present address, and so on. I gave Natty's Burbank apartment and phone as mine, signed the application under pain of prosecution for false statements, and placed my application on the desk, as directed.

Without looking up the woman said, "Be sure to know your number when called."

"I'll try. And how long might that be?"

"Hour, mebbe more."

I'd been looking at her thick glasses, so it was a few moments before I realized she was seated in a wheelchair. She had no legs. I said, "That'll be fine," and went back to the bench where I'd waited before.

After a while an obese white woman beside me said, "Sure give you the fits here, don't they?"

"They try."

"An' take their time." She shook her head resentfully.

"There's a lot of us to handle," I suggested.

"They oughta hire more help."

"You've got something there," I said, and went outside to buy a chili dog from a sidewalk vendor.

From where I munched I could look up at the pyramidal top of the Hall of Justice. Sirhan Sirhan had been held in its cells and so had Charles Manson and members of his bizarre family.

After a vigilante leveled a helicopter by Sirhan's cell and tried to shoot him with a rifle, the city positioned plate-iron shields to foil further attempts, but they were gone now. Sirhan was in some maximum security prison, annually applying for parole, his crime still unexplained. Manson was in some work farm playing guitar and writing insane cabalistic messages to the world and his particular devils.

The people on the street were young-looking, and I reflected that many had grown up unaware of Manson's night of bloody horror. How lucky they were. I had my own night of death and fire to haunt me.

I drank an orange soda and went back to the waiting bench. Twenty minutes later my number was called and I went over to a booth where a thin-faced, middle-aged woman looked up from my papers and indicated I should sit in the folding chair. "First time here?" she asked.

"First-time loser," I admitted.

"We try to place you, you know, but there's no call just now for TV writers. Seems like a lot of you around."

"It's the strike," I said.

"Know Tom Klepnik? He's in your line. Writes one of the detective programs."

"I don't know him."

"Thought you might. Well, here's what happens—your application will be verified and in two to three weeks you'll be notified to come in for your first check."

"Can't be mailed to me?"

"No." Her eyes narrowed. "You have to say where you looked for employment in that period."

"There isn't any employment," I told her. "Everything's closed down because of the writers' strike."

"You still have to tell us," she said firmly. "And if we have a job opening you gotta take it."

"Happy to," I told her, got up, and left the building.

Back aboard my boat I saw no evidence that potential buyers had come by, then remembered they wouldn't be around until later in the afternoon, led and encouraged by Maddy Gossons. I'd been tense, strained, uptight ever since seeing Melissa's photograph. The Unemployment Office had rerouted my mind, and I decided to declare siesta time to let the healing process set in.

I was going down the companionway when I saw Glenda Gray and a more attractive female strolling nearby, arm in arm. Glenda waved at me, called, "Hi, Joe," and I waved back. As they neared, Glenda said, "This is my friend, Twinkie. Twinkie, Joe."

"Hello," I said. *"Really* Twinkie?" Her lush body was nicely and evenly tanned and I could see a lot of it. She was closer to my age than Glenda's, her face yet unlined, and the sun-top she was wearing showed firm, substantial breasts. At my question they stopped and Twinkie said, "Not really—Twinkie's my stage name. I'm really Sondra . . . Sondra Starr." That sounded equally stagy, if less demure, and in the back of my mind a cog slowly began to turn.

To Glenda I said, "That drink invitation still open?"

"Sure—but what about your wife?"

"She'll be at the meeting," I said. "It's hard on a co-dependent, having to go without sauce while the addict recovers."

"Don't I know! So, sure—what time?"

"Six, seven." I cleared my throat. "After dark."

Sondra gave me a long, smouldering appraisal. "Sounds like fun," she said. Glenda waved, *"Hasta,"* and they sauntered on.

I stared after them, wondering if this Sondra could possibly be the one Melissa had told me about—the Falcon contract player Tarkos had brought to their bedroom games . . . Well, I'd known stranger coincidences, but few more welcome.

In the cabin I was taking off jacket and tie when a voice called, "Ahoy, there. Anyone aboard?"

"Ahoy yourself." I went to the companionway, looked up and saw my Mexican driver, Pancho.

A Panama hat covered much of his abundant black hair, though bushy fringes concealed his ears. There was a heavy gold chain and pendant around his thick neck, and his muscular torso showed through a long-sleeved lavender shirt. Stone-washed jeans were supported by a braided leather belt, whose large oval clasp was turquoise-studded silver. His feet were at eye level and they wore white Reeboks with black laces.

"Puddinhead! A sight to behold." I raised both hands behind the door jamb, as though to brace myself against the boat's slight roll. My right hand touched the Cobra's grip.

"Like it?" he asked. "Mind if I come aboard?" One hand was in his trouser pocket. It moved, and I saw the outline of a gun.

"I welcome all who come in peace." He started down the companionway, and as he passed into the cabin I shoved the Cobra muzzle against his ribs. "Persuade me thee cometh in peace."

His face turned to me, he frowned, and said, "Got the drop on me again, dammit."

"That I have. And I'll thank you to place that peacemaker on the table."

Daintily, with thumb and forefinger, he extracted a derringer and set it on the table. "What now?"

"We'll sit and chat and you'll specify the occasion for this visit—and how you found me."

We sat on opposite sides of the table, and Pancho said, "Last thing first, okay? I punched an IRS computer to get a copy of your last 1040. You weren't in Burbank so I thought I'd check the boat you've been deducting the past two years—along with dockage fees and so on. Bingo, here you are."

"Bingo," I echoed and shook my head. "No one says bingo any more."

"Where I come from, they do—big thing, bingo."

"Where's that?"

"Maricopa—Arizona. Population five hundred, thereabouts."

"That explains it. Am I to understand this is an official visit?"

"Could be."

"Let's see your wallet."

He dug into a hip pocket and pulled out a black calfskin billfold. Inside was a Treasury credential with his photo. The printed name was Antonio Frederick Honey.

"Honey, for God's sake. You don't look like any Honey I ever saw, few though they were. *Honey?* Is that really your name?"

"My family name was Miel until the last generation. Pop Anglicized it and it came out Honey, okay?"

"Why not go all the way—make it Anthony?"

"With *this* face?" He touched the smooth, dark skin of his Aztec features. "What do I do with this?"

"Take it to Central Casting," I told him. "Every now and then there's a call for Montezuma."

"Exactly," he sighed.

I returned his billfold. "Briefly, why are you here, Tony?"

"I thought we might work out a deal."

"On Diego?"

"Naw, he's gone—but in another month I'd have turned him."

"Another month and I'd have been dust on the forest floor."

He shrugged. "You had the right of it, Mr. Brent. We said strong words, but as far as I'm concerned that's history, too. Can we maybe start over?"

"I'm agreeable." I got up and opened his derringer, ejected the two .38 cartridges, and placed weapon and loads in a palm so large as to make the weapon look miniature.

Pocketing it, he said, "You gaffed that generator engine, sabotaged it."

"Did I?"

"Someone did. I smelled fumes and stood back. Diego didn't notice. Goodbye, Diego."

"Field office buy your story?"

"Had to. But my supervisor said it was the first time they'd ever lost two targets to anything but a car accident. He gave me two weeks off—shock recovery—and I figured it might be useful to talk with you."

"Doubtful. But being as you're on leave, let's drink to it." I poured bourbon in two glasses, added ice cubes, and we hoisted together. After swallowing, I said, "Where'd you play football?"

"Tempe—how'd you know?"

"No coach could pass up a build like yours. Scholarship?"

"How else is a poor Mex boy gonna get learnin'?"

"Merit," I said, "but that's another subject. What subject you want to pursue?"

"Ambrosino the elder, Tarkos, and the missing wife."

"She's not missing," I said, "she surfaced in the Straits of Messina."

"In the shadow of ol' Mount Etna." He raised his glass. "I saw that photo—looked like Tarkos was still chasing her. You have any idea why she went back to Tarkos?"

"Death wish, maybe." I leaned forward. "What's the deal?"

"You help me, I keep Raf Ambrosino off your back."

"You can do that?"

"I can try."

"Trying doesn't do it," I said, and added more Beam to our glasses. "What's Tarkos doing in Sicily?"

"No hard intelligence, but there's speculation he's paying his respects to the other half of the Ambrosino family. That'd be Ottavio, Raf's brother." He sipped thoughtfully. "They come from around Catania. Ottavio handles the drug side of the family business."

"Tarkos might be having to do something more than break bread with Ottavio," I mused.

"Like what?"

"Work off his debt—use that big boat to move some paste around."

"Yeah—reasonable. Mrs. Tarkos ever say anything about that?"

"Not to me. Anyway, I have a proposition that'll solve our problems: we kill Tarkos, then Ambrosino."

"Since we're only kiddin' around, Ambrosino first, *then* Tarkos."

"We'll flip for precedence." I swirled the cube around my glass. "How come you're so interested in Mrs. Tarkos?"

"Hell, the field office gets drop copies of every immunity agreement the U.S. Attorney signs. You know why she ran?"

"Do you?"

"I figured one of those dumb marshals tried to diddle her."

"I figure Tarkos's attorney passed her a message. Now they're abroad, out of U.S. jurisdiction."

"We have people abroad," he said. "Don't think we don't."

"Focused on Bern and Zürich."

"There's some free-floaters who can be targeted."

"On Tarkos's yacht? That reminds me of the title of the world's thinnest book: *Treasury Agents I've Met While Yachting.*"

"How about CIA?"

"That could be a little thicker." We drank, and I decided that holding a grudge against this offbeat Aztec would be pointless.

He pushed back his straw hat, wiped perspiration from his forehead, and said, "How about cooperating?"

"I'm good at cooperating, so long as there's a payoff."

"That's understood. The FBI wants Ambrosino. We want him *and* Tarkos."

"Good hunting."

"Know anything about Raf Ambrosino?"

"I saw his picture when they tried to get him to talk to some congressional committee—that was a few years ago."

Tony nodded. "Not long afterward a car pulled alongside his limo. Shotguns and machine guns opened fire. Raf's bodyguard was killed, driver wounded, but Raf survived a chestful of shotgun pellets and .38 slugs. The old goombah's not as robust as he used to be. Nurses his infirmities and stays out of sight."

"I'd do the same. Ever hear of Angelo DiLirio and Harold Tisch?"

He nodded. "The L.A. cops have them on suspicion of murdering Fallon and Rinaldo."

"They didn't do it."

"Who cares? Tisch is a long-time loser. They sweated him and he began talking about his employer, Borden Tarkos. That brought in my office and Tisch is now a confidential informant."

"In exchange for what?"

"The possibility of helpful words to the sentencing judge."

"How much does Tisch know?"

"He's letting it out slowly—like toothpaste from a cold tube."

"Angelo?"

"A harder case—but with Tisch, who needs Angelo?"

"So, he'll take the fall."

Tony nodded solemnly.

"What do you want from me?"

"Tisch says Tarkos keeps his financial records at home—in a safe. With Tarkos away, getting them shouldn't be an insuperable problem."

"You'd need a team of SEALS, plus a good safecracker."

A smile spread slowly across his face. "I've seen you in action, Joe. You're tough, smart, and resourceful. You could do the job alone."

EIGHTEEN

I looked at him for a long time before saying, "Listen close, Injun. I like a compliment as well as the next fellow but I'm not your guy." I spelled it out in the air: "N . . . O . . . *no.*"

"Maybe with a little help—unofficial."

"Not if the governor went with me. Forget it. There's such a thing as a subpoena *duces tecum,* you know."

"That would alert Tarkos."

"You've been drinking too much *pulque—pulque* rots the brain."

"In Maricopa we used it to run pickups during Carter's gasoline shortage."

"Be that as it may, I'm not going to turn burglar and safecracker for the convenience of a government that can conveniently forget sponsorship and responsibility."

We drank silently for a while. Then I said, "Married?"

"Not yet."

"How about a date tonight? White squaw."

"Injun like white squaws."

"Thought you might. And the way you're duded up is bound to turn her on."

His eyes narrowed. "Squaw for you, or is it a three-way fumble?"

"Yours is Glenda, mine's Twinkie."

"*Twinkie?* I don't believe it."

"Says it's her stage name, and I believe that. Twinkie Starr."

"Before I get into anything I like to know what I'm getting into. In short, other than getting laid, what's the deal?"

I described the boat set-up, and said it was just possible, *barely* possible, that Twinkie was a certain Sondra who had once worked intimately with Tarkos. "So I thought I'd massage her and keep my ears open."

"Eliciting information, we call it."

"Why call it anything? Keep Glenda occupied and I'll bring Twinkie back here."

He shrugged. "Why not? I was dubious about coming here, but who'da thought the ol' jungle fighter would fix me up with a ready teddy?"

"Tony—*nobody* says 'ready teddy' any more. Not even in Maricopa. You're seeing too many late-night movies."

"That's the truth—but on fixed surveillance there's not much to do."

I heard Maddy Gossons hailing me, told Tony prospective buyers were about to board, and suggested we adjourn to a place offering a dark, congenial atmosphere. He agreed, and as we came on deck Ms. Gossons gave him a prolonged, startled stare. She had a youngish couple with her, possibly man and wife. I nodded at them, and Tony and I took off for the beach.

Two hours later we'd run up a large bar bill that we divided, then we steered each other back to the *El Dorado*. I turned on inside lights and Tony suggested I shave. "Might go over better with the . . . um . . . broad," he hiccupped, and I agreed.

Fortunately I had an electric razor, otherwise I might have needed surgical repair. But we were in a good mood and eager to hit the targets. I got out a bottle of Beam and suggested Tony leave his Panama on my boat—the better to display the luxuriance of his hair. He agreed and, bottle in hand, we went swaying down the pier.

The ladies met us, I made first-name introductions, and we climbed aboard a fifty-foot cabin cruiser. Wagging her finger, Glenda intoned, "You started early. Naughty boys."

I planted my bottle between Twinkie's ample breasts. "Housewarmer—I mean, boatwarmer."

She laughed and fixed me with sultry eyes. "Been looking forward to this," she said. "You look like quite a guy. So what are we waiting for? Let's party."

I tended bar, giving the girls plenty and holding back on ours. Less than two hours later, Twinkie was in my cabin, peeling down shorts and panties and dropping her bra.

If you like well-rounded figures—meaning broad hips, narrow waist, large firm breasts, and solid thighs—Twinkie's was spectacular. She was tanned *all* over, and I reflected that if she was Tarkos's Sondra, I had to admire his taste in females. But if she was that Sondra, she'd also been to bed with Melissa—and that made her less attractive to me. Still, I had to find out. I stripped, kissed one erect plum-colored nipple, and asked if she had Arab blood.

"Why? You got something against Arabs?"

"Nothing at all. Arab women can be extraordinarily attractive."

Smiling, she turned slowly around to display two plump, pear-shaped buns. No cellulite. "I have Syrian blood. You like?"

"I like, Sondra." When I touched her sex it was dripping wet.

She was muscularly demanding, sturdy in the clinches and a shoulder-gnawer. She also liked spanking, so I spanked her bottom and that turned her into a panther. Pantheress.

Later, when we were lying side by side on the narrow bunk, I said, "You've got a fantastic face and figure—you should be in pictures."

"Well, I was. Sort of." She rose on an elbow and nibbled my ear. "Ever hear of Falcon Studios?"

"Vaguely."

"I had a contract there for a while. Borden Tarkos runs it—heard of him?"

"The name. Big money."

"Yeah—but careful with it."

"I know the type. Tarkos screw you?"

"Not out of any money, but he tried. As for real screwing, he wasn't a real man—get what I mean?"

"For instance?"

"He liked to watch. That was his satisfaction."

"You mean—ceiling mirrors?"

"No, stupid. A couple making it—like an exhibition. Had a video camera to photograph the action."

"And he photographed you?"

"He was my boss, wasn't he? And he paid extra for exhibitions."

"Aside from bedroom filming, did you get studio parts?"

"A few—but Borden coulda done lots more for me."

"Why didn't he?"

"Didn't want me to be a star, get independent." She lay back and stared at the dark overhead. "He used me, the bastard, shoved me out."

"But he has those action films of you."

"Yeah. If I ever told on him, he said he'd sell the films around the world." Her head turned. "You wouldn't do that, Joe."

"No, but I wouldn't take pictures in the first place. He owns a spot in Vegas, doesn't he?"

"He and some friends—heavy guys. He coulda featured me'n Glenda in the Sagebrush floor show, but he wouldn't even do that. It wouldn'ta cost him nothing extra."

"These heavy friends of Borden's—ever see them?"

"Sure—an' they saw me, too. Live. When Borden put on special home entertainment. Guinea cruds," she added in afterthought.

"Isn't he married? How'd he get away with it?"

"Oh, he'd taken pictures of his wife an' some stud makin' it."

"Ever see her?"

"*See* her? The bastard got his wife drunk and made me get in bed with her—got a real thrill outa that." Turning on her side, she reached for the Iron Duke. "I heard she ran away, then I see a newspaper photo—they're in Italy somewhere. I feel sorry for her."

She'd told me a good deal, most of it supporting Melissa's story—but not what I really wanted to know: why Melissa had surrendered and returned to her husband. Still, Sondra knew a lot about her one-time employer and some of it might be useful to Antonio Honey. We'd talk it over. Later.

Her thighs clamped around my hips, she pressed a nipple between my lips, and presently we were playing the primal game of ten toes up, ten toes down. She knew it all, and it was great.

Toward first light, I felt Sondra stir and leave the bunk. She dressed quickly, then bent over and kissed my cheek. "Good man," she said softly. "Call me anytime," and then she went away.

Having imbibed much more than my usual intake of alcohol, I went back to sleep and stayed in the bunk until Tony came down and washed up. He was in good spirits, tickled my ribs, and told me to get up and face the day. "What we need," he prescribed, "is some Bloody Marys and a big Mexican breakfast. *Desayuno.*"

"You eat, I'll drink," I said, and sat up. Carefully.

"Naw, I'm buyin'—that was a good thing you put me onto last night, 'mano—I owe you."

I pulled on clothing and we walked to the Marriott on Admiralty Way. Maxfield's restaurant served us double Bloodies, and Tony ordered *huevos rancheros,* refried beans, *chilequiles,* tortillas, guacamole, and tamales. Just the sound of it made my stomach turn over. I drank half my drink and stared at the menu. "Belgian waffles," I said weakly, "juice and coffee."

Tony said, "That ain't much—musta not worked out last night."

"It was like a night in the weight room," I said, "but satisfying. Deeply so."

He munched a soda cracker. "What'd you elicit? Give."

"She's Tarkos's Sondra," I told him, and repeated the rest of what she'd told me. "The lady has information and she needs a job. What does that suggest?"

"Recruitment."

"Giving you two girlfriends," I mused. "Poor me."

"I'm not the jealous type."

"She's all yours, Tony, a very physical person. With your muscles you can keep control. My back's bent, bruised and clawed. Don't say I didn't warn you."

Breakfast arrived, we ordered another round of drinks, and while I sipped the *jus du jour,* Tony said, "One low-level informant is okay, but we gotta do better'n that. Other thoughts?"

"Tarkos's attorney—Stanley Parsons, Esquire. Century City."

"Hey, you mean fool around with an officer of the court?"

"I mean he merits a good reaming. He knows the ins and outs of his client's illegal dealings, and he himself became an obstructor of justice when he persuaded Melissa to leave. That's heavy stuff, Tony. Consider him a wineskin waiting to be squeezed."

He frowned. Sunlight turned his Aztec beak into polished bronze. "What about lawyer-client confidentiality?"

"It doesn't exist if the lawyer is furthering an ongoing conspiracy or illegal act."

"How come you know so much about the law?"

"Research, my man, for a couple of sitcom segments I had to write. Check it out with your people."

"Hell, I'll take your word for it. So what have you got in mind?"

"Consideration might be given to having Stanley snatched and squeezed. You sop up the goodies."

His face feigned consternation. "Government agents kidnapping and abusing a citizen?"

"Well, that would be the charge *if* shiny shields were shown. But if the snatchers represented themselves as of the criminal element—Ambrosino hoods, for example—then who can Parsons and Tarkos blame but their buddy, ol' Raf?"

"Pungent thinking," he declared and bit into a tamale. The *huevos rancheros* on his plate looked like cat vomit. I closed my eyes momentarily, and when I opened them, a large puffy waffle was on my plate; honey, maple syrup and whipped butter on the side.

For a while we ate in silence, enjoying food and the second round of restorative drinks. I dabbed spiced tomato juice from my lips, and said, "Wonder if he knows Sondra—or vice versa."

"Stanley? Why?"

"Assuming Parsons is a normally conservative, straight-type fellow with a clubwoman wife, prep-school kids, and a nice suburban home, any indiscretions he and Sondra might have indulged in could be terribly embarrassing if revealed. In fact, he'd probably have to leave his law partnership and seek honest work."

"It's a thought," Tony agreed. "You gonna ask Sondra?"

"You," I said, "after you've recruited her. I can't risk having her or Glenda think I'm any way involved. I'll be around L.A. long after you're promoted to a Washington desk job."

"So what do you suggest?" His strong jaws and gleaming teeth were crunching a well-stuffed taco. "Glenda's my pal—how do I make the switch?"

"If I were doing it, I'd drop by with an armful of choice liquors and load Glenda's drinks. While she's snoring away, give Sondra satisfaction, and pitch her. Flash green and she's yours."

"Sounds feasible," he agreed. "Might save us having to grab the lawyer."

"*Us*? Uh-uh. Work the Sondra route, Tony. She's a bitter lady. If she can help ream Tarkos, she will."

"Sex and money," he said in a remote voice. "Always comes down to that, right?"

"Plus revenge."

On the way back to my boat I stopped at a pay phone and called

Mrs. Haven. Nobody had come around asking for me, and she was holding my mail. I asked her to hang on to it for the present, and ended the call before she could ask when I was coming back. If she didn't know, she couldn't tell.

Tony flopped on the unused bunk and promptly fell asleep, straw hat shielding his eyes from objectionable light. Food and drink made me feel considerably better, and I walked over to Semmes & Co. to inquire about yesterday's results.

Maddy Gossons motioned me to a chair and opened a manila folder. "Second couple didn't show, but the pair you saw made a firm offer—twenty-three." She shoved over a contingent sale form with a certified check in the sum of $500.

"Uh-uh," I said. "After all that sanding and painting, the price is twenty-five."

"I think you're being unwise, Mr. Brent. I was surprised by the offer—I think it's very fair."

"My boat, my labor," I remarked. "For twenty-five it's theirs."

"It has to be," she said thinly, "because that's our agreement. Don't try to raise the price because you've had one offer."

"Earn your commission," I told her. "Get us some serious money. If they liked my boat—and it's a dazzler now—they'll kick in the other two. I'll buy dinner at Stone's if they do."

"Well—" she said judiciously "—I'll go back to them and do a hard sell. They really liked your boat. And I guess you could use the extra two thousand."

"I don't know anyone who couldn't."

"Okay, I'll get busy."

It was close to noon when I boarded my boat, but already cocktail time aboard the *Flaminia,* on its languid, carefree cruise around the Mediterranean. Tarkos's waiters would be white-jacketed, with black bow ties. I could envision the festive setting on the yacht's broad fantail—a crescent of well-dressed guests watching colorful native dancers to the accompaniment of pipe, tambourine, and drum. Melissa, in expensive jewelry, viewing the entertainment impassively. Tarkos beside her, wet cigar clenched in his jaws . . .

Tony's snore broke my reverie. He'd be flaked out for a couple of hours, I told myself, and I'd noticed no topside movement on the girls' boat. If I wasn't around he'd do better work faster. In fact, I had to be absent so he could move in on Sondra Starr. I thought of her sculptured, Rubenesque body and the voluptuous pleasure it had given me just a few hours ago. Sex without love, of course, but plain lustful sex wasn't bad either. I'd forgotten how satisfying it could be.

I left the boat, went to my Datsun, and aired it out before driving from the Marina. I'd decided to visit my apartment and check mail; there'd be bills, and even if I wasn't ready to pay them I wanted to know their depressing sum.

In case my building was being watched, I parked on Highland, walked a block beyond Cerrito, and cut back to enter by the rear door. Old Pedro was smoking on the rear steps, a tan, hand-rolled cigarette between his stained fingers. As I passed Pedro I smelled the sweet, oily aroma of marijuana, and silently wished him happy memories of Durango, from whence he came.

Mrs. Haven gave me a handful of letters that I carried up to my place. The inside held the smell of dead air, so I opened the still-latchless window and spread my mail on the table.

Bills a-plenty: Visa, BankAmericard, American Express, I. Magnin, Getty, Texaco, and one pre-stamped white postoffice envelope addressed in graceful script.

Melissa.

My body tensed, pulse began to race, and I picked up the envelope.

My doorbell rang. I swore, dropped the letter, and opened the door, expecting to see Mrs. Haven with—

Two men I'd never seen before faced me. One held a gun.

NINETEEN

"Up with 'em," he ordered. "Back down, pal, quiet like a worm. We're comin' in."

Mouth dry, I backed to a chair, sat down while the man held a pistol on me. His partner went quickly through the apartment, came back, and said, "Clean." I had the feeling he'd been here before.

The man with the pistol was close to six feet, with broad shoulders enlarged by the jacket of a brown suit. He had the repaired nose, stitched eyebrows, and cross-hatched lips of a fighter who'd been too long in the ring. The other man wore a gray sharkskin suit with tapered trousers. He left us and went out. I could hear him going down the stairs. I said, "What happens now?"

"We wait." From his pocket he drew out a three-inch tubular silencer and screwed it into the muzzle of his handgun. I wondered if it was one that had put bullets into Rinaldo and Fallon.

I waited for what seemed a long time. If there was traffic noise on the street I couldn't hear it because of blood banging through my head. The man stood about five feet away, holding the pistol lightly, silencer trained on me. After a while I heard footsteps on the stairway, heavy footsteps. When they reached the hall, the gunman glanced back and moved aside.

Through the open doorway came three men. Two formed a chair-lift with their clasped hands, bearing an old man with a thin, cadaverous face disfigured by pockmarks.

His nose curved downward like a raptor's beak, giving his profile the appearance of a weathered gargoyle, gray and menacing. His neck was skinny, making the Adam's apple appear disproportionately large above the too-big collar of his white damask shirt. Despite his thin gray hair, his eyebrows were black and bushy. Untrimmed tufts sprouted from his ears like caterpillar spines. One eye was blindly white, the other deepset and shiny as wet opal. His men lowered him carefully onto the sofa, straightened his trouser legs, and stood behind him. "Get the door, Marco," he croaked. One man closed the door and locked it, came back into position.

Finally the old man turned to me. After licking his lips he said hoarsely, "So there's no mistakes, you're Brent."

"Right," I croaked, throat thick with fear.

His head turned, a skull on a stick, as he surveyed my apartment. "Stinks," he said scornfully. "You're nothin', know that? Nothin'."

"Whatever you say."

The lone eye examined me in a leisurely way. Lips moved and the hoarse voice said, "Know who I am?"

"No."

"No, *sir*," the gun-holder prompted me.

"No, sir," I echoed.

He grunted, swallowed, and husked, "I'm Dino's dad. I want to know about my son. Where is he? What happened?"

"I saw him in Mexico a week, ten days ago. He asked me some questions, I came back here."

"What questions?"

"Mrs. Borden Tarkos—her location, some diamonds or money she'd taken. She paid me to stay here one night, that's all I could tell him because that's all I knew."

"And my boy let you come back."

"Had his driver take me to the airport. Your son and his friend, Diego, were at the movie-set cabin when I left." I made my face as earnest-looking as I could. "Aren't they—I mean, everything's okay?"

Raf grunted. "He phoned me, said they pushed you around, what should he do? I told him to get rid of you."

"We made a deal—he'd let me go, pay my agent if I kept my mouth shut. I have."

"That part's true—you didn't snitch. Why not?"

"Two thousand dollars is a lot of money."

Raf grunted almost inaudibly. "Figures. I heard you write for TV— you write shit, right?"

"TV shit," I agreed. The eye staring out of the devastated face emanated evil. His whole presence created a force field radiating nothing but evil. His three soldiers augmented it.

I said, "If it'll help any, Dino and Diego were talking about going out for a big marlin. I don't know what they decided."

"Fishing's a day trip," said Don Rafaello Ambrosino. "They been gone too long for fishing. What else you hear?"

My turn to lick lips. "Dino said the money Mrs. Tarkos took was his—"

"Mine," Raf interjected breathily. "What you know about that money?" His one-eyed gaze traversed the room. "What'd that bitch tell you while she was here?"

"Nothing about money. Dino told me about that."

"Yeah?"

"Said Tarkos had been cheating on his—your family."

"He said that—so many words?"

"Yes, sir."

The skull seemed to shrink down into the shirt collar.

I said, "When Dino sees that photo of Tarkos and his wife on their yacht he'll know I wasn't lying."

"Lying—about what?"

"Where the wife was. Dino asked, I said I didn't know. Turns out they were together all the time, her and her husband. I couldn't know that."

The thin lips moved. "Makes sense," the voice said softly. "You thinkin' what I'm thinkin'?"

I swallowed. "Maybe. But I don't want to get dead for saying it."

"So talk."

"Since talking with your son and then seeing that picture of the Tarkoses enjoying life abroad, I thought—as writers will—that maybe they'd been putting on an act."

"Go on."

"If Tarkos was going to rip off someone—a partner, say—he'd plan carefully. When he had a lot of the sucker's money he'd—"

"Listen, I'm nobody's sucker."

"Sorry, sir. Victim, okay?" No response, so I went on: "He'd give the money—jewels, bonds, valuables, whatever—to someone he trusted, say, his wife. Or maybe he'd only *say* he gave it to her. She'd pretend to rob it and run away from him, he'd put on a big search for her—like offering a reward. She'd drop out of sight, and the next time seen, she's far away with her husband, supposedly the man she stole from."

When he said nothing I continued: "If the wife really hit the husband for several million dollars, doesn't seem likely they'd join up for a honeymoon cruise. In the meantime, he's told his partner the money's gone, wife's responsible. But having made her the scapegoat, the husband has two choices: protect her from their victim, or silence her."

"Kill her, you mean," Ambrosino said huskily. "She's still alive, ain't she?"

"But not immortal." I paused to lick my lips again because they were authentically dry. "So for now the husband is keeping her at his side, away from questions by his partners. But eventually he has to come back and face his partners—only he can't feel safe if his wife can answer questions. So she's gotta go down the chute—overboard at sea, or some crazy Greek driver runs her down . . . lot of choices and opportunities in Europe. With her out of the way he continues blaming her for stealing his partners' money. Only he's got it stashed away somewhere—a detail he could take care of while in port for a day or so. Fast flight to Zürich . . ."

I shook my head wearily. I was winding down and hoping I'd said all I intended to say. "I don't know Tarkos, don't know what he'd do in any kind of situation. You asked me to give you my thoughts and I've done that. If I blackened the name of an honest man, it was unintentional. I don't know anything, I'm not a player in this—just a guy who had the misfortune to shelter the so-called runaway wife."

For a long time the room was silent. I could hear Highland traffic now, meaning my pulse rate was lower because fear-induced tension had diminished. But the danger remained.

The opal eye fixed on me unblinkingly. "What I heard," he rasped, "is you stuck your nose in it—claiming the reward."

"Why not? I had information that could have been useful to the advertiser. Maybe others responded to Tarkos's ad, called in, I don't know. The way his gofer talked I felt I had to be careful—I'm glad I was."

Something vaguely resembling a chuckle issued from the slug-scarred throat. "You played it good. You're smart, writer, I'll say that. Just don't get too smart, know what I mean?"

"Yes, sir. I'm out of it, have been, don't want to hear any more about it."

A coughing spasm seized him. When it ended he wiped drool from his chin and his head thrust forward. "Suppose you see that dame again, what'd you do?"

"Tell me."

"You let me know." One finger lifted, the man behind him pulled out a card and wrote on it. Quickly. Very quickly. He handed me a telephone number. Not with the 213 area code for Los Angeles, but 702—Nevada.

Ambrosino said, "You wanted five large from Tarkos—finger that broad and you'll get five from me."

I slid the card into my shirt pocket. "That's very generous, sir, and I'd like to earn it." I no longer had any doubt who took Fallon's surveillance tapes.

The telephone rang, splitting the silence like a siren.

Ambrosino said, "Let it go."

Five more rings before the ringing ended. Ambrosino said, "Expecting a call?"

"No, sir—could be my agent."

"I want to hear from Dino," he said to the room. "Mother of God, where is he?" The face lifted beseechingly and an anguished cry tore from his throat. *"Where's my boy? Tell me. Where's my boy?"*

The head turned from side to side. His chest heaved spasmodically and harsh sobs wrenched from his throat. Tears welled, spilled over and flowed down his cheeks. One hand lifted, moved in a circle, and the two soldiers who'd brought him in bent over and carefully raised their boss. Ambrosino wiped his cheeks, made a snuffling sound, and was carried out like a Tonkinese emperor.

While they were going down the stairs the remaining soldier unscrewed his silencer and said, "He wasn't here. You never saw him. Right?"

"Right."

"Keeping the mouth shut is the way to a longer life."

"So I've heard."

He dropped the silencer in a coat pocket and fitted the pistol in his shoulder holster. He patted it and looked down at me with contempt. "The boss was right. You're nothin', and you write shit." Turning, he went out, slamming the door hard.

I stayed where I was until I heard an engine starting. Weakly, I got up and went to the bathroom. The face in the mirror was strained and old. I rinsed it with cold water, felt a little better. I drank bourbon from the bottle and that soothed my nerve endings enough to begin to feel anger at Tony Honey. He was going to keep Ambrosino off my back, was he? Instead, he was on *his* back in my bunk while *my* life was being threatened. I sat at the table and stared at my hands, spread the fingers. After a while the trembling stopped and perspiration began drying around my armpits. Mail lay on the table before me. I ignored the bills and picked up Melissa's letter. There was no return address on the envelope. I opened it slowly and carefully.

TWENTY

Over the years I'd occasionally wondered how it was that boys and girls who received the same penmanship instruction from the same teacher developed such different writing styles. Boys like me wrote haphazardly, but girls put care into their handwriting, developing decorative patterns that often had artistic qualities. I'd seen Melissa's handwriting once before—the note she'd left me—and it was distinctive. Lots of loops and floral curlings and unmistakably feminine. She'd had time then and wrote unhurriedly. This handwriting was different, and before I began reading I knew she'd done it quickly.

> Dear Joe,
>   I'm going away because Borden's lawyer said you'd be killed in Mexico if I don't go back to B. And he said they'd maim or kill my father so I don't have any choice. I called you three times and got no answer so I guess the lawyer wasn't lying. And my father doesn't answer his phone—the two people I care most about in this world.
>   If they let you live—and I don't know who they are—then you'll read this and you'll know why I have to do what B demands.
>   I'll always love you.
>   M.

I stared at her letter until tears distorted and blurred the words. Now I understood.

Like Ambrosino a few minutes ago, I wiped my cheeks dry, then I started for the telephone, intending to call Joel Hatfield, but remembering that my phone might be tapped. My skull felt encircled by a tightening steel band; my thoughts were chaotic. Slow down, think it out, I told myself, and with the help of more bourbon, I did.

Because my typewriter was on the boat, I had to address the envelope by hand as legibly as I could. On a sheet of typing paper I wrote:

Dear Joel:
    This letter just received from your client answers most of our questions. It might be enough to use against the lawyer who threatened her. At least you'll have something to show Ballantine by way of explanation for her flight.
    As I see it, the next step is to tell your client I'm safe. You can check on her father. Then I assume she'll come back and take care of unfinished business.
    You know how to reach me.

                                                             Joe

I folded Melissa's letter inside mine and stamped my envelope. Then I walked down to the corner letter box and mailed the envelope. Tomorrow or next day, Hatfield should have it in San Diego.

In my apartment I sat down and looked around, thinking that the place was becoming a mission flophouse, with so many ugly strangers coming in. I knew I should probably eat something, but I wasn't hungry; my stomach was too taut from the Mafia visit and Melissa's letter.

Ambrosino.

I'd sat in front of the man whose son I'd killed—and lied to him, apparently convincingly. The old Don wouldn't care that I'd had only a machete and Dino a gun. No way I could tell the truth and live. But through that confrontation with Raf I'd planted a suspicion that Tarkos had conspired against him, cheated him of money. If the time came for him to face Tarkos as he'd faced me, Tarkos would have to try to prove a lie—that he'd dealt honestly with the family, hadn't helped himself to Ambrosino funds.

Unavoidably, my tale had implicated Melissa, but Ambrosino's beef would be with the main man, his partner, Tarkos. At least I hoped he'd come to that conclusion, now that I knew Melissa still loved me, had run back to her husband to save my life.

When I remembered the tale I'd fabricated under the pressure of fear, I wondered how I'd managed to put it all together. If the old man were healthier he might have asked more questions—questions I'd have had a much harder time answering—but he had a frail hold on life, that old *mafioso*, who looked like a piece of driftwood, gray and battered. I hoped he'd die before me—a long time before. The sooner the better.

To neutralize him and protect Melissa I was going to need Tony's help, and I wondered how his afternoon with Sondra was progressing. Lawyer Parsons had to be punished, too, perhaps through Sondra, but how I got to him was less important than the consummation. I needed him to help put Tarkos away.

The telephone rang. I looked at it, and after four rings I picked up the receiver and answered with a cautious, "Yes?"

"Nero here—been calling you. Time we had another chat. Now okay?"

"Sure." I replaced the receiver and wondered if it was his call I'd been ordered to ignore. What did Nero want with me? He wouldn't be shy about telling me when he arrived.

To kill time I opened the bills on my table, sorted them out and added their totals: nearly twelve hundred dollars, and two weeks before I could pick up my first unemployment check.

The entrance buzzer rang. I went down and saw Lieutenant Jaime Nero standing outside. We went up the staircase together, and when we were in my apartment, door closed, he said, "You've had some interesting visitors. Mind telling me what you all talked about?"

I was on the point of automatically denying I'd had callers when I saw a slow smile spread across his face. "Before you make a false statement to an officer, I'll give you a break: We got a tip Raf Ambrosino was heading for L.A. He was picked up at the state line. At the city limits our O.C. squad took over and tailed him here. I've had my own men spot-checking this place while you've been away, so when Ambrosino's soldiers set up surveillance front and back, we simply watched. You arrived and they carried the old felon in." He sat down, pulled off his coat and fanned his face. "That's background. Now tell me why you merited a personal visit from the old guinea."

"I've been shaking ever since they left." I reached for the bottle and swallowed another mouthful. "If he'd come to kill me, your watchers would have been a hell of a lot of help, Lieutenant. Why didn't you have them all pulled in?"

"On what charge? I decided he ought to have his say, then you'd tell me what it was all about. I don't think the old *capo* has left Nevada in three years."

"He was looking for his son."

"And thought you had him? C'mon, tell me why."

I described the ruse that had lured me to Baja, and told it truthfully in detail. Then I repeated what I'd told Raf—Dino had let me return, and I'd left him and his *compadre* at the cabin in good health.

"Doesn't sound like Dino—maybe the kid's gone soft. He had you in an isolated place where he could erase you without a trace. Why didn't he?"

"I persuaded him I didn't know Mrs. Tarkos's whereabouts—that's what he wanted. I'll admit I was pretty scared, but once he'd heard me out, Dino had no motive to kill me. Also, he knew my agent and my lawyer knew about my trip. Eventually he'd have had to answer questions about my disappearance." I shrugged. "Easier to let me go."

"What else?"

"That Sunday photo of the yachting couple made Raf realize I couldn't possibly have known Melissa's whereabouts."

"Keep talking."

"He said it was worth five thousand if I'd finger her for him."

"Plan to collect?"

I shook my head.

"What does he want her for?"

"He needs her story—how Tarkos schemed to defraud him of casino skim."

"Nevada again," he sighed. "Anything else?"

"His soldiers killed Fallon and Rinaldo, took their wiretap tapes."

He sat forward, suddenly interested. "How do you know?"

"He had information that could have come only from the tap—calls I made to the reward number."

One hand curled into a fist and smacked his open palm. "I was right not to interfere. Now I know where to look for the shooters."

To me his smile was almost kindly. "Guess I owe you one, Mr. Brent. That lead can save a lot of police time and money."

"I'll bring you my next parking ticket."

"The next dozen." He stood up. "By the way, where you been this past week or so?"

"Aside from time in Baja, I've been filing forms at the unemployment office, and out of town looking for work."

"Any luck?"

"No."

"I always wondered—what do unemployed writers do?"

"Hang themselves on their yachts." It was an old Guild joke.

"I imagine some have. Well, this has been profitable." He began walking toward the door. "I'll stay in touch." When I said nothing he turned to look at me. "I said I'll stay in touch."

"Rather you didn't, Lieutenant. Cops and Mafia's not my game."

He grunted. "You were dealt in, *señor*, so play the cards as they come." He went out, and again I was staring at a closed door, thinking the only people who came to see me were people I didn't want to see. But my agent and ex-producer, they stayed away. In Hollywood, unemployment was regarded as a communicable disease. Maybe it was.

The phone rang. I said "Shit!" and picked up the receiver. Maddy Gossons said, "I showed your boat again—after I rousted the character who was bunking in. He's something, isn't he?"

"Exotic. Did you make a sale?"

"Well, no, but the looker said he'd consider. I think he wants something larger—more stowage space—get what I mean?"

"Like hauling from Ensenada?"

"Uh-huh. Tell me about your day-sleeper friend—what does he do?"

"If I told you, you wouldn't believe me."

"Ummm. Try me."

"He's an Indian wrestler."

"Oh. You mean he wrestles Indian-style—or he's an Indian who wrestles."

"Both," I said. "I'll be aboard later. Then if you want to rassle Tony, I'll clear the decks."

She broke the connection and I smiled. Apparently, Antonio F.

Honey had enough sex appeal to interest even latent dykes. Just the man for Sondra.

I drank a beer and relaxed enough to eat a sandwich of thawed bologna and chopped ham slathered with mayonnaise. The food made me steadier and I decided to do something about the telephone. I could lift off the receiver, or I could disconnect it at the module box. Live, the phone was a source of information to inquisitive callers. If it rang and I didn't answer, I was probably not home. If they heard a busy signal they could draw other conclusions. I opted for the latter, and laid the receiver on the floor. For a while it gave off a dial tone, then changed into a series of clicking chirps—or chirping clicks. Whatever. In the third and final stage, it died. That was how I wanted it. Dead and uninformative.

Knowing why Melissa had left protective custody and that she loved me had lifted my spirits considerably. I wasn't going to tell Hatfield how to practice law, but if I wanted to reach Melissa, I'd contact my client by radio-telephone, wherever the *Flaminia* happened to be, and pass an open-code message saying I was safe and she should come back.

Now that the wire service photo had revealed Melissa's presence aboard the yacht, Tarkos couldn't attach too much importance to a call from her lawyer, who had explanations to make to the authorities. Hatfield should be able to figure that out—he was a Phi Bete, after all.

Melissa: when Hatfield calls, don't talk, just listen.

You shall know the truth and the truth shall make you free.

I opened the refrigerator for milk, and remembered—as always, when opening the fridge—that the diamond reposed in a freezer tray, available for emergencies.

Raf Ambrosino hadn't asked me about the missing diamonds. Why not? Because his soldiers had tossed the place and found nothing. Apparently, he didn't know about Melissa's dealings with the feds—so he'd assume Tarkos had the stones. (I assumed she'd delivered them to Ballantine and Company, per agreement.) If she had, then Tarkos and Ambrosino had lost them forever, whereas Melissa was due a third of their value. Say, two million dollars for the feds, a million for her. Plus immunity.

Hard to imagine a sweeter deal, and all she had to do was get back to California.

I washed dishes, took a hot shower, and stuffed clean clothing in an athletic bag. I left the building by the rear door, and made my way back to the Datsun, wondering where Nero's and Ambrosino's watchers had been posted to see me arrive—less surreptitiously than I'd thought at the time.

I drove south through a fine afternoon, fresh breeze from the ocean dispelling coastal smog, leaving the air clean-tasting for a change. In the dockmaster's office I checked for messages, found none, and carried my bag over to the boat. As expected, Tony wasn't there, so I stowed my clothing and set up my typewriter on the table. Knowing about Melissa freed my mind for creative thinking, and after extending the Hermitage story for three hours I got up, stretched back and neck muscles, and thought about dinner. The unnerving episode with Ambrosino seemed far away: I'd survived, why review it and revive unpleasant memories?

After making and eating a salad, I put on the percolator and while coffee was brewing I got back to work. Toward ten o'clock, back aching, eyeballs sandy, I decided I'd worked long enough.

No sign of Tony who, I hoped, had found night lodging with Sondra Starr, courtesy of Glenda. Their boat was dark, not even rigging lights showing, and I felt encouraged that Tony was recruiting successfully.

I turned in, slept dreamlessly, and in the morning while I was making breakfast, Antonio F. Honey showed up.

TWENTY-ONE

Looking a little on the haggard side, Tony sat down and said, "Spare some for me? Exercise makes me hongry."

I fried another pair of eggs, toasted more bread, and divided the ham steak. He attacked his meal like a vulture. Finally his jaws stopped moving—probably from fatigue—and he sat back to swallow fresh coffee. "That Sondra's a lot of woman," he remarked. "I was thinking of calling for help."

"My, my, the Maricopa Mauler met his match."

"And then some." He wiped his mouth and drank more coffee. "Anyway, I got myself a confidential informant. Sondra can name a lot of Tarkos's associates and—putting it politely—she's been intimate with lawyer Parsons. Tarkos filmed one encounter, which to me means he had enough leverage over his lawyer to force him into visiting Melissa and threatening her."

"So you'll buy yourself a virgin videotape, wave it at Parsons and elicit his cooperation."

Tony nodded. "What I was thinking. Ever hear of a Nevada senator named Rupert Farenhold?"

"Seen the name."

"Well, Farenhold owns a newspaper—*Carson City Ledger*—which is part of his power base. According to Sondra, Tarkos money helped the senator get elected, and the senator keeps returning the favor. Again and again and again. In short, Tarkos has him in the palm of his hand."

"And behind Tarkos stands the Ambrosino family."

"Right."

"While you've been enjoying carnal pleasures, I've had a couple of unwanted visits you should know about." I added coffee to our cups and told him about yesterday afternoon.

"Jesus," he exclaimed when I finished. "You actually saw the old goombah!"

"It was a moving scene, Tony, and I don't want an encore. No way."

"I'm surprised Raf hasn't already sent soldiers down to that cabin."

"He will now. And when he's got their report he'll want me for further questioning. Any way you could have them grabbed at the Cabos airport and sent back?"

"If I had names for a watch-list it might be possible, but Raf will only send others. So it's only a question of time before he learns there was an explosion and fire. Let's hope the fire sanitized the scene." He breathed deeply, patted his belly, and stretched. "As for Melissa, wonder when she'll come home."

"When she's able to get away from the yacht. Presuming Hatfield makes contact and tells her what she needs to know."

"Meanwhile we have Parsons to set up, right?"

"Include me out, *amigo*."

"I need a driver."

"Use Sondra."

"I have more confidence in you."

"Thanks, but I'm out of it." I spelled the word in the air: "O . . . U . . . T. Besides—" I gestured at my typewriter—"I've got compelling work to do. So have you if you're going to bag Tarkos. What I know of your department, they go to the ends of the earth to nail their man."

"That's PR stuff," he said scornfully. "Maybe an occasional IRS sting operation, but mainly it's strictly by the book: Miranda, Escobedo, legal taps . . . No wonder we have trouble prosecuting offenders. Take Ambrosino—the Nevada Strike Force in various incarnations has been trying to bag his family for at least twenty years."

"Get Tarkos and you've got Ambrosino."

"Parsons is the key." He leaned forward and cracked his thick, powerful fingers. "So I need you."

"What's in it for me?"

"An opportunity to serve your country."

"I've done that," I said, "and I didn't care for it. Six weeks of psychiatric counseling and I still flash back to Beirut. No thanks. What you'd like me to do could get me six years in the slammer, no psychiatrist around to hold my hand."

"Hell, I'd be running the same risk." He got up. "Tell you what, I'll run surveillance on Parsons for a couple days, establish his movement pattern, devise a plan. If you don't like it, okay."

"I won't like it," I said, "I'll tell you that right now. By the way, how come you didn't breakfast with the ladies?"

"Glenda got a call from her friend, the boat owner. He's taking them out for the day. Catalina, or some such destination."

"Glenda resent your switch to Sondra?"

"She's philosophical—they've shared guys before." He picked up his Panama hat and pressed it down over his thick black hair. "See you." He went up the companionway and disappeared.

I made more coffee and settled down to work, thinking I'd give my letter time to reach Hatfield before phoning him for a situation update.

By mid-afternoon Hatfield hadn't received my letter with Melissa's enclosed, so I said I'll call the following day.

Ms. Gossons brought by another potential buyer and I went over to the Red Onion's Cantina Bar for Coors and a steak sandwich while she showed *El Dorado* and exaggerated my boat's extraordinary qualities. When I returned she had the guy at another slip, looking over another boat. I went back to work.

When I called Hatfield next day he'd received and digested my and Melissa's letters, and said he was going to take a photocopy of hers to the U.S. Attorney, then try to reach his client by radio-telephone. I agreed it was a good idea and he said he'd let me know what happened.

While I had him on the line I summarized Ambrosino's visit, after which Hatfield said, "You must be a very persuasive talker."

"Liar," I corrected. "Having your neck on the line concentrates your thinking amazingly."

"That brings up ramifications we ought to discuss in person. How about coming down in the next couple of days? Phone in advance so I'll be free."

"How's your schedule tomorrow?"

After a few moments he said, "Any time after, say, four o'clock."
"I'll be there."

It was well after dark when I heard Tony Honey hail me from the pier. I unlocked the cabin door and invited him aboard.

The drug-pusher togs he'd been wearing before had been replaced with a guayabera, dark trousers, and deck shoes. "How you doin'?" he asked as he slumped into a chair.

"Same as always—average."

"Well, I been busy. Fortunately, Parsons is a creature of habit. Drives off from his pretty place in Woodland Hills same time each morning, parks in a reserved slot at his office building—Century City. Lunches at Hy's, which is nearby and keeps a table reserved for Parsons's law firm. Yesterday he ate alone; today, with two other men, probably lawyers."

"Good bet."

"Yesterday he drove home at six o'clock; today, at six-fifteen. Nice house—about four bedrooms, three-car garage, satellite dish partly hidden by a tall hedge. He's got a pool—saw a maintenance truck parked outside."

"Why are you telling me all this?"

"Preface to the plan."

"Look, I don't care if it's foolproof and fail-safe. I'm not going to get involved in kidnapping a prominent citizen—even an unprominent one."

"Where's that adventurous spirit that took you down to Baja?"

"It died there," I told him. "Anyway, I'm going down to Dago tomorrow, talk with the lawyer-man. You and Sondra can take Parsons—like Bonnie and Clyde used to do."

"Thought you wanted to get Tarkos."

"It's one of my fondest hopes, Tony, but I'm betting on Melissa to bury him."

He grimaced. "Okay, assuming she comes back and nails down her husband's coffin—how does that bag Ambrosino?"

"Occurs to me Tarkos may do some plea-bargaining, finger Ambrosino. That could be rewarded with a short sentence in not-too-unpleasant surroundings."

"And a sharp shank in the spine." He looked away, then down at his buffed fingernails. "A few blocks from Parsons's house, there's a corner playground, dark at night. There's a four-way stop sign. While he's stopped, we put a gun on him and both cars go around the back of the playground. There he's shown a videocassette and Sondra, and told what's expected of him. Ten minutes does it all."

"And who does he think is putting the arm on him?"

"Like you said—Ambrosino soldiers. What could go wrong?"

"Plenty, and you know it. Starting with Sondra."

"Sondra? She's a bold bitch, never worry."

"And when were you thinking of snatching, intimidating, and blackmailing this upstanding member of the bar?"

"Sooner the better. I'm running out of leave time. Tomorrow night?"

"I'll be in Dago, remember? Anyway, I'd want to case the setting."

"Then you're on."

"I'm thinking about it, that's all. Meanwhile, I suggest you stay close to Sondra, nail down her loyalty. If she chickens out that night, someone's fuckin' had it."

He gave me his big chili-eating grin. "I've stashed her in a safehouse we keep near the racetrack." He held up a key. "Funny about these lascivious ladies—she cherished the idea Tarkos was gonna marry her. Then she reads he married Melissa. After that, when she fucked for him, she fucked for cash."

"Smarter than I thought."

"Smart enough to learn from experience."

"So may we all," I said. "I'll phone you when I get back."

He wrote down a number and said, "Anyone but me or Sondra answers, hang up."

He poured himself a drink, gulped it down, touched his hat brim in a hokey salute and departed. I locked the door and returned to a working mode. After a while, I stopped typing and considered Tony's abduction plan. Nothing novel about it, just danger for all concerned. I hadn't told him, but what I'd get out of taking part would be punishing Parsons for his role in frightening Melissa back to Tarkos. A good enough motive.

Next afternoon, I reached Hatfield's office a bit before four. His secretary/receptionist recognized me and said Mr. Hatfield would be with me shortly. I scanned *USA Today* and presently Hatfield's door opened and he beckoned me in. When we were seated he said, "That's my third call to the *Flaminia*—docked in Nice. Captain says the owners are ashore, staying at the Negresco while they visit the tables at Monte Carlo a few miles away."

"I wouldn't think Tarkos would gamble at any tables but his own."

"Could be trying to make up for the loss of his diamonds."

"So?"

"I didn't feel it prudent to leave messages for my client. I'll just hope to catch her when she's in their suite."

"What'd you tell the captain?"

"Said I was her father, Professor Anders. Okay?"

"Very good. That conveys half the information she needs."

"Unfortunately, I haven't been able to locate her father—he's not back at classes, the dean doesn't know when he's returning, but understands he's recovering from mugging injuries."

"And the U.S. Attorney?"

"Ballantine's very relieved, says he has a handle on the situation now and she'll be welcomed back, no hard feelings. As to Parsons's unethical conduct, Arch agrees with me that Melissa's unsupported statement isn't enough for the Bar Grievance Committee to act on."

I looked over at the tropical fish. Late-afternoon sun through the clear tank added brilliance to their flashing colors. I said, "Suppose a U.S. Attorney were handed Tarkos's financial records. What would happen?"

His eyes narrowed. "Much would depend on the donor—how he or she acquired them. If they were, let's say, stolen, they'd be termed fruit of a poisoned tree—legalese, meaning they couldn't be used against him any more than illegal wiretaps can be introduced into evidence."

"Since we're hypothesizing, suppose those records came to Ballantine via U.P.S. Anonymously."

"Without looking up case law, I'd say the records would be admissible evidence. Got something in mind?"

"Vaguely. Very vaguely. Ah—did I mention Ambrosino offered five large if I give him Melissa?"

"Did you accept?"

"Immediately and gratefully."

He smiled. "I'd guess Raf wants the ins and outs of Tarkos's dealings."

"My thought, too. I did what I could to convey the impression Tarkos had been stealing from Raf's portion of the skim. It's an idea that's likely to grow—one he can't afford to ignore."

Hatfield's smile broadened. "I'd love to see that miserable old *capo* in prison."

"He's in bad shape, got maybe half a lung, possibly leg-paralyzed."

"Springfield's a hospital-prison for infirm felons. Let him live out his life there."

"Before that happens he could easily take my life."

"Too bad you were so broke you took that phony job in Baja."

"Too bad his son's missing as a result. Raf'll put out a contract on me just on suspicion. That's why I'm anxious to see fast moves against Ambrosino. LAPD's handling the murder of Fallon and Rinaldo, done by Raf's soldiers. Trouble is, they don't know which soldiers to go after, neither do I. But if they could grab one of the killers, they might flip him against Raf."

"Don't expect much on that score," Hatfield said sourly. "I've had experience in that area and I'd be willing to bet a thousand no one's ever convicted of those killings. Anyway, I'm told the LA police have jailed two suspects."

"Tarkos's creeps."

"That satisfies the press and the department. Which is," he said unhappily, "a large part of the law enforcement game." He glanced at the wall clock. "Still staying on your boat? When I reach my client I'll let you know." He stood up.

We shook hands, and by way of parting he said, "Anyone handling Tarkos's financial records would leave latent prints. Defense counsel would demand print identification—and get it."

"Interesting point of law," I remarked, thanked him for his time, and went down to my car.

I fought the go-home traffic rush for an hour and surrendered at Oceanside by pulling in at Clancy's, a seafood joint I'd come to know while stationed at Camp Pendleton. I sat at the cleanly holystoned bar and consumed beer-steamed shrimp with garlic bread and a couple of chilled steins of draft Coors. Off-duty Gyrenes were working noisily flashing game tables while working girls eyed them from side booths. The familiar scene was part of my service past and replicated in a score of bar-restaurants around Pendleton. I thought about Melissa in Nice–Monte Carlo and hoped Hatfield could reach her soon.

Then I considered Tony's extralegal plan to turn Parsons against his client and wondered if the operation was really necessary. When Melissa returned she could give Ballantine pretty much what he needed to build a case against Tarkos. Still, records were irrefutable evidence, and they were what Parsons could provide if he was sufficiently intimidated. As a shaggy, zoned-out Aztec, Tony could be pretty frightening to a civilian.

I paid my bill and left Clancy's, avoiding eye contact with the booth girls, got into my Datsun, and drove the rest of the way in thinning traffic to Marina del Rey.

No messages for me, so I dialed the Treasury safehouse from the pay phone. Tony answered with a gruff "Yeah?"

"Hello, Tlaloc," I said, "can you—?"

"*Tlaloc?* What's that?"

"The Aztec corn deity—king of corn. Is your informant still under control?"

"And eager to go. I figure we've got a winning combination."

"You sound like a Little League coach. Can I say something, Coach? I think this is a crazy idea."

"It was your idea, *'mano.*"

"It was? Then it has to have merit. So what time tomorrow do we meet?"

" 'Rendezvous' is the official word. We'll *rendezvous*—hey, Sondra *likes* that word, hear her back there?"

"She's a giggler. Beware of gigglers."

"All right—*en serio,* we'll get together at five-forty, Fallbrook and Ventura, the Hess gas station, and proceed to the playground ahead of target individual."

So that was it. The snatch was on.

TWENTY-TWO

The gas station had a three-stall, do-it-yourself car wash and six pumps. I filled my tank at one of them, paid, and pulled around the side to wait for Tony and Sondra. I'd never seen his car before, but he arrived in a five-year-old Chevy two-door, Sondra beside him. Tony wore a jacket over his lavender shirt, the usual Panama hat, and a ferocious grin on his face. He got out and came over to me. "Leave the heap over there, I'll tell the owner you're okay."

"Does he know *you're* okay?"

"Silvio's a distant cousin on my mother's side." He strolled into the office, came out a few moments later, and waved me to a parking spot. I locked the Datsun and followed him to the Chevy. Sondra looked up at me, waved one hand shyly, and said "Hi."

"Hi, Twinkie," I said. She got out and fitted herself into the back seat. As Tony pulled onto Fallbrook, she said, "Isn't this exciting?"

"Thrilling."

"I bet you'n Tony've done this lots of times—but it's a first for me."

"Just do what the man says. Got the videocassette?"

She held it up. "Nothing on it, y'know. Suppose Stanley wants to see it—like, to prove he'n I are the featured players?"

From the side of his mouth Tony said, "This car didn't come with a VCR player—he'll have to trust us."

I nodded agreement and said to Sondra, "Your role is largely a silent one, honey. Smile guiltily, whisper you're sorry you were forced into this, and keep clutching the cassette."

She nodded. "That's what Tony said. An' for your information, Joe,

I'm glad to cooperate with the government. Borden Tarkos is a stinkin', lyin', jerkoff bastard, an' I *hate* him."

Laconically, Tony said, "And Stanley Parsons is a scumbag, too, remember?"

"Right," she said firmly, "an' a lousy lay."

Tony flipped back the side of his jacket, exposing a shoulder holster. From it he drew a snub-nosed .38 revolver and laid it on my lap. "Feel in my pocket," he said. I groped and pulled out two black ski-masks. "We're in business," he said, hunched over the steering wheel, and drove to the Topanga Canyon Boulevard exit, turning south into Woodland Hills.

By now dusk was enveloping the hills and canyons of West L.A. Lights were coming on in hillside homes. Tony glanced at them, and said, "Nice to live around here. Not a hut under five hundred thou and a satellite dish on every one. If they ever kick out all the illegals, these people'll have to wash their own dishes, iron their own clothes, and mow their own lawns."

"So you've got a social conscience."

"Only as regards my own people. There's programs for blacks; nothing for wetbacks, so they have to work. Take a Mex—any Mex. All he wants is a chance to work, a job, so he crosses the line and comes north. The scummiest, dirtiest job in L.A. is better than the best he could hope for south of the line." He sighed. "A big country down there, with all that potential . . ."

After a while we came to a four-way stop with a large, empty playground on one corner. "This is it," Tony said, and looked at his big gold Omega watch. "We'll be parked over yonder, and in about half an hour Stanley's dark green Jaguar oughta show. You get in with him and follow me around behind the handball court. The Jaguar stops, I pull alongside and the chat begins." He looked around at Sondra. "*Chica*, you hearing this?"

"I got it all, Tony," she said in an almost worshipful voice. "You took me through it before."

"Okay, I'm hungry." He drove several blocks to a MacDonald's drive-through and ordered a Big Mac with fries and Coke for himself. I was too tense to eat—coffee for me, Coke for Sondra. While we were parked, Tony munching away, I unloaded his revolver and dropped the cartridges in his pocket. "To avoid accidental death," I explained, and stuck the empty weapon in my belt.

We returned to the playground corner and pulled over beside the curb, lights on. Tony watched the rearview mirror as occasional cars came up, stopped, and crossed the intersection. After a while he muttered, "I'da tailed him from his office, but I didn't want him spooked. Now I don't know when the bastard's coming."

Sondra leaned forward, face between us, and whispered, "I gotta go. I get nervous, I *gotta* go."

"Just hold it," Tony said severely. "Go when we get behind the handball court. Think of something else. Anyway, why be nervous? This is a piece of pizza. Federal agents gotta have big bladders."

She sat back and subsided into silence.

Two more cars came up, stopped, and drove on.

I said, "Tony, suppose things don't work out and you get busted out of Treasury?"

He turned to me and said thoughtfully. "Silvio would give me the car-wash concession. Says it's a real money-maker and the tips are good. Also, it's cash income—report what you want and keep the rest."

"Sounds ideal." His future looked assured. And if I was prosecuted for this unsound caper, maybe Joel could get me off with a first-offender's suspended. Maybe.

"Mexicans," Tony went on, "learn how to beat the system. They have to."

"Survival," I said, but he wasn't listening. His eyes were fixed on the mirror. Suddenly he began pulling the ski-mask over his head. I did likewise, adjusted the eye slit so I could see, and pulled out the short-barrel revolver.

"He's late," Tony growled, "but he's here."

"How—?" I began.

Tony said, "Jag headlight shape and spacing. It's him. Ready?"

Before I could answer, a sleek Jaguar salon model pulled up beside us. I shoved my arm over the doorsill and leveled the revolver a foot from the driver's face. "Hold it right there," I snapped, got out quickly, and opened his rear door. From behind the driver I pressed the revolver muzzle into his neck. He squealed like a rabbit and I thought he was going to faint. "Take it easy," I told him, "and nobody gets hurt. Follow the other car."

"Take my money," he babbled, "but don't hurt me. Take my money, the car—God, *please* don't hurt me!"

Tony moved out and turned down alongside the playground. I jammed the muzzle into Parsons's neck. "Move!"

Obediently, Parsons steered after Tony's Chevy, and when both cars were in the darkness behind the handball court I said, "Stop. Lights out."

Tony came over, followed slowly by Sondra. She said, "Hi, Stanley," and got in beside me. Tony got in the front seat beside the lawyer, who said, "What's this—blackmail?"

"Good thinking," Tony replied. "Sondra, show him the tape." She lifted it so he could glimpse the videocassette, and returned it to her lap. I heard Parsons sucking air between clenched teeth. "Borden photographed us," she said, "I guess you know that. I'm sorry, Stanley, they're making me do this." Having delivered her message, Sondra faced away, staring into the darkness. Tony said, "You can go now. Don't linger or I'll come after you."

She got out of the car and walked away. I said, "Stanley, you visited Melissa Tarkos, after which she disappeared and showed up abroad with Borden. What message did you give her?"

My eyes were adjusting to the darkness. As Parsons turned his head I saw thinning blond hair, rimless glasses, a long, thin nose, and a weak chin. He licked his lips and croaked, "I just told her that her husband was concerned about her well-being and wanted to see her."

I placed the revolver muzzle against his ear. "Uh-uh. You frightened her. How?"

Closing his eyes, Parsons inhaled deeply. "Who are you working for?"

"Guess."

He shook his head. "I don't want to."

Tony chuckled. "In Vegas there's an old man who's losing confidence in his partner. You being the partner's lawyer, he wants straight talk from you. He also wanted a sit-down with Mrs. Tarkos, but she ran away. He thinks you're responsible and he wants to know what you told her. Don't lie, Stanley."

"All right," Parsons said resignedly. "Okay. I was ordered to tell Mrs. Tarkos her boyfriend and father would be killed if she didn't go back to Borden."

"With the money," I said.

"If she still had it."

"Did she?" I asked.

"By then she'd turned over most of it in diamonds to the U.S. Attorney." He shivered. "That's not my fault. Tell Raf, will you? Borden sent me too late."

"Sure," said Tony, "we'll tell Don Rafaello but he won't like it worth a damn. He figures Tarkos's been dipping into the skim. You can square yourself with the family by turning over Tarkos's books and financial records. Otherwise, that tape of you and Sondra goes to your wife, copies to your partners."

"Oh, God," he breathed, "you'll ruin me."

"You ruined yourself," I said, "by taking part in an ongoing crime and threatening a government witness. Now it's make-up time. Cooperate, Stanley. The books and financial records."

"Tarkos'll kill me," he blurted.

"Not if we tell him not to," Tony said. "We're your best hope—your only hope—of living to a respectable old age."

Sondra came toward us through the darkness and got in beside me. She said, "I could phone your wife, Stanley, have lunch with her and tell her all the kinky things you like. Remember my leather boots and bra? I'll bet she's not into leather the way you like . . ."

Tony picked up, adding, "The tape shows it all, Stanley. It could be put out commercial all over the world. Someone'll recognize the big L.A. lawyer giving head to this lovely lady."

Parsons began hyperventilating. *"My heart,"* he gasped. *"Weak heart."*

"Take it easy," Tony soothed. "Cooperate and put all this behind you. What's to worry about?"

"Tarkos—what do I tell him?" His breathing slowed.

"Nothing," I said.

"He keeps his records at home."

"But you've got copies," Tony said. "Your firm handles his financial reporting. Tell you what, Stanley, lend us those files for a few days, we'll make copies and give the files back to you."

"You'd do that?" he said beseechingly. "Can I trust you?"

"Have to," I said. "Like you have to trust us with the porno tape. Everything private. Between us, you, and the Don."

I thought he was going to cry. Instead he managed to whimper, "I don't have any choice. Borden's a terrible man anyway. I can do it with a clear conscience."

"Good thinking," Tony remarked, "and now we'll go back to your office and collect what we want—all of it, Stanley, no holding out."

"Oh, God, no," he wheezed. "I'll do just what you say. Only, please, *please* don't show that tape to anyone."

Tony looked back at me. "I'll ride with Mr. Parsons. You and Sondra follow."

I passed Tony his revolver, and Sondra and I got out of the Jaguar. We got into the Chevy. Presently the Jaguar engine started, headlights flared, and when it cleared the playground I started the Chevy and followed. Sondra said, "Better take off the face mask, Joe."

"Yeah," I said, "I forgot," and pulled it off.

"What a wimp," she said after a while. "The way he rolled over for you guys. Just like you said."

"We haven't got the records yet," I said, turning east on Ventura. "Stanley could try something."

"I'm betting on Tony," she said admiringly. "What a guy. What a macho male!"

"He's okay," I agreed, a little miffed that my performance hadn't matched his.

There was no traffic to speak of, and we reached Century City in about twenty minutes. At the building entrance Parsons got out, and Tony drove the Jaguar off into shadows. I wondered if he was still wearing the face mask, and followed, parking about fifty feet away—in case Parsons emerged with a crowd of cops.

Lights off, we waited.

After ten minutes Sondra said, "How long does it take to open a file drawer and empty it?"

"Shouldn't take long, but Parsons probably has to turn off the alarm system and all that. And there could be people still working in the office."

"That's true," she said uncertainly. "Joe, I did okay, didn't I?"

"Letter perfect," I assured her.

"Can I go now?"

"You'll go home with Tony."

"And you?"

"Back to my floating palace."

One finger touched the side of my face. "We had fun there, didn't we?"

"Fantastic," I said truthfully. "You're all woman, never doubt it."

Six minutes more and Parsons came out of the office building. Unaccompanied, I was glad to see, and carrying a large litigation bag. He walked directly to the Jaguar and I started the Chevy. Tony got out, took the bag from Parsons, and said a few words. I steered toward them, but not so close Parsons could see my unmasked face. As Tony walked toward me he pulled off the ski mask, gave me a thumb-up sign, and got into the rear seat. We ducked Parsons's headlights as he turned the Jag around and headed out, and when he was on Santa Monica, Tony slapped my shoulder exultantly. "We did it!"

"We did it," I echoed. "Are you really going to copy all that stuff?"

"Sure—there's an all-night copy center near the university. We'll drop you off at Silvio's and Sondra'n me'll do the rest."

At the Hess station I got into my Datsun while Tony gave Cousin Silvio a big *abrazo*. There being nothing more to discuss, I drove to the nearest bar, gulped down a double Beam, and headed south to the marina.

My sleep was shallow, and as I turned on the bunk I wondered what we'd have done if Parsons *had* suffered a heart attack. Any way I looked at the episode, we were lucky to get out of it unscathed and with what we were after. How Tony got the records to where they'd be welcomed was his problem, but he was resourceful enough to do it. SuperMex, I thought, and fell asleep.

Two mornings later I stopped typing and went to the marina office for messages. There was only one: *Call Joel*, it said. *Urgent.*

When I got him on the line, Hatfield asked, "Read the papers?"

"No. What's happened?"

"Tarkos fell, jumped, or was pushed from his hotel balcony—five stories. He's dead, and the police are holding Melissa."

Her words, *I hate him enough to kill him*, flashed through my mind as Hatfield continued: "I'm on a five o'clock flight to Paris, but before that, maybe we ought to talk."

"I'll fly down," I said. "Be there in a couple of hours."

"Good. Bear in mind, French law is different than ours. Under the

Napoleonic Code, you're presumed guilty—have to prove yourself innocent."

The thought of Melissa behind bars sickened me. At that moment I didn't care whether she'd killed her husband. The only thing that mattered was getting her free.

TWENTY-THREE

Seated before Joel Hatfield, I said, "I'm going with you."

Slowly he shook his head. "I considered that and found it a very poor idea. The boyfriend shows up to console the widow who may be charged with murder. Think about it."

"All right," I said reluctantly, "I guess you're right. But tell Melissa I wanted to come."

"I will. And for your information, I reached her by phone just after you were last here. Tarkos wasn't around so we were able to talk freely. I told her you and her father were safe and Ballantine would welcome her back. Tarkos must have come in then, because she hung up."

"Then she called you from Nice—from the jail?"

"No, the U.S. Consulate phoned me, saying she wanted me there to represent her. Of course, I can't do that in French courts, but on the Consulate's recommendation I've retained a well-known *avocat*, Emil Desjardins. I'll give him some background on the couple's troubled marriage, try to buck up Melissa's morale, and come back." He spread his palms upward on the desk. "Nothing more I can do."

"So Melissa knew from you that Tarkos had no further leverage on her."

"And the next night, about two o'clock in the morning, Tarkos took a header off their balcony. The French, of course, don't know about my call to her. If they did, they'd theorize cause and effect."

"What are the grounds for jailing her?"

"Their form of preventive detention—for questioning, is the reason given." He eyed me speculatively. "You think she killed Tarkos?"

"I don't think I should answer that. Obviously, it's a possibility, unless circumstances rule it out. On the flight I read the press account of the incident. The couple went to bed as usual after an evening at Monte Carlo, and Melissa was wakened by a cry. When she didn't find her husband beside her she went to the balcony—door open, curtains blowing—and saw his body lying below."

Hatfield breathed deeply. "Not much, eh?"

"Anyone else in the room? Did she hear a struggle going on?"

"I don't know what she's told the police, but I hope very little. Besides, Joe, that unknown intruder bit has been done to death. It's a tale with no future."

"Tarkos could have lost heavily at the tables, then killed himself. That's not unknown in Monte Carlo."

"Desjardins's investigators will determine how much Tarkos won or lost. But a man who can afford a large pleasure yacht and owns a variety of lucrative businesses is probably not going to take a dive because of gambling losses. At least, that's what the French are likely to presume. So, preliminarily, it comes down to whether Tarkos jumped or was pushed. And the only one around who could have pushed him was his wife."

"Maybe Tarkos was drunk, got up in a daze, wandered onto the balcony, lost his balance, and fell."

He dismissed my suggestion. "Another negative point—they were to have left Nice next morning. It was their last night ashore." He sat forward, folded his hands together, and studied them. "I want the truth to this question: did she ever tell you directly or by implication that she was sufficiently alienated from Tarkos that she wanted to kill him?"

"No," I lied. "And consider this—if she planned to murder Tarkos she'd have stayed around him, not fled as she did."

"That can be adduced," he said, "but it's balanced by her motive."

"Motive? You mean the way he degraded her?"

"No, and I hope *that* aspect will never surface. I mean money as a motive. I don't know how she's provided for in Tarkos's will—she might be slated to inherit everything—but under California law she'll get at least half of his estate, unless she's convicted of murdering him. And the estate probably runs to, oh, say, fifty million dollars. Many, many people have been murdered for much, much less." He leaned back in his chair, looked upward at the soft, midday lighting. "Other than a sister floating around somewhere in the background, Tarkos has no known relations. The sister's got a long history of mental illness, been in and out of institutions most of her adult life. She could create a problem by asserting a claim to Tarkos's estate, but provable mental incompetence should invalidate such a claim."

"Out of fifty million, Melissa can afford to provide for her."

"Except that crazies are unpredictable—but she's not an immediate problem; others are more pressing. For example, the French will interview the yacht crew and hotel employees to ascertain whether there was any appearance of hostility between Melissa and her husband. If there was, she's in deep trouble."

A chill spread from my inner core. To suppress it I said, "There's another possibility, Joel: Ambrosino had reason to suspect Tarkos cheated him. Ambrosino could have sent a soldier from Sicily to waste him."

"How would that benefit old Raf?"

"He collects what's due him from the widow."

Hatfield thought it over. "The French wouldn't attempt to investigate Raf Ambrosino. Why should they when this country, with all our resources and manpower, has hardly laid a finger on him?"

"Her lawyer could assert it, create doubt about her guilt."

He made a note on a scratch pad. "I'll mention it to Desjardins. Have you talked with her father?"

"Haven't tried."

"He's back at classes. I spoke with him this morning."

"Is he going to Melissa?"

"Like you, he wanted to, but I don't want him subjected to questioning. He knows too much about that bizarre marriage and what went on. Under pressure he might talk—and put his daughter's neck on the guillotine. No, Professor Anders is going to stay put and profess his daughter's innocence to the media every chance he gets. At least that's what I recommended." His gaze traveled to the office vault. "That package you left—should I take it to her?"

"Leave it here, just tell her it exists."

He made another note on his pad, his secretary buzzed, and Hatfield spoke into the intercom: "I'll be with him shortly." He turned to me. "I'm trying to take care of other clients' affairs before I leave. Anything we missed?"

I shook my head.

"Follow the case in the papers. I'll phone you when I get back."

"When's that likely to be?"

"I'm estimating a week."

I got up and placed my hands on the desk edge. "Tell her I love her."

"I will."

Three clients were in the waiting room. I nodded at the receptionist and took an elevator to the street. A taxi rode me to Lindbergh Field, where I caught the next flight to Los Angeles.

I was back at Marina del Rey before Hatfield's flight left for France.

Toward evening, Tony Honey came aboard, tossed his Panama on a bunk, and slouched down beside it. "How's your morale?"

"Not good. Yours?"

He shrugged. "If I'd known Tarkos was going to be disposed of, squeezing Parsons wouldn't have been necessary."

"So I've been thinking." I shoved aside the typewriter. Nothing good had come out of it since I'd learned Melissa was in jail.

"While his estate's being probated, IRS will examine his financial records. Maybe they'll lead to Ambrosino, maybe not. I looked them over but I'm not an accountant. I learned one thing, though. The widow gets everything."

"Everything?"

"Except a hundred thousand Tarkos left to a sister in Anaheim. She might contest the will. But if your lady is convicted of murder, the sister gets it all."

"The sister's supposed to be a nut case, but a crack at fifty million could restore sanity in a hurry."

Tony nodded agreement, and I went on to summarize my session with Joel Hatfield. "So how do you weigh Melissa's chances?"

"I think her lawyer will have a hard time proving she didn't kill Tarkos—if it comes to a trial. You figure she did it?"

"She had strong motives," I conceded, "but why do it in a way that would cast immediate suspicion on her?"

"Opportunity," he suggested. "She sees Tarkos gazing at the soft Mediterranean moonlight, tiptoes up behind, and over he goes."

Tony got up and went to the liquor cabinet. "Other wives have done it, husbands too." While he was pouring a drink I said I'd like the same. Holding our glasses, we looked at each other until Tony said, "Seems that was their last night ashore, Joe. She could have figured it was then or never." He drank deeply and so did I. "Anyway," he went on, "her future is your problem, not mine."

That was true, and I was powerless to resolve it. "You place Parsons's files in the hands of duly constituted authorities?"

"Copies, and indirectly. Now I'm glad I didn't claim credit." He drank moodily. "Sondra was pleased about Tarkos's demise—less pleased when I advised her her career as confidential informant had come to an end. I paid her a few hundred and wished her a brilliant future." He gestured with his head. "I see their boat's gone."

"Hadn't noticed."

"So long, Glenda, so long, Twinkie," he muttered, and drank again. Tony seemed as dispirited as I was.

To break the silence I said, "The scenario I like is that Ambrosino was out big bucks due to Tarkos's chicanery. Tarkos wouldn't pay him back, so Raf puts out a Sicilian contract on Tarkos. The job is done smoothly and Melissa takes the blame."

"It's possible," he said, "but even if it happened like that, who's to prove it?"

I couldn't answer that. Instead, I said, "Raf's now had plenty of time to get an on-the-scene report from the Baja cabin. No one knows who Pancho, the Indian driver, is, but Raf damn well knows who I am and that worries me plenty."

"It should."

"So?"

"Watch your back, stay out of dark places. Anyway, my leave's over and tomorrow I report for assignment. Whatever it is, it won't be Ambrosino. Dino was my target, and you took care of him. Raf belongs to the Vegas Strike Force. They're all white-collar, three-piece-suiters, and this Indian wouldn't fit in." He shrugged philosophically. "I came to say goodbye, *'mano*—it's been an interesting relationship."

"Share the good times, share the bad," I intoned. "Take care of yourself, *amigo.*"

"You, too." He drank the last of his drink and, carrying his Panama hat, went up the companionway. I stood at the bottom looking after him, and heard him step onto the pier.

Moments later came the sharp crack of a high-powered rifle, the unmistakable sound of a body hitting concrete, then squealing tires and racing engine. I bolted up the companionway and looked out.

Tony's body lay crumpled a few feet away on the pier.

Even in the near-darkness I could see that half his head was blown away.

TWENTY-FOUR

The prowlies came first and roped off the crime scene, then the ambulance arrived. Homicide made up the third echelon, and while the Crime Unit was photographing everything in sight, Lieutenant Pendergast and Sergeant Dolfuz sat in my cabin, asking questions and taking notes.

After I'd satisfactorily identified myself, Pendergast said, "This fellow—the deceased—have any enemies you know of?"

"He may have, may not. I hardly knew him. We met in the bar over there—the Beachcomber—about two weeks ago, maybe less. He came by a couple of times, and we'd drink here or at the Beachcomber. Said his name was Tony Honey."

"Antonio F. Honey," Dolfuz supplied. "Weird name for a Latino. Tell you where he worked?"

"Said he was a government employee with a couple of weeks' leave."

"How about you?" Pendergast asked. "You have any enemies?"

"Why? Think he was mistaken for me?"

"I don't know—just covering bases, Mr. Brent. How about it? Enemies?"

"None who want to kill me," I lied. "I'm just an unemployed TV writer, separated from my wife."

"Ah," said Dolfuz, scratching his right ear, "how big an insurance policy you carry?"

"G.I.—ten thousand. A skilled marksman would want at least half that to make the hit."

"You heard a car tearing away. Did you see it?"

"No. I was staring at the body."

"How many shots? Just the one?"

"One's all I heard."

"From how far off, would you say?"

"Seventy yards—under a hundred."

The lieutenant looked at his notebook and repeated what I'd said before. "This friend—Tony—came by for a drink—"

"He was less friend than acquaintance."

"—and about fifteen minutes later he walked up these steps and you heard the shot. That it?"

"Right."

"What were you—more important, he—talking about that quarter-hour?"

"Mainly he was saying he wouldn't be around anymore—vacation was over, he had to go back to work."

"Then?"

"Then he finished his drink—" I pointed at our two glasses. "He went topside, and you know the rest."

"I wish we did," said Pendergast, "like who shot him and why." He put away his notebook and got up. Sergeant Dolfuz also rose. Pendergast said, "You'll be around?"

"I'm living aboard until the boat's sold." I grimaced. "Trying to write a novel."

He gestured at the pier. "Maybe that'll give you inspiration."

"I doubt it," I said. "Just the shakes."

They nodded at me, climbed the companionway, and disappeared from view.

I picked up my empty glass and looked at Tony's. I couldn't bring myself to touch it—not yet. A good man had taken a bullet intended for me. I knew it and I'd take the knowledge to my grave. As I poured liquor into my glass I heard another police car growl up—probably the medical examiner; the body couldn't be moved until he okayed it. I reached up and locked the cabin doors, then opened my small refrigerator and took out Tony's Treasury credentials.

While I was kneeling beside his body I'd removed the card from his jacket pocket because I didn't want his Treasury connection publicized—not right away. And a vague thought had flashed through my mind as I stared at his blown-apart head—I might be able to use his official I.D. in some way to avenge him.

Anyway, I'd removed it, hidden it, and had it now.

The Maricopa Kid, I thought, and my eyes filled with tears.

I could visualize the sniper waiting in the car, rifle ready, expecting me to come up from the cabin. He hadn't seen Tony arrive, so he sighted on the man who appeared topside. I hadn't turned on any of the normal rigging lights, and in the dimness the rifleman mistook Tony for me. Well, the late edition would clear that up, and a hit man would come again.

Inevitably, Treasury investigators would also come and ask the same questions I'd answered for Pendergast and Dolfuz, but they might have more background than I was willing to give the police. And they would want to know what the hell Tony had been messing around with during his two weeks' leave. Without implicating myself in the Parsons snatch, I couldn't tell them.

Somehow I'd been located; however it was done, my refuge was known and no longer safe. I had to leave and travel light. And as I reflected on what faced me, I realized that my situation was much the same as Melissa's when she fled from Tarkos. Both of us running to save our lives.

And, like Melissa, I knew exactly who wanted my life: Don Rafaello Ambrosino, avenging the death of his son.

Voices filtered in from outside: police shouting commands; media reporters asking questions, taping on-the-spot reports; crowd noises —and finally the ambulance sirening away, bearing one D.O.A.

My mind flashed back to Beirut and I saw blood and crushed, fragmented bodies, smelled the smoke and heard the cries of the dying. And for a moment, surmounting it all like a black sun, was the turbaned head and whiskered cheeks of Satan himself, only the face wasn't the Ayatollah's—it was the pale, hook-nosed visage of Raf Ambrosino. Breathing quickened and my pulse began to race. Finally, I forced my mind back to here and now, and strength seemed to drain away.

It took a while to shake off shock-induced lethargy, and by then the cops and medics were gone, the crowd dispersed. Two TV crews remained, focusing on the blood-stained concrete until some boater with a sense of decency hosed it clean.

While that was going on, I forced myself to focus on my situation, evaluate it, and put together an initial course of action. After that, I washed the two liquor glasses, straightened the rumpled bunk, and snapped the top on my portable.

I laid draft pages in the cabinet, from which I took my revolver, and fitted on the shoulder holster. Then I put a clean shirt and shaving kit in an athletic bag and wrote a note to Madeleine Gossons saying I'd be away for a while and out of touch; take the first offer for twenty-five. I figured I had an hour to clear the marina before black hats came around to correct the marksman's mistake, so I moved fast.

After locking the cabin doors I went to the marina office and checked for messages. None. From there I walked back to the Datsun and drove over to Semmes & Co. The yacht brokers' office was dark, but I stuffed my note under the door—Maddy had a duplicate set of keys. Then I got into my car and began driving toward L.A. and my apartment.

I tuned the A.M. dial to an all-news station, and within five minutes heard a flash report—unidentified man killed by sniper fire at Marina del Rey harbor. No witnesses to the shooting, but a friend of the slain man heard the shot. Police officials had no comment, pending identification of the victim and notification of next-of-kin. He was described as a Hispanic-appearing male, between thirty and thirty-five. Anyone having knowledge of the victim of the apparently random crime was requested to contact police immediately.

Damn it, they were telling too much. Raf and his thugs knew I wasn't Hispanic-appearing—so did the sniper. I prayed he'd return to the marina and give me time in my apartment.

A surge of adrenalin purged fear from my brain, and I felt driven, compelled, invincible. My mood was vengeful, dangerous.

I went into my apartment, hand on my Cobra's grip, ready to blast anyone in my way. But the apartment was as I'd left it; dark, air stale. I took the ice-cube tray from the freezer and carefully melted out the diamond. Cashed in, it would pay for a lot of travel. I rolled down my left sock and taped the diamond behind my ankle bone, in the hollow by the Achilles tendon.

Next, I pocketed Tony's Treasury credentials, ready to impersonate a federal officer if it took that to get within shooting range of Raf Ambrosino. Talk alone wouldn't do it.

For twenty years and more the old Don had lived untouched by the law, but he wasn't immune to those who didn't follow the law's rigid rules. He'd been blasted by determined enemies but not killed. I proposed to finish what they'd failed to do.

Not only to avenge Tony's murder, but to save my own life. For, until Don Raf was dead, I'd never sleep a night, walk a block, or drive a mile without fearing assassins. Death was preferable to living in fear.

And there was Melissa to consider. She was Raf's target, too.

I dropped a box of .38 soft-point cartridges in my carry-bag, added socks and underwear from my drawer, and scanned the apartment for perhaps the last time. It wasn't much of a place, I hadn't enjoyed its cheap confinement, but I'd always remember how it sheltered Melissa the night we met.

Nothing left to do.

Feeling freed and purposeful, I exited the building by the back door and walked to where I'd left the Datsun. From there I followed the Santa Monica Freeway east to Boyle Heights, then north on the feeder highway through East L.A. and onto the San Bernardino Freeway. I drove just under the speed limit, not wanting to be stopped for speeding, maybe get frisked and found with Tony's I.D. Uh-uh.

Rosemead, Covina, Bonnell Park, Ontario, and finally, the interchange where Route 15 slanted northeast through San Bernardino National Forest, and on across the state line into Nevada. The car's AM radio bands had been keeping me aware of changing cultural zones: from sobbing mariachi and pounding congas the theme shifted to L.A. rappers, Hammer, Sting, Bon Jovi, and Mariah Carey, eastward into Willie Nelson, Tammy Wynette, Garth Brooks, Reba McIntyre, the Mandrells, Randy Travis, the funky folk of Judy Collins, and the soaring, incandescent flute of Nestor Torres.

Far from the City of Angels, moonlight whitened the bleak Mojave. Stars glittered, the straight road made driving effortless, and I felt as though I were speeding through space. Then I noticed the white line drifting, and quickly centered the car, realizing I'd come close to road hypnosis.

At the next diner I pulled in for two cups of black coffee and gasoline. Hit the road again.

At eleven I crossed the state line, and by midnight I was entering the brilliant starburst that was Las Vegas.

McCarran Airport offered long-term parking. I took the automatic ticket and located a dark corner, where I left the car. Carrying my bag, I walked to the bus stop and rode an air-conditioned bus to the edge of town. I got off by an old motel, the kind built in one long row of ten-by-twelve rooms, single window, toilet, shower, and basin. I paid the grizzled clerk for three nights in advance, lay down on the sagging bed, and slept until bright sunshine seared my eyelids apart. I showered, shaved, put on a clean shirt, my holstered .38 and jacket, and left my room.

Ready to hunt down Raf Ambrosino.

Buona sera, goombah.

Adios, capo.

TWENTY-FIVE

As I rode the bus toward Sin City, I thought back over the past three weeks, reflecting that chance had dealt me a very strange hand. Whereas before meeting Melissa I had been a law-abiding, unemployed writer leading an unexciting, pedestrian life, I had since become a killer, an obstructor of justice, the lover of a woman suspected of murdering her husband, and the target of Mafia hit men. I had taken part in abduction and extortion with a buddy whose death was intended to be mine.

And now I was getting my act together so that I could liquidate one of the nation's most notorious gangsters.

Everything incongruous to the placid, innocuous life I had known. Without Dr. Jekyll's potion I had turned into Mr. Hyde.

The shoulder holster prodded my ribs, and I shifted position to get more comfortable. From time to time the bus stopped for boarding or dismounting passengers. The morning air was diamond-clear and the distant mountains were as sharply defined as a meticulously painted backdrop. I liked the space of the desert, the openness that translated into easier human relationships. And I'd always felt sorry for city kids who'd grown up in apartments, played hazardously on city streets. Lacking horizons as children, they matured with limited vision, contented with narrow boundaries, fearful of the unconfined.

As a boy I'd hiked the hills and valleys of Schoharie County, shot fat black squirrels in autumn hickory copses with my first .22, heard the resonant drumming of grouse deep within pine woods, folded thundering ringnecks in their frantic flight, and trailed big snowshoe rabbits over fields deep with new-fallen snow. And I'd learned there was no silence like the stillness of a forest in the grip of winter.

At the time I'd never thought I had a privileged upbringing, but now, in retrospect, I realized how rich it really was.

We were entering America's Babylon. I went forward and asked the driver to recommend a good place for breakfast.

He smiled and said, "Where I eat—One-Eye Jack's. A dollar ninety-nine buys all you can hold, free coffee refills."

"My kind of place. Thanks."

"I'll tell you where to get off."

A few minutes more and the bus pulled to the curb. The driver pointed down the intersecting street and said, "Halfway down the block. Have a good day, friend."

"You too," I said, thinking few New York or L.A. drivers would have called me—or anyone—"friend."

The restaurant was fronted with plate glass, painted in foot-high letters with its name, and two depictions of its namesake: a bushy-haired man wearing a pirate eyepatch and handlebar mustache. If the painting lacked versimilitude, I didn't care. The aroma of frying ham, bacon, beans, and coffee as I entered was enough to make a dead man salivate.

Breakfast was served from a buffet behind which white-capped Mexican chefs fried, scrambled, or poached eggs to your taste. There were pitchers of cold juice; thick, delicately browned biscuits; warming pans of bacon, sausage and ham; hash browns, French toast, flapjacks, applesauce, syrup, baked beans, chili beans, and a ten-gallon coffee urn beside a pitcher of fresh cream. I helped myself lavishly, gave the cashier two dollars and carried my heavy tray to a table with a penny change.

Seated, I could see more deeply inside the place. Inevitably, the walls were lined with slot machines, electronic games, and big wire birdcages with six-inch plastic dice. No baccarat, no wheels or card games, just the bread-and-butter bandits whose profits made up for the loss-leader food.

There were the proverbial little old ladies who cranked and fed the slots from change-heavy carpenter aprons frayed from wear. Now and then I'd hear the bells and jingling burst of a noisy payoff, but mostly it was the steady rhythm of crank, whirr, click, crank, whirr, click.

One-Eye Jack's wasn't Harrah's, the Sands, or any of the other famous big casinos, and wasn't competing with them. It drew proletariat who could venture twenty or thirty bucks at the quarter slots, and like almost every other business in Vegas, it was open 'round the clock.

Immediate hunger satisfied, I ate more slowly, enjoying the hearty food. Two cups of coffee cleared my pipes, and as I dabbed my lips with a paper napkin I reflected that my cholesterol/triglyceride count had hit emergency-room levels. Well, so be it; I might not have long to live, so why not enjoy available creature pleasures? Life itself was brief, and I'd be dead forever.

Beside a pay phone I checked the yellow pages and found what I was looking for. The cashier told me the place was four blocks away and went to considerable trouble giving me directions.

As I went out, two weary-eyed showgirls pushed in, looking as if they'd hiked all night from Reno in their black vinyl boots, purple crotch-hugging shorts, and magenta tank-tops. They and their sisters were the sparrows who fed from the fringes of the big casinos' heavy action. They flocked to Vegas hoping to be noticed by a producer or claimed by a big spender, revalidating the showgirl's perennial dream.

Walking away from Jack's I thought about Melissa and wondered if Joel Hatfield and the French lawyer had been able to do her any good. If she were tried for murdering Tarkos, a jury of Nice townspeople would probably convict her out of envy over her wealth and beauty, evidence aside. So it seemed paramount that *avocat* Desjardins elect trial by judge if he couldn't prevent her indictment. But what did I know about French law or judicial procedures? A good deal less than I knew about American legal process.

Without realizing it, I'd almost walked past the Blue Star Theatrical Costumery, so I went back and turned in. A bald man wearing spectacles and a checkered vest had his elbows on the counter, reading a newspaper. The entrance bell jangled as I opened and closed the door. Looking up he said, "Morning, sir. What can I do for you?"

"Everything, I hope." I walked to the counter and sat down. "I bet a friend I could ride a bus with him and not be recognized."

He nodded. "So you need a disguise." Stepping back, he studied my face. "How about a Hasidic costume—hat, beard, spectacles?"

"Little too noticeable around Vegas," I demurred. "I was thinking more of a wig and mustache . . . glasses . . . makeup tends to run in this heat."

"You're right there. Come on back with me."

I followed him into a small makeup room whose mirror was framed with lightbulbs. I sat down and waited, and in a little while he brought in half a dozen wigs and an assortment of matching mustaches. The red wig was too garish; the gray too old for my face, so I settled on a wig with long black hair, and a broad black mustache. He brushed and combed the wig hair, sprayed it from an aerosol can, and applied spirit gum to the mustache backing.

While I was studying the transformation in the mirror, he handed me a pair of black-rimmed glasses, saying, "Nonrefractive lenses." I put them on and studied myself again. "Well," he said, "think that'll do it?"

"My friends won't know me, much less my enemies. How much?"

We went back to the counter, he added the items on his calculator, and said, "One seventy-eight. Mind if I ask how much the bet is?"

"Two hundred," I told him, "so if I win I clear twenty-two bucks profit—but it's the satisfaction of winning."

He smiled. "You gamblers are all the same," he remarked, took my money and made change. He resumed reading his paper while I borrowed his Classified directory and looked up jewelry appraisers. I read three addresses aloud and the costumer told me the nearest was two blocks away. I thanked him and went out.

The appraisal fee was one percent of appraised value, a counter plaque informed me. The jeweler took my diamond, fitted on his loupe, and studied it under a high-intensity lamp. After that he disappeared into the back of the store for refractive analysis, he told me, and came back five minutes later, returning the diamond in a small, velvet-lined box. "At retail," he said, "your stone would be priced around five thousand dollars. Wholesale, three thousand to maybe three-five. If you pawn it, you might realize two thousand. That'll be fifty dollars, please."

"How much would you give me for the stone?"

He removed the loupe and pocketed it. His right index finger tapped slowly on the counter top. "Two thousand."

I laid a twenty-dollar bill beside his hand. He looked at it, then his eyes met mine. "Fifty."

I pointed at the plaque. "You get one percent of the appraisal figure. You've appraised its worth at two thousand. So you get twenty dollars." I dropped the boxed diamond in my pocket.

"Wait a minute," he said, "what's the hurry? I underestimated you." His shoulders slumped and he sighed, "Me and my big mouth. Okay, I'll give you twenty-two for the stone."

"Twenty-five—you can sell it for double."

"Not much demand for diamonds. Divorcees and gamblers flood the market. Twenty-four."

I picked up my twenty-dollar bill and tucked it away. "Twenty-four. Cash."

"I can give you a check."

"Casinos don't take checks. We'll go to your bank."

He locked up the place and we went to his bank a block away. I waited while he got the cash and we made the exchange at a customer counter. "Mind a piece of advice?" he asked. "Put plane fare home in a separate envelope and leave it in your room. Blow the rest but never touch travel money."

"Thanks," I said, "I won't."

"That was the voice of experience you just heard. These casinos weren't organized to transfer capital to the public. The odds are against you."

I nodded. Only I knew how heavy the odds were. "How far's the Sagebrush from here?"

"A taxi ride." His eyes narrowed. "Why drop your roll at Mafia headquarters?"

I put on a surprised expression. "That what it is? I heard the food and entertainment were good."

"Naturally. Because the big chief lives in the penthouse. Well, be lucky." He sauntered off, calculating future profits from the stone, and I counted my bankroll. With the sale money I had over three thousand dollars—enough for a medium-priced coffin with fifty for the padre. I left the bank and taxied to the Sagebrush Hotel Casino.

The façade was mission-style architecture for the first two floors, then a setback from which rose twelve undistinguished stories of windowed rooms, topped with a railed penthouse. I could glimpse a couple of sun umbrellas beyond the topmost railing and nothing else.

The lobby had a terrazzo floor and a few potted palms near the registration desk. There were no reading chairs or sofas in the lobby. Management wanted customers on their feet and moving around the gaming area, which began immediately beyond the lobby. That early in the day not all tables were manned, but there were four scantily clad girls dealing blackjack, the dice tables were busy, and one roulette wheel was in operation. No uniformed security types in view, but I spotted three husky young men in leisure suits whose invisible weapons had worn shiny places on their coats. Widely spaced, the three guards moved counter-clockwise around the big room, which was back-up surveilled by video cameras. Other cameras looked down on the wheels and faro tables. In the far corner there was a convenience bar for gambling patrons, and beyond that a large, darkened restaurant with a band pit and a raised, curtained stage.

I turned my back on all this and scanned the lobby again. There was a double bank of elevators beyond the registration desk, and just by the casino entrance a single elevator door set almost flush with the wall. A neatly dressed man in a black suit stood beside it. No call buttons—the elevator responded to the turn of a key.

Ambrosino's private access to his headquarters, not for public use.

I walked toward it and saw a telephone box set into the wall behind the black-suited guard. I assumed it was there so the guard could clear visitors to the penthouse. And I recognized the guard as Marco, one of the three soldiers who had invaded my apartment with their *capo*. When his gaze swept across me, I nodded genially as any out-of-town rube might do, and walked past him to the registration desk.

The clerk was a smooth-shaven, olive-skinned young man whose black hair was teased into a swept-up pompadour. He regarded me with faint interest, said, "Sir?" as I planted my hands on the counter edge. "How much's a room cost here?"

"Single, sir? That's a hundred dollars a night. With it you get continental breakfast and twenty in chips."

"So let's see, that breaks out at about seventy-five for the room, right?"

"About that. Checking in?"

"I might at that. Where do I sign?"

He flicked a registration card across the counter and I printed the name Michael Z. Phillips with a fabricated address in Kansas City. I signed and pushed the card back. He scanned it and said, "Credit card?"

"My wife would scream at the charges, see? Has to be cash."

"Then I'll have to ask for two nights in advance."

I extracted my wallet and laid two bills on the counter. The clerk took them to the cashier and returned with a receipt.

"I'd like a high-up room—for the view."

Turning around, he surveyed the room-key boxes. "Tenth high enough?"

"How many floors you got?"

"Twelve plus penthouse, but that's private."

I grinned stupidly. "That where Howard Hughes died?"

"No, sir, this hotel wasn't Hughes property. And he died in the Bahamas." He handed me the key to room 1002 and four yellow chips. "Baggage?"

"I'll get it from the bus station."

"Enjoy your stay."

"I aim to."

Between guest elevators an easel displayed a large photograph set against white poster cardboard. I assumed it was advertising a cabaret entertainer until the word *tennis* caught my eye. Hand-printed in bold tempera colors, the announcement read:

> Our tennis pro is available for private or group instruction by appointment. See Social Director for details.

The name below the photograph was Rene Keats.

I remembered him now—Melissa's lover until Tarkos discovered the affair and transferred Rene from Beverly Hills.

Rene Keats's face was smooth, tanned, handsome, and utterly without character. His hair was dark brown. Tight ringlets cascaded down the back of his neck almost to the collar of his white Lacoste shirt. Sensual lips smiled at the world invitingly and I thought that he was probably making a good living from his female students after hours. The Lakeside Tennis Club would doubtless object to such liaisons, but not the Sagebrush or any other Vegas hotel, where anything goes.

I filed the face in the back of my mind, thinking that if I came across him I might bust a racket on his gleaming teeth.

I rode a guest elevator to the tenth floor and entered my room. It was a sterile place with a double bed, writing table, and an elaborate TV set that offered adult movies at five dollars per viewing, according to the week's printed program.

I turned down the a/c to seventy degrees and pulled off my wig to let collected perspiration evaporate from my skull.

The hotel's security set-up was about what I'd expected. Short of coming by helicopter or parachuting onto the penthouse, there was no easy way to get there. Taking out the guard, Marco, and using his key to the penthouse elevator would be a readily noticeable action. And when I reached the penthouse, there would be the palace guard waiting with drawn guns. I might manage one step out of the elevator, no more.

I stretched out on the bed and reviewed the situation. Getting to the penthouse was out; had to be another way to access the Don. And as I lay there, my mind filled with the image of Tony's crumpled body, the blown-apart skull, and the pooling blood. His Panama hat lying a few feet away.

Had he worn that atrocious hat, the sniper might not have shot Tony, I reflected, but all the ifs in the world wouldn't bring him back.

After a while I pulled on my wig and went down to the street. From a pay phone I dialed 911 and said huskily, "If you start now, you can get to the Sagebrush before the bomb goes off." I hung up and returned to the hotel.

After crossing through the lobby, I went into the casino area and began playing blackjack with a red-headed dealer. She chewed gum and dealt cards like an automaton. Before the first hand ended, a loud buzzer sounded and an amplified voice advised patrons to leave the area while a fire threat was investigated. Women shrieked, men groaned, and overhead lights began flashing to an intermittent horn. There was a general rush for the lobby. My dealer pulled in the cards and said, "Better go." I picked up my chips and managed to be the last to leave the casino before steel fire doors closed, shutting off game tables from the lobby.

Guests poured out of elevators and fire stairs, many in pajamas. Security guards began shepherding us out to the street where a fire engine and police bomb disposal truck had screamed up. Firemen were shouting at us to stay calm as bomb squad specialists in protective masks and clothing pushed through the crowd. Before I was shoved onto the sidewalk, I looked back and saw the private elevator open. Two men emerged, pushing an old man in a wheelchair. Marco led the way, blocking people aside like an offensive lineman.

Rafaello Ambrosino was hunched forward in his wheelchair, holding an oxygen mask to his face. The green oxygen bottle rested on a tartan throw across his legs. His good eye stared straight ahead as he passed six feet from me, face grayer than ever.

There was a sovereign cure for his infirmities, and I planned to supply it: a soft-nosed bullet in the head.

Having learned what I wanted, I let myself be pushed and shoved into the street. Free of the apprehensive crowd, I walked to a drugstore where I bought a bottle of potassium chlorate, a candle, a roll of tape, and a pint bottle of rubbing alcohol. I carried my bagged purchases to another drugstore and added a bottle of powdered sulfur. "For my complexion," I explained to the cashier.

"They say it does wonders," she remarked, and handed over my change.

I crossed the street, walked a block and went into a large hardware store that advertised mining supplies. The counter clerk was listening to a radio report of a bomb scare at the Sagebrush, where guests were being evacuated.

"Sounds bad," I said.

Shrugging, he turned off the radio. "Not unusual around here. Some kook gambles away the rent money and gets even with a bomb scare. What can I do for you?"

I asked for a pair of pliers and a yard of fuse cord. He cut the cord from a large reel and dipped into a bin for pliers. "Sure that's enough cord? Burns an inch per second."

"I'm sure."

"Blasting caps? Primers?"

"Got plenty," I lied. To buy them you needed a license, which I didn't have.

He totaled the bill: seven-eighty. I paid and left.

A toy store sold children's painting and decorating sets. I examined several sets before finding one that included a vial of powdered aluminum among the varicolored glitter. I bought two of those and walked back to the Sagebrush, where bomb squad and fire engine were pulling away. Elevators were busy taking relieved guests back to their rooms, and I noticed that Marco was at his post again beside the penthouse elevator.

When my turn came I got into the guest elevator and punched ten, carrying in my shopping bags all the components of an incendiary bomb.

TWENTY-SIX

In my bathroom I drained the plastic bottle of rubbing alcohol and opened the hotel courtesy package containing a shower cap. After fluffing it out on the writing table, I began measuring chemicals into it, using proportions from a terrorist manual I'd studied in Beirut: fifteen parts potassium chlorate, three parts powdered charcoal, and two parts sulfur. From the play sets I added both vials of powdered aluminum and, as with a cake recipe, mixed well.

From my Cobra I took a .38 cartridge and used pliers to extract the bullet. I scattered powder grains over the other ingredients, and dropped in the empty shell—its primer would add force to the detonation.

The interior of the alcohol bottle was now dry. I ran fuse cord inside until it touched bottom. Then I funneled the explosive mixture into the bottle, sealing it with melted candle wax. The rest of the fuse cord I laid in tight longitudinal loops along the outside of the bottle, and taped it in place. The end of the fuse cord extended just above the bottle's neck.

My face was wet, hands damp from tension. I got up from the table and looked down at what I'd manufactured: the equivalent of a thermite bomb.

The debris I gathered into shopping bags for disposal away from the hotel, carefully removed my mustache, and took a hot, relaxing shower. After drying off, I wrapped the bottle-bomb in a towel and laid it in the bureau's bottom drawer. Then I turned on an early soap opera, got into bed, and watched the incomprehensible storyline until I fell asleep.

Outside it was dark—for Vegas—when I dropped my leftovers in a sidewalk trash receptacle. Back in the hotel I rode to the twelfth floor—just below the penthouse—and reconnoitered the fire stairs, figuring there had to be an emergency exit from Ambrosino's refuge if catastrophe cut off the elevators.

From the twelfth-floor level, stairs led up to a landing jog, turned, and ran the rest of the way up to a steel-shod door. I tested it gently and found it locked, probably barred as well. As I walked down I stopped at a large electrical box set into the wall. A steel door closed it off, but the lock was open. Inside there was a maze of cables, knife switches, and commercial-size fuses. Connections were labeled telephone, electric mains, and elevator. Nearby a large copper fire extinguisher hung in a wall rack. Above it, a shielded, battery-run emergency lamp. I took down the extinguisher and loosened the hose coupling so the connection would blow away if anyone activated the extinguisher. Then I replaced the extinguisher and walked down two flights to my room.

The time was seven-fifteen. I washed my hands, combed my wig, and went down to the street. Two blocks away I found a modest-looking French restaurant and sipped Beam over ice while I studied the menu. I ordered petite marmite, sole amandine, and endive salad, dined enjoyably, and finished dinner—perhaps my last—with espresso and Martell brandy.

On the way back to the Sagebrush I stopped at a drugstore and bought a small, disposable halogen flashlight and a copy of the *Los Angeles Times*. In the lobby I heard the brassy blast of the pit-band—showtime in the restaurant—and saw that all gaming tables were busy with bettors. Nothing there for me; any luck I might have going I wanted to preserve for later.

In my room I spread out the *Times* and found the stories I was looking for on pages two and three. The larger one was datelined Nice:

MILLIONAIRE'S WIDOW
DENIES KILLING SPOUSE

Flanked by her American and French lawyers, Mrs. Melissa Tarkos, widow of American financier Borden Tarkos, appeared at a guarded press conference in the Nice city jail where she is being held for questioning concerning the death of her late husband. Mrs. Tarkos, who arrived at this city last week aboard the Tarkos yacht, *Flaminia,* told an international group of reporters that she had been asleep when her husband left their bed, and was awakened by the sound of a cry. She rushed to the open balcony and saw her husband's body lying five stories below. Mrs. Tarkos declined to speculate as to whether Mr. Tarkos had fallen or jumped from the balcony. Appearing tight-lipped and distraught, she said she knew of no reason her spouse might have taken his own life. The couple had begun the evening dining at the Monte Carlo casino, then played roulette for several hours. "I won a few thousand francs," Mrs. Tarkos said, "and Borden lost several thousand dollars, a sum he could easily afford to lose. During dinner we drank wine, and at the roulette table a few champagne cocktails over several hours. Neither of us was inebriated."

A police source who requested anonymity said that preliminary questioning of *Flaminia* crew members had failed to produce evidence of hostility between the couple, and it is expected that Mrs. Tarkos will be released after the judge studies available evidence and makes his ruling.

As principal heir, Mrs. Tarkos will become owner of a Beverly Hills estate, a motion picture studio, and a professional basketball team, as well as other interests including shares in a Las Vegas, Nevada, hotel-casino. Overall, the Tarkos estate is said to be worth in excess of fifty million dollars.

On that pecuniary note the story closed, and I felt almost euphoric at the likelihood of her forthcoming release. Why had I doubted crew members would testify favorably for Melissa? Even if they had witnessed physical abuse and bitter words, it was in their interest to remain employed. Trial of the yacht's new owner could leave its title in doubt, and salary checks would stop. Practical seafarers were like the three monkeys, neither hearing, speaking, or seeing evil, and I silently applauded their tact, if not their truthfulness.

"Baby," I said aloud, "when will I see you again?"

Then I moved to page three where the story was headed:

TREASURY AGENT'S DEATH PROBED
MEXICAN MAFIA INVOLVED?

The shooting death at Marina del Rey pier of U.S. Treasury Agent Antonio F. Honey, at first thought by police to be the result of random sniping by an unknown gunman, may be related to Agent Honey's undercover work in Mexico, according to police sources who asked that their names not be disclosed. These sources say they had little to go on until the Los Angeles Treasury Field Office revealed that Agent Honey was recently conducting an undercover investigation in Mexico, details of which the Treasury spokesperson declined to reveal.

Shortly before his death, Agent Honey had visited a friend aboard the friend's sailboat at a marina pier. Moments after leaving the boat Agent Honey was struck by a single rifle bullet and died instantaneously, according to the Medical Examiner's report. The owner of the sailboat has been identified as Joseph M. Brent, writer of the successful television sitcom *Frankie's Follies*. Marina sources said they understood Mr. Brent was unemployed due to the current Writers Guild strike and was living aboard his boat while preparing it for sale. Since initial questioning by police, Mr. Brent has not been seen, and one marina source said he may have left the Los Angeles area in fear of his life. Another source was quoted as saying Mr. Brent was probably in shock owing to his friend's sudden violent death. Whatever the motive for his disappearance, Mr. Brent is sought by Homicide detectives for further questioning concerning possible knowledge of enemies Agent Honey might have incurred during his undercover activity in Mexico, where a combination of powerful drug-traffickers and corrupt army and police officials make up what has become known as the "Mexican Mafia."

Mr. Brent's wife, Natalie, from whom he is separated, has told police she has no information concerning his whereabouts.

And lucky for me she hasn't, I thought as I folded the paper, or she'd spill it to the world.

So, the cops were looking for me, and they might have word of me much sooner than expected.

Like tonight—if anything went wrong upstairs.

It was now nine o'clock. I turned on a local TV channel for the hourly newsbreak and learned that a citizen from Canton, Ohio, had won half a million dollars betting a big Trifecta at the Hilton casino. At the payoff cage the winner would be braced by IRS agents for the federal share, so he'd go back to Canton with about half what he won, and even that wasn't bad.

In a different way Melissa was coming out a winner and on a much larger scale, making the desert island I'd proposed to her seem trivial compared to the resources she would soon command.

And I wondered how great wealth would affect her . . .

Time would tell.

Time.

At eleven I was going to activate my plan. Two hours from now Don Rafaello would be asleep and his guards, if not sleeping, would at least be dozing and unprepared for disaster.

As I put on my disguise I went over my plan again, reviewing it step by step. I would have one shot at him, two at most, but only this one chance to take his life.

Raw justice for the Don, but as a Nobel Prize writer once put it, raw justice is better than none.

Much better. Reprisal for a man whose entire life was nothing but evil. Raf was scum to be eradicated and buried.

As I sat there I remembered telling both Melissa and her father that I wasn't a gunslinger, but now I was entering the trade. If I survived, I'd hang up my gun like Gary Cooper in *High Noon*, and leave town. I made that promise to myself.

I got out my Cobra, opened the cylinder, and twirled it. Replacing it, I lowered the hammer on the empty chamber. Five shots for the Don and his escorts. How many would they get off at me?

I was counting on darkness and surprise to bring it off. This time I was going to be the invisible gunman, emulating the sniper who'd blown apart Tony's cranium. Eye for eye, tooth for tooth, skull for skull.

Subconsciously I'd been psyching myself with an inner monologue, like a boxer readying for the Big Fight, but I didn't want to peak too soon. Slow down, Brent, try to relax.

Fuse cord burns one inch per second. Mine was thirty-six inches long, less six inches inside the bottle, giving me thirty seconds between fuse ignition and bomb detonation. Ample time to take cover from the blast. Right? Better count on only twenty-five. Safety margin for error.

News program over, the channel was showing *White Nights,* one of my favorite movies. Baryshnikov and Gregory Hines acted as superbly as they danced. I watched the compelling story unfold, watched it to the end, and by then the time was ten-fifty. Time to get organized.

I switched off the set, got the bomb from where I'd cached it in the bureau drawer, and checked to make sure the fuse was in place, the wax layer compacting the explosive mix.

My palms were damp as I reholstered the Cobra under my left arm. I took a book of hotel matches and lighted one to make sure they weren't too damp to strike when I needed flame.

I used two more matches to jam my door lock's spring bolt so I wouldn't have to use precious seconds fitting key in lock when I returned.

If I returned.

Still inside the room, I let the door swing shut and drew it open again. The jammed bolt hadn't moved. Fast access was certain.

I rolled the bottle-bomb in a section of the *Times* and looked around the room. Anything else? Anything forgotten?

Satisfied I had everything I needed—luck was the imponderable—I looked up and down the corridor, saw no one, and crossed the carpeted corridor to the fire-stair door.

In semi-darkness I went quietly up the steps to the electrical junction box, got out my small flash, and shined it on the interior, finding ledge space for the bomb.

It was ironic, I reflected, that because I couldn't breach the Don's palazzo and get to him, his soldiers were going to deliver him to me.

Eleven o'clock.

Watching the seconds on my digital watch, I struck a match and held it to the end of the fuse cord. The powder core caught at once and ignited like a sparkler. I closed the steel door on the hissing fuse, and watching the seconds run, went down the stairs to the twelfth floor.

Eight, nine, ten . . . the seconds were tolling.

I stepped into the corridor and closed the stair door behind me.
Fourteen, fifteen, sixteen . . .
Nine to go . . .
I closed my eyes, bracing for the blast.

TWENTY-SEVEN

. . . twenty-three, twenty-four, twenty-five, twenty-six—
BLAM!

The door beside me bulged. I heard the junction box door slam against the opposite wall, clatter down stairs. Ears buzzing from the blast, I opened the hall door and looked up. The stairway was filled with thick gray smoke and the stench of gunpowder. At the top, the junction box was a hole in the wall where flames licked out and cables sparked and sizzled. The emergency lamp had been blown off, the fire extinguisher hung askew, swaying with a grating noise. I played my flashlight beam through the smoke and saw that the interior of the wall box was utterly destroyed.

I could feel air rushing around me into the upper stairwell. It fed the cables' flames and diminished the heavy smoke. I took a deep breath and stepped into the stairwell, locking the fire door behind me. From just below the concrete landing jog I took up firing position, Cobra in my right hand, flashlight in my left. Smoke still issued from the box, the acrid fumes stung my eyes, etched my dry throat.

I had figured it would take the palace guard around three minutes to realize their elevator wasn't running, and this was the only way out. Fire bells were clanging throughout the hotel, and I'd seen a rehearsal for the general confusion I wanted to prevail. My watch showed two minutes gone. I thumbed the hammer halfway back, and it seemed as though all the moisture in my body had drained into my hands.

The Don's wheelchair wouldn't take the stairs, so his soldiers would have to carry him as I'd seen them do. With their hands supporting the *capo,* they couldn't come out with drawn weapons.

I hoped.

Footsteps were coming rapidly toward the steel-shod fire door at the top of the stairs. Heavy footsteps. I heard an inner barrier scrape away, the click of drawn bolts, and then the heavy door swung inward. I didn't need the flashlight to show me the three figures who emerged. Two men carrying a third, and the third was the Don himself, no oxygen bottle, no breathing mask.

They couldn't see me through the smoke, none of them.

The carriers' voices were hoarse, excited. "What a break!" one said. "Holy God, what a break! Lookit the box there, the shit's blown out of it."

The other man coughed, smoke shifted, rushing around them into the fresh penthouse air, and then he said, "Well, are we going to carry him all the fucking way down?"

"Hell, no. I've had enough of this shit."

"Now!"

Together they swung their passenger back, then forward so that his body arched far over the slanting staircase, and struck the wall with a sickening sound. It dropped, crumpled like old rags onto the jog. One side of his skull was flat, crushed by impact. Blood trickled from his mouth. The Don was dead before I could kill him. The two soldiers started down the stairs. I had no quarrel with them. I let the Cobra hang by my side, not threatening, but ready.

One of them spat on Ambrosino's body. "Tragic," he said nastily, "and who's to know?"

They stepped around the body and came face to face with me. The spitter went for his gun but I shoved mine in his belly.

"Easy," I said, "the stairs are clear. Get the hell out of here."

His eyes widened, he gasped and jerked his head around toward the demolished box. *"You* did that?"

"Tarkos's contract. Yours?"

Breathing heavily, they exchanged glances. "L.A.," he said. "Ever since Dino disappeared, the old shit's been acting crazy, wanted to waste everyone in sight. The Council let him sit here like an old king so long as didn't get outa line. But he got outa line." He coughed spasmodically.

"That include the Treasury agent?"

"Yeah—that mistake finished Raf. We got orders yesterday."

"You collect, I collect, right?"

"Right." He looked over at Ambrosino's body. It hadn't moved. "Couldn't walk worth a shit, shouldn't have tried."

I moved aside, they hurried past me down the stairs, and I holstered my .38. People were beating on the fire-stair door.

After a final glance at the man I'd come to kill, I went to the fire door, unlocked it, and people in pajamas began pouring through, heading down to the lobby. When they were gone I wiped my prints from the inner knob, and walked two floors down.

The tenth floor corridor was empty. I went unhindered to my room, unjammed the bolt, and locked the door behind me. The room was lighted, telling me I'd cut only the palazzo cables, and the sprinkler system wasn't spraying.

I hadn't heard fire engines arrive—my mind had been tuned to other sounds and action—but when I looked down from my window I could see three units outside the hotel, firemen running around like crazed beetles. I didn't know why it was taking them so long to check the topmost floor.

Then I heard the faint chuffing of chopper rotors, looked up, and saw a pair coming toward the Sagebrush, searchlights pointing down. If there was a helipad by the pool, one would land firemen to investigate. If not, firefighters would be lowered.

I wondered how long it would take them to find the *capo*'s corpse.

I sat down, feeling strength leave my body. I'd been keyed up, tense, for what seemed like hours—in reality only a few minutes—and I'd been in control. Now as I looked at my hands, they were trembling. I made fists of them and the trembling stopped. I needed a bottle of Beam more than I'd ever needed one in my life—except for those frightful, sickening days and nights in the Beirut rubble. Then I'd run on nerve alone. I didn't have to now.

The choppers were thundering overhead. Thirst was overpowering. I ran cold water in the basin and gulped water like an animal, splashed more over my face, and soaked my hands and wrists.

I dried my face and hands, adjusted my wig and glasses, made sure my mustache wouldn't fall off, and left the room.

It took a long time for the elevator to reach the tenth floor, and while I was waiting, I rested against the wall. The adrenalin in my system had dissipated, and I felt like a wired skeleton hung with loose clothes.

Finally the elevator door opened. There were only five guests in it, three with blankets wrapped around them. They were talking rapidly in high-pitched voices. I slumped in a corner until the elevator stopped at lobby level.

As earlier today, steel doors isolated the gaming area, and the lobby was generally empty but for firemen, uniformed police, and hotel staff. I noticed that Marco was not at his post beside the Don's private elevator, and I wondered if he had been in on the L.A. contract.

Walking toward the street, I felt the irony of the Don's own men killing him, and I reflected that in a way I owed them. They'd spared me an act of murder, the Don's blood-quest was finished, and I was still alive. That was all that mattered.

I made my way through fire and police lines across the street, walked two blocks, and almost staggered into the first saloon. I wasn't sure I had enough strength to sit on a bar stool so I took a side booth and ordered two double Beams, no ice, water on the side.

When the waiter brought my drinks, he said, "Wonder what's happening down at the Sagebrush? Second ruckus today."

"Probably another false alarm." I gulped down half of my first drink.

The old man shrugged. "People can get hurt in false alarms," he observed. "Trampled on . . . blood pressure, bad heart . . . You can die." He looked out at the street. A few pajamaed guests were coming in.

I sipped water to ease the smoke-rawness in my throat, followed it with the second half of my drink. Thoughts that had been on fast-forward were slowing now, focus gradually returning. The waiter went off to serve the hotel refugees, leaving me alone in a booth for four, my thoughts for company.

When the two carriers flung their Don against the wall I'd been too astonished—shocked—to react. And what was there to react to? They'd taken advantage of a situation I'd created to carry out their L.A. contract. Should I have gunned them down?

By letting them live I'd been able to verify Ambrosino's responsibility for Tony's murder. I'd been ninety percent sure since that bloody moment, but the two soldiers had filled the gap and I was satisfied the way things had worked out.

Had to be, because I was out of it now. Finished with the *capo* and Borden Tarkos. I had a future to organize and Melissa was to be part of it, a very significant part—if she didn't get the guillotine. But according to the *Times* story, there was no evidence against her, and a judge in France would decide.

I wanted desperately to be with her, just to see her, touch her hand if warders allowed that. But not tonight; I was too shot, too tired even to get my car at McCarran and drive to the junky motel where my clothing was.

I drank my second drink more slowly, and midway through it, decided I was hungry. The waiter brought me a hot pastrami on rye with a jar of Dijon mustard, and I ate as hungrily as a jackal. I finished the drink, and as I paid the bill I gave him the four freebie chips. He picked them up, said, "Thanks, mister, I can use them. So you were at the Sagebrush—not going back?"

"A place like that scares me," I told him. "Two alarms in one day is two too many."

"You got something there." He started to turn away. "Liquor stores open?" I asked.

"Do they ever close? Good one in the next block. Jimmy's—my brother-in-law."

I bought a liter of Beam and trudged back to the Sagebrush. Fire and police lines were clear, but medics were stretchering a blanketed shape into the rear of a police ambulance. A small body, about the size of Don Rafaello's in life. Alive or dead, the old Don was a *pezzo di merda*. Cameras flashed, the double doors gave off a heavy metallic crash as they closed, and the ambulance whined away.

D.O.A.

I went up to my room, took a long draw from the bottle, pulled off my shoes, and lay down on the bed, lights out, too tired to take off my disguise and holstered gun.

That was for morning.

Along with other things.

TWENTY-EIGHT

The morning paper, delivered to my room along with a dry croissant and bitter coffee, described the death of Rafaello Ambrosino as accidental. A semi-invalid, Mr. Ambrosino had tried to descend the hotel's fire stairs, stumbled in the dark, and fallen to his death. The darkness was ascribed to a brief power failure caused by a malfunctioning fuse, and I imagined the hotel's PR person had struggled hard with that one. Fire-bombing was not likely to give potential guests a feeling of security; a major power outage was almost as bad. So the latter was chosen and minimized. And true to local code, the Sagebrush was not even mentioned by name. Had forty guests expired of cholera in the lobby of any Vegas hotel, the paper—if it mentioned the event at all—would have reported simultaneous attacks of indigestion due to gross eating habits.

So it goes in a tourist town, I thought, where image is the draw.

Page two carried a Reuter's story from Nice, where the sister of Borden Tarkos, Ms. Sophie Letterman, had arrived to claim the remains of her late brother and allege that her brother's widow, Melissa, was solely responsible for Borden's death. "My brother was no foolish moongazer," stated Ms. Letterman, "and would not have put himself in a position of danger. His wife pushed him, no doubt about it. She killed him."

A small photo of Sophie Letterman showed a middle-aged woman with a prominent nose, unkempt hair, and wild-looking eyes.

Given the provisions of Tarkos's will, I supposed the sisterly outburst was to be expected. But how much did Sophie Letterman know about her brother's marriage? What would she tell the court—and the press?

For Melissa the timing was bad; how much weight would the judge attach to Sophie's outburst? Surely *avocat* Desjardins could challenge it as disappointment over her small inheritance. Even so, the unexpected development was a potential setback for Melissa, delaying her release while the judge pondered what Sophie had to say. Moreover, Sophie's charge would be exploited by the tabloid press, turning Melissa into a notorious figure in the minds of too many people.

Still, the situation had to be dealt with and I could only hope that the French lawyer would promptly and effectively discredit Sophie Letterman's ravings. Again, there was nothing I could do to help Melissa.

After shaving and dressing, I got rid of my wig, mustache, and glasses in the service trash chute, left my room key in the lock, and took a taxi to the motel just outside town. I had the taxi wait while I transferred my Cobra to my carry-all, checked out of the motel, and rode to McCarran Airport.

While waiting for a flight to Phoenix, I had breakfast in the airport restaurant. The food wasn't bad but couldn't compare with yesterday's feast at One-Eye Jack's. My one good memory of Vegas.

The flight to Sky Harbor Airport took just an hour, another half hour had me in a rental Ford and on my way south along the Gila River to the village of Maricopa.

A policeman directed me to the Honey home, and asked, "You another reporter?"

"Why?"

"Antonio was buried yesterday. He was well-liked here, we were proud of him—still are. So don't give his folks a hard time, hear me?"

"That's a promise," I said, and drove to the outskirts of the small town.

A battered mailbox bore the Honey name. It stood at the side of the dirt road in front of a fence that consisted of several strands of barbed wire running from the gate and enclosing the yard.

Surrounding land was sandy desert, flat except for a few distant buttes. On one side of the house two rusted junkers rested on their axles. Through and around the wrecks, nopal cactus had grown up, and a family of goats was browsing on the spiny leaves. A couple of mesquite trees provided thin shade for a flower border, and I could make out a well and outhouse set back from the house. Wind had piled tumbleweeds against the side fencing.

The house itself was one-story adobe, painted white with projecting roof poles, weathered gray. The setting reminded me of an Alvarez oil of the bleak Sonora desert.

The air was clear, sky almost cloudless. As I walked up the dirt path I saw a black wreath fixed to the wood-slab front door, and both front windows were draped with black cloth.

There was a ranch-style porch of warped, heat-grayed timbers, a brown-and-white mongrel sleeping at one end. No doorbell, so I rapped on the heavy door and waited. After a while a middle-aged, white-haired woman in a black dress opened the door and looked at me. Her eyes were red, eyelids puffy from tears. "No more reporters," she said in an accented voice. "Please go away."

"I'm not a reporter," I said. "I was Tony's friend. I tried to come for the funeral but I was delayed. I'm sorry."

Wordlessly, she opened the door wider and stepped aside to let me in. The room was cool and dark, its furniture heavy wood with a handmade look. A wicker birdcage was hooded. In the far corner sat a man who looked like an older version of Tony—as Tony might have appeared had his life not been cut off. I said, "My name is Joe Brent. Tony was visiting me just before he was killed."

At the sound of my voice, the man's face turned. To the woman he said, "Refreshments for our guest, Julia. What do you take, Mr. Brent?"

"Anything wet, and please call me Joe."

The man rose. "Manuel Honey," he said, and we shook hands. His was hard, muscular, and calloused. "Any friend of our son's welcome here. *Estas en tu casa, señor.* A soft drink? Tequila?"

"Tequila," I said, "with a little ice."

"Salt? *Limon?*"

"Just ice, thanks."

"Please be seated." He resumed his chair while his wife went into the kitchen. "We don't know what to do," he said in a listless voice. "He was our son, all we had. A good boy, we were proud of him. Now—he's gone. Taken by God." He crossed himself.

"He was a good man," I said. "We didn't know each other long, but we became friends." Mrs. Honey glided in, her soft leather *huaraches* making slight whispering sounds over the polished wood floor. Her skin was less coppery than her husband's, and her nose less pronounced. Her hair was the whitest I had ever seen. After bringing my drink she sat in an *equipal* slightly behind and to one side of her husband, hands folded over her spotless apron. I lifted my glass, said, *"Salud,"* and sipped. The pot-cured liquor was smooth and viscous, with a slight tangy taste. Tony's father said, "Your name was in the paper. Reporters asked about you but I said truthfully we never met. But you were with Tony when he died?"

"Below deck in my cabin. I heard the shot and found him lying on the pier."

"And the man who shot him?"

"He got away unseen." I sipped again. "I have no information beyond what was said in the papers. I came to extend my condolences, be with you, share your grief, if such a thing is possible."

"It is enough to know that his death brought sorrow to others, that my son will be well remembered." He looked away. "Government friends honored him at the funeral."

"Antonio was a fine man, an honest man, and a patriot who served his country honorably. He was proud of his heritage—of you."

His mother spoke in a voice soft and resigned. "Was it his work that caused his death?"

"I have to think so," I told her. "Antonio was an enemy of everything evil."

Manuel turned to his wife and reached for her hand. *"Oyes? Como te dije,"* he said quietly.

"Verdad, mi amor." Tears gathered, coursed down her cheeks.

Manuel turned back to me. "Was he killed because of his work in Mexico?"

"Probably," I said. "There's no other explanation."

"And these men—the killers—will they ever be found?"

"I can't tell you that. In Mexico, as in this country, justice is very slow."

"And sometimes—*verdad?*—there is no justice at all," said his mother.

"Unfortunately so," I admitted. "Nevertheless, we must go on with our lives."

For a time there was silence in the low, cool room. Motes drifted through a shaft of sunlight, and I had the sensation of having been here before—a hundred, two hundred years ago. Must be the liquor, I told myself, coupled with brain fatigue. I'd been pushing myself hard, knew I was nearing exhaustion.

I drank more of the smooth, pungent tequila and said, "Although I knew Antonio only a short time, I know he loved you both."

His mother said, "He spoke of us?"

"Frequently."

"A good boy," his father said reminiscently. "Never a troublemaker like others. Worked as we all worked, made something of himself."

Someone knocked at the door. His mother rose and went outside. Manuel said, "The padre, I believe. Is there something you came to tell me—while we're alone?"

"There is." I went over and sat in his wife's chair. "In Baja California your son was working against a gangster named Dino Ambrosino. This Ambrosino is dead. His father, a powerful Mafia leader in Las Vegas named Rafaello, blamed Antonio for his son's death. He hired a sniper and the sniper killed Antonio." Manuel started to speak but I said, "*Momento*. Dino's father, Rafaello, was killed last night in Las Vegas. That is what I wanted you to know. In time, tell your wife, but I think she is not yet ready to know the truth."

Manuel nodded slowly. "I agree." He sat forward. "Between *hombres*, in confidence, did you have a hand in the father's death?"

"It was necessary," I said, "for Antonio, and for myself. There was a blood debt. The debt is purged."

When he spoke again he said, "It is good to know that my son had friends—a friend—like you. What you did makes my sorrow less hard to bear."

"There's one other thing. Remember that your son Antonio died in the performance of his duty—'in line of duty.' If the government fails to give you what is yours in accordance with the law, there are lawyers who specialize in those matters. And I will help the lawyer as much as I can." I handed him Tony's Treasury credentials. His father gazed at the card and put it in his pocket. "Thank you," he said, "*Gracias.*"

"Before I go I would like to visit his grave."

Slowly he rose from his chair. "It is beside our church—the padre will show you the way." He gave me a cheek-to-cheek *abrazo* and we went outside where Mrs. Honey was talking with a dark-skinned priest in long black habit. Manuel spoke to them in rapid Spanish, the priest nodded and fingered a large silver crucifix set with turquoise bezels. Around the waist of his habit was a loose silver chain from which the crucifix hung.

I said my goodbyes to Tony's mother. *"Gracias* for coming," she said. *"Vaya con Dios,"* and crossed herself.

The priest got in the car beside me. "Good people," he remarked. "Your coming meant a lot to them."

"It meant a lot to me. You knew Tony?"

"We were boys together, but in recent years I hadn't seen much of him—not as much as I wanted. Did you know him long?"

"A few weeks," I said as we pulled up at the small Mission-style church. We got out and the padre led me to the edge of the burial ground.

Sun-dried flowers were strewn over a long earthen mound. At the head of it an iron cross had been stuck into the ground. High in the distance a hawk rode updrafts from the heated earth. A quarter mile away a windmill clanked as the blades slowly turned. The padre said, "Desolate, isn't it? A hundred years ago, maybe more, the Great White Father—and I emphasize the color of his skin—gave much of this worthless land to the Gila Indians. The reservation isn't far away. My people raise goats and cactus, grow beans, corn, whatever grows in arid country. They are very poor."

"Why did you come back, padre?"

He shrugged. "I felt I was needed. Isn't that why you came today?"

When I said nothing, he said, "You brought them solace—in some fashion. They'll be better able to manage now."

"I hope so," I said, and he walked away and entered the little church.

I went to the new grave, knelt, and said a prayer. Wind stirred the desiccated flowers, rustling them as though to acknowledge my words. I picked up a handful of earth and let the breeze carry it across the grave. "Goodbye, friend," I said and got up.

In the flatness beyond the church, dust devils were forming, whirling briefly and disintegrating. Symbolic of human life?

Walking back to the car, I thought how different Raf Ambrosino's funeral would be: long lines of hearses and expensive limousines, open cars filled with wreaths and floral offerings; notables from city and state expounding on Raf's charities, his contributions to the greatness of Las Vegas and his chosen home, Nevada. Perhaps Senator Farenhold would speak the eulogy. There would be well-fed priests in abundance, a bishop or two, a monsignor to say a final mass, a benediction.

But none of that mattered; Raf was as dead as his victim, and could never harm the helpless again.

At Phoenix Airport I returned the rental Ford, and drank in the air-conditioned barroom until my flight was called, slept through the hour-long flight back to Vegas. At McCarran Airport I bought an afternoon paper and scanned it on the bus ride to where I'd parked my Datsun. Carrying handbag and paper I walked to the car, paid at the toll gate, and started back the way I'd come. On the highway a few miles from town I pulled into a filling station for gas and a quart of oil. A directory listed the Treasury Field Office and I dialed it from a pay phone. I asked to be put through to a supervisor, and when a man's voice answered I said, "I have information concerning the deaths of Treasury Agent Antonio Honey in Los Angeles and Raf Ambrosino at the Sagebrush."

"Wait a minute, lemme get this down."

"Just record it," I said, "which you're probably doing anyway. Okay? Honey was working against the Ambrosino family in Baja. Dino was killed there, and old Raf blamed Honey. He put out a contract on Antonio and got results. The Council didn't like Raf's hitting a federal agent, so they ordered two of Raf's soldiers to kill him. They did it during a fire alarm by throwing him downstairs. End of story."

"That so? Who're you?"

I grimaced. "The proper phrase is 'Thank you, sir,' " I said, and hung up.

By day the drive back through the Mojave was considerably less enchanting than by night. Heat waves distorted the highway, dust and tumbleweed blew across it, an occasional jackrabbit made me brake or veer, but I kept the speedometer at a steady sixty-five until I reached the L.A. city limits, and dropped back to a normal commuter crawl.

It was dusk when I pulled into the marina parking lot. I locked the Datsun and carried my bag to the marina office, where I paid the dockage bill and checked for messages. There weren't any, but the lady with whom I'd shared beer and a TV game whispered, "I think your boat is being watched."

Cold gripped me. "Who?"

"Two men—they didn't say."

"Many thanks," I said. "Forewarned is forearmed."

Before leaving the office I transferred my Cobra from holster to side pocket, and held its grip in my hand. I headed for the pier and my boat.

I'd almost reached it when two men emerged from shadows. One called, "Hold it right there."

TWENTY-NINE

As I turned, I pulled out my revolver and covered them. "Who says so?"

"Police."

"Prove it."

The nearest man reached into his coat, I said, "Very, very slowly." He grunted, and tossed a credential toward me. It fell open on the pier. I knelt to pick it up, scanned it, and said, "Okay, what's on your mind?" I gestured him closer and returned his I.D.

His partner said, "You got a license for that piece?" I recognized him as Sergeant Dolfuz.

"Sure as shootin'," I said. "You got a warrant?"

"Gonna play tough? Where you been the past couple of days?"

"Out and around. Any objections?"

"Lieutenant Pendergast told you not to leave town," Dolfuz said sternly.

"Hell he did. He asked if I'd be around."

"Same thing."

"Uh-uh." I holstered my revolver. "Not by a long shot it isn't. And speaking of long shots, have you collared the sniper who shot Agent Honey?"

"That's what the lieutenant wants to talk to you about. Maybe you forgot somethin', like the dead man was Treasury."

"I didn't know it until I read the papers. Big deal."

"What do you know about what the agent was doin' in Mexico?"

"How's your investigation going? Find the rifle shell? Identify the car?"

Dolfuz said, "You're stonewalling, Brent, an'—"

"*Mister* Brent to you, pal, and any other public servant. Meanwhile, I'm not going to be interrogated here by a pair of gofers, so you tell the Loo he can drop by tomorrow—alone—and unburden his mind. If it's to be a friendly chat, okay. If not, we'll have my lawyer present. *Capisce?* Two words: alone and friendly. Goodnight."

I walked across the pier to my boat, not looking down at the place where Tony's body had lain. I unlocked the cabin doors, went down the companionway, and turned on cabin lights.

I felt played out, ragged from the drive, the flight, the tension of being with Tony's folks. And being braced by two cops was far from relaxing.

After a substantial slug of Beam I turned out the lights and got into my bunk. I lay there trying to clear my mind for sleep, but memories crowded in, and I saw myself putting together the firebomb, carefully placing it in the junction box, and igniting its fuse. I could almost hear the wall-shaking explosion, smell the after-smoke, and see the penthouse escape door open.

I remembered my stunned astonishment when Ambrosino's body arced through the air, heard again the water-bag sound of his skull smashing against the wall.

The Council, having ordered Ambrosino's liquidation, would follow through with the hitman who'd killed Tony. They would leave no loose ends traceable back to the Nevada operation. Too much was at stake for the families. Killing federal agents was outside their code—unless an agent on the pad had betrayed them. Then he had to go.

I didn't expect to learn the hitman's identity but I was satisfied he would soon be permanently out of business. One of the nameless corpses found in California alleys or bleaching in desert sand. In any case, the sniper was a technician; Raf Ambrosino was the intellectual author of Tony's death—the last one he had ordered.

Melissa.

Days and nights would pass slowly until she was with me again. I didn't want her money, her yacht, or her Beverly Hills mansion. I just wanted her as she'd come to me; as I'd known her. As we'd made love. Simply, openly, unreservedly.

I didn't allow myself to contemplate her prison cell. I made myself visualize her lying beside me, our hands clasped, bodies touching . . .

And with that comforting fantasy, sleep came.

In mid-morning I was polishing topside brightwork when Lieutenant Pendergast came down the pier, looked over, and said, "You in a mood to talk?"

"You in a mood to listen?"

He nodded and I motioned him aboard.

As he came down the companionway he sniffed and said, "Coffee smells good."

"Just making it. There's sugar, not sure about cream."

"Black's fine."

Perking completed, the coffee was simmering on the range. I poured two cups, added sugar to mine, and carried both to the table. Pendergast sipped, said, "Thanks," and put down his cup. "Last evening you were kinda rough on my boys."

"I could have been rougher, Lieutenant. This is a new day."

"Right—let's start over." He sipped again. "Good coffee." He glanced around the cabin before saying, "Now that we know your friend Antonio Honey was a Treasury agent, I'd like any info you might have about what he was doing in Mexico and who he might have got mad enough to kill him."

I took a long pull from my cup, stirred in more sugar, and said, "Wired?"

He opened his jacket. I went over and felt under it, around his waist, and resumed my chair. "If you'll bear with me, I'll tell a story that's true as far as I know it. There's no basis for indictments and if I'm ever asked, I'll deny I told you. Okay?"

He nodded. "I wouldn't bother you if I had anything to go on but I have a case to close. Treasury tells me nothing. That means either they know everything they need to indict someone for assassinating a federal officer, or else they don't care."

"Probably a mix." I took a deep breath and began. "Antonio Honey was working against the Ambrosino family—you've heard of it?"

"Sure—in fact, the old Don just died in Vegas."

"In some fashion Honey got next to Raf's son, Dino, in Mexico. When Dino didn't return, his father went ape and—"

"Wait a minute—what about Dino?"

"Tony said he disappeared, so let's presume he's dead."

"You mean Honey disappeared him?"

"That's conjecture. Maybe Dino will turn up, maybe not. The point is, the old man put a price on Honey's head and he was hit—here."

"Treasury know all this?"

"I assume they do."

"Anyone know who fired the shot?"

"Maybe just Raf Ambrosino, and he's not talking. But to round it out, the Council decided Raf had gone too far with his vendetta, killing a federal agent. So Raf was whacked in his hotel during the panic of a fire alarm."

"Actually," said Pendergast, "it was a bombing. They found Ambrosino's body near where the bomb went off. You won't read that in the papers, but it was on the police wire. Accidental death, according to the Vegas coroner." He looked away. "Anything else?"

"I figure the Council has to liquidate the marksman, if they haven't already."

He grunted. "Leaving me with a story that explains a good deal, but lacks any evidence whatever. You happen to be in Vegas yesterday?"

"Yesterday," I said, "I visited Tony's bereaved parents in Maricopa, Arizona, talked with the village priest, and paid my respects at Tony's grave. More coffee?"

"A splash—thanks, that's fine. So the killers—presumed killers—are dead, no one to indict, case closed." He drank from his cup and looked at me. "You satisfied with things?"

"We have to be. Nowhere else to go."

"Guess so. And I'm wondering how to write a report that doesn't sound like I've been taking controlled substances."

"Don't write one."

"And how do I get away with that?"

"Anyone checking your progress, remind them killing a government officer's a federal crime. Bureau jurisdiction and Treasury's. Besides, this would be a fine opportunity for the Nevada Strike Force to toss Ambrosino's place—they might find incriminating material."

His eyes narrowed. "Such as what?"

"No idea. But it's something the government has been itching to do for a long, long time."

Pendergast drank silently. He seemed to be watching water reflections playing across the overhead. Finally he said, "Goes against my grain just to leave it and walk away. Maybe I'll give the Strike Force a call, offer cooperation—and a theory."

"For a piece of the credit."

"That's what careers are made of."

"So I've heard. Just leave me out of it."

"Naturally. Can't have civilians sharing credit." His smile carried a shade of embarrassment. "I appreciate the coffee and your hypothetical tale."

"My pleasure, Lieutenant."

He stood up and stretched. "Anything I can do for you?"

"Not now—maybe some other time."

"I'll remember," he said, went up the companionway, and stepped onto the pier. A shot had dropped my last visitor; Pendergast walked away unharmed.

I finished my coffee, rinsed our cups, and decided to pick up a morning paper. Until Hatfield returned, press reports from Nice were all the information I could get.

Maddy Gossons hailed me halfway to the office. I waited for her, and when she was a yard away she said, "So you're back. Where on earth have you been?"

"Attending my friend's funeral. Long drive."

"Well, your note could have said so. Anyway, I've been showing your boat and I may have a deal. The customer likes it for twenty-five. Will you be around to close?" Maddy was displaying the persistence of a Javanese nest-builder.

"I was thinking of going out for a final cruise."

"I'm supposed to hear yes or no tomorrow."

"If I'm not here, say I've taken the boat on a presale shakedown."

"Which you're going to do?"

"Which I'm planning to do."

"So—"

"Maybe bring up a load from Ensenada."

"Please—" she covered her ears"—I don't want to *hear* it." Turning, she strode away and I continued walking towards the office. I fed the vending machine outside and scanned the paper on the way back to the boat. The Tarkos death was page four now. Nothing new, just a rehash of what had been printed before, with a few more details on Tarkos's holdings. A talent agency, a building on Rodeo Drive, a fashion magazine, and substantial equity in an FM station that broadcast classical music and opera—a sure money-loser unless the demographics were as fine-tuned as the fiddles.

Truthfully, I hadn't given much thought to taking *El Dorado* on a farewell cruise, and mentioned it largely to nettle Ms. Gossons. But as I boarded my boat the idea expanded into one of my better inspirations.

A few bottles of Beam, some supplies for the galley, and gasoline for the engine were all I needed. Besides, anchored in a lee cove at Santa Catalina, I'd have the tranquility that only the sea can provide, plus the serenity of mind I needed to develop ideas for my lagging novel.

I was starting down the companionway when I heard my name called. Looking around I saw Sondra Starr hurrying towards me. She was wearing salmon slacks, a loose batik blouse, white ballet slippers, and a scarf around her long dark hair. I helped her to the deck, and when her breathing slowed I said, "Hi—how're things going?"

"With *my* life? Terrible. I kept thinking about you and Tony, mostly Tony. It's just terrible, isn't it? *Terrible.*"

I nodded agreement, put my arm around her shoulders and guided her down into the cabin. She looked around and her eyes grew moist. "Did that Parsons prick kill him?"

"No, honey, it wasn't Parsons. Could you use a drink?"

"Sure could." She knuckled tears away as I poured two drinks, no ice. She gulped half of hers, licked her lips, and said, "I been looking for you, Joe. Where you been?"

"At Tony's funeral."

She shook her head self-reprovingly. "Shoulda known, you bein' such good friends. Where was it at?"

"A small place in Arizona. Sit down, you look pretty ragged."

"Thanks." She downed her drink and held out her glass. I poured an equal amount and sat beside her. "How's Glenda?"

"Glenda? Who knows? Gone with the wind—the boat, I mean." She suppressed a giggle. Fast mood shift, I thought, but isn't that one of alcohol's virtues?

"So what have you been doing?" I asked. "Since that exciting kidnapping we shared?"

"Not much, really. I had to leave that place of Tony's—not that it was much, anyway—an' I been here'n there." She looked at me coquettishly. "How about you?"

"I told you about me, remember? Arizona."

She sighed heavily. "So much on my mind, Joe. Grief, job worries . . ." Her voice trailed off.

"I guess you can't work without Glenda."

"We're an act. I can't do chorus because I'm—well, amply built—as you well know." Her smile was even more coquettish. "Dance directors want those skinny pipes, y'know—no tits, no buns, just matchstick legs, and that's not Twinkie Starr." Her elbow nudged me.

"Well I know. How about stripping?"

"Y'mean here? Now?" Her eyes widened, whether from apprehension or anticipation I couldn't tell.

"What I meant," I said in a patient voice, "was a strip act—on stage. Like belly dancing."

"Oh, I can do that but there's not much call for it. As for nude bars, well, they draw a pretty stinkin' crowd, if you've been to one."

I nodded and drank some Beam. "So you're at—what, loose ends?"

"You got it. *Very* loose." One hand reached up and undid the batik scarf. Her hair tumbled down over her shoulders. "How about you?"

"Finally got a buyer for this boat."

"That's good, isn't it? I mean, you've been wanting to sell."

"To beat the sheriff."

"Oh." She looked around, her expression vague.

"I was thinking," I said, "of a final cruise—Santa Catalina, San Clemente . . . ever been there?"

She shook her head.

"Come with me?"

A long sigh. "Joe, I'd love to, I mean that, but I get awful seasick . . . wouldn't be any good to you or me."

"Shucks."

"Yeah. Besides, it's time I got outa here, moved along. Know what I mean?"

A thought occurred. "What's the matter with me? I've been holding money for you, and if you hadn't showed up I'd of probably forgot."

Her face brightened. "Money? From who?"

"Tony. A gift, he said—since he had to go back on duty and wouldn't be around." From my wallet I got out three hundred-dollar bills and gave them to her. Eyes watering, she pressed them to her breast. "Whatta guy," she breathed. "What a wonderful-type guy."

I nodded agreement.

"This'll take me a long way," she said as she tucked the money into her cleavage. "Help a lot."

"Then it's lucky you stopped by." While she was dabbing at her wet cheeks I kissed her forehead. "Whatever you do, kid, don't sell yourself short, okay?"

"Okay," she said hesitantly, "but—"

"No buts, honey. Think well of yourself and so will others."

Her head angled sideways as she eyed me. "You're quite a guy yourself, Joe. Real sentimental."

"When there's just cause."

She breathed deeply and sighed. "I'm no good at goodbyes, Joe, so I'll go now." She rose and gave me a warm, lingering kiss. "Thanks for everything, and especially what Tony—" her voice quavered, broke, and she went quickly up the companionway. I downed the last of my drink and glanced down the pier. Sondra was disappearing into the dock office.

I washed our glasses, tidied up the cabin, and when I went topside I saw Sondra near the shore end of the pier. She was pushing one of those stolen shopping carts that adorn every marina, and in it was a bulging suitcase. Probably held everything she owned, I thought, and because it looked heavy I jogged after her. "No cabs here," I told her. "We'll try the hotel."

Wordlessly, she let me push the cart across the street, and at the nearest cab I stopped and lifted down the suitcase. While the cabbie was putting it into the trunk, Sondra hugged and kissed me in silent desperation. When the cabbie opened the rear door for her I said, "Good luck, honey."

"Take care of yourself, Joe." She began to cry, dabbed at her makeup, and got quickly into the cab. I heard the driver ask, "Where to, lady?" And her choked reply: "I'll think of someplace. So move, dammit, move!"

For a few moments I watched the taxi draw away, and then I crossed the street and walked down the pier, reflecting that Sondra's companionship would have made my contemplated cruise a hell of a lot more enjoyable than a solo sail. There were two messages for me at the dock office, one from Hatfield, the other from Lieutenant Nero. From the outside pay phone I called Hatfield's office, found the line busy, and dialed Nero at police headquarters.

THIRTY

They put me on hold while they located Lieutenant Nero. When he came on the line I said, "Joe Brent returning your call, Lieutenant. How'd you track me down?"

"Your wife suggested the marina, okay? I guess you know the Don is dead."

"So I understand. And good riddance."

"Right. And you've been away from your usual haunts."

"Whatever that's supposed to imply. I went to a funeral in Arizona. Any objection?"

"Not really. But because of your special relationship with the old guinea and what you once told me about Fallon's taps, I thought you might have an idea or two."

"I'm not reading you," I told him. "Ideas about what?"

"How to proceed. Referring to the Fallon-Rinaldo murders."

I considered the proposition before saying, "Been in touch with Nevada authorities? Cops? Strike Force?"

"The Vegas police faxed me a report on the old man's accidental death—nothing that wasn't in the papers. Why the Strike Force?"

"Because I assume they've got enough combined smarts to seal off wherever the Don lived and go through the place with comb, brush, and microscope."

There was a pause before he said, "Looking for what?"

"Anything, for Lord's sake. A major crime boss dies—a guy who's been a federal target for decades—and suddenly the feds have access to his files and records."

"Okay, that's the federal angle—what's in it for me?"

"What's in it for you, Lieutenant," I said with forced patience, "is the chance a search will turn up the tapes recorded by Fallon and Rinaldo. They were killed for those tapes, remember?"

"Your theory."

"Well, I don't think they presented the tapes to Ambrosino in a gift-wrapped package, no charge. They were trying for early retirement. So the tapes make the connection between the two murdered men and Ambrosino."

"He's dead," Nero objected, "no one to indict—unless I can somehow build a case against the trigger-men."

"Last week," I said, "you were holding Tisch and DiLirio for those murders. Not that they did it, but at least you had two warm bodies in jail. What happened?"

"The D.A. declined to prosecute—insufficient evidence."

"Doesn't that sort of let you off the hook? You came up with a pair of probable perpetrators and the D.A. said 'no, thanks.' Anyway—oh, just had a flash: you're looking for some way to nail the actual killers without revealing the fact that Fallon was involved in a felonious wiretap for shakedown purposes. That'd trash departmental pride."

Nero said, "Without confirming anything you've said, any tapes that might be found would have to be tied to the actual killers—and they could be anyone. Could even be dead."

"Doubtful," I said. "Of the three soldiers who brought Raf to my apartment, I got only one name—Marco. Grab him, and maybe he'll flip—now the *capo*'s dead."

"That's Marco Amiglione," he said thoughtfully. "It's an idea."

"An idea that's going nowhere," I said thinly, "because you can't convict without introducing the tapes to establish motive, and the why and how of who made them would reveal the late Sergeant Fallon as an extortionist—which you and your superiors don't want. So get off my back, will you? Anyway, Borden Tarkos is dead, as you damn well know, and can't be revived to identify the tapes—leaving you no place to go."

"Tarkos," he said, sounding relieved to get away from Fallon. "He's dead, all right, and the French seem to think his wife—your lady friend—did the deed."

"It's theory, lacking elements of proof."

"Think she did it?"

"I have no opinion, Lieutenant, and you can quote me. Anyway, what have we been talking about? The dialogue reminds me of one of those little theater productions where two or three Ionesco characters sit around and gabble endlessly without reaching a sensible conclusion. The curtain drops and the audience staggers out barfing all over the curb. The curtain is now dropping." I hung up, shaking my head, and went into the office, where I got a cold Coke from the machine. Sipping it gave me something else to think about, reducing my anger at Nero's deviousness.

Maybe Hatfield had good news for me. I fed the pay phone and called his office again.

His secretary put me through and Hatfield's first words were, "I'm back."

"I know. Because the toll to San Diego is three quarters, not the twelve dollars it costs to call France. Okay? We've established your location. Mine is Marina del Rey."

"Hey, easy does it, don't get uptight over a cliché."

"Sorry, I'm still tensed up from a nonsensical police conversation. What's happening with Melissa?"

"Things were shaping up nicely when I left—"

"How nicely?"

"Desjardins says the *juge d'instruction* is inclined not to indict our client. He's keeping her locked up to satisfy public opinion but he'll let her out pretty soon. Possibly today."

"Terrific! You talked with her—any word for me?"

"There is, and I'm coming up today, reservation at the Marina Beach. How about meeting me there at, say, three o'clock?"

"I'll be there."

Hatfield's news thrilled and excited me. Conceivably, Melissa could be flying back tomorrow. Blue skies ahead.

I was working hard on the remaining brightwork when a young man on a bicycle pedaled up to the boat and said, "Hello there. By any chance are you Joseph Brent?"

"In the flesh."

"Got something for you." He set the bike's kickstand and came to the edge of the pier, envelope in hand. I reached for it, he said, "Service performed," and stepped back to his bike. I opened the envelope and found a legal document inside. My wife was filing for divorce. The process server gave me an apprehensive glance as he got on his bike. "What kept you so long?" I called, and tossed the notice down the companionway.

Whistling, in good spirits, I resumed polishing.

The Marina Beach was one of the newer hotels, probably financed by Asian investors. The marble-floored lobby was spacious enough for a large cocktail area, and beyond it was a carefully tended enclosed garden with a waterfall. At the far end, opposite the registration desk, doors opened into Stone's, the excellent French restaurant I'd enjoyed in affluent times.

After getting Hatfield's suite number I crossed to the elevators and noticed several sharp-eyed Japanese men unobtrusively watching employees. Performance control, I thought, protecting their investment.

Joel Hatfield had assembled a tray of drinks from the suite's Servi-Bar, and after we'd touched glasses he said, "Good news and bad, Joe. But before that you should know I'm here to retain a law firm to represent Melissa's new interests—probate, financial management, tax and debt consolidation, and so on." He sipped from his glass. "Now the good news is, Melissa is being freed tomorrow."

I grinned. "After that, what could be bad?"

"Well, she's not coming here directly. I thought—and Emil agreed—that flying out of Nice could appear as though she was afraid to stay in French jurisdiction. Strictly a PR touch, understand."

"Hell, her husband died there. Seems only natural she'd want to get all that behind her."

"The press hasn't been kind to Melissa," he remarked. "Emil and I—and for that matter, Melissa—don't want to give them any pretext for alleging she's fleeing the scene of her possible crime. After all, she had no witnesses to her innocence—just an absence of evidence against her. The yacht crew was solid, thank heaven, no bad-mouthing the mistress."

"For which accommodation," I suggested, "she'll express appreciation in a material way."

"No doubt of that," he said, "while recovering from the trauma of abrupt widowhood, the publicity and humiliation of jail." He drank from his glass. "The plan is for her to leave Nice as she came—by yacht—and stay aboard at least as far as Gibraltar. She may fly back to the U.S. from there, or she may take the Atlantic crossing on the *Flaminia*. It's undecided."

"So the bad news is, I won't see Melissa for a while."

"Afraid not." He looked away. "She hasn't taken the experience well, Joe. It's been very hard on her and she's bitter."

"She has a right to be. Anything else on your mind?"

"After I get her affairs into Ed Jacobson's hands I'll bow out. Ed's got a big firm downtown, specializes in the sort of overall representation she'll need." He looked at his thin gold watch. "I worked for Ed when he was U.S. Attorney, so I have confidence in him."

"Is he honest?"

"I said he'd been U.S. Attorney," he said, face reddening.

I rolled my eyes. "I can remember an Attorney General who went to prison, Joel—two of them."

"Well, so can I, but Ed's got a good track record and plenty of smart, able people around him. Satisfied?"

"I raised the question because here in California large estates are known to melt down to nothing in the hands of avaricious lawyers."

He thought it over and decided against defending the legal profession. Instead, he said, "I've read that old Raf Ambrosino is no more."

"Gone to tread grapes in that big vineyard in the sky."

"I was afraid he'd go after Melissa for what Tarkos owed him."

"So was I. Not to mention what he could have done to me had he lived."

The telephone rang. Hatfield answered, said, "Come on up, Ed, been waiting for you." He replaced the receiver and looked at me. "So how's it been with you while I was gone?"

I put down my unfinished drink and got up. "The same," I said. "My wife's filed for divorce but that was expected. Strike's still on . . . Thanks for filling me in."

Without getting up, he shook hands with me and I left the suite. As I neared the elevator, a large man with gray, theatrically wavy hair stepped out and walked briskly toward Hatfield's door. He had a neatly trimmed mustache, polished black shoes, and a gray, three-piece cheviot suit. He radiated an aura of success and the power bred by success. Maybe I should have gone into law, I reflected as I pressed the Down button. Down seemed to be my general direction anyway.

In late afternoon, while I was taking inventory of galley supplies, there was a knock at the cabin door, and when I opened it I saw the bearded face of Professor George Anders looking down at me. "Am I interrupting anything?" he asked.

"C'mon in," I said, and he came carefully down the companionway. "Drink?"

"Please—anything you've got handy."

I set out two glasses and the Beam bottle. Anders poured first—a good four ounces—and I gave myself about half his dosage. We clinked glasses and I asked, "What brings you up from academe?"

"Joel Hatfield wanted me to meet Lissa's new lawyer—Edward Jacobson—did you meet him?"

"In passing. He may be just the power attorney she'll need."

He thought it over. "Does she really need a lawyer?"

"Lawyers run the world, Professor. Melissa has to hire a big one to protect her from the pack."

Anders was looking considerably better than at last viewing. His face was no longer swollen and discolored and the arm sling was gone. Red-rimmed, watery eyes, however, suggested that the professor was a latent alcoholic, if not a practicing one—an evaluation supported by the eager way he downed straight bourbon, smacked his lips, and asked if another splash was okay. "Why not?" I said. "It's that time of day." Besides, how could I deny my prospective father-in-law something he obviously craved? As he poured another stiff one I said, "Where'd you go, Professor?"

"Oh, up around Sonoma. The family of a former student owns a winery there and made me welcome."

"Been in touch with Melissa?"

"Not directly—only through Mr. Hatfield." He drank deeply. "It's been a terrible experience for her."

"Yes, and it's fortunate she's being freed. But all that inherited money should compensate for stress and anxiety—in time."

"I hope so," he said, licking his lips to absorb a lingering drop of sauce. "My daughter affects a shell of toughness but that's to protect an inner sensitivity."

"I don't think Tarkos will have many mourners."

"There's his sister, and of course Lissa will have to dissemble grief." He leaned forward. "Do you think she did it?"

"Did what?"

He swallowed. "Killed her husband."

"Strange question coming from someone who's known her all her life. What's your opinion?"

He drew in a deep breath and exhaled slowly. "I'm troubled by the possibility. She loathed Tarkos and with ample reason. So there was motive, and apparently, opportunity as well. I—I don't know what to think."

"I don't think it's something you ought to brood about. Tarkos was a rotten human being by all accounts—and I've heard more than Melissa's version. If she shoved him over the balcony it'll be on her conscience and she'll have to wrestle with guilt or sublimate it. Anyway, the judge is saying she's not guilty."

He held up one finger, teacher-style. "Ah, not quite that conclusive. More on the order of a Scottish verdict: not proven."

I shrugged. "If there's a problem, it's hers exclusively, so don't fret it. Leave that to store-front philosophers who equate an act of justifiable vengeance with general social dissolution. Besides, Professor, considering the beating you took from Tarkos's men, I wouldn't think you'd worry over how he passed from this world into the next."

"Oh, it's not that, it's my daughter's character that concerns me. I wouldn't want to see her life warped by . . . by any . . . ah . . . traumatic memories." He had trouble phrasing the euphemism but that could be due to liquor. I said, "Nor would I, and I'll do my best to see that she's reconciled to the world as it exists."

"That's good to hear," he said, and picked up the bottle. "One for the road?"

"Sure. Heading back to Dago?"

"Morning classes." He half-filled his glass. "Nice boat, you keep it up well."

"Mainly because it's for sale." When he looked at me blankly I said, "I'm unemployed and need the money."

"Well, why don't you wait for Lissa to come back? I'm sure she wouldn't hesitate to—ah, help out." He tilted his glass and drank.

"I wouldn't want that," I told him. "Call me chauvinist, but I pay my own way." That wasn't quite true because I'd accepted money and one shiny diamond from his daughter, but I saw no need to confide in her father. Anyway, I'd had so much recent practice that I was becoming an accomplished, unblushing liar.

"I should be going," he said.

"Glad to drive you to the airport," I offered.

"Thanks, but I'll just take a taxi." He drained his glass and stood up. "I guess we'll be seeing more of each other after Lissa returns."

I helped him up the companionway and onto the pier, watched his unsteady progress toward the taxi stand until he was in one, and the taxi drove away.

So he had doubts about Melissa's innocence, I mused as I went back to the cabin. So had the French police. But as far as I was concerned she was cleared, and having killed two men and provoked the death of a third for reasons I deemed sufficient, I would be a hypocrite to entertain suspicions of Melissa's guilt. Let Sophie Letterman's mad fantasies suffice.

I was warming the galley oven for a TV dinner when Maddy Gossons came aboard, wearing a broad smile. "Sold!" she exclaimed. "As soon as the check clears, the buyer takes possession."

"How long'll that take?"

"Three days, four, so you can start moving out gear whenever it's convenient."

"Not much to move," I told her, "and I'll leave bedclothes and such. Plenty of gas in the tank."

"Shall I mail your check or will you pick it up at the office?"

"Call me when it's ready and I'll decide."

"And you'll pay off the bank lien?"

"Sure will. How about a celebration drink?"

"I won't refuse." She glanced at the bottle. "Bourbon's fine—with a little ice, if you don't mind."

As we drank together I had the feeling she'd have stayed for dinner and more if I'd suggested it. But losing my boat depressed me now the realization had set in, and I wanted to be alone with it for the final hours.

Drink finished, she said goodnight in a rather wistful way, and I locked the cabin doors when she was gone.

Dinner was pretty tasteless, and after washing dishes I pushed Natty's divorce filing aside and set up my typewriter on the table. Before resuming work I read all I'd written, to reprise the story line, and then I rolled a fresh sheet in the portable and picked up where I'd left off.

Scenes and dialogue came slowly because my mind was flashing back to Vegas and Maricopa and Nice and the woman I loved aboard a big seagoing yacht. So I stopped for a while, made coffee, and decided it would be nice if Melissa's next husband was a published author, since I was bringing so little else to our marriage.

That self-stimulus opened mental doors, and for the next three hours I beat the noisy keys, cranked in sheet after sheet of pristine paper, and ended the session with a rewarding stack of typed pages beside me.

I treated myself to a bourbon nightcap, and as I undressed for my last night aboard, I thought about Professor George D. Anders, my father-in-law-to-be. I wouldn't have selected him had there been a world to choose from, but he was what I was going to get and I felt I had him sized up pretty well. A man of above-average intelligence, long-widowed and old-maidish, settled into an undemanding tenured job in a nonselective institution, liquor his substitute for wife and the goals he might have set in his youth but which by now were faded or forgotten dreams. Doubtless, he had guilty feelings over insufficiently nurturing his motherless daughter—having a living to earn—but I couldn't fault him for that. In his circumstances I probably couldn't have done better.

So I saw him as *l'homme moyen*, and hoped he'd visit Melissa and me by invitation only, wherever we made our home.

In the morning I filled a spare sail bag with my belongings, added odds and ends to my suitcase, and piled everything into my Datsun. At the dockmaster's office I advised the clerk my boat had been sold, and any questions concerning it should be referred to Ms. Gossons at Semmes.

I treated myself to a large, high-calorie breakfast at the Holiday Inn, remembering Tony sitting across from me, and feeling vacant and morose. He and the padre had made it out of dusty, sunbaked Maricopa and only the padre had returned alive.

As I paid my bill I looked at my watch and calculated that the *Flaminia* would have cleared Nice by now and be well outside

French jurisdiction underway to the Pillars of Hercules; Melissa's long ordeal was behind her.

When I got to my apartment, no cops or hoods were waiting for me, just a scattering of mail and the usual musty air. I collected laundry for the Chinaman and picked up what I'd left there, made the bed, and hung up fresh towels, remembering the night Melissa had emerged from her shower wearing one.

By the back steps I roused old Pedro from Durango dreaming, and paid him five dollars to replace my broken window latch. I felt I could afford his services, for I was coming into money—as soon as the boat check cleared.

After Pedro had hammered and screwed the latch in place—not a sturdier one, just a new one—I made a routine call to Morry Manville, letting him know I was alive and available for general assignment. He said, "Y'know, Joe, I've decided this strike'll *never* end. The studios will close, real estate will be sold off for condos and office buildings, and the movie industry will be an historical memory like the ox-cart road."

"It's certainly a possibility."

"With Borden Tarkos dead there's a lot of unrest and uncertainty over at Falcon. No one knows what his widow plans to do with the place. Sell it or try to run it."

"I understand she's hired a heavyweight named Ed Jacobson to straighten out Tarkos's affairs. If she's smart, she'll listen to his advice."

"I think I heard she had some sort of show-biz background before she married Tarkos."

"Could be. Making the kind of success story Hollywood loves to tell and retell."

"And film and film and film." He paused. "There aren't any new stories, you know, just revisions of the old standbys. Ah—how's your novel going?"

"I've finished a hundred pages—draft, of course."

"You like it?"

"It's readable. I started it as make-work, you know, but now that I'm really into it I want to see it through."

"If it's got a sustained story line and isn't hard porno, my brother-in-law might be interested. He's made big bucks publishing those weight-control booklets you buy at checkout counters—you know, calorie count, how to keep lard from clogging your veins. Good health for the elderly; how to turn leftovers into duck *à l'orange.*" Morry chuckled. "Don't knock it, Joe, and the point is, Aaron wants to go literary. If I like your book and *he* likes it, maybe we can cut a deal."

"Well, it's something to think about." If Morry was as busy as he used to be he wouldn't have time to think about connecting my draft novel with his brother-in-law. But the strike had skewed everyone's thinking and made the remotest possibility seem like present opportunity. Still, if Morry wanted to try for ten percent of the gross, why not show him the finished book? He was my agent, after all, and deserved first refusal.

Morry said, "I don't expect perfection, understand; just give me a clean draft to consider."

"I'll do that," I said, "but it'll be a while."

I set up my typewriter and took the phone off the hook. It was noon when I started typing, three o'clock when I broke for lunch. I bought beer and groceries from Ruben Gomez, went back to my place and worked until eight PM, when the basketball games began.

Generally, that was the schedule I followed for the rest of the week. By then I had two hundred typed pages and enough confidence to write the final hundred.

When I'd moved in, Mrs. Haven mentioned that her married daughter did professional typing at home on a word processor. The daughter, Janice ("Call me Jan") Rentgen, looked over my pencil-corrected pages and said they looked better than most writers she worked for, shoved them in an envelope, and promised a clean copy in a week.

After Jan left I was visited by a Treasury agent named Fred Onderdonk—according to his I.D.—who politely asked if I could throw any light on the murder of Agent Antonio Honey. I said I'd told several detectives what little I knew and he said, yes, he'd read their reports but perhaps, at a distance, I had something to add.

"Frankly," I said, "I've tried to put it out of my mind. From what I've read, Tony was tracking some bad people in Mexico. Have you investigated that angle?"

"To some extent," he admitted, "but there's a Vegas angle, too."

"Oh? Tony leave markers at the casinos?"

His expression registered distaste. "No, no," he said quickly. "Organized crime. Ah—he ever mention the Ambrosinos to you?"

"Ambro—?" I shook my head. "Except for talking about his home town, Maricopa, Tony was pretty tight-lipped. I gathered he wasn't supposed to talk about his work."

"That's so. Did he have a girlfriend?"

"None he exposed to me." By now they'd have learned he'd stashed a girl at a safehouse and I hoped they'd never identify her as Sondra Starr. "That Ambro . . . sino—the old Mafioso who died not long ago—that who you mean?"

"That's the one. The remains of his son and another soldier were found down near Los Cabos. That's where Tony—Agent Honey—was working."

"So you think maybe he killed those men and was hit in reprisal?"

"The suggestion's been made, but everyone involved is dead." He shrugged. "Guess we'll never know."

"Sorry I can't help."

"Appreciate your time, Mr. Brent. We all liked Tony—you did, too. It's a loss we'll remember."

For the rest of the day I stayed close to my place, typed a dozen pages, and turned in, eyes feeling like hot gravel.

In the morning, while I was washing breakfast dishes, the phone rang, and I heard the voice of Joel Hatfield.

"Thought you'd want to know," he said. "She's flying in today."

"*Where?*"

"Los Angeles International, United from Barcelona. There'll be a hell of a lot of media, so I don't think you ought to be there. She'll get in touch when she's settled in. Jacobson's reserved a suite for her at the Picasso."

"Nice place."

"She can afford it—and anything else her heart desires. You're a lucky guy, Joe."

"Am I? We'll see."

I hung up feeling even happier than when Melissa was let out of jail a week ago. She'd gone through a lot since that afternoon when I'd taken her to the feds, and her father said she was bitter. But I loved her, I hadn't changed.

Had she?

Through the day's long hours I waited for her call. It came at four-thirty and her voice was husky as she said, "Darling, I've missed you so, and I love you."

"I love you, Melissa. How soon can I see you?"

"The press is leaving now—my new lawyer, Ed Jacobson, thought we ought to invite reporters in for an informal conference and get it behind me. So six o'clock ought to be about right. Then we can be alone. We'll have dinner by ourselves, and—"

"It's the 'and' I'm eager for."

"So am I, dear. It's been awful without you."

I took a third shower, having perspired a lot from nervous excitement, dressed in my best available clothing, and drove out Sunset Boulevard to rendezvous with my long-absent love.

THIRTY-ONE

Two years ago, when the Picasso was built, it enraged Angelino preservationists and traditionalists, for the builders had torn down and bulldozed a famous old Hollywood restaurant that had served film people from silent days onward. In its place had risen a tall glass-and-marble structure, all planes and angles, that looked as hard and impenetrable as the entertainment industry it served.

Because the hotel was located near two major recording studios, it was a favorite of rock musicians, their entourages, and groupies. The least expensive room went for more than two hundred a night and there were few of those. Most of the lavish lodgings were two- and three-bedroom suites with large reception rooms, dining areas, and fully equipped kitchens for international personalities who brought their own chefs, maids, and butlers. Servant quarters were located at the rear of the hotel above service entrances.

The lobby was a glare of marble broken by framed modernist paintings, and from it a narrower corridor led to a dim cocktail lounge that adjoined the restaurant. Hung against the corridor wall and tastefully illuminated was the hotel's showpiece—a four-by-five cubist painting by Picasso, purchased by the hotel's Arab owner and displayed, for tax write-off, to public view. At the time of its hanging, several gossip columnists sniffed that the owner was showing a reproduction, while keeping the multimillion-dollar original in his penthouse, safe from Hollywood's Visigoths and vandals.

I'd seen the blue, pink, and gray painting several times when I'd met Morry for drinks in the nearby lounge—Morry had musical clients as well as writers—and I didn't care whether it was original or reproduction. What I cared about, and resented, was the ostentatious wealth displayed by the rockers, punk and mainstream, who swirled around the lobby and corridor after being offloaded from their stretch Mercedes limousines. A gaggle had just arrived, males and androgynes wearing tapered black leather trousers and tight black leather sleeveless tops. They and the squealing females who followed were barefoot, their feet none too clean. They pressed like lemmings toward the elevator bank, pushing and elbowing aside lesser mortals; crowding into the elevators, eager and anxious for the lines and needles waiting in their suites.

I waited for an elevator's return and took it to the eleventh floor. Muffled rock music drifted through the corridor from the floor below, following me to the inset double doorway of Melissa's suite.

A neatly dressed hotel security man stood in the shallow alcove. He looked me up and down and said, "You expected?"

"Mrs. Tarkos is expecting me." I gave my name and he said, "Yeah, you're expected. Go on in."

I depressed the brass handle and the oak door gave inward.

The entrance hall was marbled floor and sides. A hanging lamp was filigreed to resemble a ball of golden fire. The hallway gave out into a large step-down living room, in the center of which was an eight-foot coffee table. Parallel with it, on both sides, were white leather sofas. On the nearest one, back to me, sat two people, both of whom I recognized. At the sound of the closing door, their heads turned. Melissa cried, "Joe!" and hurried to meet me. We put our arms around each other, but in place of the warm embrace I'd expected, she kissed my cheek chastely and pulled away. "Later," she whispered, took my hand, and led me to the sofa.

"Joe, this is my lawyer who's going to handle everything. Ed Jacobson, Joe Brent."

The lawyer rose in stately fashion and offered me a large, moist hand. "Glad to meet you," he intoned. "Melissa's told me so much about you."

So already it was "Melissa." How soon they move in and take over, I thought, and said, "Not everything, I hope."

He chuckled tolerantly and gestured at the drinks tray on the table. "Help yourself. Melissa?"

"Whatever Joe's having."

I moved in between sofa and table, poured Jack Daniel's into two

Baccarat glasses, added ice, and gave one to Melissa. "It's been a while," I said, touched my glass to hers, and heard the crystal chime. "Too long," she said, and sighed. "Ed's been wonderful, helping me through that confrontation with the press."

"But I didn't do all that much," Jacobson said modestly. "My client is a natural-born performer and the media loved her. This is a good start in building her new image." He regarded her with what seemed like more than paternal fondness.

"And what image is that?" I inquired as pleasantly as I could.

"Oh, we have to neutralize all that adverse publicity the sensationalist press put out while Melissa was in Nice. Once that's accomplished, she becomes a patroness of the arts and charities, a gracious hostess whose invitations are eagerly sought."

He sipped from the glass he'd been fondling and winked at Melissa, as though to remind her of secret covenants. To Melissa I said, "That what you want?"

"I—I think so—I don't know. Everything's happened so suddenly, I've been so rushed . . ."

"You just leave everything to me," Jacobson said with the assurance of a fixer who could turn base metal into gold. "You'll be amazed at the results."

Melissa smiled uncomfortably. She was wearing a white wool skirt with a top knitted of gold thread. Around her neck was a pearl necklace I hadn't seen before—but then I'd never seen any of her strung or mounted jewelry. Just the loose diamonds she'd taken from her late husband.

Jacobson studied me through narrowed eyelids. "Haven't I seen you someplace, sir?"

"As recently as yesterday. I was leaving Hatfield's room—you were on your way in."

He snapped his fingers. "That's it! Of course. I like to get everyone in place."

Or put everyone in his place, I thought, but said, "So the press conference was a big success. That's great, dear."

Jacobson, who seemed to have become her spokesman, said, "They were drawn to Melissa like ants to honey. Hardly a hostile question, and that's rare for filmland's press corps. Don't believe me? Read tomorrow's papers."

"Oh," I said, "I never doubted your ability to get what you wanted."

His eyes narrowed again but he decided against going against me. Instead, he said, "Well, I feel we've accomplished enough for one day, don't you, Melissa? And you must be exhausted."

She nodded.

"Then I'll take my leave. Dinner engagement with Judge Reamer and Judge Podakis at the club." He forced me to clasp his plump, moist hand again. "Glad to meet a friend of Melissa who's helped her along the way."

He began walking toward the exit and Melissa followed. Before Jacobson opened the door, he said, "Remember, don't be seen in public places for a while—unattractive people and pushy press are bound to be annoying. Rest, relax, and think of the boundless future that will soon be yours."

"I will," she said, and gave him her hand—which, amazingly, he didn't bend over to kiss—and closed the door behind him.

"Thank God," she exclaimed as she turned to me. "I thought he'd never go."

"He sees himself as a chaperon—maybe more than that. Is he married?"

"I don't know, it never occurred to me to ask."

"Well, he's having a bachelor dinner."

"Maybe the judges don't have wives."

"True—but it's worth a query before he establishes himself too comprehensively."

She put down her drink and laced her fingers behind my neck. "You don't like him, do you?"

"I don't like him and he doesn't like me. I had the feeling he was here for the night if I hadn't arrived."

"Oh, Joe, you're making something out of nothing."

"I hope so," I said. "Now how about a *real* kiss?"

She pressed her lips to mine and murmured, "You don't know how often I've longed for this."

"Am I still part of your life, your future?"

"Of course you are—how could you even think otherwise?"

"You were with your husband, and a long ways away."

"But you know I went back to him only to save you and my father."

"I know, honey, and it was a noble thing to do. Still, it's worked out for the best, hasn't it?"

"I can't deny that—but don't, *please* don't ask about Borden's death—I'm not ready for that yet—I'm just trying to get it all behind me. And that awful jail—" She shivered in my arms. "I was cold all the time, had to wear a canvas uniform—and the food was sickening."

"Well, you'll never have to look at sickening food again. And on that subject, I suppose we'd better have dinner here—since Jacobson doesn't want you seen with unattractive people."

"Joe, he didn't mean *you*, for heaven's sake. He was talking about nosy people who might try talking to me in a restaurant."

"So you'll be a princess in a golden cage. Until Ed lets you out."

"Joe, *please* don't talk that way. We're getting off to a dreadful start."

I kissed her again. "Sorry, but that Jacobson set me on edge. He looks too damn perfect and he treated me like a delivery boy."

"Oh, he didn't at all, he's just being protective."

"Too damn protective," I said. "The son of a bitch regards me as a rival—an ineligible rival at that. And if he ever gets condescending with me again I'll bust that perfect nose of his."

For the first time since my arrival, Melissa laughed. "Can't help it—it's so funny to think of. The proper lawyer wearing a big bandage on his nose." She laughed again, the pealing, unrestrained laughter I remembered so well.

"So let's think of him as a fun figure," I suggested, "and not take him too damn seriously."

"Exactly."

I reached around and unclasped her pearls, laid the strand on the table. "Expecting anyone else? More appointments tonight?"

"No one but you."

I unbuttoned her gold-knit blouse and drew it off, then her bra. I touched her nipples and kissed them. They swelled between my lips. Throatily she said, "You do things to me, darling. Wonderful things. I want it to be just the way it was in that funny little motel—where was it?"

"El Cajon," I said, unzipping the white wool skirt.

"What were you doing all these weeks?"

"Fighting crime," I said, "but that phase is history. Actually, I've been perishing for you to return."

"And now I'm here." The skirt dropped to the carpet and I picked her up in my arms. "Which way to the bedroom?"

"Choose one of three—I'm in the one with the white door."

"That's for me." I kneed the door open and lowered her gently onto the king-sized bed. "No ceiling mirrors?"

"Gold door, but I don't want us there—Borden—too many nasty memories I want to forget." Her hands were busy at my belt buckle. I kicked off my shoes, bent over, and kissed her open mouth. It was warmer than mine and her tongue lashed like a trapped eel. I smelled her perfume, the sweet scent of her womanhood, and then we were in each other's arms, the world forgotten as we made love hungrily, almost desperately, absorbing each other as though this encounter had to make up for all we'd missed.

In jail she'd lost enough weight that my fingers could feel each rib, but that made me closer to her inner core where I wanted to blend my being with hers.

Panting, sighing, murmuring, we clung to each other long after passion dissolved, and it seemed there were just the two of us alone, detached from the rest of the world.

Sleepily she whispered, "Hungry?"

"For you. And a restorative drink."

Rising on one elbow, she smiled down at me. "That guaranteed to do it?"

"Plus your inexhaustible charms."

"Champagne okay?"

"Perfect."

Naked, she walked lightly from the bedroom and I heard the refrigerator door open. She returned with two flute glasses and a bottle of Dom Pérignon. I peeled off the seal, twisted away the wire retainer, and pried up the cork with my thumbs. The cork exploded against the ceiling and bubbles poured forth. I filled our glasses and we drank with linked arms, as lovers do. She picked up the cork from the bed and said, "I'll keep this always—a souvenir of our first night together. Joe—it's just as exciting as the first time we made love."

"And the last," I said nostalgically.

"Yes—when we thought it would be only a week or so apart." She sipped from her glass. "Were you really a prisoner in Mexico, as that lawyer said?"

"Stanley Parsons. Yes, I was lured there to be killed but I managed to get away. Let's not go into that now."

"No—there'll be time to tell each other many things. Were you worried about me when I was in jail?"

"Crazy with worry."

"They couldn't prove anything against me—not a thing. And I don't ever want to go back to France."

"Ten years from now," I said, "we'll go there with our children, show them the Louvre, Versailles, the Arc de Triomphe. Assuming we can afford it."

"Oh, that's no worry. Jacobson says I'll have millions to spend."

"If he knows that he's a fast worker and I'll bet he's got your inheritance figured to the last dime. But I won't be unemployed forever—I intend to support you."

"Oh, don't be foolish. What I'll have is yours to share—has to be that way." She sipped again, thoughtfully. "Are you still married?"

"My wife's filed for divorce and I'm not contesting it."

"How long before you're free?"

"No idea—I've never been divorced before. Probably a month or two for the paperwork. Is the time important?"

She looked away. "It corresponds to a period of—let's call it 'waiting time,' which Jacobson thinks I ought to observe for public consumption."

"Observe how?"

She touched the side of my face. "Now, don't get tense and resentful, Joe. But as a recent widow I should dress modestly, not be seen in fun places, and for a while not be with men."

I couldn't help feeling stressed and resentful. "Men meaning me but not Jacobson. Right?"

"Joe—"

He calls you Melissa—why not call him Ed? You're on a first-name basis."

"I *wish* you'd drop the hostility, can't you *please?*"

"Look, I didn't expect us to get married immediately—certainly not until I'm divorced—but there are plenty of places we could dine where you won't be recognized."

"I know, I know that, and we will, but we'll have to be discreet when we're together. If I'm photographed with a man, any man, Joe, Ed—like that better?—*Ed*'s worried Borden's sister might try to take legal action against Borden's will and slow things up." She paused. "I assume you read what she's been screeching to anyone who'd listen?"

"I read it and gave it the same credence I'd give any crazy who'd spent a lot of time in padded walls."

She looked at me quickly. "So you know about that?"

"Word gets around."

"Darling, I just don't understand this chilly mood you're creating. We're together, we've made wonderful, satisfying love, and suddenly it's almost as though we were strangers."

"Not my intention," I said truthfully, "it's that having you away so long I want to reclaim you now, be with you as much as possible. I don't like restraints, never have."

"But it's only a few weeks, darling, and then we'll have total freedom to go and do as we like."

"Does Jacobson know we're lovers?"

"He may suspect it, having seen you—the only person I've invited here. What does that matter?"

"Because I think he'll go to special lengths to keep us apart. From the moment I stepped inside here I sensed he was a rival and I know damn well he feels the same about me. So let's not be manipulated by him, okay?"

"Okay." She divided the rest of the champagne between our glasses. "Even though it's conceivable you could be wrong about him."

"I've lived in a man's world, sweetheart, I know men." I drank from her glass. "No more Jacobson."

"Thank heaven," she sighed.

"Would it be . . . too indiscreet if I stayed the night? You could always hide me in another bedroom—like a Restoration play."

"Darling, I expected you to stay with me, counted on it. Of course you will."

I smiled and kissed her full, champagne-moist lips. "Where else could I go but back to our Cerrito love nest?"

"Suddenly I'm hungry—ravenous. Can I order?"

"Surprise me. Ah—is there enough champagne to last the night?"

"Six bottles in the fridge. Why don't you open one while I check the menu."

By the time I'd gotten the cork out Melissa was replacing the room-service phone. "They say half an hour. Shall we share a shower?"

It was a large, marble-faced hexagonal stall, with spray coming from all directions. We soaped each other's bodies, and soaped them again with frank, erotic rubbings and probings. New terrycloth robes hung on the wall—a Picasso amenity—and after drying each other we put them on with shower slippers and lay on the bed working on our second bottle of champagne. After a while she said, "In Mexico —was it bad?"

"Bad," I agreed. "Ambrosino's son got me there to question me about you and kill me."

She shivered. "Did you tell him anything?"

"I played dumb, convincingly enough that he phoned his dad in Vegas for further instructions. While they were gone—"

"They?"

"He had a soldier with him. Anyway, I managed to get free, and when they came back, I killed them." My hands tightened at the repressed memory.

Her eyes were wide. "You . . . killed . . . two . . . men?"

"Them or me, honey. But this is no time to talk about death. We're alive and we have a life to live—together. By the way, I had a talk with your father yesterday."

"Was he sober?"

"Less so when he left."

"He drinks too much," she said bitterly. "Always has."

"He's a lonely man, Melissa. Lonely people tend to drink, if only to pass the time. How do you think I've managed without you? Push-ups and cold showers?"

"That's sweet," she said and kissed my cheek. The buzzer rang and Melissa got off the bed. Through the closed hall door the security guard called to ask if room service was authorized to come in. Melissa said it was, and after the waiters had set the dining table and gone away I came out of the bedroom.

Two candles illuminated the glass-topped table that was set with starched linen and gleaming silver. The first course was shrimp cocktail, the second, Oriental-style shrimp sauteed in soy and wine.

"I thought red meat and potatoes might be too filling," she said, "if you get my meaning."

"Perfect choice. Shrimp's light on the stomach, especially when consumed with sufficient champagne."

"How much is sufficient?"

"Thought you'd know. Isn't that all that's served at Monte Carlo?"

She laid down her fork. Very levelly she said, "Please don't mention that place—or anything connected with the cruise."

"My mistake, and no offense intended."

"I'm still very sensitive about all that—you understand."

"Truly sorry." I ate another shrimp before saying, "Your father wants to see you."

"Probably—now that I have money."

"It's more than that. Give him a break. He has no one, nothing. You're his daughter and he's proud of you."

"Does he think I killed Borden?"

"He didn't discuss it," I lied.

"What do *you* think?"

"I believe the French wouldn't have absolved you if you had."

For a while she said nothing, as though there was nothing more important than cutting the next large shrimp into bite-size pieces. Then she said, "We quarreled that night—after we got back to the Negresco. Fortunately, no one heard us. Then we went to bed and I fell asleep. I lied about one thing, though. I was aware that Borden got out of bed. At the time I was barely awake and thought he was going to the bathroom, as he often did at night."

"That's not much of a lie."

"It's one that worried me."

"Then forget it. One less worry for you is the death of Raf Ambrosino."

"Joel Hatfield told me. And he said Raf had gone after you."

"We had a conversation," I admitted, "but I persuaded him I knew nothing of his son's disappearance." I drank deeply. "That was before the bodies—remains, I should say—were discovered." I looked away. "There was a fire . . ."

She took my hand and held it firmly. "Because of me so many things happened to you—bad things. A thousand times I've wished I hadn't run away—but then I remembered I wouldn't have met you with your bag of Gomez groceries. I'll make it up to you, I promise."

"Your being here is all the compensation I'll ever need."

After dinner we watched an Italian soft-porn movie on the big TV projector screen until I realized that Melissa was uncomfortable with the actors' writhings and simulated lovemaking, and I turned it off. More negative memories to keep buried deep.

We stood hand in hand before the wall-high window and watched the Hollywood skyline, the multicolored lights that merged into the cold pure light of the stars. I thought of my boat's rigging lights and wished we were together on the foredeck surrounded by silence, sea, and night breeze. But the boat was gone now, along with my job and my marriage. Memories . . .

Melissa murmured, "Two weeks ago I didn't dare dream I'd ever be here. I was terribly afraid of what could be done to me; I could hardly sleep and I began to treasure every breath, counting them as the hours went on."

I took her in my arms and held her as a distant searchlight swept the sky. "No yesterdays," I said gently. "Just tomorrows and forever."

We went back to bed then and lay together for a long while before we began making love. This time was less frantic, much longer, and more profound. The thrilling excitement was there, and after I'd climaxed, waves continued running through Melissa's body while she gasped with each succeeding high. Then in the dark I heard a long, drawn-out sigh of contentment, her body relaxed completely, and I realized she had slipped into sleep.

Much later I was wakened by bed movement. I opened eyes sleepily and saw Melissa sitting upright, clawing at her chest. At first I thought she was ridding her flesh of biting ants, then her mouth opened and an anguished wail tore from her throat. Sobs came in choking spasms. I put my arms around her but she shook them off and writhed away.

"*I killed him,*" she screamed. "*I can't lie any longer. I killed my husband!*"

THIRTY-TWO

I slapped her face.

The screaming broke off, her mouth opened and closed emptily. Her eyes were large, staring at me as though I were a stranger. One hand touched her cheek. "You hit me," she said in a querulous voice. "Why did you hit me?"

"To break your nightmare." I drew her into my arms and this time she didn't resist but began sobbing brokenly, desolately.

I held her tightly, kissed her face, and gradually her spasm ended. She dried her eyes with the edge of a sheet and kissed my lips. "Thank God you were here. I thought I was going crazy. I can't shake the memory . . ."

"It's too soon," I said. "In time even the worst memories fade. By morning you won't remember your dream."

Lying back, she stared up at the ceiling. "It was more than a dream," she said in a strained voice. "It happened."

"It happened in your dream." I lay back beside her, holding her hand in mine. "You know how real a dream can seem—especially a bad dream, a nightmare. Let it go."

Her head turned toward me. "You don't understand, Joe. I knew I'd have to tell you and it might as well be now."

"Midnight confessions aren't valid," I said, "and I don't want to hear anything about it."

"But I must, don't you see? If I don't tell you the truth, there'll always be doubt in your mind after we marry."

"No. Just a few hours ago we said what's past is past and started a new beginning. Don't rake it up, darling. Let it die."

"But I have to tell you. I've kept it within myself and it's torturing me . . . the lies . . . the deception . . ." She looked away. "We *did* quarrel that night. It began at the casino when we were gambling. Borden spotted a young man who was losing heavily. While I was placing bets I saw Borden take him aside and talk to him. The man looked over at me and nodded, and I knew what was happening. When Borden came back he whispered to me that the man was coming back to our room. 'You'll entertain me,' he said, 'the two of you. I need it, I must have it.'

"I left my chips and walked away. Borden caught up with me and I told him I was finished being his whore. He said he knew I'd been sleeping with you, what difference did another man make? I'd done it before—he had proof.

"I felt nauseated. I told the man to get lost, I wouldn't screw him or anyone, and I went to the car. Borden got in beside me, twisted my arm until I screamed, and called me a bitch. I called him worse names and slapped his face. That made him quiet down until we got to our room. Then it started all over again, and he began to drink. He was sullen, resentful, said he was finished with me, he'd get rid of me."

"Did he demand the diamonds?"

"I'd told him what I'd told his lawyer—Parsons—that I'd turned them over to the U.S. Attorney in San Diego. That was no longer a problem between us—it was between him and Ambrosino. Borden knew he'd have to square himself with Ambrosino after we went back to the States. He didn't like it, of course, but he had no alternative—too many people knew how he'd been skimming and cheating his partners and the government."

My mouth was dry but I managed to say, "Go on."

"So I got into bed—a separate bed from Borden's—and managed to doze off. After a while—an hour, maybe two hours later—he shook me awake and said he wanted me to see the view from the balcony, the moon over the Mediterranean. It was our last night there, a memory he wanted to share.

"He was unsteady on his feet as he went to the balcony doors and opened them, and the way he looked back at me—Joe, it was *evil*. Suddenly I realized he planned to kill me."

"Why didn't you run from the room?"

"I've wondered—thought about my movements—but I felt completely helpless. His eyes—God, his *eyes*–they *compelled* me—I can't explain. But I didn't go willingly. I was almost paralyzed with fear."

"So you joined him on the balcony."

"His manner changed abruptly. He spoke softly, coaxingly, said he'd been wrong to insist on something so distasteful to me, even promised not to do it again. By then we were standing side by side just by the railing—a low railing, put there for children, I thought—and then his hand shot out and caught my wrist. He was pulling hard, and almost automatically I dropped to my knees, resisting. My other hand chopped his wrist, he let go and staggered backward. The railing stopped his legs but the rest of him kept moving. I saw his feet fly up, heard a scream, and he was gone."

Her voice was choking, her breathing fast, spasmodic. "I got to my feet, I looked down and saw him lying on the paving. I knew he was dead—no one could live through such a fall—and I realized I had to think of myself." She paused. "Maybe the worst part is that I was grateful he was dead. Glad."

"You didn't murder him. You defended yourself and by trying to kill you, he killed himself," I said urgently.

"I'm guilty."

"*No.* What was the alternative? Let him kill you?"

Her head moved wearily. "I hurt his wrist, made him let go."

"You're not thinking straight. You had an absolute right to protect yourself."

"Joe—I had to lie. As I hurried down to Borden's body I *knew* the truth wouldn't be believed."

"You did all the right things."

"By the time I reached the body I'd made up my mind. If I said I hadn't seen him go to the balcony, I couldn't be blamed for what happened. And later I said he hadn't been drinking much, so when alcohol was found in his blood, Emil Desjardins pointed out Borden must have been drinking while I was asleep, so it bore out what I'd said. Was that in the papers?"

"If it was I missed it, but stop torturing yourself with details. I'd never have asked, darling."

"But you'd have wondered."

I knew I would have; hell, I'd wondered all along. But her story satisfied me. More: Tarkos deserved to die.

I held her close until her flesh warmed and the memory began to dissolve. I turned on the bedside reading lamp and poured cognac into two glasses. "Gulp it down," I told her, "it's not for sipping—medicinal," and provided an example to follow.

She coughed a few times, smiled weakly, and said, "You always know what to do—from that very first night. Some instinct told me I'd be safe with you."

"The same instinct told you Tarkos had murder on his mind. Intuition, instinct—whatever it is, don't suppress it, nourish it. Trust it."

"As I trust you."

It didn't take long for the liquor to dull my brain. Melissa turned on her side, and laid one arm across my chest. Her head rested on my shoulder, her eyes closed, and her breathing became hardly audible. I tried to think of things I could have said to comfort her, erase the needless guilt that etched her mind, and while my subconscious was exploring those things, alcohol took over and washed me off to sleep.

Morning dispelled nightmares, and we made love as though we'd never made love before. We showered together, dried each other with warm, huge towels, and dressed for breakfast.

After the serving table was wheeled into the dining room, I removed the morning paper and set it aside. After sipping nectarine juice Melissa said, "I have an appointment at ten—Jacobson's office. Apparently, I have a lot of papers to sign—bank account transfers, ownership of Falcon and the Rebels to consider. He said it would be about two hours." She glanced at her wristwatch. "A limousine will pick me up. Let's meet back here at noon, lunch together. And . . ."

I smiled. "I'll be here."

"How will you spend your morning?"

"I'll go back to Cerrito and shave, pick up laundry at the Chinaman's, and straighten my apartment. I've been staying on my boat," I explained. "A boat that's now been sold."

"Oh, Joe, that wasn't necessary!"

"I'll clear enough to keep going—maybe until the strike ends."

"Can you cancel the sale—give back the money? I'll give you whatever you need, you know that."

"I know that, and I suppose I'll have to become accustomed to being a kept man. But for now let me cling to what's left of my integrity."

"Integrity—foolishness is what it is," she said sharply. "Don't get hung up on words."

I refilled our coffee cups and worked away at my fluffy cheese omelette. After a while the door buzzer rang and Melissa looked at me. "I'm not expecting anyone."

"Ask the guard."

She left the dining room, crossed the living room, and when she was by the door, I heard her call, "Who is it?"

"Man to see you, ma'am. Says you know him."

"What's his name?"

A few moments passed before I heard the guard's voice again. "Rene Keats. I.D. checks out."

Turning, Melissa leaned back against the door. Her gaze found me and I motioned her nearer. Quietly she said, "That's the tennis pro who—"

"I know who he is. Have him come in—I'll listen from the bedroom." I went there, leaving the door ajar. Melissa unbolted the entrance door and stood aside while Handsome sauntered in. He was wearing white Gucci loafers, white flannel trousers and a white Polo shirt. "Hel-*lo*, honey," he purred, and reached for her. Melissa stepped back and said icily, "What do you want?"

He shrugged and slouched down in an overstuffed leather chair. "Too bad about Borden, right? I'm gonna miss him. Y'know, he coulda had me wasted when he found out about you'n me, babe, but that wasn't his style. He gave me the best job I ever had."

"So I see. You never dressed that well before."

"Lakeside paid peanuts—an' I never got rewarded for servicing you when you needed it." His eyes rolled upward. "Great times in that cabana, right?"

"Mediocre. And I was a fool to have anything to do with you." I could see her hands curl into small fists. "What do you want, Rene?"

He sighed. "I thought I oughta pay my respects to the widow, find out if she needs more lessons."

"What kind of lessons?"

"*Any* kind—you know. Private instruction, like before."

"I don't play tennis any more. Now go."

He didn't move. Languidly he crossed one knee over the other, looked up at Melissa, and ran one hand through his curly locks. "Yesterday I had a talk with Sophie Letterman—you know, Borden's sister."

"She's crazy."

He shrugged. "Who's to say? Anyway, she wants to know everything about you. With enough dirt she could contest your late husband's will."

"And what did you tell her?"

He looked down at his fingernails. "So far, nothing. I thought you oughta know—maybe make me a better offer."

"How much?"

"Oh," he said with forced casualness, "you can spare a hundred thousand for your old tennis pro."

"A hundred *thousand?* And for that you'll keep your mouth shut?"

"Like the grave."

"It's an . . . interesting proposal," she said in a thoughtful tone. "It would be worth that never to see you again. And of course you're easy to buy off. Borden knew that. But how can I be sure Sophie won't top my offer?"

He smiled. "I'd be the first to let you know."

"Wouldn't that make it into an auction?"

"That's life, babe. Gotta face reality."

"How true that is, but before I enter into any agreement with you I'll ask my lawyer." Rene sat up quickly, but before he could speak Melissa turned and called, "Ed—did you hear this man's proposal?"

I opened the door and came out, adjusting my tie as though just finishing dressing. "Heard it all," I said, walking toward them, "and, like most lawyers, I have a counter-proposal to make."

Rene Keats stood up. He was a couple inches taller than I, but his frame was thin and his face soft. He blurted, "Who the hell's he, Melissa?" and his cheeks whitened.

"Ed Jacobson is my lawyer. Ed, Rene thinks he has a story to sell to my sister-in-law—*ex*-sister-in-law. About how after a tennis lesson we'd freshen up in my cabana and get it on. Rene thinks his silence is worth a hundred thousand dollars. What do you think?"

I stared at him and frowned.

"I think he'd be well-advised to maintain his silence, my dear." I faced the tennis lad. "No hundred thousand, no nothing. Just this: extortion's ten-to-twenty-five years' hard time in this state, and because you came here from Nevada, that adds a federal rap. You'd be middle-aged when you got out, not half so attractive to lonely wives, and clumsy on the court. Mrs. Tarkos is in charge of the Sagebrush, where you work, courtesy of her late husband, and if you want to go elsewhere, try to get a letter of recommendation."

I didn't think he'd go for me, but that was my mistake. Going for me was his.

"You fucker!" he yelled, bounded off the chair and threw an unguarded right. I half-turned, his forearm grazed my left shoulder, and I grabbed his wrist with my left hand. My right elbow slammed back into his thorax. He grunted in pain and surprise, and then I dropped forward, taking his bent arm with me. The rest of his body followed, cartwheeling over me, landing hard on the marble floor. He was wheezing, blowing hard, but he wasn't quitting. He got up on his knees, shaking himself like a wet dog while he decided what to do.

I stood a few feet away looking at the would-be blackmailer, and as I remembered that he'd made love to Melissa, a surge of fury made me want to kill him. He lunged at me, arms outstretched. I stepped between them and kicked his chin. His head snapped back and dropped hard on the gleaming stone. Melissa cried out, "God, don't kill him!" She grabbed my arm and pulled me back.

I was breathing hard. "I'd like to," I said, "but it's his lucky day."

Blood was running from his chin. His eyes were open but glazed and sightless. I probed his carotid and felt hard, driving pulse. "Temporarily absent," I said, got up and flexed my fingers. "If he'd done military service he'd know something about close combat, hand-to-hand. Hell, he doesn't even know basic boxing." I went to the door and told the security guard to come in. The guard looked down at Keats, then at me.

"The caller had a fall. If he requires medical attention, bill Mrs. Tarkos. Just get him out of here."

"Yes, sir." He stooped over, got his hands under Rene's armpits, and dragged him over the smooth floor. I noticed that he handled the unconscious man none too gently; probably he'd heard Rene's yell and Melissa's cry. They disappeared into the corridor and the door closed.

Melissa took a deep breath and came to me. Her body was trembling. I hugged her and said, "You were great, just great the way you handled him. And you even used Jacobson's sacred name."

She managed a slight smile. "I liked that touch, too. But what will Rene do now?"

"He's probably smart enough not to go back to Vegas and the job you control. After that chin's stitched he'll probably limp 'round to Sophie and talk out of spite. But he'd have done that anyway."

She sighed heavily. "I guess so. What time is it?"

"About a quarter of ten."

"I'll put on my face and go see Jacobson. Here—" she handed me a door key "—this is for you. The guard will always let me in."

"He better had," I said, "or Mr. Picasso will hear about it. And while you're with Jacobson, tell him to refuse any claims Parsons may lay against the estate."

"Can I do that?"

"He's been your adversary," I said, "and if he balks I'll have another talk with him."

Her eyebrows raised. "You had one?"

"That I did."

"You didn't tell me about it."

"One day I will."

She smiled, disappeared into the powder room, came back, kissed me again, and went out.

After pouring coffee for myself I scanned the morning paper and found what I was looking for.

The reporter might not have asked Melissa hostile questions, but the story she wrote was acidulous. The text didn't meet the test of libel *per se* but it was filled with sickening innuendo that the paper's legal staff must have vetted very carefully. Melissa came off as a glitzy fortune-hunter whose murderous guilt had not quite been established in a French court hearing. Borden Tarkos's standing as a benefactor of the arts and charities was emphasized, as was the estimated value of the estate that would soon pass into the young widow's inexperienced hands.

And in the spirit of liberal journalism, equal space was given to an adjoining interview with Sophie Letterman, whose photo showed a middle-aged woman with combed bangs, thin cheeks, piercing eyes, and a twisted smile. The journalist who wrote up Sophie's interview was careful to describe Sophie's renewed charges that Melissa had murdered her brother as "allegations". Sophie was quoted as saying "The Nice trial [sic] was a farce because that bitch paid everyone off, then fled on my brother's yacht."

Further, Ms. Letterman said she was gathering evidence to contest her brother's will, and was in the process of selecting an attorney "who couldn't be bought off by Melissa."

If the interviewer knew of Sophie's frequent institutionalization for mental illness, that aspect was kept from the public—to make Sophie a more credible adversary, I suspected. But whatever the rationale, I was glad I'd kept the paper from Melissa. After last night's nightmarish episode she didn't need negative news this morning. And I took covert satisfaction from Master Media Manipulator Jacobson's erroneous prediction that the press conference would produce sympathetic stories. I'd needle him about that but not today; I'd reserve it for his next try at talking down to me.

And for Melissa's sake, I hoped the power lawyer was more effective in court than with the media.

At my apartment I did what I'd told Melissa I was going to do, and also weeded out *passé* food from the refrigerator. There was no mail to open and no message from Maddy Gossons confirming the buyer's check had cleared. Before leaving, I pocketed a razor and shaving cream and admired the starched points of my shirt collar artfully ironed by the ever-reliable Madame Chu.

Then I drove back to the Picasso.

The door guard said, "The hotel doc stitched up that fellow who slipped on the floor and made him rest a while."

"Then?"

"The doc had him sign a release protecting the hotel from lawsuits and the guy went away."

"If he comes back," I said, "give him a toe in the crotch—or if that's beyond your duties, call me."

He smiled. "Yes, sir," and I unlocked the suite door, confident we'd seen the last of Rene.

During our absence maids had cleared away press conference debris, made the bed, and straightened the bathroom. I put my shaving gear in the big mirrored cabinet and went into the bedroom with the gold door. As Melissa had said, the ceiling was covered with mirrors. These were antiqued with gold foil, and for Borden Tarkos the Italianate décor would have had immense appeal, but none for me.

I poured a mild drink for myself, turned on the TV, and watched a midday news report on Channel 7. Today's feature story focused on youth-gang warfare and killings that the LAPD seemed unable to end. There were scenes of jacketed ruffians battling each other and riot police, and for the finale the camera panned across bodies lying amid debris. A secondary story came from the *barrio,* where banged-up Mexican illegals complained of border-patrol brutality—prompted, naturally, by the bilingual TV reporter.

At twelve-thirty a chef told us how to convert leftovers into attractive and appetizing casseroles that the whole family would appreciate. Much of his formula had to do with cream sauce and browned breadcrumbs, and an oven set precisely at 300° Fahrenheit.

I wondered why Melissa was so late, and hoped she hadn't forgotten our luncheon plans.

The leftover expert was followed by Donal of Doheny Drive, a fluttery hair stylist who invited volunteers from the largely female studio audience to treat themselves to the magic of his nimble fingers and flashing comb. The program was one of those dead-time fillers the studio figures is better than a blank screen. I felt otherwise, and turned it off.

I was pouring a second drink when the door opened and Melissa came in, cheeks flushed, shaking her head. "Sorry I'm late, and may I have that? I really need it."

I gave her my glass and made another drink for myself. She flopped down in a chair—the one from which Rene had lunged at me—and fanned her face. "I've never *seen* so many lawyers or so many papers to sign!" She wiggled her fingers. "Writer's cramp, would you believe it?"

"Price of power." I bent over and kissed her damp forehead. "While you cool off, I'll order lunch."

She looked up. "Would you mind? Chef's salad for me."

"Wine?"

"What's the saying—'A day without wine is a day without sunshine.'"

I picked up the leather-bound menu and began examining it. Melissa said, "And I had *another* bad experience just now. There were photographers and TV cameras on the sidewalk, and a crowd of people, and I was terrified they were all waiting for me." She breathed deeply. "Thank heaven they were waiting for some rock group and paid me no attention at all." She pulled off her neck scarf, kicked off her shoes, and walked to the bathroom shedding clothes all the way.

I could hear the shower running while I phoned our room service order: chef's salad for Melissa, king crab claws for me and a bottle of chardonnay. Melissa emerged, fluffing out damp hair, and I guided her into a chair, massaged her neck and shoulder muscles. She sighed contentedly and after a while purred, "That feels just marvelous. Can you manage to stay around, sir?"

"Depends on overtime."

"I'll take care of that—to your complete satisfaction." She got up, faced me, and opened her robe, then pressed against me. I said, "I like flashers—unless they're teasers."

"Not me," she declared and nibbled the tip of my tongue.

During lunch Melissa said Jacobson's lawyers were concerned about Borden's Sagebrush shares totaling forty percent of the privately held stock. Her name would have to be submitted to the Nevada Gaming Commission, which was also looking into allegations that Organized Crime figures secretly controlled the other sixty percent. "Frankly," she said, "I'd just like to get rid of the place, sell my shares to anyone who'll buy."

"Don't act hastily, the place is a goldmine," I counseled. "A day's take could put our children through Exeter and Harvard, with new Ferraris every year."

"And I'm definitely going to sell the Beverly Hills place."

"I'm with you on that."

"Falcon Productions needs restructuring, they tell me, and I'll need your advice. Get rid of Borden's contract whores and bring in competent new management with new ideas."

"That's always the cry when a studio changes hands, but in this case we'll make it work." I refilled our wine glasses. She sipped and said, "Jacobson recommends I hire an investment counselor—what do you think?"

"If the guy's honest, you need him. I've never made an investment bigger than the bank's Christmas Club."

She smiled and dimples appeared. "Neither have I. Oh, darling, we'll have such a *wonderful* life together!"

"We would even without your money—but it'll be nice to enjoy."

"Now the bad news is, I told Jacobson he could bring over more papers at three o'clock. What time is it now?"

"Ten to two."

"Is that time enough for a quickie?"

"It is," I said judicially, lifted her from the chair, and carried her into the bedroom I'd come to think of as our own.

Afterward, as she lay quietly in my arms, I knew that I loved her very deeply and told her so. She said she loved me and kissed the tip of my nose to prove it.

We got dressed then and I ordered coffee brought up for Jacobson and ourselves. He was there promptly at three, a large genial smile on his features, briefcase in left hand, right thrust out to clasp mine. I was always going to remember the sensation of pawing a walrus.

We sat around the big coffee table and Jacobson spread out papers for Melissa's signature. To her he said, "I've drawn up a short-form will as you instructed—a more detailed one will be prepared after the estate is probated." To me he said, "Mr. Brent, Mrs. Tarkos has named you principal beneficiary. Her father will receive income from a life-long trust fund, but aside from that, Mrs. Tarkos's holdings in their entirety will pass to you."

I looked at her. "I don't want to see that day, believe me."

"You'll sign there, Melissa, but we'll need another witness in addition to myself—as a beneficiary, Mr. Brent can't be a witness." He thought for a moment. "I might ask the door guard to perform that service, Melissa, if you don't object."

"Fine with me," she said. "What else?"

"Mainly to do with real estate—and there's a lot of it."

"Can you arrange to sell the Tahiti Way place right away?"

"I can certainly try, and I know the right realtor to handle it." He looked at her. "As is?"

"Furnished—everything. I want everything to go."

He made a note on his yellow-lined pad.

While he was doing that the door buzzer sounded and Melissa called, "What is it?"

"Flowers, ma'am."

"Can't you take them?"

"Messenger says you have to sign."

"All right."

As she rose I got up and said, "You take the flowers, I'll speak to the guard about witnessing."

We walked toward the door and she said, "I wonder who they could be from?"

"Your father?" I suggested, but she shook her head. "Anyway," she said, "it'll be fun to find out."

I opened the door for her and she went to the delivery woman, a little old lady wearing a brown, peaked cap and a brown uniform, who extended a large tissue-wrapped bunch of roses toward Melissa. Something about the woman's face alarmed me, but I didn't make the connection in time. Melissa took the flowers with both hands. I said, "No!" and started to move. But by then the revolver was out of the woman's pocket and thrusting at Melissa.

She fired once and stepped back, fired a second shot as Melissa gasped and crumpled. *"From Borden,"* she screeched as the security guard grabbed her from behind, wrestling her for the revolver. A third shot went into the ceiling. I knocked the revolver away and dropped to my knees beside Melissa. There were two blood-rimmed holes in her chest and a trickle of blood at the corner of her mouth. I got my arms under her back and lifted her. I kissed her mouth and forehead, hearing inchoate sounds from the struggling murderess, and choked, "Don't die, darling, don't die, please don't die, you can't die, I love you so . . ." words babbling out in a mindless rush.

I thought I saw her lips try to smile, but already the glaze of death was dulling her eyes. Holding her frantically tight I wept, my tears splashing on my darling's face.

Vaguely I was aware of Jacobson nearby and feet pounding toward us along the corridor. The lawyer bent over and said, "The doctor will be here right away."

My hands were wet with her blood. I gazed at him blindly and blurted, "Don't you see? She's dead!"

From Sophie Letterman came a hoarse cackle of triumph. I picked up the revolver and strode toward her, but Jacobson held me back. "Don't," he said. *"Don't* make it worse than it is."

I stared at the faded cheeks, the glittering insane eyes, the twisted, off-center smile, the cords in her chicken-neck, and handed the revolver to Jacobson.

As they dragged Sophie Letterman away, she jerked around and screamed at me, *"They'll never touch me, never harm me. I'm crazy, you know."* Then she was gone.

I lifted Melissa again and kissed her closed eyelids. Held her until police medics pulled me away.

THIRTY-THREE

What happened afterward became a chaotic blur—still is. I was struggling, shouting I was going with Melissa, then the hotel doc stuck a needle in my arm and the world went blank.

When consciousness returned I was lying on a sofa, white leather —I was still in the room where it happened.

Night. The only light in the big room came from a table lamp. My eyes weren't focusing, I couldn't make out the man who sat in a chair beside the lamp. Dazedly I managed to get upright, saw the chalk-outlined place where Melissa died, and felt my throat choke off. Tears welled, streamed down my cheeks, and I wept. Wept for her youth, our lost future, my utter loneliness.

When the spasm ended a voice said, "Don't mind me."

A voice I recognized. I wiped my eyes and saw the long figure of Lieutenant Jaime Nero. He sat forward and said, "I'm terribly sorry. It shouldn't have happened."

"What are you doing here?"

"Watching over you." He cleared his throat. "It's reported you said that because you didn't kill Sophie you were going to kill yourself. Suicide is a crime, you know. I have respect for you—I don't want to see you take that route." He gestured at the other sofa. "Take his."

Huddled on the sofa, eight feet away, lay a bearded man. Professor Anders. Melissa's father. Anders snored and twitched. There was a bottle near his fallen hand. I didn't care what was in the bottle. I reached for it and drank deeply. The liquor burned my raw throat. I set down the bottle and spoke in a dull voice. "It wouldn't have happened if you people had kept her behind bars where she belonged."

He held up one hand. "Easy—we only arrest them. The courts and shrinks decide how long they stay. In Sophie's case they made a mistake. They were very wrong."

"Dead wrong." I drank again. My head buzzed. It was hard to control my thoughts; my vision wasn't clearing.

Nero looked away. "Those places are overcrowded—they let a percentage go when the courts require it. Sophie knew how to manipulate the system. She was plausible . . . Five months ago they let her go. No supervision—it's not like parole."

"No excuse for it."

"Insane she was and is. But with the craftiness of the demented. Clever enough to steal that uniform from a dry cleaner and make her plan."

I swallowed, licked drug-dry lips. "The gun she used?"

"An effort will be made to trace it, but you know this city—you can find weapons in trash barrels, if you're looking." He shook his head. "The antigun people are already yelling for stricter enforcement, abolition of handguns. But hell, Sophie didn't apply for a license to buy a handgun—she acquired one. Which makes the point so few want to hear—almost anyone, crazy or sane, who wants a weapon can get one. And I've been in Homicide long enough to know. Want some coffee?"

I shook my head. "Want to question me, get my version of what happened?"

"Don't need to—Mr. Jacobson and the guard gave statements. There'll be no trial for Sophie Letterman—she'll end her days at Camarillo."

"That doesn't bring Melissa back."

"No, but Sophie will never kill again. And, Joe, remember you're not the only one to lose a loved one. Be thankful for what you had together. You've got memories—and a future."

"We had so little time together . . . hardly any time at all . . . just a few days and nights . . ." My throat tightened, and my mind rewound in time. When I could speak again I said dully, "I recognized that crazy bitch but I was a second too late to stop her. I'll never forgive myself for that."

"Joe—listen to me. She was disguised to avoid recognition. How can you blame yourself? You mustn't."

"Words don't mean anything." I lay back and closed my eyes. My mind drifted farther back in time.

At Balboa, Navy psychiatrists explained to me that those who live through a disaster can experience survivor's guilt, a persistent inner questioning of the rationale for one's survival when others perished; often a subconscious feeling of somehow having contributed to the causes of the disaster, no matter how groundless the feeling was. Unless the delusion was psychologically resolved, the most traumatized cases convinced themselves that expiation was required: self-mutilation, suicide.

Nero said, "Don't read papers or watch TV. The coverage is enough to make even me throw up."

I opened my eyes and looked over at Melissa's father. "How's he doing?"

"He's a rummy—rummies survive. He's out of it for now and he's lucky."

"I don't want to stay here," I said huskily. "I never want to see this place again. It's a cruel place. Cold. Impersonal. A death-house."

"Where do you want to go? Home?"

"Cerrito," I said. "Where I took her in. Where she was safe . . ." I choked, couldn't say any more.

Lieutenant Nero drove me home, one of his men following in my car. At the building entrance I thought he'd leave, but he said, "We'll go the rest of the way—just to make sure everything's okay."

"Nothing's okay, never will be."

He steadied me up the staircase—the knockout drug still flowed through my veins—and opened the door with my key.

He turned the lights on and locked the door. "Mind if I have a drink?"

"All you want. And one for me."

He sat down and loosened his tie, drank from his glass, stretched out and closed his eyes. "Long day," he said tiredly.

"Longest day of my life. Aren't you expected home?"

"Home?" He laughed shortly. "I haven't had a home in three years.

Homicide marriages don't last . . . the hours, no time for the kids, the wife . . ." He yawned.

Gradually my mind was clearing. He and I, we were like two men on a raft, no land in sight. I said, "Why don't you stay here, Lieutenant—I could use the company." I pointed at the sofa. "I'll get a blanket and pillow." Remembered that was where I'd slept that first night when Melissa . . . Tears filled my eyes again. I got up and brought back blanket and pillow for him. He had his shoes and jacket off. Stretching out he said, "I appreciate this—anything I can do for you—if the night gets too dark we'll have coffee together . . . talk . . ." He yawned again and I saw his eyelids flutter and close.

After a while I got up and walked around the apartment touching places she'd touched, remembering how she'd looked, her smile, her tinkling laughter . . . the dimples so seldom seen . . .

When I woke, Nero was frying eggs and bacon in the kitchenette. He poured coffee for me and said, "No matter how bad it is, no matter how bad it gets, we have to keep going . . . go on."

"Why?" I looked at him curiously.

"Because that's the kind of men we are, you and I. You were in Beirut, I was in Cong prison for nearly two years. The easiest thing in the world would have been to let go—die. Sick, hurt, half-dead, I wouldn't. You're that way now. Just don't let go." He served our plates, sat across from me. "I've made some calls—the funeral will be at Forest Lawn day after tomorrow. I'll pick you up, okay?"

"Okay."

The telephone rang. Nero looked at me, got up, and answered. Turning, he said, "A Miss Gossons—about your boat."

I picked up the receiver, said "Brent," and heard Maddy say, "I apologize for calling at such a bad time, but I wanted you to know—I'm afraid it's all bad news. The buyer's check bounced. No sale. Shall I keep trying?"

"Let it rest a while," I told her. "Maybe next month."

I went back to the table and sat down. Nero poured more coffee in my cup. "If you feel up to it," he said, "and I'm not pressing, understand, there's a question you could answer, and it could prove very useful—for her memory."

"Ask it."

He swallowed. "It's—well, did she murder her husband?"

"What could I say that would be useful?"

"I could leak it to the press—to counter all that's being said, speculated."

"She didn't murder Tarkos—she killed him. Self-defense." I told him what had happened on the balcony, and before. The telling seemed to tear away a fragment of sorrow. Now someone else knew the truth. In time I'd tell her father—in a sober moment—but that would be a while.

"Before the professor passed out he called his brother in Minnesota—only relative, I guess. They're trying to reach Melissa's cousin—skiing somewhere in Argentina. Winter down there, you know."

"I hadn't thought about it. Didn't know she had a cousin."

"We'll establish a police line at the grave, keep the curious away."

"Thanks." Even with a few hours' rest my mind was too tired to function. Maybe it would never really function again. I looked at my typewriter and wondered if I'd ever write again, finish the novel. I couldn't think of anything I wanted to do less.

Nero washed our breakfast dishes, saying he was used to it, while I sat listlessly and watched. I had strength for nothing.

He pulled on his jacket, knotted his tie. "One more question?"

"Why not?"

"That Treasury agent—Honey. Was the sniper after him—or you?"

"It's Pendergast's case. Why stir it up?"

"I could do him a favor—in an unofficial way. Just like real life, favors are traded within the PD."

I thought about it for a while. "Without attribution?" I asked.

"If that's how you want it, sure."

"Raf Ambrosino put out a contract on me. In Baja I killed two men who were going to kill me—his kid was one of them."

He nodded thoughtfully. "So the sniper hit the wrong target—now old Raf's dead, rounding it out."

"And Melissa's dead, too—as though she were sacrificed for what I did." Again tears filled my eyes. I turned away, brushed my sleeve across my face. Nero said, "No, no, don't ever think that. It doesn't happen that way, not ever. You have no guilt, Joe, none at all."

I said nothing. Nero patted my shoulder, said he'd come by later, we'd have dinner somewhere. I watched him go.

In a little while I got out the bottle and began drinking, drank through the morning and slept through the afternoon, drank all evening until the hours became meaningless, without reference to day or night.

And through it all, the remembered sorrow, instant flashbacks to the gun going off, the fading smile on her lips; my mind became detached from reality and I felt disembodied, as though I were a silent observer watching a Greek tragedy relentlessly unfold, powerless to change the ending.

Until on the morning of the funeral, Nero came for me, got me shaved and dressed, and drove me to the cemetery.

During the burial rites I stood beside Professor Anders, and before the coffin was lowered we each placed a yellow rose on it, later, a handful of earth. Ed Jacobson was there, as was Joel Hatfield; and the police, true to Nero's promise, kept press and photographers a decent distance away.

Hatfield walked from the graveside with me and said, "When you feel up to it, Joe, we should talk."

"That won't be soon," I told him, "I'm going away."

"Where?"

"I don't know. I've got a boat . . ." My voice trailed off.

"How soon?"

"Tomorrow . . . next day. I can't think yet, make plans . . . it's as if I was lobotomized."

"I thought you'd sold your boat."

"Nothing's worked out." I got into Nero's car. "Goodbye, Joel. You did all you could for her, and I'll never forget it. You were a good friend—to us both."

After Nero left me at the apartment I paid Mrs. Haven what I owed her and told her I wouldn't be needing the place anymore. She gave me the typing her daughter had completed and I paid for that, too. Then I collected everything I owned from the apartment, loaded the Datsun, and drove down to Marina del Rey.

I moved the boat to another slip—away from where Tony had died—and busied myself unpacking and stowing my possessions. I bought a good supply of liquor and provisioned the galley for a couple of weeks. By then it was late afternoon and the tide was running against me, so I decided to lay over for the night and leave next day. Or the day after . . . what difference did it make?

I didn't buy a paper or listen to the radio, but mainly to distract my mind I got out what Jan had typed for me and read it from beginning to end. To my surprise the story was pretty good, and I began outlining the last third of it, calculating I could complete the draft in two weeks, working undisturbed.

So I set up my typewriter and began work that night, ideas unfolding as if they'd been long suppressed, and after I turned in I slept through the first wholesome, restful night I'd known since the catastrophe.

In the morning I tried the engine and thought it sounded rough. A check of the tachometer confirmed diagnosis, so I went over to the boatyard for a set of new points, pulled off the distributor and got to work.

I was standing ankle-deep in bilge water when someone called, "Mr. Brent? Joseph Brent?" I looked up and almost fainted. The same face, hair a shade more golden, leg muscles a trifle more defined but it was . . . *Melissa*. In a trance I stared at her until she said, "No, no, I'm not a ghost. I'm Lissa's cousin, Karen." She stepped lithely aboard. "I hope I'm not interrupting you, but Mr. Hatfield said you were going away and I—"

I couldn't believe what I was seeing. I tried to say something and got out only, "Hello." Weakly I sat down. The impact was overwhelming. I was in shock.

"I couldn't get here until yesterday afternoon—wires were down in Bariloche, heavy snowfall in the high Andes."

"You were skiing," I said, grasping for anything that halfway made sense. "Your father's in Minnesota . . . When they said 'cousin,' I just assumed it was a man." I ran a clean hand through my hair. "You've come a long way. The resemblance is . . . stunning."

"We were often taken for twins," she said shyly, sitting on the stern transom and crossing long, tanned legs. She was wearing bermuda shorts and a loose pink shirt. "Our fathers married sisters—it happens, you know—and that's why Lissa and I looked so much alike." Her face sobered. "I don't mean to chatter inanely, Mr. Brent, but it's . . . difficult. Not really knowing what to say."

"How long are you here for?"

"That . . . depends. I want to spend some time with Uncle George—help him through this bad period. And then—"

"You must be a pretty good skiier."

She actually blushed. "In downhill I've been an Olympic possibility, but I couldn't put in the necessary training time, take all the competition trips because of my doctorate." She shrugged. "So I tell myself I never really could have competed at world-class level, and I have my Ph.D. to keep me warm."

I laid down my tools and got up on deck. "Doctorate in what?"

"Entomology—I know it sounds daunting, but it's just about insects."

"Oh."

"It's a fascinating, revealing field. Not many people realize that, for their weight and size, insects are incredibly stronger than man. And in some ways much smarter."

"I'm one who didn't know that," I said. "And what are you going to do with all that knowledge?"

"I have until summer to decide where I'll teach."

My throat was tight. "It must be nice—satisfying—to have choices."

"It is. The universities of Minnesota and Washington are two possibilities—then there's Southern Cal, UCLA, and Duke."

"Great institutions," I said, awed. "Have you had breakfast?"

She smiled. "It's almost noon, Mr. Brent."

"Please—it's Joe. Then how about coffee?"

"Love it."

While the coffee was perking she sat on one of the bunks and looked around. "Everything's so neat . . . Lissa?"

"She was never here," I said, and got out two mugs and sugar. "I'm afraid there isn't any cream."

"Don't need any." She waited until I'd poured before saying, "Uncle George told me a few things about you—so did Mr. Hatfield—all adding up to a very unusual man. It's no wonder my cousin was in love with you." She sipped and looked away. "You were to be married, I know."

"That was the plan," I said emptily.

"Well, I didn't come to dredge up terrible memories, but I didn't want to miss meeting you either. You're going for how long?"

"I've got supplies for two weeks," I told her, and pointed at my typewriter. "And a book to finish."

"I didn't realize you were an intellectual as well as a man of action."

"One unfinished book doesn't qualify me as anything," I said, "so we'll leave that aside. What was your dissertation on?"

She blushed again. "The monarch butterfly. Near Morelia, Mexico, there's a preserve for them, a winter haven. Can you imagine a green biosphere sheltering zillions of those gorgeous creatures? Well, I spent almost a year there—and that's what I wrote about."

"So you speak Spanish."

"*Como no.*"

I didn't want conversation to end, because just looking at Karen gave me new life . . . new hope. "Have you time for lunch?" I asked.

"Afraid not today—I'm helping Uncle George at the Picasso. Then I'll go down to San Diego with him." She sighed. "It's all so unbelievable, and I cared deeply for Lissa, though we hadn't seen each other in several years. I couldn't stand her husband and he knew it. So . . ." She emptied her cup. "After you get back, we could lunch together. I want to know more about you, and about my cousin. Secondhand isn't at all satisfactory."

"Will you be in San Diego?"

"I'm—well, I'm interviewing again at UCLA and Southern Cal, to meet the department people, really, see if we're compatible."

"I hope you are," I said, and got up as she did. We shook hands rather formally, she said, "Good luck with your writing," and went away.

For a long time I sat in the cabin, overcome by a sensation of Melissa's presence. I knew I wanted to see Karen again—had to see her—but time had to elapse. There had to be space for a while. For both of us.

As soon as I'd replaced the points and checked out the engine, I cast off lines and sailed out of the channel.

By late afternoon I was anchoring in a cove not far from Avalon. I went swimming, pried off a good-sized abalone, and baked it for dinner. The exercise left my body tired but my mind active, and I typed a good episode before turning in.

Then at night came memories. Remembering Melissa became a fever that had to burn itself out.

Sometimes I'd wake thinking Melissa was there beside me; then I'd realize there was only darkness, emptiness. Other times I'd begin talking aloud as though she were there to listen and respond . . .

And I wondered how things would have gone for us had she lived. Melissa, the newly created woman of money, power, and influence—me, the nothing writer tagging along . . . How long could it have lasted? I knew so little about her, she so little about me. Pitifully little in retrospect, but while she was alive it didn't seem important and perhaps it wasn't. But I'd felt all along there was a protective shell around her, transparent and resilient to the touch, that she'd never fully opened to me. In time it might have vanished—I wanted to think that—but again it might have remained.

I wanted to remember her as she had been in those few days we'd shared together. Tried in my mind to recapture her voice and smile, relive the happiness we'd known.

I didn't want to let go.

But I knew I'd have to if I was ever to get on with my own life, come to grips with whatever lay ahead. Live without her.

For fourteen days I stayed there, away from bottled liquor, breaking a Beam seal only for the voyage back—not to Marina del Rey, but down to San Diego's Shelter Island Yacht Basin, where *El Dorado* was only one of a thousand boats, most of them larger than mine.

Ashore, I phoned Hatfield's office, said I was back and ready to talk. He said he'd be in the office all day; I should come when I could.

"I look like old Ben Gunn," I told him, "if you don't mind a seafaring bum in your office." When he didn't pick up I said, "Gunn—ah, that's *Treasure Island,* Joel. A basic book."

"I only saw the movie," he said. "If your novel's finished, bring it along."

"Be there in a couple of hours."

I phoned George Anders's apartment and Karen answered.

"I was afraid you might have left," I said, "but if you're free, how about dinner?"

"Lovely idea. On your boat?"

"I'm a little tired of cooking," I admitted, "and supplies are low. I'll pick you up at six. Steak or Mex?"

"Steak—I've eaten my last tamale, believe me."

So I went to Hatfield's office and laid my novel on his desk. He said, "I've been thinking about you—thinking a lot." He got up and went over to his safe. After opening it he took out the mailer envelope I'd intended for Melissa. "No one has claimed this, Joe. I don't know what's in it, and I don't want to know. As far as I'm concerned it's your property."

I took the envelope from him and thanked him, wondering how much the diamonds would bring. Much more than I could earn in a year, I was sure—five years, even.

"I'm taking Karen Anders to dinner."

"Glad to hear it. She's a remarkable young woman. Kept her Uncle George off the sauce while the estate's sorted out. Done everything that needed doing."

When I didn't react, he said, "I forgot you've been out of touch. Well, because Melissa died intestate—without making a will—everything that would have gone to her goes to her next of kin, her father."

"I'm glad," I said. "I was afraid California would get it all."

"Some, but nowhere near all. Now tell me about your novel."

I summarized the plot for him, he thought it over for a while, and said, "Sounds publishable—and I've got some contacts in entertainment law, if you'd like me to check around."

"Best offer I've had." The mailer envelope lay on my lap, far weightier than gold.

"As I said, I've been thinking a lot about you. And I'm going to make a suggestion that could do you good in several ways. Therapy plus money. Interested, Joe?"

"Let's hear it."

"There's a story that'll never be written, never be told unless you do it. Know what I mean?"

I looked over at the aquarium fish. Light flashed from their iridescent colors. Beautiful captives. When I said nothing, he said, "*Your* story, Joe, you and Melissa. What happened—all that *really* happened—Tarkos, the Ambrosinos, Baja . . . It all needs telling. You have to do it, just as it took place. Names suitably disguised, of course."

"You may be right," I said, "but I'm too close to it now. Not for a while, Joel. And now I've a date for dinner."

The Guild strike lasted five months, and by the time it ended, my life was much different than when the strike began.

Natty's divorce application was granted with a minimum of paperwork, and she and Bryon moved in with Prem at Long Beach, where she became his production assistant.

Publishers reacted to my Hermitage-heist novel with unanimous indifference, despite Joel Hatfield's networking. And Morry's brother-in-law lost a bundle putting out a paperback on weight-loss through meditation, making Aaron unreceptive to a first novel by an unknown author. So in the late fall I started writing the story Joel wanted me to write, working out of a comfortable house in Westwood Village, a short walk to the UCLA campus, where Karen had begun to teach. It took me months to get it all down, tell everything the way things really happened, Karen encouraging me when I faltered or suffered emotional blocks I couldn't get through alone.

She said it was a learning experience for her, learning about Melissa and me. So when I finished in the spring, Karen was the first to read it all, and approved—subject to my toning down certain passages concerning Sondra Starr.

So that's how this book came to be.

My wife is a meticulous critic of everything I write and I respect her comments and perceptions, never argue or complain.

I figure I'd lose the debates anyway, and it's a wise man who knows when he's overmatched. Because besides being beautiful, athletic, and intelligent, my wife's a Ph.D.